Harlequin R

Saddle up and get ready, these wealthy cowboys set out to wrangle the hearts of the women of their dreams!

Riding the range and herding cattle are only a couple talents these irresistible heroes have. Fiercely protecting their loved ones and stopping at nothing to win the adoration of a good woman are some of the reasons we can't get enough of them.

These ranchers hold honor above all else, believe in the value of a hard day's work and aren't afraid to make the tough decisions. In fact, they have everything under control...except their hearts! And once these men of the West give their love, there's no walking away.

If you enjoy these two classic stories, be sure to look for more books featuring rich, rugged ranchers in Harlequin Special Edition and Harlequin American Romance.

USA TODAY Bestselling Author

Judy Duarte
and
Barbara White Daille

IN THE RANCHER'S CARE

H HARLEQUIN® RICH, RUGGED RANCHERS

Recycling programs
for this product may
not exist in your area.

ISBN-13: 978-0-373-60118-9

In the Rancher's Care

Copyright © 2015 by Harlequin Books S.A.

The publisher acknowledges the copyright holders
of the individual works as follows:

The Rancher's Hired Fiancée
Copyright © 2012 by Judy Duarte

Honorable Rancher
Copyright © 2012 by Barbara White-Rayczek

This edition published by arrangement with Harlequin Books S.A.

For questions and comments about the quality of this book,
please contact us at CustomerService@Harlequin.com.

Printed in U.S.A.

CONTENTS

THE RANCHER'S
HIRED FIANCÉE

Judy Duarte

To Mark Winch, who reads every book I write.
I hope you enjoy this one, too, Mark.

Chapter 1

Catherine Loza napped in a child's bedroom at the Walker family's ranch in Texas, dreaming of sold-out nights on Broadway, the heady sound of applause and the pounding of her heart after a well-executed performance.

She took a bow, then straightened and glanced out into the audience, only to see an empty stall and a bale of straw in an illuminated old barn, where a group of children clapped their hands in delight.

Their faces were a blur until two of them glided toward the stage, greeting her with red rosebuds, their long stems free of thorns.

Recognizing Sofia and Stephen, Dan and Eva Walker's youngest twins, Catherine knelt and received the flowers. Then the darling two-year-olds wrapped their pudgy arms around her and placed soft, moist kisses on her cheeks, on her forehead, on her chin.

How strange, she thought, but so sweet.

She'd no more than thanked them and sent them on their way when she heard a light tapping noise in the distance.

Thoughts and visions tumbled together in her sleepy mind—until another knock sounded, this time on the bedroom door.

"Yes?" she said, realizing she'd dozed off after reading a storybook to the children. Now, as she scanned the empty room, she saw that they'd both slipped off, leaving her to nap alone.

Eva opened the door and peered into the darkened bedroom. "I'm sorry to bother you, but we're having company for dinner tonight, and I thought you might want to know."

Catherine glanced out the window, which was shuttered tight, only a faint light creeping through the slats. She tried to guess the time of day but didn't have a clue—other than it was obviously nearing the dinner hour.

"A lot of help I am," Catherine said. "I wasn't the one who was supposed to fall asleep."

Eva chuckled softly. "Sofia and Stephen woke up a few minutes ago. Now they're in the kitchen, coloring and playing with their sticker books."

Catherine never had been one to nap during the day. Apparently the fresh air, sunshine and the rural Texas setting had a calming effect on her.

"If you'd like to rest a little longer," Eva said, "it's not a problem. You've been burning the candle at both ends for so long. Your body probably needs the sleep."

"Who's coming for dinner tonight?" Catherine asked.

"Ray Mendez. He's a local rancher and a neighbor. In fact, he'll be here any minute."

"Thanks for the heads-up." As Eva closed the bedroom door, Catherine raked her fingers through her hair, her nails catching on a couple of snags in her long curls. She probably looked a fright, with eyes puffy from sleep, but she wouldn't stress about it. This was supposed to be a vacation of sorts.

Ever since her arrival on the ranch, she'd decided to go au natural—no makeup, no fancy hairstyles. She was also kicking back for a change—no schedules, no grueling workouts, no rehearsals. And quite frankly, she was looking forward to having a break from the hectic life she'd once known in Manhattan.

Catherine rolled to the side of the bed and got to her feet. Then she straightened the pillows, as well as the coverlet, before opening the door and stepping into the hall.

She'd taken only two steps when the doorbell rang. The rancher had just arrived. Wanting to make herself useful, she detoured to answer the door. What had Eva said his name was? Ray something.

Catherine had never met any of the Walkers' neighbors, but she assumed Ray must be one of Hank's friends. Hank, Dan's elderly uncle, who'd once owned the ranch and now lived in a guesthouse Dan had built for him, always ate dinner with them in the main dining room.

Not seeing anyone else in the room, Catherine opened the front door.

She expected to see a weathered rancher who resembled Dan's uncle, a sweet but crotchety old cowboy who reminded her of Robert Duvall when he'd played in *Lonesome Dove* or *Open Range*. But nothing had prepared her for the tall, dark-haired visitor who stood on the porch.

The man, whose expression revealed that he was just as surprised to see her as she was to see him, didn't look anything like the grizzled Texan she'd envisioned just moments before. At first glance, he bore enough resem-

blance to Antonio Banderas to be his younger brother—
all decked out in Western wear, of course.

A sense of awkwardness rose up inside, and she tried
to tamp it down the best she could. She might be dressed
like a barefoot street urchin in a pair of gray sweatpants,
an old NYU T-shirt and no makeup to speak of, but she
was actually an accomplished woman who'd performed
on Broadway several times in the past—and would do
so again.

"I'm Catherine Loza," she said. "You must be Ray...?"

"Mendez." His voice held the slightest bit of a Spanish
accent, which made him all the more intriguing.

She reached up to flick a wild strand of her sleep-
tousled curls from her eyes, only to feel something
papery stuck to her face. She peeled it off, and when she
looked at her fingers to see what it was, she spotted a
child's butterfly sticker.

Oh, for Pete's sake. How had that gotten there?

It must have been on the bedspread or pillow, and she'd
probably rolled over on it.

Determined to shake the flush from her face and to
pretend that her ankles weren't bound together with duct
tape, that her brain hadn't been abducted by aliens, Catherine forced herself to step forward and reach out to shake
the neighboring rancher's hand. "It's nice to meet you,
Ray. Eva said you'd be coming to dinner tonight. Please
come in."

The handsome rancher's smile deepened, lighting his
eyes, which were a vibrant shade of green.

As he released his grip on her hand, leaving her skin
warm and tingling, he lifted a lazy index finger and
peeled another sticker from her face.

Her lips parted as he showed her a little pink heart.

"You missed a couple of them," he said.

Huh? A couple of...what?

He removed a gold star from over her brow and a unicorn from her chin.

Catherine blinked back her surprise, as well as her embarrassment. Then she swiped her hand first over one cheek and then the other, discovering that either Sofia or Stephen had decorated her face while she'd slept.

Goodness. What else had the twins done to her while she'd been asleep? Surely they hadn't used their Magic Markers on her, too?

She hadn't felt the least bit self-conscious in years, but it all came rushing back at her now. She must look like a clown. What must the man be thinking?

Calling on her acting skills and her ability to ad-lib on stage, she gave a little shrug, as if this sort of thing happened all the time. "Well, what do you know? The sticker fairies stopped by while I napped."

Ray tossed her a crooked grin, humor sparking in his eyes. "You've got to watch out for those fairies, especially on the Walker Ranch. There's no telling what they'll do next."

"I'm afraid he's right about that," Dan said as he entered the living room. "Our younger twins can be little rascals at times."

Before Catherine could respond, Dan greeted his friend with a handshake, then invited him to take a seat, suggesting that she do the same.

But there was no way Catherine wanted to remain in the living room looking like a ragamuffin, so she said, "I'd better help Eva in the kitchen."

"I was just in there," Dan said. "And she has everything under control."

Catherine didn't care where she went—to the kitchen, her bedroom or the barn. All she wanted to do was to disappear from the handsome rancher's sight until she could find a mirror before dinner.

"Well, since Eva doesn't need my help, I'll just go freshen up." She lobbed Ray Mendez her best, unaffected smile. "It was nice meeting you."

"The pleasure was mine."

The sound of the word *pleasure* on the lips of a man who not only resembled a Latin lover but sounded like one, too, was enough to knock her little Texas world off its axis.

And until she flew back to Manhattan, she'd do whatever it took to keep her feet on solid ground in Brighton Valley.

One screwed-up world was more than she cared to handle.

Ray Mendez had no idea who Catherine Loza was, why she'd been napping this late in the afternoon or why she'd been included to have dinner at the Walkers' ranch. He watched her leave the room, turn down the hall and walk toward the bedrooms.

The minute she was out of hearing range, he turned to his neighbor and friend. "You're not starting in on me, too, are you?"

"*Starting in* on you? What do you mean?"

Ray crossed his arms and tensed. "Is this dinner supposed to be a setup?"

Dan looked a little confused by the question—or rather the accusation. "A *setup?* You mean, with you and *Catherine?* No, I wouldn't do that." Then he glanced toward the kitchen, as if realizing his pretty wife might have had a plan of her own.

But why wouldn't she? Every time Ray turned around,

one of the women in town was trying to play match-maker.

"Eva called and asked you to dinner because we hadn't seen you in a while," Dan said. "Why would you think we had anything else in mind?"

"Because ever since word got out that my divorce was final, the local matchmakers have come out of the wood-work, determined to find the perfect second wife for me. And the last thing I'm looking for right now is romance. I've got my hands full trying to run my ranch from a distance and finish out the term of the previous mayor."

"Has it been that bad?" Dan asked.

"You have no idea."

"For the record," Dan said, "Catherine is a great woman. She's beautiful, talented and has a heart of gold. But she's just visiting us. Her life is in New York, and yours is here. So it would be a waste of time to try my hand at matchmaking."

That was a relief. Thank God Ray's friends hadn't joined every marriage-minded woman in town—or her well-intentioned best friend, mother or neighbor.

He unfolded his arms and let down his guard.

As he did so, he glanced down the hall just as Catherine returned with her hair combed, those wild platinum curls controlled by a clip of some kind.

She'd changed into a pair of black jeans and a crisp, white blouse—nothing fancy. She'd also applied a light coat of pink lipstick and slipped on a pair of ballet flats.

For a moment, Ray wondered if she had romance on her mind. But the cynical thought passed as quickly as it had struck.

If Catherine had expected to meet someone special tonight, she wouldn't have opened the door with her hair a mess, stickers all over her face and no makeup whatsoever.

Although he had to admit, she'd looked pretty darn cute standing at the door, blue eyes wide, lips parted....

As Catherine crossed through the living room on her way to the kitchen, she gave him a passing smile.

And when she was again out of hearing range, Ray turned back to Dan. "Where'd you meet her?"

"She used to be Jenny's roommate."

Dan's sister, Jenny Walker, had left Brighton Valley after graduating from high school. She'd gone to college in the Midwest, majored in music or dance and moved to New York, where she'd done some singing and acting off-Broadway.

About eight or nine years ago, Jenny gave birth to twins, although she died when Kevin and Kaylee were in kindergarten. Dan and Eva adopted the kids and were now raising them, as well as their own younger set of twins.

"Catherine has come out a time or two to visit," Dan added, "but she never stayed long. She's an actress and a dancer, so she usually has a Broadway show of some kind going on."

"Is that what she's doing here now? Visiting the kids?"

"Actually, this time I'm not sure how long she'll be with us. She broke up with some hot-shot producer back in New York and wanted to get away for a while. I don't know all of the details, but it really doesn't matter. She stepped up to the plate and helped me and the kids out when we really needed her, so I'm happy to return the favor now."

Ray raked his hand through his hair. "I'm sorry for jumping to conclusions. I should have known you wouldn't have invited me to come over with more than dinner on your mind."

Dan studied him for a moment. "Is the matchmaking really that bad?"

He chuffed. "I can't make it through a single day without someone trying to set me up with a single daughter, niece or neighbor. And that's not counting the unmarried ladies who approach me on their own behalf." Ray grumbled under his breath, wishing he'd stayed out of politics and had remained on his ranch full-time.

"Well, I guess that's to be expected." A grin tugged at one side of Dan's lips, and his eyes lit up with mirth. "You're not a bad-looking fellow. And you've got a little cash put away. I guess that makes you an eligible bachelor in anyone's book."

"Very funny." Ray had never been full of himself, but most women considered him to be the tall, dark and handsome type. He also had a head for business, which had allowed him to parlay a couple of inheritances into millions. As a result, he had more money and property than he could shake a stick at, something that made every unattached female between the ages of 18 and 40 seem to think he was a prime catch.

He could always give them the cold shoulder, but his mother had taught him to be polite and courteous—a habit he found hard to shake. Besides, he didn't know how to keep the women at arm's distance without alienating half the voters in town.

"To top it off," Dan added, "you being the mayor gives you a little more status than just being a run-of-the-mill Texas rancher, which the ladies undoubtedly find even more appealing."

Ray sighed. "That's the problem. I'm not looking for romance. And if the time ever comes that I'm interested again, I'm perfectly capable of finding a woman without help."

Dan, who'd been biting back a full-on smile, let it go and chuckled. "There's got to be a lot of guys who'd be happy to trade places with you."

"Maybe, but only for a couple of days. Then they'd get fed up, too. This has been going on since…well, since word got out that my divorce was final. And now I can hardly get any work done—in town or on the ranch."

"Why *not* date someone, just so word will spread that you're already taken?"

Ray shook his head. "No, I'm not going to do that. After the marriage I had, I'm steering clear of women in general. But even if I wanted to ask someone out, I don't have the time to add anything else to my calendar. As it is, I've been spending the bulk of my day driving back and forth to the ranch, making sure Mark and Darren have everything under control, then zipping back to town for one meeting or another."

"I don't blame you for not wanting to jump back into another relationship, especially after the hell Heather put you through over the past two years."

Dan had that right. Ray's ex-wife had not only cheated on him, she'd turned out to be a heartless gold digger. And after the long legal battle she'd waged, Ray wasn't about to make a mistake like that again.

"You know," Dan said, "it might not be a bad idea to spread the rumor that you're already taken. Maybe that way, the matchmaking mamas and their starry-eyed daughters will give you a break and let you get some work done."

"That's an idea, but as simple and easy as it sounds, I'm afraid it won't work."

"Why not?"

"Because I'd keep showing up alone at all the various community events I'm required to attend, and people will begin to realize the woman is only a myth. And then I'll be right back where I started. I'm afraid I'd need the real thing, and that would defeat the purpose of creating a fictitious woman."

"Too bad you can't rent an escort," Dan said.

"Yeah, right."

At that moment, Catherine reentered the living room and called Dan's name. "Eva said to tell you that dinner's ready. She's already called Hank, and he's heading over here now."

"Thanks," Dan said. "We'll be right there."

As Catherine returned to the kitchen, Ray watched the sway of her denim-clad hips. It was hard to imagine her as a woman who was at home on the stage, especially since she had a wholesome, girl-next-door appeal. But then again, she *was* an actress....

Suddenly, an idea began to form.

"How long does Catherine plan to be in town?" he asked.

"I'm not sure. Why?"

"Do you think she'd want a job?"

"Probably. Just this morning she mentioned that she'd like to find something part-time and temporary. Why?"

"Because I want to hire her, if she's interested."

"What did you have in mind? Something clerical?"

"No, it would be an acting job."

Dan looked confused. "I'm not following you."

A slow smile stretched across Ray's face. "I'd like to hire Catherine to be my fiancée."

After dinner and dessert had been served, Dan's uncle thanked Eva for another wonderful meal, then headed back to his place so he could watch his favorite TV show.

Eva sent the older twins to get ready for bed, then

she and Dan gathered up the preschoolers and told them it was bath time, leaving Catherine and Ray in the dining room.

"Can I get you another cup of coffee?" Catherine asked.

"That sounds good. Thanks."

Minutes later she returned with the carafe and filled his cup, then her own.

"Dan told me that you might be interested in some part-time work," Ray said.

Catherine had no idea how long she'd be in Brighton Valley, but it would probably be at least a month. So she'd thought about trying to earn a little cash while she was here.

Of course, if truth be told, she didn't have many skills that would come in handy in a place like Brighton Valley.

"I'm interested," she said, lifting her coffee cup and taking a sip. "As long as it was only temporary. Do you know of a position that's open?"

"Yes, I do. And it's probably right up your alley."

Catherine couldn't imagine what it might be. She was just about to ask for more details when she realized that Ray had zeroed in on her again, as if mesmerized or intrigued by her.

If she were in Manhattan, dressed to the nines, she might have taken his interest as a compliment. As it was, she didn't know what to think.

"What kind of job is it?" she asked.

"It's a little unorthodox," he admitted, "but it's only part-time, and the money's good."

"Who would I be working for? And what would I be doing?"

"You'd be working for me. I need an actress, and you'd be perfect for the part."

"I don't understand." Catherine lifted her cup and took another sip.

"I need a fiancée," Ray said.

Catherine choked on her coffee. "*Excuse* me?"

"I want people in town to think that I'm in a committed relationship. And Dan thinks you have the acting skills to pull it off."

"Why in the world would a man like you need to hire a girlfriend?" Once the words were off her tongue, she wanted to take them back. "I'm sorry," she said. "I'm not sure I'm following you."

"Okay, let me explain. I need a temporary escort to attend various community functions with me, and it would be best if people had the idea that we were serious about each other."

Did he think that was an explanation? He'd merely reworded the job description.

"There are a lot of single women in town who've been making my life difficult," he added. "And for some reason, they seem to think I'm actively looking for another wife."

"But you're *not?*"

"No. At least, not for the foreseeable future. My divorce became final a month ago, although my ex-wife moved out nearly two years ago. So I'm not in any hurry to jump into another relationship. I've tried to explain that to people, but apparently they don't believe me."

"Maybe you should be more direct."

"I thought I was. And I'd rather not alienate or anger any of my constituents."

Constituents? Oh, yes. Eva had mentioned he was also the mayor of Brighton Valley. So that meant he was dealing with small-town politics.

Either way Catherine thought the whole idea was a

little weird—if not a bit laughable. But then again, she could use the work—and she *was* an actress.

"How long do you need my help?" she asked.

"Until my interim position as mayor is over—or for as long as you're in town. Whichever comes first."

He seemed to have it all planned out.

"I'll pay you a thousand dollars a week," he added.

Catherine was still trying to wrap her mind around his job offer, which was crazy. But the money he would pay spoke louder than the craziness, and against her better judgment, she found herself leaning toward an agreement.

"What would your fiancée have to do?" she asked.

Ray sketched an appreciative gaze over her that sent her senses reeling and had her wondering just how far he'd want her to go in playing the part.

"I have to attend a lot of events and fundraisers, so it would be nice to have you go with me whenever possible. I even have a ring for you to wear on your left hand, which you can return when the job is over."

He was including the props?

This was wild. Pretending to be engaged to Ray Mendez was probably the craziest job offer she'd ever had, but she supposed it really didn't matter. If he was willing to pay for her acting skills, then why not go along with it?

"All right," she finally said. "You've got yourself a deal. When do I start?"

"Why don't you meet me for lunch at Caroline's tomorrow? A lot of the locals will be there, so it'll be a good way to send out the message that I'm already taken."

"And then...?"

"I don't know." He stroked his square-cut jaw. "Maybe I could greet you with a kiss, then we'll play it by ear. Hopefully, the rumor mill will kick into gear right away."

"What if it doesn't?"

He gave a half shrug. "I guess we'll have to take things day by day."

"So you just want me to have lunch with you tomorrow?"

"Actually, later that evening, I also have a charity event to attend at the Brighton Valley Medical Center. It's a benefit for the new neonatal intensive care unit, and it would probably be a good idea if we walked in together, holding hands. Maybe, if you looked at me a little starry-eyed, people would get the message."

"You want me to look at you *starry-eyed?*"

"Hell, I don't know how to explain it. You're a woman—and an actress. Just do whatever you'd do if we were actually engaged or at least committed to each other. I want people to think we're a real couple."

"Okay. I can do that. But what's the dress code tomorrow night?"

"I'll be wearing a sport jacket."

She bit down on her bottom lip, then glanced down at the simple blouse and black jeans she was wearing now. If truth be told, it was the fanciest outfit she'd brought with her.

"What's the matter?" he asked.

"If we were in New York, it wouldn't be a problem for me to find the right thing to wear. But I'm afraid I didn't plan to do anything other than kick back on the ranch and play with the kids while I'm here, so I only packed casual outfits."

"That's not a problem." He scooted back his chair and reached into the pocket of his jeans. He pulled out a money clip with a wad of bills, peeled off three hundred dollars and handed it to her. "After lunch tomorrow you can walk down the street to The Boutique. It's a shop located a few doors down from the diner."

Catherine couldn't imagine what type of clothing she'd find in Brighton Valley, but then again, she'd chosen to come to Texas because it was light-years from Manhattan and her memories there. She supposed she would have to adjust her tastes to the styles small-town women found appealing—or at least affordable.

She stole another glance at the handsome rancher seated across the table from her to find that he was studying her, too. Sexual awareness fluttered through her like a swarm of lovesick butterflies.

But that shouldn't surprise her. Ray Mendez was a handsome man. No wonder every woman in town was after him.

Of course, he was paying her to keep the other women at bay.

It would be an easy job, she decided—and one she might actually enjoy. Her biggest Broadway role had been the mistress of a 1920s Chicago mobster. The actor who'd played her lover had been twenty years older than she and about forty pounds overweight. His ruddy appearance had suited the character he'd played, although it had taken some real skills on her part to pretend she was sexually attracted to him.

Ray Mendez was going to make a much better co-star, though—especially if her role was going to require a few starry-eyed gazes, some hand-holding and maybe a kiss or two.

For the first time since leaving Manhattan, she was actually looking forward to getting on stage again.

Chapter 2

At a few minutes before noon, Ray stood in front of Caroline's Diner, waiting for his hired fiancée to arrive. The plan had been for Catherine to borrow Eva's mini-van, then to meet him in town.

To his surprise, he was actually looking forward to seeing her again—and not just because she was the solution to one of his many problems.

Even when she'd been wearing sweatpants and an oversize T-shirt, the tall, leggy blonde with bed-head curls had been a lovely sight. Her blue-green eyes—almost a turquoise shade, really—and an expressive smile only added to the overall effect.

Of course, those little heart and flower stickers that the younger Walker twins had stuck on her face while she'd slept had been an interesting touch.

When Ray had pointed them out, she'd made a joke of it without missing a beat. And that meant she would probably be able to handle anything the townspeople might throw at her. If anyone quizzed her about their past or their plans for the future, she'd be quick on her feet.

They hadn't talked much after dinner last night, since Dan and Eva had returned to the table once they'd gotten the kids in bed. But they'd managed to concoct a believable past for their imaginary romance.

Fortunately, she wasn't a well-known Broadway actress, so they'd agreed to tell people they'd met in Houston six months ago and that they'd been dating ever since.

The day Ray's divorce had been final—after two long years in legal limbo—he'd proposed over a glass of champagne during a candlelit dinner in the city. She'd accepted, although they'd decided not to make an official announcement of their engagement until she could take some vacation time and come to Brighton Valley.

So now here he was, standing outside Caroline's Diner, ready to reveal their phony engagement to the locals who'd already begun to file into the small restaurant and fill the tables.

Ray glanced at his wristwatch again, knowing that he'd arrived a few minutes early and realizing that Catherine really wasn't late. Rather, he was a little nervous. Could they pull it off?

"Hello, Mayor," a woman called out in a chipper voice.

Ray glanced up to see Melanie Robertson approaching the diner wearing a smile.

Aw, man. This was just the kind of thing he'd been trying to avoid. Where was his "fiancée" when he needed her?

"Are you waiting for someone?" Melanie asked. "Or would you like to join Carla Guerrero and me for lunch?"

"Thanks for the offer, but I am meeting someone."

"Is it business or pleasure?" she asked, her lashes fluttering in a flirtatious manner.

"It's definitely pleasure." Out of the corner of his eye he spotted Catherine walking down the street. At least, that tall, blonde stranger striding toward him appeared to be the woman he'd met last night.

She'd told him that she hadn't brought anything fancy to Texas, but…hot damn. She hadn't needed a shopping trip for their lunch today. A pair of tight jeans, a little makeup and a dab of lipstick had made a stunning transformation from attractive girl next door to dazzling.

"Hi, honey." Catherine burst into a smile as she reached him. "I'm sorry I'm late."

Then she leaned forward and brushed her lips across his, giving him a brief hint of peppermint breath mints.

Her fragrance—something light and exotic—snaked around him, squeezing the air out of his lungs and making it nearly impossible to speak.

Then she turned to Melanie, offered a confident, bright-eyed smile and reached out her hand in greeting. "Hi, I'm Catherine Loza."

The same pesky cat that seemed to have gotten Ray's tongue appeared to have captured Melanie's, as well. He could understand her surprised reaction to Catherine's arrival and greeting, but not his own. Not when he'd been the one to set up the whole fake fiancée thing in the first place.

So why had Catherine's performance set *him* off balance?

Because she was so damn good at what she was doing, he supposed.

Shaking off the real effects of the pretend kiss, he introduced the women, adding, "Melanie's family owns the ice-cream shop down the street."

"It's nice to meet you," Catherine said.

Melanie, whose eyes kept bouncing from Ray to his "date" and back again, said, "Same here. I...uh..." She nodded toward the entrance of Caroline's Diner. "I came to have lunch with a coworker, so I guess I'll see you two inside." Then she reached for the door and let herself in.

Well, what do you know? Catherine had been on the job only a minute or two, and the ploy was already working like a charm.

When they were alone, she asked, "So how did I do?"

"You were great." In fact, she was better than great. She both looked and acted the part of a loving fiancée, and even Ray found himself believing the romantic story they'd concocted was true.

"Now what?" she asked. "Did you want to go inside?"

"Yes, but I've got something to give you first. Come with me." Ray led her to the street corner, then turned to the left. When they reached the alley, he made a second left.

Once they were out of plain sight, he reached into the lapel pocket of his leather jacket and removed a small, velvet-covered box. Then he lifted the lid and revealed an engagement ring.

"Will this work?" he asked.

Catherine's breath caught as she peered at what appeared to be an antique, which had been cleaned and polished. The diamond, while fairly small, glistened in the sunlight.

"It was my grandmother's," he said.

"It's beautiful." She doubted the ring was costly, but she imagined that the sentimental value was priceless. "I've never had an heirloom, so I'll take good care of it."

Then she removed the ring from the box and slipped

it on the ring finger of her left hand, surprised that it actually fit.

For a moment, she wondered about the woman who'd worn it before her, about the relationship she'd had with her husband—and with her grandson. She suspected they'd been close.

When she looked at Ray, when their eyes met and their gazes locked, she asked, "What was her name?"

The question seemed to sideswipe him. *"Who?"*

"Your grandmother."

He paused, as if the reminder had surprised him as much as the question had, then said, "Her name was Elena."

Catherine lifted her hand and studied the setting a bit longer. It was an old-fashioned piece of jewelry, yet it had been polished to a pretty shine.

When she looked up again, he was watching her intently.

"What's the matter?" she asked.

He didn't respond right away, and when she thought that he might not, he said, "I know that ring isn't anything most people would consider impressive, but it meant a lot to my grandmother."

Catherine's mother had worn a single gold band, although she wasn't sure it had meant much to her. And when she'd passed away, the family had buried her with it still on her finger. As far as Catherine knew, not one of her siblings had mentioned wanting to inherit it.

But Ray's ring was different—special.

"It's actually an honor to wear this." She studied the setting a moment longer, then turned to Ray, whose gaze nearly set her heart on end.

So she repeated what she'd told him before, "I'll take good care of it while it's in my possession."

"Thanks. I'm glad you can appreciate the sentiment attached to it. Not all women can."

He'd mentioned being recently divorced, so she couldn't help wondering if he was talking about his ex-wife.

Had she worn it? Had she given it back to him when they'd split?

Not that it mattered, she supposed.

"So," he said, "are you ready to have lunch now?"

When she nodded, he took her hand and led her back to the diner, where they would begin their performance. They were a team, she supposed. Costars in a sense.

They also had something else in common—hearts on the mend.

Ray opened the glass door, allowing Catherine to enter first. While waiting for him to choose a table, she scanned the quaint interior of the small-town eatery, with its white café-style curtains on the front windows, as well as the yellow walls that were adorned by a trellis of daisies on the wallpaper border.

To the right of an old-fashioned cash register stood a refrigerated display case filled with pies and cakes—each one clearly homemade.

She glanced at a blackboard that advertised a full meal for only $7.99.

In bright yellow chalk, someone had written, *What the Sheriff Ate,* followed by, *Chicken-Fried Steak, Buttered Green Beans, Mashed Potatoes, Country Gravy and Apple Pie.*

The advertised special sounded delicious, but she'd have to watch what she ate today. When she'd gotten dressed back at the ranch, she'd struggled to zip her jeans and found them so snug in the waist that she'd been tempted to leave the top button undone or to wear something else.

If she didn't start cutting out all the fat and the carbs she'd been consuming since arriving in Brighton Valley, she was going to return to New York twenty pounds heavier. And where would that leave her when it came time to audition for her next part?

Of course, after that stunt Erik Carmichael had pulled, she'd be lucky if other producers didn't blackball her by association alone.

How could she have been so gullible, so blind? The one person she'd trusted completely had pulled the cashmere over her eyes. And while she feared that she'd been hard-pressed to trust another man again, it was her own gullibility that frightened her the most.

As Ray placed his hand on her lower back, claiming her in an intimate way, she shook off the bad memories and focused on the here and now.

"There's a place for us to sit." With his hand still warming her back, he ushered her to a table for two in the center of the restaurant, then pulled out her chair.

It was the perfect spot, she supposed. Everyone in the diner would see them together, which was what Ray had planned—and what he was paying for. So as soon as he'd taken the seat across from hers, she leaned forward, placed her hand over the top of his and put on her happiest smile. "I've missed you, Ray. It's so good to be together again."

His lips quirked into a crooked grin, and his green eyes sparked. "It's been rough, hasn't it?"

When she nodded, he tilted his hand to the side, wrapped his fingers around hers and gave them a gentle, affectionate squeeze. "I'm glad to have you with me for a change."

Before Catherine could manage a response, a salt-and-pepper-haired waitress stopped by their table and smiled. "Hello, Mayor. Can I get you and your friend something to drink?"

"You sure can, Margie. I'd like a glass of iced tea." Ray gave Catherine's hand another little squeeze. "What would you like, honey?"

"Water will be fine."

At the term of endearment, Margie's head tilted to the side. Then her gaze zeroed in on their clasped hands. Instead of heading for the kitchen, she paused, her eyes widening and her lips parting.

"We'll need a few minutes to look over the menu," Ray told the stunned waitress.

Margie lingered a moment, as if she'd lost track of what she was doing. Then she addressed Catherine. "I haven't seen you in town before. Are you new or just passing through?"

Catherine offered her a friendly smile. "I'm visiting for the next couple of weeks, but I'm not really passing through. I plan to move here before the end of summer."

"Well, now. Isn't that nice." Margie shifted her weight to one hip, clearly intrigued by Catherine. "Where are you staying?"

"With *me*," Ray said. "You're the first one outside the Walker family to meet my fiancée, Margie."

"Well, now. Imagine that." The waitress beamed, her cheeks growing rosy. "What a nice surprise. Of course, there's going to be a lot of heartbroken young women in town when they learn that our handsome young mayor is...already taken."

"I doubt that anyone will shed a tear over that," Ray said, turning to Catherine and giving her a wink. "But

I'm definitely taken. And I was from the very first moment I laid eyes on her in Houston."

Catherine reached for the menu with her left hand, taking care to flash the diamond on her finger. Then she stole a peek at Margie to see if the older woman had noticed—and she had.

When the waitress finally left the table, Ray said, "Margie is a great gal, but she's a real talker. By nightfall, the news of our engagement will be all over town."

As Catherine scanned the diner, which had filled with the lunch crowd, she realized that Margie might not have to say much at all, since everyone else seemed to be focusing their attention on her and coming to their own conclusions.

"So what are you going to have?" she asked as she opened the menu and tried to get back into character.

"If I hadn't already eaten a good breakfast at the Rotary Club meeting this morning, I'd have the daily special. But Caroline's helpings are usually more than filling, so I'll probably get a sandwich instead."

Moments later, Margie returned with her pad and pencil, ready to take their orders. "So what'll you have?"

"I'd like the cottage cheese and fruit," Catherine said.

Ray asked for a BLT with fries.

After jotting down their requests, Margie remained at the table, her eyes on Catherine. "So what do you think of Brighton Valley so far?"

"It's a lovely town. I'm going to like living here."

"I'm sure you will." Margie smiled wistfully. "My husband and I came here to visit his sister one summer, and we were so impressed with the people and the small-town atmosphere that we went back to Austin, sold our house and moved out here for good. In fact, it was the single best thing we ever did for our family. Brighton Valley has got to be the greatest place in the world to raise kids."

"That's what I've been telling her," Ray said. "So I'm glad you're backing me up."

"Well, let me be the first to congratulate you on your engagement," Margie said, "and to welcome you to the best little town in all of Texas."

"Thank you."

Margie nodded toward the kitchen. "Well, it was nice meeting you, but I'd better turn in your orders before you die of hunger."

When the waitress left them alone again, Ray reached into his pocket, pulled out a single key, as well as a business card, and handed it to Catherine. "This will get you into the apartment I keep in town, which is just down the street. I'll point it out to you later."

She placed the key into the pocket on the inside of her purse, then fingered the card with his contact information at both the Broken M Ranch and City Hall.

"After you go shopping at The Boutique," he added, "you can hang out and wait for me at my place. I should be home by five or five-thirty."

"All right. I'll be dressed and ready to go by the time you get there."

"Good. I've got some snacks in the pantry and drinks in the fridge. But if there's anything else you need, give me a call and I'll pick it up for you."

Anything she needed?

For the hospital benefit? Or was he talking about the duration of her acting gig?

She recalled the day Erik Carmichael had given her the key to his place, pretty much telling her the same thing, so she wasn't sure.

"Did you bring an overnight bag?" he asked.

No, only her makeup pouch. He hadn't said anything about spending the night.

Where are you staying? Margie had asked Ray just moments ago. And without batting an eye, he'd said, *With me.*

Was he expecting Catherine to actually move into his apartment while they pretended to be lovers? He hadn't mentioned anything about that when they'd discussed the job and his expectations last night.

"We'll probably be out late this evening," he added, then he bent forward and lowered his voice to a whisper. "It'll be easier that way."

She supposed it would be. And if they wanted everyone in town to assume they were lovers, staying together would make the whole idea a lot more believable.

They could, she supposed, talk about the sleeping arrangements later, but she assumed that she'd be using the sofa.

Of course, she wasn't sure what he had in mind, but she'd have to deal with that when the time came. Right now, she had a job to do.

She had to convince everyone in town that she was Ray Mendez's fiancée.

After Ray had paid the bill and left Margie a generous tip, he opened the door for Catherine and waited for her to exit. Once he'd followed her outside, they would be the talk of the diner, and that was just what he'd wanted.

Catherine had done all he'd asked of her. She'd looked at him a little starry-eyed, and she'd also used her hands when she'd talked, which had shown off the diamond his grandfather had placed upon his grandmother's finger more than seventy-five years ago.

She'd seemed to be genuinely impressed by the ring,

although he supposed that could have been part of the act. But something told him that wasn't the case, which was more than a little surprising.

Before offering the ring to Heather, he'd had it cleaned and polished. But she'd turned up her nose at wearing something that wasn't brand-new and expensive. So, like a fool, he'd gone into Houston and purchased her a two-carat diamond, which she'd taken with her when she'd told him she wanted a divorce and moved out of the ranch house.

He supposed he'd have to be thankful for Heather's greed in that respect. Otherwise, he would have lost his grandmother's ring completely—or paid through the nose to get it back, since Heather had known how much it had meant to him. And if she'd had one more thing to hold over him, they might still be in the midst of divorce negotiations.

On the other hand, Catherine seemed to have a lot more respect for the family heirloom. When she'd studied the diamond in the sunlight, she'd even asked his grandmother's name, although Ray had been so caught up in the memory of Heather scrunching up her face at the ring that Catherine's question had completely sideswiped him.

Now, as they stood outside the diner, in the mottled shade of one of the many elm trees that lined Main Street, Ray pointed to his right. "The Boutique is located right next to the ice-cream shop. And several doors down, you'll see the drugstore. There's a little red door to the left of it, which is the stairway that leads to my apartment."

"Thanks. After I buy the dress, I'll probably do some window shopping while I'm here. If anyone asks me who I am, I'll tell them I'm your fiancée. And that I'm staying with you."

"That's a good idea." He probably ought to start the

walk back to City Hall, but for some reason, he couldn't quite tear himself away.

Outside, even in the dappled sunlight, the platinum strands of her hair glistened like white gold. And when she looked at him like that, smiling as though they were both involved in some kind of romantic secret, he noticed the green flecks in her irises that made her eyes appear to be a turquoise shade. It was an amazing color.

And she was an amazing...*actress.*

In fact, she was so good at what she did that he'd have to be careful not to confuse what was real and what wasn't.

"Thanks for helping me out," he said.

"You're welcome." She didn't budge either, which meant she was waiting for him to make the first move. But there were people seated near the windows of Caroline's Diner, people who were watching the two phony lovers through the glass.

"Well, I'd better go," he said. "I've got to get back to City Hall before it gets much later. Do you have enough money to cover the dress and any incidentals you might need?"

She patted the side of her purse. "I sure do. And it's plenty. I'll probably have change to give you this evening when you get home."

Change? Now, that was a surprise. Even when they'd only been dating, Heather would have spent the entire wad and then some. And once he'd slipped a ring on her finger...well, things had just gone from bad to worse.

He was just about to say goodbye and send Catherine on her way when she eased forward, rose on tiptoe and lifted her lips to kiss him goodbye.

Of course.

Great idea.

There was an audience present, and they were two people in love. A goodbye kiss was definitely in order.

Ray stepped in and lowered his mouth to hers, but as their lips met, he found himself wrapping his arms around her and pulling her close, savoring the feel of her in his arms, the scent of her shampoo, the taste of her....

Oh, wow.

As he slipped into fiancé mode, the kiss seemed to take on a life of its own, deepening—although not in a sexual or inappropriate public display. In fact, to anyone who might be peering at them from inside the diner, their parting kiss would appear to be sweet and affectionate.

Yet on the inside of Ray, where no one else was privy, it caused his gut to clench and his blood to stir.

She placed her hand—the one that bore his grandmother's ring—on his face and smiled adoringly. As she slowly dropped her left hand, her fingers trailed down his cheek, sending ripples of heat radiating to his jaw and taunting him with sexual awareness.

Damn she was good. She even had *him* thinking there was something going on between them. No wonder Hollywood actors and actresses were constantly switching partners.

He'd best keep that fact in mind. The last thing in the world he needed to do was to get caught up in the act and to confuse fantasy with reality.

Chapter 3

When Ray entered his apartment at a quarter to five, he found Catherine seated on the sofa, watching television.

"You're home early," she said, reaching for the remote. After turning off the power, she stood to greet him.

But just the sight of the tall, shapely blonde wearing a classic black dress and heels made him freeze in his tracks.

"What do you think?" She turned around, showing him the new outfit she'd chosen.

"It's amazing," he said. And he wasn't just talking about the dress. Her transformation from actress to cover model had nearly thrown him for a loop.

Each time he saw Catherine, she morphed into a woman who was even more beautiful than the last.

Is that what dating an actress would be like? Having a different woman each time they went out?

If so, the part of him that enjoyed an occasional male fantasy sat up and took notice.

"I even found a pair of heels and an evening bag," she said, striding for the lamp table to show him a small beaded purse.

"You found all of that at The Boutique?" He'd expected her to complain about the out-of-date inventory at Brighton Valley's only ladies' dress shop. Heather, who wasn't even from a place as style conscious as New York, certainly had.

"No," Catherine said, "I had to go to Zapatos, the shoe store across the street, for the heels and bag. What do you think? Will this do?"

Would it *do?*

"Absolutely." She looked like a million bucks, which had him thinking he'd better reach for his wallet. "I couldn't have given you enough money to pay for all of that."

"Oh, yes, you did." She smiled, lighting those blue-green eyes and revealing two of the prettiest dimples he'd ever seen. "I even have a few dollars change for you."

Again, the compulsion to compare her to his ex-wife struck him hard, but he shook it off. Heather was long gone—thank goodness. And now, thanks to Catherine, Ray wouldn't need to weed out the gold diggers from the dating pool until he was ready to.

"I'll take a quick shower," he said. "Just give me a couple of minutes."

After snatching his clothes from the bedroom, he headed for the bathroom. Then, once inside, he turned on the spigot and waited for the water to heat.

Surprisingly, he was actually looking forward to attending the hospital benefit tonight, especially since he would walk in with Catherine on his arm. A man could get used to looking at a woman like her—and talking to her, too.

Of course, he was paying her to be pleasant and agreeable. If they'd met on different terms, it might be another story altogether.

He had to admit that he'd gone out on a limb by hiring a fake fiancée, but after all he'd been through with Heather, after all their divorce had cost him, he wasn't ready to date again. And even when he was ready to give it another go, he didn't think he'd ever want to get married again.

What a nightmare his marriage had turned out to be.

Of course, if he wanted to have a child, he'd have to reconsider. After all, as the only son of an only son, Ray had no one to leave his ranch and holdings to unless he had an heir. But he was still young—thirty-six on his next birthday—so he had plenty of time to think about having children.

He reached into the shower stall and felt the water growing warm, so he peeled off his clothes and stepped under the steady stream of water. As he reached for the bar of soap, he found Catherine's lavender-colored razor resting next to it, along with her yellow bath gel.

It was weird to see feminine toiletries in his bathroom again. He'd been living without a woman under his roof for nearly two years, so he'd gotten used to having the place to himself.

Still, he reached for the plastic bottle, popped open the lid and took a whiff of Catherine's soap. The exotic floral fragrance reminded him of her.

Again he realized that he could get used to coming home to a beautiful blonde like Catherine, to having her ask how his day went, to stepping into her embrace and breathing in her scent. But the Catherine who'd spent the lunch hour with him earlier today wasn't real.

He'd employed her to be the perfect fiancée, and she was merely doing her job.

Even if he got caught up in the act, if he let down his guard, believing Catherine was different and allowing himself to see her in a romantic light, he'd be making another big mistake.

After all, he'd made up his mind to steer clear of big-city women from here on out—and cities didn't get much bigger than Manhattan.

Besides, he now realized that he needed someone with both of her feet firmly planted on Brighton Valley soil.

And Catherine was only passing through.

Ray snatched one of the brown fluffy towels from the rack on the wall and dried off. After shaving and splashing on a bit of cologne, he put on his clothes—black slacks and a white dress shirt, which he left open at the collar.

After he'd combed his hair, he removed his black, Western-cut jacket from the hanger and slipped it on. Then he returned to the living room where Catherine waited for him.

She wasn't watching television this time. She was standing near the window, looking out onto Main Street. She turned when she heard his footsteps, gave him a once-over and smiled. "You look great."

He didn't know about that, but he figured people were going to think that they'd planned coordinating outfits.

"Thanks," he said. "So do you. You're going to knock the socks off every man at the benefit—married or not."

"Well, you're no slouch, Mayor. Especially when you get all dressed up. So maybe I ought to worry about running into a few jealous women tonight." A slow smile stretched across her face. "I might have to charge hazard pay."

He chuckled. "There might be a few who'll be sorry to learn I'm taken, but they'll be polite about it." He nodded toward the bedroom door. "I need to get my boots. I'll be right back."

Minutes later, he returned to the living room, ready to go.

"So tell me," Catherine said, as she reached for her small, beaded evening bag. "What made you decide to run for mayor of Brighton Valley?"

"I didn't actually run for mayor. Six months ago, after a couple of beers down at the Stagecoach Inn, I had a weak moment and agreed to run for a vacant city council seat. I'd never really wanted to get involved in politics, so I almost backed out the next day. But then I realized I might be able to make a difference in the community, so I went through with it."

"Apparently the citizens of Brighton Valley agreed with you."

"I guess you're right, because I won hands down. Then, a few weeks ago, Jim Cornwall, the elected mayor, was trimming a tree in his backyard and fell off the ladder. He suffered a skull fracture, as well as several other serious injuries. He'll be laid up for some time, so I was asked to fill the position until he returns."

"That's quite the compliment," she said.

"You're right, which is why I reluctantly agreed. Trouble was, I had enough on my plate already, with a land deal I'm in the midst of negotiating and a new horse-breeding operation that's just getting under way."

Then, on top of that, his life had been further complicated by all the single women coming out of the woodwork, now that he was single again. And if there was anything he didn't need in his life right now, it was more complications—especially of the female variety.

"Something tells me you'll be able to handle it."

She was right, of course. Ray Mendez was no quitter. He was also an idea man who could think himself out of most any dilemma.

So here he was, preparing to go to a charity event at the Brighton Valley Medical Center with a hired fiancée, albeit a lovely woman who was sure to make a splash when they walked into the hospital side by side.

Ray had never been one to want center stage, yet he didn't really mind it tonight, since he knew he'd be in good hands with an accomplished actress. So, with their employment agreement binding them, they were about to make their evening debut.

Now, as he opened the door of his apartment, the curtain was going up and the show was on. He probably ought to have a little stage fright, but he wasn't the least bit apprehensive.

Catherine, as he'd found out at their matinee performance earlier today, just outside Caroline's Diner, was one heck of an actress. All he had to do was to follow her lead.

In fact, he was looking forward to being with her tonight, to watching their act unfold.

When it was over, they'd head back to his place. He wasn't sure what would happen after that. They'd have a debriefing, he supposed. And maybe they'd kick back and watch a little TV.

He really hadn't given the rest of the evening any thought. Yet something told him he should have. He was finding his hired fiancée a little too attractive to just let the chips fall where they might.

As Catherine and Ray entered the hospital pavilion, which had been decorated with blinking white lights, black tablecloths and vases of red roses, she instinctively reached for his hand.

She wished she could say it had been part of the act, but the truth was, she was having a bit of stage fright— as unusual as that was.

He wrapped his fingers around hers and gave them a conspiratorial squeeze. "Good idea."

She wished she could have taken full credit for the hand-holding, but she'd done it without any forethought.

During the ten-minute drive from his downtown apartment to the medical center, she'd been so engrossed by the tall, dark and handsome man across the seat from her, so mesmerized by his sexy Texas drawl, that she couldn't help thinking of this evening as a date, rather than a job. So when they'd entered the pavilion and she'd spotted a sea of strangers, she'd reached for a friend.

At least, that's the way it had felt at the time.

But he was right; slipping her hand into his had been the perfect move—under the circumstances.

So what if his warm grip was actually comforting and she found herself feeling energized by the connection, strengthened by it.

Ray led her toward a petite Latina who was greeting an older man dressed in a gray suit and bold tie.

"I want to introduce you to Dr. Ramirez," he said upon their approach. "She's one of the major players trying to fund a neonatal intensive care unit at Brighton Valley Medical Center."

The attractive doctor who, even in high heels, didn't appear to be much taller than five foot two, was stylishly dressed in turquoise and black.

"Selena," Ray said, "I'd like you to meet my fiancée, Catherine Loza."

The doctor brightened, and as she reached out in greeting, Catherine released her hold on Ray long enough to give the woman a polite shake.

"I didn't realize Ray was engaged," Selena Ramirez said, "but it's no surprise. He's a great guy."

"I couldn't agree more." Catherine wondered if Selena had been one of the single women in town who'd been after Ray, although she certainly wasn't giving off those kinds of vibes now.

Even Melanie Robertson, the woman she'd met in front of the diner, had seemed a little disappointed—and maybe even envious—when she'd gotten the message that the handsome, single mayor was now taken.

"Selena is an obstetrician," Ray added. "She's been actively working with the city council to support the efforts to build the NICU."

"As it is," Selena explained, "our smallest preemies have to be airlifted to Houston. And I'd like to provide our mothers with the assurance that their babies are getting the best care available here at the medical center."

Ray nodded in agreement. "That reality really hit home for all of us when one of the councilmen's granddaughter was born. She had some serious problems at birth and had to be transported to the nearest neonatal unit. That's when we agreed to open our wallets and do whatever we could to help."

"That must have been a scary time for the councilman's family," Catherine said.

"It was." Selena's face grew solemn. "And sadly, their baby didn't make it."

Just hearing of a new mother's loss tore at Catherine's heart. She loved children and had hoped to have one or two of her own someday, but she'd had so many female problems in the past, including cysts on one of her ovaries and surgery to remove it, that the doctors had told her years ago that she wasn't likely to conceive. So her chances of having a baby of her own were slim to none.

She'd been more than a little disappointed upon learning the news, but she'd come to grips with it.

"I'd be happy to lend my support," Catherine said. "When Jennifer Walker's twins were born, they were several weeks early. But thanks to their time spent in a top-notch neonatal unit, they came home healthy and were soon thriving. So I know how valuable it is to have a NICU at the medical center."

"Jennifer Walker's twins? Are you talking about Kaylee and Kevin?"

Catherine nodded. "I used to be Jenn's roommate in New York."

"So that's how you met Ray," Selena surmised, "through Dan and Eva."

Uh-oh. That hadn't been part of the story she and Ray had created last night, but it was the truth, so she nodded in agreement. "That's how we first met, of course. But nothing came of it. Then we ran into each other again in Houston six months ago. He attended one of my performances and came to visit me backstage—just to say hello. He asked me to have a drink with him, and one thing led to another."

"You're a performer?" Selena asked.

"I sing a little and dance." Catherine thought it might be a good idea to downplay the acting.

"That's wonderful. Our next benefit is a talent show, so it would be nice if you took part in it."

Catherine was at a loss, and she glanced at Ray, hoping he'd toss her a lifeline of some kind.

"That's on the second Saturday of this month," Ray said. "Right?"

Selena nodded. "Can we count on you to perform?"

Good grief, Ray was leaving it up to her. But then again, she supposed that was only fair. He couldn't very well schedule her every waking moment.

"I'll see what kind of act I can come up with," Catherine said.

"That's great," Selena said. "Clarissa Eubanks is in charge of the talent show. I'll tell her to call the mayor's office for contact information."

"I'll make it easy on both of you," Ray said. "Catherine's staying with me."

They made the usual small talk for a while, then Selena saw someone else she needed to greet.

"Congratulations on your engagement," she said as she prepared to walk away. "I hope you'll be very happy together."

"Thank you. I'm sure we will." Catherine turned to Ray and blessed him with a lover's smile, which he returned in full force.

For a moment, as their gazes zeroed in on each other again, something she couldn't quite define passed between them, something warm and filling.

He reached to take her hand again, and as his fingers wrapped around hers, the shattered edges of her heart, which had been damaged by Erik's deceit, melded into one another, as if beginning a much-needed healing process.

Coming to Brighton Valley had been a good idea, she decided.

With her hand tucked in Ray's, reinforcing whatever tentative bond they'd forged just moments ago, her past turned a brand-new corner, revealing a future rife with promise and possibilities.

And for one brief moment in time, she could almost imagine that future including Ray Mendez.

* * *

Ever since Ray had agreed to take the job as the interim mayor of Brighton Valley, he'd spent more time at various benefits, ribbon-cutting ceremonies and dinner meetings than he'd imagined possible.

In fact, just thirty-six hours ago, he'd dreaded attending this very event.

Not that he didn't fully support the building of a new neonatal intensive care unit. He did, but he'd been waking up each morning at four, just so he could tend to his personal business commitments, as well as the political obligations that now filled his calendar.

Yet tonight, with lovely Catherine on his arm, the hospital benefit had not only been tolerable, but surprisingly pleasant.

Of course, now as the evening was winding down, he and Catherine had become separated once again. Usually they'd split up due to someone wanting to speak to him privately about one matter or another. But a couple of times, someone else had whisked Catherine away to introduce her to somebody she "just had to meet."

However, they'd always managed to find each other in the midst of the milling crowd.

Even from across the room, their gazes would meet. And when they did, Catherine would look at Ray with a lover's yearning. At least, that's the way it felt to him.

The first time it had happened, he'd been so unbalanced by the expression on her face that his breath had caught. But after a while he'd actually come to look forward to their eye contact.

What was with that?

He knew that their so-called romance was all an act, but he'd gotten so caught up in their performance that he'd found himself seeking her out, just to catch her eye.

And there she was now, standing next to a potted palm, talking to one of the doctors' wives. And here it came—the glance his way, the look, the smile, the expression that announced she would much rather be curled up in bed with him.

She was good. *Really* good. And it was all he could do to remember that they'd only just met, that she was his employee, that they hadn't slept together—and that they would never even consider it.

Well, hell. Okay, so he probably would consider it—if it ever came to that. But it wouldn't.

The affectionate glances, the touches, were all just for show. Things would be much different when they returned to his apartment.

So why was all that phony longing driving him nuts now?

Because she was such a good actress that he was buying it all—hook, line and sinker. How was that for bad luck and a lousy roll of the dice?

Still, he planned to take one last opportunity to claim his fiancée this evening. Then he'd take her home and end it all.

After checking his wristwatch and deciding now was the time, Ray made his way across the room to where Catherine was speaking to Margo Reinhold, the wife of one of the city councilmen.

"Your fiancée and I have been talking," Margo said to Ray. "I suggested that she join the Brighton Valley Women's Club. We're having a luncheon and fashion show next month, so it would be a fun meeting to attend. We're also looking for more models, so I hope she'll consider volunteering for that, as well."

There was no guarantee Catherine would still be in town this summer, so she couldn't very well commit to anything that far in advance without letting someone down.

Realizing her dilemma and seeing the indecision in her eyes, Ray stepped in to help. "I'm sure Catherine would love to join you ladies, but she has plans to...take a cruise with a couple of her girlfriends."

"Oh, yes," Catherine said, taking the baton he'd passed. "When is the fashion show?"

"It's on August the tenth."

Catherine's expression fell—just as if she were shattered that her previously made plans wouldn't allow her to take part in the event.

"Wouldn't you know it?" she said. "That's the day I set sail for the Caribbean."

"I'm so sorry to hear that," Margo said. "But there's always next year."

"Oh, of course." Catherine tossed Ray another one of those bright-eyed, I-love-you grins. Or maybe it was one of those saved-by-the-bell smiles.

"Since you won't be leaving until mid-August," Margo continued, "maybe you'd like to help with the high school dance recital. It's on the last Saturday in July. I'm sure the young people would love to have some advice from a pro."

Had Catherine told Mary that she was a dancer? And a professional? Or had Selena Ramirez spread the word?

Ray supposed it was okay that the news was out, but something told him they'd better go over their story again so they didn't get mixed up and tell on themselves.

"I'd love to work with the kids," Catherine said.

Now, wait a minute. Catherine was working for *him.* How was she going to schedule practices at the high school when he might have need of her? And what if...

Well, what if she decided to stick around in Brighton

Valley indefinitely? What would happen when he decided to end…her employment?

Of course, that could become a problem whether she started volunteering in the community or not.

Catherine placed a hand on his arm. "You don't mind, do you, honey?"

Had she read something in his expression? If so, he hadn't wanted anyone to know he was a little uneasy about their future together in Brighton Valley.

"Of course I don't mind," he said.

The women chatted a moment longer, then Margo handed Catherine a business card with her contact information. "Give me a call sometime tomorrow, and I'll schedule a meeting between you and the dance teacher at the high school."

At that point, Ray decided it was time to cut out. Who knew what else Margo had up her sleeve or what she might try to rope his pretty fiancée into?

"Are you ready to go home?" he asked Catherine.

"Yes, I am." Then she slipped her arm through his and said goodbye to Margo.

Five minutes later they were in his Cadillac Escalade and headed back to his apartment.

"Something tells me you didn't want me to volunteer to work with the dance recital," she said.

"It just took me by surprise, that's all."

"Why?"

He glanced across the seat and saw her studying him, her brow furrowed.

"I don't know," he said. "I'd hate to see you get more involved with the locals than you have to."

"Actually, I'd love to work with the kids. It will be a way for me to pay it forward."

"I don't understand."

After a beat, she said, "I grew up in a family that was both large and dysfunctional. Music was my escape from the noise and hubbub. I would have loved to have taken dance or piano lessons when I was a child, but my dad was chronically unemployed, and my mom used to spend her extra cash on beer and cigarettes for the two of them. So there wasn't any money available for the extras."

"So how'd you become a dancer?"

"In high school, I chose every music, dance or drama class I could fit into my schedule. The teachers insisted I had a natural talent, and after a while I began to believe them. I also knew that an education was my way out of the small town where we lived, so I studied hard and landed a scholarship at a small liberal arts college in the Midwest."

"And from there you decided to go to New York?"

"In a way. I met Jenn Walker at college, and she insisted that we try our luck on Broadway. But it was Miss Hankin, my high school dance teacher, and Mr. Pretz, the choral director, who convinced me that I could actually have a career doing what I loved."

So that's what she meant by paying it forward. She wanted to encourage other talented students to reach for their dreams. He had to admire that, he supposed.

"Do you miss it?" he asked. "Being on Broadway?"

"Yes, although I was ready for a break."

Dan had mentioned that she was recovering from a bad relationship. And now that Ray knew her better, he was curious about the details. And about the guy who'd broken her heart.

"Why did you need to get away?" he asked.

She paused for the longest while, then said, "The man I was involved with turned out to be a jerk. So I wanted to distance myself for a while."

"From him?"

"And from everything that reminded me of him."

She didn't say any more, and he didn't want to pry. After all, he'd had his own ways of shutting Heather out of his life after their split. So who was he to criticize someone else's way of dealing with a bad and painful situation?

After he pulled into the parking lot in back of the drugstore, he found a space and turned off the ignition.

When Catherine reached for the handle to let herself out, he said, "Hold on. I'll get it for you." Then he slid out from behind the wheel, went around to the passenger side and opened the door for her.

"I could have gotten it," she said. "There's no one around who'd see me do it."

"We don't need an audience for me to be polite."

She graced him with a moonlit smile. "Then thank you."

A shade in one of the upstairs windows opened, letting a soft light pour out from the apartment over Caroline's Diner.

Apparently they weren't entirely alone and unnoticed.

As they started back across the dimly lit parking lot, Catherine's ankle wobbled, and she reached for Ray to steady herself.

As her fingers pressed into his forearm, setting off a surge of hormones in his bloodstream, he asked, "Are you okay?"

"Yes. I stepped in an uneven spot and lost my balance."

"Those high heels look great on you, but it's got to be tough walking in them, especially out here."

"Yes, it is." Still gripping his arm, she looked up at him. And as she did so, their gazes met—and held.

There it went again, that rush of attraction. And while he knew whatever they were feeling for each other was purely sexual, he couldn't help basking in it longer than was wise.

Then, as one heartbeat lapsed into a second and a third, he reached for her waist.

"We've got an audience," he whispered, making an excuse to hold her, to draw her close.

He doubted that was really the case, though. But he didn't care. All he wanted to do right this moment was to extend the act they'd been playing a little while longer. To push for just a bit more of that heated rush.

To maybe even push for another brief kiss…

As his blood began to race, he didn't think one that was brief would be quite enough.

Besides, he told himself, a kiss from Catherine, albeit a phony one, just might help him forget all the crap Heather had put him through.

Oh, what the heck. Who was he trying to kid? He wanted to kiss Catherine senseless—even if he'd pay for it later.

So he lowered his mouth to hers.

Chapter 4

The last thing Catherine expected this evening was for Ray to kiss her goodbye while they stood in the parking lot behind his apartment.

Not that she minded.

In fact, as she stepped right into his arms, her heart raced in anticipation as if she'd been waiting all evening to get her hands on him.

And maybe, somewhere deep inside, that's just what she'd been doing, because the moment their lips touched, the kiss, which she assumed was also a thank you for a job well done, intensified.

As tongues met, their breaths caught and desire sparked, turning something that began tender and sweet into something heated and sexual.

Before long, Catherine wasn't so sure who ought to be thanking or praising whom.

In fact, right this moment, all she wanted to do was to kiss Ray back and let nature run its course. And if truth be known, she wasn't doing this for the benefit of any neighbors who might be watching.

No, her motive was a bit more selfish than that.

Over the years, she'd kissed quite a few men—most of them her costars on stage. And not a single one of those kisses had come anywhere near to moving her as much as Ray's did.

She supposed this was a nice perk that went along with the job she'd been hired to do.

As the kiss ended, Ray placed a hand on her cheek. "You were great tonight."

He'd been *great,* too—especially right now.

Somehow, she managed an unaffected smile. She'd planned to thank him and tell him it had been easy, yet as his gaze settled on hers and his fingers trailed along her cheek, she found it difficult to speak.

On the other hand, his eyes were speaking volumes to her—if she could trust them. Maybe she was misreading something that was merely appreciation for affection.

The acting was over for tonight, wasn't it?

Sometimes, when she really got into a role, she became the character she portrayed. Is that what was happening now? Had she actually become Mendez's fiancée for the past couple of hours?

If so, she'd better shake that role on her drive back to the ranch.

"Well," she said, finding the words to segue back to reality. "I guess I'd better go. I don't want Dan and Eva worrying about me."

"I hate to have you drive back to the ranch this late at night. The road isn't well lit, and some of those curves are tough to make in the daylight."

So what was he suggesting?

"You're more than welcome to stay in town with me,"

he added. "We can call the Walkers and tell them you'll be bringing the car back in the morning."

He wanted her to spend the night with him? She probably ought to be a little concerned by his expectations, yet she didn't find the idea of a sleepover all that out of line. And she wasn't sure why.

The kiss maybe? The temptation to see where another one might lead?

No, she needed to keep things a little more professional than that.

"Thanks for the offer," she said, "but I think I can make the drive without any problems. If I'd had more to drink than club soda, I might take you up on it."

Still, in spite of the decision she'd made, Catherine knew it wouldn't take much of an argument from Ray for her to call Eva and tell her there'd been a change of plans. Her knees were still wobbly from the kiss. And the chemistry the two of them shared—on or off the stage— promised to be explosive.

"Just for the record," he added. "I'll sleep on the sofa and you can have the bed."

"That's tempting," she admitted. And not only because she was tired and didn't want to make the drive back to the ranch.

"Then what's holding you back?"

The truth? Not trusting herself when her senses were still reeling from that last kiss.

Instead, she said, "I don't like to change plans after they've been made, but I'll keep your offer in mind next time—assuming there'll be another event we need to attend together."

"It's going to take more than a couple of sightings for people to realize I'm engaged."

He was probably right.

"So what's next on the agenda?" she asked.

"How about lunch tomorrow? We can meet at City Hall around noon, then walk a couple of blocks to an Italian restaurant that just opened up. The owner's grandfather is a member of the city council, and I'd like to be supportive of a new local business endeavor."

"All right. I'll see you then."

She started toward the parked minivan, and Ray followed. When she reached the driver's door, he placed his hand on her shoulder. She turned, and as their eyes met, she sensed another goodbye kiss coming her way.

"Just in case someone's watching from one of the apartment windows," he said, as he slipped his arms around her.

Yet as their lips met, she had a feeling he would have kissed her a second time tonight, even if no one was looking down at them.

And if that had been the case, she would have let him.

The chemistry between them was much stronger than she'd anticipated, which might prove to be a real problem for her in the very near future.

The handsome Brighton Valley mayor was paying her to keep the single women at bay—not to join their ranks.

Sofia, one of the younger Walker twins, had awakened with an earache. So Eva had needed her car to drive the child to the pediatrician, which meant Catherine's only mode of transportation was one of the ranch pickups.

So, after getting directions to the Brighton Valley City Hall, an ornate brick building that the town fathers had built nearly a hundred years ago, Catherine drove into town to meet Ray for lunch.

As the beat-up old pickup chugged down Main Street, past Caroline's Diner and the other quaint little shops,

Catherine held tight to the steering wheel, looking for town square and the public parking lot Dan had told her about.

Sure enough, it was right where he'd told her it would be. Once she'd found the automatic dispenser and paid for the two-hour minimum, she took the ticket back to the pickup. Then she crossed the street, entered the hundred-year-old brick building and made her way to a reception desk, where a middle-age woman with graying hair sat.

"Can I help you?" the woman asked.

Catherine offered a friendly smile. "I'm here to see Ray Mendez."

The woman's pleasant expression faded. "Do you have an appointment?"

"Not exactly. I came to have lunch with him."

"You don't say." The woman arched a brow, as if she found that hard to believe. "I'm not sure if he's available. I'll have to give him a call."

Did she treat every visitor this way?

Catherine crossed her arms and shifted her weight to one hip. "Tell him that Catherine Loza is here."

The woman lifted the telephone from its receiver, then pushed an intercom button. When someone on the other end answered, she brightened. "Hello, Mayor. It's Millie. There's a young woman named Catherine here to see you."

Millie's smile faded, and her eyes widened.

"Your...fiancée?" She took another gander at Catherine, her expression softening. "Of course. I'll tell her you'll be right down."

Millie hung up the phone, then offered Catherine a sheepish grin. "I'm *so* sorry, Ms. Loza. It's just that I had no idea he... That you..."

"That's okay." Catherine lifted her left hand and flashed the diamond. "We haven't told many people yet."

"Still, I'm sorry. I didn't mean to be rude. It's just that I was asked to screen his calls and his visitors."

"I understand," Catherine said, realizing that Ray hadn't been exaggerating when he'd said the single women in town were making it difficult for him to get any work done.

Millie pointed to a row of chairs near her desk. "You can have a seat, if you'd like. But he said he'd be right down."

"Thank you."

Within moments Ray came sauntering down the hall, a dazzling smile stretched across his face. "Hi, honey. Did you have any trouble finding the place?"

"No, not at all."

They kissed briefly in greeting, then Ray turned to the receptionist and said, "Thanks, Millie. I see you met Catherine. What do you think?"

"I think the local girls are going to be brokenhearted, especially when they realize they can't compete with the future Mrs. Mendez." Millie chuckled. "And once word gets out, it'll make my job easier. Now I won't have to stretch the truth and come up with excuses for you anymore."

"I guess my engagement is a win-win for all of us." Ray placed a hand on Catherine's back. "Are you ready to go, honey?"

"Whenever you are."

Ray took her by the hand, and after a two-block walk, they crossed the street to a small restaurant that offered curbside dining under the shade of a black awning.

"It's a nice day," Ray said. "Why don't we sit outside?"

"That sounds good to me."

After Ray told the hostess their preference, they were led to a linen-draped table and handed menus.

Ray held Catherine's chair as she took her seat. Then he sat across from her.

"I heard the manicotti was pretty good," he said.

Catherine scanned the menu, tempted to choose the pasta, but knowing she didn't need the carbs when she wasn't having regular workouts each day.

"What looks good to you?" Ray asked.

"I'd like the vegetarian antipasto salad—the oil and vinegar on the side. And a glass of water with lemon."

"That's it?"

"Yes, but I might try to steal a bite of whatever you're having—as long as it's high in carbs and covered in cheese."

He tossed her a boyish grin. "Be my guest."

Fifteen minutes later, after several of the townspeople stopped to say hello to the mayor and were pleasantly surprised to meet his "future bride," the waiter brought out their meals.

"Can I get you anything else?" the young man asked.

"No, this is fine for now." Ray glanced down at the lasagna he'd ordered. "I had no idea the servings would be this large. I'll give you half of it."

"Oh, no you don't. I just want a taste."

Ray cut off a good size chunk anyway, placed it on a bread plate, then passed it to her.

It was, she decided, just the kind of thing that lovers and friends did while eating. Yet she hadn't given their roles any thought when she'd asked to sample his meal.

Were they becoming friends?

Before she would even risk pondering the idea of them ever becoming lovers, she asked, "Do you have anything special on the calendar this week?"

"There's a community barbecue in the town square on Saturday afternoon. Besides having the best rib eye you've ever tasted, they'll have a pie-eating contest and a line-dance competition."

That sounded like fun. "What's the dress code?"

"I suppose you'd call it country casual, with denim being the only requirement."

"I can handle that." Catherine cut into the lasagna Ray had given her with a fork and took a bite. The minute it hit her mouth, she wished she'd agreed to split their meals.

"Do you have any Western boots?" Ray asked.

"No. Do I need a pair?"

"Not really. You'll be fine in jeans."

Maybe Eva would have a pair she could borrow. She'd ask her as soon as she got home.

They ate in silence for a while, and when Catherine reached for her glass of water, she caught Ray staring at her.

"What's wrong?" she asked.

"Nothing."

She didn't believe him.

Finally, he said, "You're a good sport."

She always tried to be. But something told her his comment held a deeper meaning. "What makes you say that?"

"Because you're a big-city girl. All this country-bumpkin stuff has to be pretty foreign to you. Are you that good of an actress?"

She laughed. "I'm a pretty good actress, but I wasn't always a big-city girl. I grew up in a small town in New Mexico, although it wasn't anything like Brighton Valley."

"You mentioned that to me before, but I still have trouble imagining you as anything other than a big-city girl."

"Why is that?"

He shrugged. "The way you carry yourself, I suppose. And because of your background on the Broadway stage."

"I've spent the past ten years surrounded by bright lights and skyscrapers, but that wasn't always the case."

"What was it like growing up in a small New Mexico community?" he asked.

"It was dry, hot and dusty for the most part. And I couldn't wait to leave it all behind."

He took a bite of garlic bread. "What about your family? Do they still live there?"

"A few of them do. My dad died when I was twelve, and my mother passed on about five years ago. Most of my siblings cut out the minute they turned eighteen, just like I did."

"*Most* of them? How many brothers and sisters do you have?"

"There were seven of us—three boys and four girls."

"I was an only child," he said. "I always wondered what it would have been like to have had siblings."

"Big families aren't always what they're cracked up to be. Mine was pretty loud and dysfunctional, and so I escaped through reading or listening to music."

"Is that when you decided to be an actress?"

She'd been gone so long and traveled so far, that whenever she looked back on those days, it was hard to believe she'd ever been that lonely girl with big dreams.

"I knew that an education was my only way out of that town—and school provided the lessons I wanted. So I studied hard and landed a scholarship."

"At the college where you met Dan's sister?"

"Yes. Jennifer was determined to perform on Broadway, and her dreams were contagious. I began to think that I might be able to make the cut, too."

"And you did." He smiled, his eyes beaming as though he was proud of her.

Her heart skipped a beat at his belief in her, at his pride in her accomplishment. She hadn't had a cheerleader since Jenn died. And while Dan and Eva had always liked hearing about her successes, she'd never been able to share her failures with them in hopes of getting a pep talk.

She offered Ray a wistful smile. "After we graduated from college Jenn and I moved to New York, rented a small apartment in the Bronx and then tried out for every off-Broadway play or musical available. In time, we began to make names for ourselves, first with bit parts, then with an occasional lead role."

"Sounds like the perfect world—at least, for you."

"Yes and no. When Jennifer got pregnant with the twins and feared she'd have to call it quits, I was afraid I couldn't make it on my own. Not because I didn't have the talent, but Jenn was the one with the determination and the perseverance, the one who kept me going when things didn't work out as hoped or planned. So I offered to support her any way I could—*if* she'd stay in New York."

"Support? You mean financially or with the kids?"

"Both. I had no idea how difficult it would be to bring home two newborns."

"I'll bet that changed both of your lives."

It certainly had. And in a good way. A lot of roommates might have had qualms about having crying babies in the house, but Catherine and Jennifer had become a team—and a family.

But then again, Catherine had suffered a lot of female problems in the past. Since she'd been told that having a child of her own wasn't likely, it was only natural that she grew exceptionally close to Kaylee and Kevin.

"It must have been tough when Jennifer died."

Catherine nodded. Just the thought of losing the young woman who'd been both her best friend and a better sister than the three she'd had brought tears to her eyes.

It might have been four years ago, but the grief sometimes still struck hard and swift.

She could still recall that awful day as though it had been yesterday. She'd been home watching the kids and practicing the lines for a new part in an off-Broadway production when the doorbell rang. And when she'd answered, she'd found an NYPD officer on the stoop, who'd told her the news: Jennifer had been killed while crossing a busy Manhattan street—struck by a car.

At that time, Jennifer and her brother Dan, the twins' only surviving relative, had been estranged. He'd been devastated to learn of his sister's death and had flown to New York to do whatever he could. But the twins weren't quite five years old and hardly knew him. So Catherine had volunteered to keep the children for a few months to help them through the grieving process and to allow them time to get to know their uncle better.

When the kids finally moved to Brighton Valley, Catherine had missed them terribly, but she knew it was for the best. Still, she called regularly and visited them in Texas as often as her work would allow—although it wasn't nearly as often as she would have liked.

"I'm sorry," Ray said. "I didn't mean to bring up something painful and turn your afternoon into a downer."

Catherine lifted her napkin and dabbed it under her eyes. "That's okay. It happens sometimes. We were very close. And I still miss her." Then she managed a smile. "I really don't mind talking about her. And I don't usually cry."

As Ray watched Catherine wipe the tears from her

eyes, he regretted the questions that had stirred up her grief. He'd only wanted to learn more about her, to get to know her better.

If they'd actually been dating, if he'd had the right to quiz her about her past, it might have been different.

She glanced at the napkin, noting black streaks on the white linen.

"My mascara is running," she said.

"Just a bit."

"I probably look like a raccoon." She smiled through her tears, relieving the tension, as well as his guilt. "Excuse me for a minute. I'm going to find the ladies' room and see if I can repair the damages."

Catherine had no more than entered the restaurant when Ray spotted Beverly Garrison getting out of her parked car. Beverly was the president of her homeowners' association and made it a point to attend every city council meeting, whether the agenda had anything to do with her neighborhood or not.

When Beverly saw him, she brightened and waved. "You're just the one I wanted to see, Mayor. I have something to give you."

Then she reached into the passenger seat and pulled out a yellow plastic tub.

What the heck was in it? Margarine?

"I looked for you over at Caroline's Diner," she said as she bumped her hip against the car door to shut it. "But you weren't there. Someone suggested I look for you here."

She headed for his table. "I brought you a treat."

"What is it?" Ray asked.

"Two dozen of the best homemade oatmeal-raisin cookies you've ever eaten in your life. My daughter baked a fresh batch this morning. Carol Ann is a little shy, so she asked me to give them to you."

As Ray glanced down at the yellow tub, Beverly reached for the lid, peeled it off and revealed a stack of cookies that certainly looked delicious.

"Thanks for thinking of *me*," he said, a little surprised that she'd go so far as to chase him down.

"Oh, it wasn't me." Beverly's hand flew up to her chest, as she took a little step back. "It was my *daughter*. You remember Carol Ann, don't you? She's the pretty blonde who showed up at the last city council meeting with me."

Ray remembered, but poor Carol Ann, who'd spent most of the time with her nose stuck in a book, was neither pretty nor blond. At best, she was a rather nondescript woman with stringy, light brown hair. She was also in her forties, which meant she was five to ten years older than him.

Not that age was that big of an issue. But Ray wasn't looking for a date.

Of course, he didn't want to hurt the woman or her daughter's feelings, so he kept those thoughts to himself.

"You'll have to thank Carol Ann for me," he said.

"I can certainly do that, but why don't I give you her telephone number instead? That way, you can call her yourself. It'd be a nice thing for you to do."

Ray took a deep breath, then glanced to the doorway of the restaurant, where Catherine stood, watching the matchmaking mama do her thing.

Catherine's lips quirked into a crooked grin, clearly finding a little humor in the situation.

Beverly reached into her black vinyl handbag and pulled out a pen and notepad. Then she scratched out Carol Ann's contact information, tore out the sheet she'd written upon and handed it to Ray. "Carol Ann has plenty of time on her hands these days. She and Artie Draper broke up a few months back, and…well, what with your recent divorce and all, I'm sure you understand how tough it is to get back into the dating world again."

It actually wouldn't be tough at all for him to start dating—if he were inclined to do so. There were single women ready, willing and able at every turn.

"I'll be sure to call Carol Ann and thank her for the cookies," Ray said, getting to his feet and glancing to the doorway where Catherine stood by.

"That would be wonderful," Beverly said.

Taking her cue, Catherine approached the table.

"Beverly," Ray said, "I'd like to introduce you to my fiancée, Catherine Loza."

"How do you do," Catherine said. "Goodness, will you look at those yummy cookies."

Beverly's eyes widened and her lips parted as she ran an assessing gaze over Catherine. "I…I…um, didn't know you were engaged, Mayor…."

"It's only been official for a few days," Catherine said with a gracious smile. "And we haven't made any formal announcements."

Beverly took a step back, then fingered the top button of her blouse. "You know, I can probably thank Carol Ann for you, Mayor. There's probably no need for you to call her. She's pretty shy. And well, I'd hate to see her embarrassed. She…uh…"

"I understand," Ray said. "I wouldn't want to cause her any discomfort, especially after her recent breakup. But please give her my best. Tell her the right guy will come along. And before she knows it, she'll be happy again."

"Well," Beverly said, nodding toward her car. "I really need to get going. I have a lot of errands to run."

"Thank you for the cookies," Ray said. "Do you want me to return the container?"

"No, don't bother. You can just recycle it when you're through." Then she turned and strode to her car.

Ray pulled out Catherine's chair, and when she took a seat, he followed suit.

Once Beverly had closed her car door and backed out of her parking space, Ray glanced across the table, his gaze meeting Catherine's.

"See what I mean?" he asked. "That kind of thing happens to me all the time. And most of them don't know how to take a polite no for an answer."

"Well, hopefully, once word gets out that you're taken, you won't have to deal with those kinds of distractions anymore."

That was his plan. Having a hired fiancée seemed to be working like a charm, thank goodness. Although he had to admit, another actress might not have been able to pull it off with Catherine's grace and style.

Ray studied the beautiful blonde as she ate the last of her salad.

The sunlight glimmered in her hair, making the strands shine like white gold... The teal-colored blouse she wore made her blue-green eyes especially vivid today.

While in the restroom, she'd reapplied her mascara, as well as her pink lipstick.

Damn, she was attractive. And not just because of her appearance. In a matter of two days, she'd added something to his life—smiles, camaraderie...

Of all the women he'd met since his split from Heather, Catherine seemed to be the only one who might not complicate things.

Of course, she was an actress, so who knew if he was seeing the real Catherine. She also lived—and no doubt thrived—in Manhattan, which was worlds away from Brighton Valley.

Still, if things were different...

If he could trust that the woman who'd revealed herself to him was real...

If she were a normal, down-home type...

If she planned to escape the city lights and excitement and move to a small Texas town...

...then Ray would be sorely tempted to ask her out on a real date.

Chapter 5

On Saturday afternoon Catherine climbed into the same old ranch pickup she'd driven before and headed for Ray's apartment, but she wasn't sure if she would make it or not. Each time she stopped at an intersection, the engine sputtered and chugged as though it might stall at any moment.

Thankfully, she reached the alley behind the drugstore and parked in the lot next to a battered green Dumpster.

Before climbing out of the cab, she reached into her purse, pulled out her cell and called Dan.

"I'm sorry to bother you," she said, "but there's something wrong with the pickup."

"Are you stranded along the road?"

"No, I made it. But I'm not sure if I'll be able to get home or not."

He paused a moment, then said, "The ranch hands have all left for the day. And I'm still waiting for the vet. But I'll try to get out there as soon as I can."

Dan had a broodmare that was sick. And earlier this

morning, while climbing on the corral near the barn, Kevin had fallen down and sprained his ankle, which was why Dan, Eva and the kids wouldn't be coming to the town barbecue.

"Don't give it another thought," Catherine said. "I just wanted to let you know. I'll ask Ray to look under the hood. And I'll also have him bring me home this evening."

"Don't bother asking Ray to look at the truck," Dan said. "As long as it won't put you in a bind or strand you in town, you can leave it right where it is. I'll call a towing service and have it brought home on Monday."

After she ended the call, Catherine got out of the pickup and crossed the parking lot. She'd borrowed a pair of cowboy boots from Eva, as well as faded jeans and a blue-and-white gingham blouse. She was certainly going to fit right in with the other Brighton Valley residents today, which ought to please Ray.

A smile tugged at her lips as she climbed the stairs to the small apartment, then used the key Ray had given her. She was a few minutes early, so once she was inside, she made herself at home—just as he'd told her to do.

The sparsely furnished apartment, while clean, tidy and functional, lacked any artwork on the walls or accent colors. She was tempted to pick up a couple of throw pillows, something to brighten up the place and make it a bit homier. But she supposed it didn't matter. Ray stayed here only on the nights he didn't want to drive all the way back to the ranch.

Catherine turned on the television. Then after finding the Hallmark channel, she took a seat on the brown leather sofa and watched the last half of a romantic comedy about a woman who was snowbound in a cabin with her ex-husband.

It wasn't until the ending credits began to roll that she heard another key in the lock, alerting her to Ray's arrival.

"I'm sorry I'm late," he said as he closed the door and stepped into the small living area that opened up to a kitchen and makeshift dining room. "I meant to get here sooner, but I was at a funeral of an old friend of my parents, and his widow asked me to meet with her and her attorney."

"Please don't apologize." Using the remote, she shut off the power on the television, then got to her feet. "I'm so sorry to hear that."

"Thanks. It wasn't a surprise. He'd been sick for a long time, so it was probably for the best." He loosened his tie.

Not only was Ray a successful rancher, he was also a loyal friend, which Catherine found admirable. No wonder he'd been elected to the city council and appointed mayor.

"Look at you," he said, breaking into a smile. "You're going to be the prettiest cowgirl at the barbecue."

Catherine didn't know about that, but she thanked him just the same.

"I need to change into something more appropriate," he said. "I'll only be a minute or two."

She knew he'd planned to be home a lot sooner than this. "Is there anything I can do to help? I know you'd wanted to arrive early."

"I was going to welcome everyone before the music started, but that's not going to happen now. I'll just have to do that at the halfway point." His steps slowed. "In fact, I'm even going to take time to get a drink of water."

"Is your life always like this?" Catherine asked as she returned to her seat on the sofa. "Do you run from one event or meeting to another?"

"Yep. That's pretty much the way each day goes."

She smiled. "I'll have to keep that in mind if I ever decide to run for public office."

"Actually," he said, removing his jacket, "I never planned on going into politics, but a few of my friends and neighbors—including Dan Walker—had been urging me to run for the city council. I'd put them off for a while, but…"

"Now here you are," she said, "the mayor of Brighton Valley."

"The *interim* mayor," he corrected. "I'm covering for Jim Cornwall, remember?"

"Are you sorry you took on the extra work?" she asked.

"I really don't mind the job itself. The biggest problem I have is balancing all of my other responsibilities."

"Such as…?"

"The day-to-day duties on my ranch, as well as the new horse-breeding operation I'm just starting up with Dan." He blew out a sigh, and his shoulders seemed to slump a bit. "I hate leaving others to do the work I should be doing myself. And it's not easy being pulled in a hundred different directions. But I can handle it. Besides, now that you've stepped in as my 'fiancée,' things are a lot easier. I don't have to fend off the single ladies in town."

"That surprises me."

"What does?" He hung his jacket on the back of one of the dinette chairs. "That the women are interested in me?"

"No, not that." Goodness, not *that*. The man was successful, well-respected, personable and drop-dead gorgeous. "I'm just a little surprised that you're not the least bit interested in dating."

"I don't have time for a relationship. And even if I did, I'm not ready to get involved in another one."

If that was the case, then his ex-wife must have done a real number on him—just as Erik had done to her.

"Not that it's really any of my business," she said, "but why aren't you ready to start dating?"

"My divorce got ugly." He strode to the kitchen area, pulled a glass from the cupboard, then filled it with water from the tap. "And when the one person in the world you depend on to have your back kicks you in the ass instead…well, even a cowboy isn't too eager to get back in the saddle again."

She knew exactly what he meant. That's why she was in Brighton Valley these days, rather than in Manhattan.

After Ray had quenched his thirst and put the empty glass in the sink, Catherine said, "You mentioned that your divorce got ugly. I assume your marriage started out all right. When did things go south?"

"Probably after the first few weeks. But our relationship was wrong from the get-go. And it's my fault for not realizing that."

Catherine should have seen Erik's flaws, too, but love—or whatever she'd felt for him—had blinded her to them. She'd not only been hurt, but she'd felt pretty stupid, too. So it was nice to know she wasn't the only one who'd been snowballed by someone she'd cared about, someone she'd trusted.

"What clues did you miss?" she asked.

"First of all, Heather was a city girl who didn't like living on a ranch. And I was crazy for thinking she'd eventually get used to it." He clucked his tongue and shook his head. "She was also selfish and greedy. I'd noticed it going in, I suppose. But I hadn't realized just how bad it really was." He pointed to Catherine's left hand. "When

I asked Heather to marry me, she turned up her nose at the ring you're wearing. I know it isn't much, but she couldn't see the value in it—the vows made and kept over the years."

Catherine lifted her finger, studied the small stone. Again she thought about Ray's grandmother, the woman who'd worn it and cherished the love and the promises it had represented.

"I should have taken a step back and reconsidered my proposal at that point," Ray said as he left the kitchen area, "but I stuck the ring in the safe, then went out and purchased a two-carat diamond for her instead."

Catherine had always believed there were two sides to every story—until she'd met Erik and fallen for his lies. So she found herself disliking Ray's ex-wife, even though they'd never met.

"Were the two of you ever happy?" she asked.

"At first, but once we got home from our honeymoon, the complaints started. And it became clear that she hated everything about my life—and me, too. Before long, she was spending more time in the city than she was in Brighton Valley. The day we split, she finally admitted that she was having an affair with a plastic surgeon."

"I'm sorry."

"About the divorce? Don't be. It was for the best. Trouble was, she hired a high-priced attorney out of Houston, and even though I'd expected to pay a hefty settlement, I hadn't been prepared for a legal battle. Each time I thought we'd reached some kind of agreement, she'd ask for something else. The whole thing dragged on for nearly two years."

Catherine didn't know what to say. Another *I'm sorry* seemed not only redundant but inadequate.

"I'm just glad it's finally over," he said. "So you can

see why I'd be hesitant to get involved with someone else again—especially a woman who's only interested in me because she thinks I'd make a good catch."

Ray Mendez would make a *wonderful catch* for any woman, so Catherine could certainly understand why every Tamara, Diane and Mary in town was trying her best to snag his attention or set him up with someone she knew.

Yet Ray had a lot more going for him than his financial portfolio and political standing in the community. And he deserved a woman who'd be true blue and a helpmate to him.

"Dan said you'd been through a breakup, too," Ray said.

Catherine hadn't meant to bring up the subject. Goodness, she was trying to forget Erik and all he'd put her through. But after Ray's heartfelt disclosure, it seemed only fair to admit that she'd been hurt and disappointed, too.

"Last year I met a producer who'd recently moved to Manhattan from London. He asked me out, and we started dating. Before long, he promised me a starring role in the play he was producing, and I was thrilled. In fact, he also gave me an opportunity to invest in the production, which meant I'd reap some of the profit.

"For the first time in my life, I began to believe that I might finally be able to have it all—a successful career and a happy marriage. But he turned out to be a scam artist who ran off, taking the funding for a production that never came to pass."

"I'm sorry to hear that."

Catherine had not only been crushed and embarrassed by his deception, but she'd also lost a large chunk of her savings to the lying jerk.

"So you decided to get away for a while?" Ray asked.

That was about the size of it. She'd sublet her brownstone for three months and flown to Texas to stay with Dan and Eva.

"I figured that Brighton Valley would be a great place to lick my wounds and to sort out my options," she admitted.

And while she was here, she'd use the downtime to allow her body to mend. Like many professional dancers, she'd suffered a couple of injuries that made it difficult for her to continue performing in musicals.

To be honest, she hoped to land more singing or acting roles from now on. But she'd deal with that once she got back to Manhattan.

In the meantime, she tossed Ray an appreciative smile. "And thanks to you, I'll not only be able to stay longer, I'll also be able practice my acting skills while I'm here."

"I'm glad to do my part. You've been a real godsend. If things continue to go well, I'll have to give you a bonus."

With finances being what they were, she could certainly use the extra cash, but she couldn't take any more money for doing a job that came so easily to her.

"That's not necessary," she said. "I get a lot of perks working for you."

"Such as…?"

"Meals and entertainment."

As their gazes met, as their time so far together came to mind, another perk crossed her mind: heart-spinning kisses that turned her every which way but loose.

Her cheeks warmed at the memory. Afraid to let him know what she was thinking, she turned away, walked several steps to the window and peered at the street below just so she could break eye contact.

"When do you plan to return to New York?" he asked.

"I don't know. In a couple of months, maybe. I don't have a return flight scheduled."

She liked knowing she could leave whenever she grew tired of being in Brighton Valley, although she found the rural Texas setting both quaint and restful. But she'd grown up in a small town and had found it to be stifling.

In Manhattan, she'd thrived and had finally become the woman she was meant to be.

"Well, I'd better get into my boots and jeans," he said, removing his wristwatch and leaving it on the dinette table, "or we'll end up arriving even later than we already are."

Minutes later, Ray sauntered into the living room in his Western wear, his Stetson in hand. His bright-eyed, sexy grin was so mesmerizing that Catherine couldn't help thinking that he made the perfect cowboy hero to play opposite her.

How did Brighton Valley's most handsome and eligible bachelor get better-looking each time she laid eyes on him?

"I'm sorry I kept you waiting," he said.

She offered him a breezy smile and said, "No problem," even though she could see a huge one looming on the horizon.

Ray had hired her to keep the local ladies from setting their romantic sights on him, and she had no reason to doubt that they'd respect the phony engagement.

Catherine would respect the role she was playing, too. And there was the problem.

As Ray opened the door for her, she grabbed her purse and proceeded downstairs. In a matter of minutes she'd be strolling along the street with the hottest cowboy in town.

She'd pretend to be in love with the handsome mayor,

although it wouldn't take much acting on her part to feign her affection or her attraction to him.

No, the real difficulty would be in forgetting that it was all part of the act.

Ray and Catherine decided to walk to the community barbecue, since the town square was just down the street. In fact, it was so close that they'd barely stepped onto the sidewalk when they caught a hearty whiff of mesquite-grilled meat and heard the sound of bluegrass music.

"It sure smells good," Catherine said.

"Wait until you taste it. Brighton Valley goes all out for this event."

Ray, who'd been fighting the urge to hold her hand while they'd made the five-block walk, reached for it now.

It was all part of the act, he told himself. Yet there was something very appealing about Catherine. Something that made him happy to be with her.

Maybe it was the fact that she wasn't batting her eyelashes at him, that she wasn't delivering homemade cookies and hinting that she'd like more than a friendship.

Yeah, he told himself. That had to be it.

But as she slipped her hand into his, as their fingers threaded together, a burst of pride shot through him.

Or was it more than that?

Unwilling to let the possibility of anything "more" take root, he said, "I think you'll have a good time. Besides having the best barbecue food you've ever eaten, several of the local bands will be playing and trying to outdo each other as a way of promoting themselves for future parties and performances."

"Is it all bluegrass and country-western music?" she asked.

"For the most part. You'll hear some banjo groups

and a couple of fiddlers. But there'll probably be some classic rock, too."

"It sounds fun."

He'd always liked attending the event, but something told him he was going to enjoy it a whole lot more with Catherine as his date.

Well, not a date in the classic sense of the word.

As they turned the corner and caught the first glimpse of the town square, Ray gave her hand a gentle squeeze. "Here we are."

The parklike area had already begun to fill with local residents, who stood in small groups on the grass or sat in some of the white chairs and tables they'd gotten from the party-rental company.

Near the courthouse, the Barbecue Pit, a local restaurant known for its great sauce, had set up an old-style chuck wagon, as well as a portable barbecue grill, where several men with white aprons watched the meat cook over mesquite chips.

Over by the restrooms, Charlie Biller's bluegrass band played their last set, as the Dave Hawkins Trio stood by, waiting to take their place on stage.

Now would be a good time for Ray to walk up to the microphone and welcome everyone to the event that had become one of the highlights of the year.

They'd barely stepped off the sidewalk and onto the grass when they were met by Buddy Elkins, one of the older city council members. Buddy was dressed in his cowboy finest—complete with boots, a silver buckle and a Stetson.

As recognition dawned, the silver-haired councilman headed straight for Ray with a big grin on his face. "I'd heard you snatched up the prettiest little gal in these parts, but I gotta tell ya', Mayor, the rumor mill didn't do this young lady justice. You really hit the jackpot this time."

Ray winked at Catherine, then released her hand so he could shake Buddy's. "You've got that right. I'm a lucky man. Catherine has renewed my faith in women."

That same surge of pride returned as Ray watched Buddy tip his hat to Catherine. "I'm pleased to meet you, ma'am."

She thanked him, then blessed him with a pretty smile.

Buddy elbowed Ray. "There'll be a hundred young men who'll be chomping at the bit to take your place— and a few my age who'd like to give you a run for your money. So you'd better treat her right."

"You can bet on it." Ray stole a glance at Catherine, and she gave him one of those starry-eyed smiles he'd suggested she throw his way every now and again. But this one shot right to his heart—or somewhere thereabouts. In fact, if he didn't know better, he'd think it was real.

Too bad it wasn't. He could get used to having a woman look at him like that—especially if the lady was her.

Shaking off the effects of their playacting, Ray said, "I'm going to head over to the stage and welcome people to the barbecue. But I'll be right back, Buddy. So don't try to steal my girl from me."

Buddy, who was nearing seventy, chuckled. "I'll keep my eye on her and chase off any riffraff who might not be as honorable as I am."

Ray brushed a kiss on Catherine's cheek, but as he did so, he caught a whiff of her floral scent, which taunted him to distraction. But he didn't dare stray from his task, so he excused himself and headed for the bandstand.

Along the way, several of the local townspeople

stopped him to ask about one thing or another—but mostly to congratulate him on his engagement. For the first time in what seemed like ages, no one tried to hit on him or introduce him to the perfect woman.

Apparently the Brighton Valley residents had begun to realize that he'd already found her.

Of course, when it came to hired fiancées, he certainly had. Catherine was not only classy and sophisticated, but she also seemed to have a down-to-earth way about her.

Ray reminded himself that she was a talented actress who was able to immerse herself in a role. And even though a bucolic setting and small-town personalities held little appeal to a woman who'd moved on to the big city, Catherine appeared to be in her element and charmed everyone she met.

In fact, Ray felt a little bewitched by her, too.

When Charlie Biller, the leader of the bluegrass band, noticed Ray standing near the stage, he nodded to acknowledge him.

As soon as the song ended, the audience broke into applause. Charlie thanked them, then announced, "Let's all give a hand to Mayor Mendez."

Once Ray stood at the microphone, he welcomed everyone to the barbecue, then thanked the committee members who'd worked so hard to put on the event, as well as the local businesses and citizens who'd made donations of both money and goods.

"Before I turn the stage over to Dave and his trio," Ray said, "I'd like to take a minute to thank you for offering your best wishes on my engagement."

A brief hush fell on the crowd, followed by a gasp or two and some startled looks.

Ray scanned the grounds, looking for Catherine, finding her in the same place he'd left her. "Honey? Where are you?"

The townspeople, many of whom hadn't heard the news, began to crane their necks, seeking the woman in question.

Catherine, who wore a pretty smile, lifted her hand and fluttered her fingers. Then she blew Ray a little kiss.

Damn. She was good. And so *natural*....

So believable.

But Ray couldn't very well stand there and gawk at her like everyone else. So he said, "Let's get on with the show."

As the trio of banjo players took their place onstage, Ray stepped onto the lawn, only to be stopped by Clyde Wilkerson, one of the local ranchers.

"I had no idea you were engaged," Clyde said. "When in the world did that happen? My wife was planning to invite you to dinner so she could introduce you to our niece."

"I kept things quiet until I popped the question and she said yes."

Clyde took another gander at Catherine. "Lucky you. She's certainly a pretty one."

"Yes, she is." Ray found himself craning his neck, looking for her. And wanting to make his way back to her.

"Where'd you find her?" Clyde asked.

"In Houston. I saw her dance on stage at the Yellow Rose Theater, and I knew right then and there that I had to meet her. We've been seeing each other for several months now."

"I don't suppose she has a sister," Clyde said. "I'd sure like to see my son Grady find a lady like that."

Catherine, who'd managed to break free of Buddy,

made her way to where Ray and Clyde were standing. She offered Ray an I-missed-you-baby smile, then slipped her arm through his.

Trouble was, Ray had kind of missed her, too.

He supposed he ought to be glad his ploy was working—and he was. The whole town square was abuzz with whispers about the mayor's new lady and nods of approval, indicating they were all clearly impressed by the match.

Thank goodness for that small miracle.

Some bachelors might find it nice to have nearly every single woman in town trying to catch their eye. And while Ray had spent more than his share of lonely nights during the months leading to his divorce and the two years after he and Heather had split, he'd put it all behind him now. And it grated on him to have anyone assume that he'd never be a whole man until he landed another wife, when that couldn't be any further from the truth.

Heck, even if he were the needy kind, he wasn't interested in complicating his life with romance until long after his job as interim mayor was finished. And to be honest, the jury was still out on whether he ever wanted another wife or not. His divorce had left him more than a little gun-shy when it came to trusting his heart to anyone again. So he wasn't going to give matrimony another try anytime soon.

Of course, it was a little weird and disconcerting to think that he'd not only had to pay through the nose to divorce the ex-wife who'd made his life a living hell, but that he was now paying a fake fiancée to keep his life simple and maintain his privacy.

On the other hand, he found himself enjoying Catherine's attentions far more than he could have imagined.

So he placed his hand on her lower back. "Come on, honey. Let's get something to eat."

They'd no more than taken a couple of steps when an old pickup started up, then backfired.

Catherine jumped. "What was that? A gunshot?"

Ray slipped his arm around her and smiled. "No, it was just an old truck that needs a tune-up."

"Oh, thank goodness." As they walked toward the chuck wagon, she leaned into him, just as if it was the most natural thing in the world to do.

And maybe it was.

"Speaking of old trucks," she said, "I completely forgot to mention this. Dan's pickup, which I drove into town today, isn't running very well. So I'm going to need a ride home this evening—unless you don't mind me sleeping on your sofa."

No kidding? Ray would love to have her stay the night with him in town. And she didn't need to take the sofa. She could sleep anywhere she liked.

"If you spend the night," he said, "I'll take you to Caroline's Diner for breakfast in the morning. The Brighton Valley Rotary is meeting in the back room, and that way, people will assume we're not only engaged but sleeping together."

It was kind of a lame excuse, especially since Ray hadn't even planned to attend the meeting. But if it meant having Catherine to himself this evening, then so be it.

"Sounds good to me."

It did? Was she feeling that comfortable with him, too? Or did spending the night just make her job easier?

The only way to find out for sure was to ask, and he wasn't about to do that.

They continued on to the chuck wagon and the spread of food that had been set out on long tables, but it took nearly twenty minutes to get there, thanks to all the folks who stopped them to offer their congratulations.

Each time it happened, Catherine lit up like a happy bride at her wedding.

Needless to say, the phony engagement was working beautifully, and Ray couldn't imagine anyone thinking that Catherine wasn't in love with "her man."

He supposed he ought to be pleased, but for some reason, he felt compelled to steal her away from the crowd, to find someplace quiet and romantic where they could spend the rest of the evening alone.

And he didn't dare contemplate why.

Chapter 6

As the sun set over Brighton Valley, black, wrought-iron gas lamps that had been spaced throughout the town square came on, bathing the parklike grounds in a soft glow.

An hour earlier, Ray had introduced Catherine to Shane and Jillian Hollister, then asked the couple to join them at their table when they ate dinner. Shane, who'd once been a detective with the Houston Police Department, had worked on Dan Walker's ranch prior to being appointed as the Brighton Valley sheriff.

Shane was off duty today, yet he continued to make the rounds, just as Ray did. But Catherine didn't mind fending for herself. She'd hit it off with Jillian. And she also enjoyed holding Mary Rose, the Hollisters' three-month-old daughter.

"It must be tough leaving the baby with a sitter while you do your student teaching," Catherine said.

"Yes, it is, but my grandmother recently moved to Brighton Valley and watches Mary Rose for me. In fact, Gram loves providing child care and even has her own little nursery set up. So I'm really fortunate in that respect."

Catherine studied the infant in her arms and smiled. "It seems like ages since I've held a little one."

"Did you have brothers and sisters?"

"Yes, but by the time I left for college, I was so eager to get a break from them that I didn't think I'd ever want to have kids of my own."

"Have you changed your mind?"

"I suppose," Catherine said wistfully, "but I've had a lot of female problems, including endometriosis. The doctor told me that I'd probably never conceive."

"I'm sorry to hear that," Jillian said.

"Me, too." Catherine glanced up and gave her an I've-accepted-it smile. "But the Walker twins have become the children I'll never have. After Kaylee and Kevin were born, I fell in love with them. And since their mother was my roommate, the kids lived with me for the first five years of their lives. So at least I've had the whole baby experience—times two."

Catherine glanced down at Mary Rose, realizing that holding someone else's child wasn't the same as holding her own.

The thought of adopting someday struck again, which was comforting. At least she had options available to her.

"You know," Jillian said, "my doctor, Selena Ramirez, is a great obstetrician/gynecologist. She was a resident at the Brighton Valley Medical Center, but started up her own practice last year. You might want to check with her and get a second opinion. She also treats infertility."

If Catherine were going to stay in town, she'd give it some thought. But she had no business even thinking about home and hearth and families at this point in her life.

Still, she scanned the town square, searching for Ray and finding him talking to Jillian's husband. As their gazes met, a warm feeling spread throughout her chest, setting off a yearning she couldn't quite explain.

What was that all about? It's not as though she and Ray actually had a future together.

Jillian glanced at the bangle watch she wore on her wrist, then sighed. "As much as I'd like to stay here, I need to take Mary Rose home. It's getting close to her bedtime."

Catherine took one last look at the precious infant in her arms, then handed her back to her mommy.

"I need to let Shane know I'm leaving," Jillian said. "That is, if I can find him."

"He's over there," Catherine said, pointing toward the chuck wagon, "talking to Ray."

"Oh, yes. I see them." Jillian reached for the diaper bag, then paused. "I hate to leave you sitting by yourself."

"Don't feel bad about that. I like sitting here, listening to the music." She'd also enjoyed talking to Jillian, as well as the various townspeople who occasionally stopped by to introduce themselves and to welcome her to Brighton Valley.

"Shane and I will be inviting you and Ray for dinner one day soon," Jillian said, as she prepared to leave.

"I'd like that." Catherine had found it easy to talk to Jillian. And the fact that she was also a friend of Eva's made it all the nicer.

"Hopefully, Ray will come back soon."

"I'm sure he will." Catherine offered her new friend a smile. "And even if he doesn't, I'm in no hurry to leave. I'm having a good time."

As Jillian crossed the lawn and approached her husband, Catherine watched her go. Once she'd reached Shane's side, Ray spoke to them both for a moment longer, then he softly stroked Mary Rose's dark hair before returning to Catherine's table.

"How are you holding up?" he asked as he took a seat beside her.

"I'm fine. How about you?"

"Winding down." He lifted his Stetson with one hand, then combed his fingers through his dark hair with the other. "It's been a long day, and I'd really like to say my goodbyes and get away from the crowd and all the noise."

It must have been especially tiring for him. Even though he wasn't being bombarded by matchmakers, a lot of people continued to drag him off to talk about a project or a problem they had.

"Will you be able to leave soon?" Catherine asked. "Or do you need to stay until it's over?"

"It's supposed to go on for another hour, but I don't need to stay that long."

As she studied him in the soft light created by one of the gas lamps, she noticed that his expression had turned serious, creating a furrowed brow.

Was something weighing on his mind? Or was he just tired, as he'd implied?

When his gaze caught hers, he seemed to shake the serious thoughts. "You've got to be worn to a frazzle."

"Not really." She'd been able to kick back and enjoy the day, but he hadn't been that lucky. He'd had to work.

In a sense, she supposed she'd been working, too. But being Ray's fiancée hadn't required much effort on her part. It had been an easy role to fall into. In fact, at times it felt as though the two of them were a real couple.

But even if it was real, long-distance relationships had

two strikes against them already. Not that Ray had indicated he'd like to become involved in something like that.

As the country-western band began to play a slow and sultry love song, Catherine stood and reached out her hand to him. "Okay, Mr. Mayor. I've been patient long enough. You've been so busy with your civic duties that you haven't even gotten around to dancing with the woman you love, and I think it's high time you did."

He tilted his head slightly, then when he caught her wink, he smiled, slipped his hand into hers and let her lead him to the dance floor.

On the stage, an attractive young brunette vocalist sang "Breathe," the hit song that had earned Faith Hill a Grammy.

The local singer certainly wasn't as talented as Faith, but she gave it her all, and the other couples who'd gathered on the dance floor seemed to appreciate her efforts.

"I should have thought of this earlier," Ray whispered, as they walked across the lawn. "People are probably wondering why I haven't been courting my fiancée properly."

"I'm not so sure about that," she said, lowering her voice to match his. "We put on a believable act for them."

In fact, there'd been times throughout the day that she'd nearly forgotten that she really wasn't his lover, that he'd only hired her to play the part.

When they reached the dance floor, Catherine turned to Ray, whose smile had lit his face and completely chased away that furrowed brow.

"I'm not a bad dancer," he said as they came together, "for an amateur. But I'm sure you're used to guys with a lot more talent than I've got. So take it easy on me, okay?"

As she peered into his eyes and saw them sparkle with mirth, she returned his grin. "I'm not looking for any fancy footwork, Ray. All you need to do is sway to the music, and I'll follow your lead."

As he opened his arms, she stepped into his embrace, savoring the warmth of his body and the musky scent of his cologne.

It's an act, she told herself. But as she felt the strength of his arms, as they melded into one on the dance floor, she couldn't help wishing there was something more going on between them.

If things were different…

If she were going to stay in Texas indefinitely…

If she didn't have a career waiting for her in New York, directors who'd like to cast her again…

But how crazy was that? If she stayed in Brighton Valley, she'd have to give up all she'd ever wanted, all she'd worked so hard to achieve.

No, they just had this time together—today, tonight, next week. Who knew how long she'd stay in town? Who knew when the urge to return to the stage would strike?

The song, it seemed, ended all too soon. And as Ray released her, she hadn't been ready to let him go.

That is, until their eyes met and she spotted the intensity burning in his gaze.

Well, what do you know? The dance had affected him, too.

"Come on," he said, taking her by the hand. "Let's go home."

Her heart skipped a beat, then slipped into overdrive.

Home, he'd said. But right now, she'd follow him anywhere—no matter what role she was playing, even if she were merely being herself.

* * *

Ray had taken Catherine's hand when they'd walked off the dance floor, and he continued to hold it as they left the town square and headed back to his apartment.

He wasn't sure what he'd expected when he'd taken her into his arms—just a run of the mill slow dance, he supposed. But when his hands had glided along the curve of her back and he'd drawn her close, there'd been more than a seductive tune and lyrics swirling around them.

No one ever told him that acting could be so much fun—or so arousing. He could almost imagine their phony romance taking a turn toward the real thing.

Would he ever find a woman like Catherine—or like the woman she was pretending to be?

Again, he wondered how much was acting and how much of it was genuine. After all, he was only human. And he'd been celibate for nearly two years.

Damn, had it really been that long?

He had no idea what to expect when they returned to his apartment—a good-night kiss or maybe one of appreciation? It was hard to say, but something told him that any kiss they shared was going to consume him with lust for the beautiful woman who had the ability to turn him inside out with just a smile.

Still, he was glad to know she'd be going home with him. Even if it meant one of them would be sleeping on the sofa.

As they walked down Main Street, which was quiet now that the stores had closed, their boot soles crunched along the sidewalk.

"There's something appealing about Brighton Valley," she said.

"I think so."

"How'd you like growing up here?"

He wasn't sure why she'd asked, but he gave her an honest answer. "It was great. I can't imagine living anywhere else."

She seemed to think on that for a moment, then she nudged her arm against his. "You mentioned being an only child. That must have been nice—and peaceful. The house I grew up in was just one drama after another."

"My home life was nice and quiet, but it was lonely at times."

She smiled. "Sometimes people can be lonely in a crowd."

He supposed she might be right about that. "It wasn't so bad, though. My parents wanted me to socialize, so they let me invite plenty of friends to come to the ranch."

"Did you have any cousins?" she asked.

"Nope. It was just one set of grandparents, my folks and me. In fact, I was the only son of an only son."

"I'm sorry," she said.

"Don't be. It wasn't so bad." A smile tugged at Ray's lips, as he thought back to the loving home in which he'd grown up. "I was a late-in-life baby, whose birth was an answer to my mother's prayers. Needless to say, all the adults in my life doted on me."

Catherine's smile deepened, setting off her pretty dimples. "I'll bet they're proud of the man you've grown up to be."

"They were. They sat in the front row of every school play I was in, every Little League game I played. And they cheered, even if I messed up, telling me that it didn't matter."

"Do they live with you?" she asked. "I mean, it being a family ranch and all."

"No. My grandpa passed away when I was a junior in high school, and my dad died three years later. I lost my grandmother next, and my mom right before my thirtieth birthday."

"That's too bad. I'm sorry."

He was, too. "I guess that's the downside of having older parents. You usually lose them a lot sooner than most of your friends."

He sensed her grieving for him, and he appreciated the sentiment—whether sincere or not. Heather hadn't fully understood or sympathized with his loss—and she hadn't even tried to fake it. Instead, she'd thought he was lucky to have been the sole heir of the family ranch, the biggest spread in Brighton Valley and all the investments his family had accrued over two generations.

But he would have given it all up just to have his family still with him.

As they neared the drugstore, he realized they'd be at his apartment in no time at all and he found himself looking forward to having some time alone with the woman who was unlike any other he'd ever known.

"So what about school?" she asked. "Did you attend college?"

He wasn't sure what had triggered her curiosity, yet he didn't mind her interest in his past. So he said, "I went to Texas A and M."

There didn't seem to be any reason to mention that he'd graduated at the top of his class and received several job offers before his last semester—a couple in the Dallas area and one near Houston. He'd turned them down, though. Instead, he'd come home and taken over the family ranch, which he'd made even more successful than his grandfather and father had made it.

As they continued to hold hands and to make their way down the quiet, deserted downtown street, Ray relished the intimacy they shared.

"What about you?" he asked.

There wasn't much to tell—at least, when it came to her childhood—but Catherine supposed it was only fair that he quizzed her, too.

"I don't have too many good memories of growing up. By the time I graduated from high school, all I wanted to do was get on the first bus heading to Ohio."

"Ohio?" he asked.

"I had a scholarship to Crandall School of Fine Arts. It wasn't my first choice of colleges, but it had offered the best scholarship and was the farthest from home. So I jumped at it."

"And that's where you met Jenny Walker?"

She nodded. "Then we both moved to Manhattan."

Once she'd left New Mexico, she'd really begun to thrive in the college setting—and even more so in the metropolis, where she'd finally become the woman she was meant to be.

"I've never gone to New York," he said. "Brighton Valley must be a huge culture shock for someone used to a city that's open twenty-four hours a day."

"That's for sure."

Their boots continued to crunch on a light film of grit on the sidewalk that lined the empty street, reminding her just how huge the difference was. Still, there was something appealing about the community, as well as the people she'd met so far.

When they reached the drugstore and the stairwell that led to Ray's apartment, his steps slowed. Then he withdrew his hand from hers and motioned for her to go first.

As she started up the lit steps, she wondered what the evening would bring. More disclosures, she supposed.

Would he kiss her again? Probably not. Once they were

completely out of sight from any passersby, it wouldn't be necessary.

Still, she couldn't help but hope that he would, and by the time they reached his front door, her heart rate kicked up a notch.

Ray pulled out his keys, slipped them into the lock, then let her in. Once inside the small apartment, he hung his hat on the hook by the door.

She scanned the sparsely decorated living area, again tempted to do something to help him add a little color. In one of several small apartments inside of an old brownstone in Greenwich Village she called home, she'd done her best to brighten up the drab rooms by using vivid shades of red, yellow and blue, then adding a splash of purple here and there.

Even her furniture back home—a selection of black, glass and chrome—was modern in style.

Still, she supposed there was no need for him to go all out on the decor of the place when he spent only occasional nights.

She wondered what his ranch was like—and whether he'd ever invite her to go out there with him. She'd really like to see it.

"I can put on a pot of coffee or decaf," he said. "I also have a bottle of merlot."

Coffee probably was the safest bet, but she liked the idea of kicking back with him and having a glass of wine.

"The merlot sounds good," she said.

"I think so, too. Why don't you have a seat while I open the bottle."

Catherine made her way to the leather sofa and settled herself near one of the armrests, leaving room for Ray to join her. Then she watched him move about in the kitchen area as he removed a wine bottle from the pantry, two goblets from the cupboard near the sink and a corkscrew from the drawer.

He wasn't at all like the men she'd known in Manhattan, although he was pure eye candy, no matter how he was dressed. His dark hair, which was mussed from the Stetson he'd worn earlier, was a bit long and curled at his collar. She supposed some women might think it needed a trim, but she wasn't one of them. In fact, she didn't think she'd change a thing about the man.

Broad shoulders tapered down into a narrow waist, and—

Before she could continue her perusal, he turned and smiled at her.

Did he realize she'd been making an intense assessment of his lean, cowboy body, appreciating both his form and his style?

She hoped not, yet her cheeks flushed warm.

He carried the wineglasses to the sofa, then handed her one. "Here you go."

When she thanked him, he took a seat beside her.

The lamplight cast a romantic glow in the room, but it was the handsome cowboy who'd set her heart spinning, her hormones pumping and her imagination soaring.

She remembered something one of her friends had told her in Manhattan. *Once you meet another man—even if it's just a one-night stand—you'll forget all about Erik Carmichael.*

At the time, Catherine hadn't been interested in anyone else—not even to go out for a cup of coffee.

But what about Ray? Would he make the perfect transitional relationship?

She took a sip of wine, hoping to shake the thoughts that began to plague her. She couldn't very well suggest that they have an affair while she was in town, could she?

No, that would have to be Ray's idea.

"You know," he said, "I'd like to make a toast to the best hired fiancée I've ever had."

Catherine smiled, then clinked her wineglass against his. "And to the best male lead an actress ever had."

Did she dare tell him how easy her role had been? How tempted she was to stop playacting and see what developed between the two of them?

Not that she'd want to actually be engaged or marry him one day, but would making love with him be out of line? After all, if the man's kisses turned her inside out, what would a full-on sexual encounter be like?

Just the thought of it shot a warm, intoxicating buzz right through her, and she hadn't taken more than a couple of sips of wine.

"I'll sleep on the sofa tonight," he said. "You can have my room."

"That isn't fair."

"What isn't?" A boyish grin tugged at his lips, and a spark of mischief lit his eyes. "Did you want to fight me for the sofa?"

"Maybe," she said, teasing him right back.

Truth was, she'd seen his room—and the size of his bed. It was plenty big enough for both of them.

She told herself that she was just being thoughtful when she said, "There's no reason for you to sleep out here and be uncomfortable. I don't mind sharing the bed, if you don't."

The mischievous glimmer in his gaze disappeared, and something else took its place—something intense. Something masculine.

"It's not like we'd do anything other than sleep," she added by way of explanation. Yet the moment the words left her mouth, she realized she wouldn't be doing much sleeping if he were lying beside her, just an arm's reach away.

Goodness. What had she done?

She wished she could blame it on the wine, but her thoughts had taken a sexual turn the moment she'd entered his house.

When they finished their first glass, Ray poured them a second.

"Just half for me," she said. "Thank you."

After filling his glass, he walked over to the stereo and turned on the radio to a country-western station. She didn't recognize the artist or the song, but she liked the music.

"This is really nice," she said, lifting her glass and studying the deep burgundy color in the lamplight.

Yet she was talking about more than the music or the wine. She meant this moment, this man.

She was tempted to suggest something they might both regret. And with a man who was her employer. Wasn't there something unethical or inappropriate about that?

"You know," she said, "I'm going to need something to sleep in tonight. Do you have an old shirt and a pair of shorts I can use?"

"Sure." He placed his goblet on the coffee table, then strode to the bedroom.

She heard the closet door open and shut, followed by a bureau drawer.

When he returned, he held a large maroon T-shirt that sported a white Texas A and M logo on the front, as well as a pair of black boxer shorts. "How's this?"

"Perfect."

"I've also got a new toothbrush you can use," he added. "It's in the right-hand drawer in the bathroom."

"Then I'm all set." She got to her feet and took the makeshift nightwear he'd given her. "Thanks."

"You may as well take the bathroom first. You'll find clean towels hanging on the rack, in case you'd like a shower."

She offered him an appreciative smile, then headed for the bathroom, wondering what he'd say if she offered him a lot more than a smile upon her return.

Chapter 7

While Catherine was in the bathroom, Ray walked to the window and looked out into the darkened street below. He'd been both surprised and pleased when she'd agreed to stay with him tonight. But that had nothing to do with the long drive back to the ranch and everything to do with the fact that he wanted to spend more time with her, to have her to himself for a while.

He actually looked forward to being around her, and not just because she was a pleasure to look at. He enjoyed talking to her, too. There was something very appealing about her, something alluring that went beyond sexual fascination.

Maybe it was due in part to the fact that he was safe with her. She understood that he didn't want to get romantically involved with anyone right now, so she hadn't pressed him for anything other than friendship.

Of course, if things were different, if she planned to

stay in Brighton Valley—and more important, if he could be sure that the persona she'd revealed to him wasn't just part of an act—he might even ask her out on a real date, complete with soft music, candlelight, roses and wine.

But even if she was just as sincere, considerate and sweet as she appeared to be, she was going back to New York one of these days. So he'd just have to enjoy their friendship and whatever time they had left.

Now here they were, tiptoeing around all the sweet dreams and bedtime stuff.

The water shut off in the bathroom, which meant she was probably climbing from the shower and reaching for a towel, naked and wet.

That particular vision was a lot more arousing than it ought to be, but then again, the tall, leggy blonde was a beautiful woman who also seemed to have a good heart.

To top that off, he'd been serving a nearly two-year term of self-imposed celibacy, which was really starting to eat at him now—big time.

He tried to shake it off—the sexual thoughts, the arousal, but he wasn't having much luck.

Had she dried off yet? Had she slipped on his shorts and his shirt?

She'd mentioned that they could sleep together tonight, although he supposed she was only being practical. But the moment she'd suggested sharing the bed, his thoughts had taken a sexual detour.

And that's exactly where his thoughts were right now.

He could almost see her in the bathroom, wrapped in a towel and facing the fogged-up mirror. In his mind, he stood behind her, damp from the shower, too. His hands reaching for the edge of the towel, tugging it gently, removing it. Revealing that lithe dancer's body in the flesh.

He was going to drive himself crazy before she even left the bathroom.

As a soft, country love song began to play on the radio, setting off a romantic aura in the room, his libido began to battle with his good sense. In spite of his better judgment, the idea of making love with Catherine grew stronger by the heartbeat.

He probably ought to change the station and find something with a livelier beat, but he didn't make a move toward the stereo.

Instead, when the bathroom door opened, he turned to face the woman he'd envisioned naked just moments before.

Her platinum-blond hair had been swept up into a sexy twist, revealing a ballerina's neck, just begging for hot, breathy kisses.

She smiled when she spotted him, her eyes lighting up. He probably should have responded with a platonic grin of his own. Instead, he allowed his gaze to sweep over her, amazed by those long, shapely legs that could wrap around a man and make him cry uncle. Or aunt. Or whatever else she had in mind.

"It's a little steamy in there," she said.

Hell, it was even steamier out *here.* And while he had no business making any kind of sexual innuendo, he couldn't help speaking his mind. "Seeing you like that..." His gaze sketched over her again, making it difficult to continue without acting upon his arousal.

"I can change into something else," she said, glancing down at the shirt she wore, "if you'd be more comfortable. Or..."

Or *what?* Was she going to suggest that they let nature take its course this evening?

Sure, why not? he wanted to say.

She didn't continue the open-ended option, but the way she was looking at him—which had to be the same way he was looking at her—didn't leave a whole lot of doubt that her thoughts had taken a sexual turn, too. But hey, why shouldn't they?

He could throw out the idea, he supposed, laying it on the table—or wherever else they might end up. But what would he do if she told him it wasn't in her job description?

Then again, he might kick himself later for letting a once-in-a-lifetime opportunity slip through his hands.

"How long has it been for you?" he asked, stepping out on a limb that swayed under the weight of the question.

"Since I've had sex?" She gave a little shrug. "Quite a while. How about you?"

Had he actually been celibate for two long years?

After he and his ex had split, it had seemed like a good way to avoid getting caught in another bad relationship before he had time to get over the last one. But now?

He couldn't imagine going without sex for a minute longer.

They stood like that for a moment—too far away from each other to touch, yet connected in a way he hadn't expected.

"I know that a short-term affair wasn't part of our bargain," she said, "but I wouldn't be opposed to it."

At that, his pulse rate shot through the roof, and his mouth went dry, then wet. Before meeting Catherine, he hadn't really missed sex all that much. Not that he'd planned to give it up for good.

But now? When the opportunity of a lifetime was knocking?

He took a step forward, then another. "I wouldn't be opposed to it, either."

"It might actually help us both move along in the healing process," she said.

There was no doubt about that. Just the thought of taking Catherine in his arms had his heart spinning—and all in one piece—strong, vibrant, whole.

"We've definitely got chemistry," he said as they met in the middle of the room.

"That's true. If the kisses we shared were any indication of how good it would be between us…"

He finished the thought for her. "Then making love is going to be off the charts."

She nodded.

Still, he didn't make a move.

And neither did she.

When she bit down on her bottom lip, he wondered if it was a shy reaction to what was going on between them or if it was… No, it wasn't part of her act. Neither of them were playing a role right now. This—whatever *this* was—had to be real.

For a while, he'd wondered where fantasy ended and reality began when it came to his feelings for her. But when push came to shove, he had to admit that he'd quit playacting about the time of their very first kiss.

In fact, he'd even become intrigued by the idea of dating her and… What? Pursuing her?

Maybe so—at least, that was his game plan tonight.

When Ray opened his arms and Catherine stepped into his embrace, he relished her clean, fresh-from-the-shower scent, as well as the feel of her soft breasts pressed against his chest.

He realized she must be entertaining a similar game plan because she wrapped her arms around his neck and drew his lips to hers. As their tongues met, their kiss exploded with passion, with heat.

She tasted of peppermint, of sunshine and dreams, and he couldn't get enough of her. His hands sought, stroked and explored every uncovered inch of her, but still he wanted more, needed more. He reached for the hemline of her T-shirt, lifting the fabric, revealing her bare waist, her taut belly, her perfect curves....

When his hand reached her breasts, he cupped the soft mounds, caressed them. As his thumb skimmed across her nipple, her breath caught.

Damn. He couldn't believe his good fortune. They were actually going through with this, and he couldn't be happier—no matter what tomorrow brought. And by the way Catherine was responding to his touch, to his kiss, he had a feeling she felt the very same way.

Caught up in an amazing swirl of heat and desire, Catherine leaned into the rugged cowboy and gripped his shoulders as if she might collapse if she hadn't. And who knew? Maybe she would have.

Never had she wanted a man so badly, so desperately. If she didn't know better, she'd swear that they'd been made for each other—their bodies, their hearts, their souls.

She kissed him back for all she was worth, wanting him, wanting this.

There might be a hundred reasons they shouldn't allow themselves to get carried away tonight, but tell that to her raging hormones. Right now, all she wanted to do was let him work his cowboy magic on her and take her someplace she'd never been.

As the kiss ended, they clung to each other, their breaths ragged, their hearts pounding.

"Let's take this to the bedroom," Ray whispered against her cheek.

She didn't trust herself to speak, so she slipped her hand in his and allowed him to take her anywhere he wanted to go.

They padded across the hardwood floor, and moments later, when they reached the bed, he took her in his arms again and kissed her until her thoughts spun out of control, until nothing else mattered other than this man and this night.

His hands slid along the curves of her back, then he pulled her hips forward, against his erection. She arched forward, showing him her need, as well as her willingness to make love to him.

When she thought she'd melt into a puddle if they didn't climb into bed and finish what they'd started, she ended the kiss, then she removed the T-shirt he'd loaned her. As she let the garment drop to the floor, she stood before him in nothing but the boxers he'd loaned her.

His gaze caressed her as intimately as his hands had done just seconds earlier. "You're beautiful, Catherine."

Her only response was to reach for his belt buckle and to begin removing his clothing, too. She needed to feel his bare skin against hers, and she couldn't wait another minute.

Together, they removed his shirt, and she marveled at his broad chest, his six-pack abs.

Catherine wasn't a novice at lovemaking. She'd had lovers before—two, in fact. But neither of those men had been built as strong and sturdy as Ray, whose muscles were a result of both genetics and hard work.

"You're beautiful, too," she said.

After they'd drawn back the spread and slipped into bed, Ray showed her how a cowboy loved a lady, creating a memory she'd never forget.

They moved together in rhythm that built until they

reached a breath-stealing peak. As she cried out with her release, he let go, too, climaxing in a burst of fireworks and spinning stars.

Never had she felt such passion or experienced such an earth-shattering orgasm.

As she lay in Ray's arms, relishing the stunning afterglow, a sated smile stretched across her face. She'd expected their lovemaking to be good, but she'd never imagined it would be like this.

She tried to tell herself that it was merely a physical act, that there wasn't anything emotional going on. Making love with Ray had been a great way to completely shake any lingering disillusionment she'd had after her breakup with Erik. Yet she found herself wading through a rush of emotions she hadn't expected.

As she pondered those budding feelings, Ray stiffened, then rolled to the side.

Was something wrong?

"I, uh…hate to put a damper on things," he said, propping himself up on an elbow and casting a shadow over the sweet afterglow she'd thought they'd both been enjoying.

Her stomach knotted, and disappointment flared. Just moments ago, everything had seemed right—perfect, if not promising. Was he regretting what they'd done?

The possibility sent her tender emotions into a tailspin, making her question the value she'd placed on their lovemaking. As her mind scampered to make sense of it all—not only the budding emotion their joining had stirred within her, but also her agreement to enter into a fake engagement in the first place. What had she been thinking?

Determined to protect herself, she decided to downplay their joining and her unexpected emotional reaction to it.

"It was just a physical act," she said, "something we both needed."

"Yes, I know." He brushed a strand of hair from her brow in a sweet and gentle manner, yet the look on his face remained serious, sending her a mixed message.

"This doesn't mean we have to change our employment agreement," she said, taking a guess as to what might be bothering him. "And don't worry. I'm not going to ask for any kind of commitment or chase after you like some of the local women have done."

"I know that." While his expression seemed to soften, his demeanor remained tense, maybe even defensive.

"Then what's bothering you?" she asked.

"You don't know?"

No, she didn't. That's why she'd assumed that he was regretting what they'd done. And why she'd tried to assuage whatever worry he might have.

As he slowly shook his head and clicked his tongue, she braced herself for the worst.

"We didn't use any protection," he said.

Oh, no. He was right. They hadn't.

"And it's not like me to be irresponsible."

It wasn't like her to neglect something important like that, either. But apparently, they'd gotten so carried away with the passion that they'd lost their heads.

"You might have gotten pregnant," he added. "And that's a complication neither of us needs right now."

She appreciated his concern, but at least she could put his worries about that to rest. "It's not the right time of the month for me to conceive. And even if it were, it isn't likely. I've been told my chances of having a baby are slim."

"I'm sorry to hear that."

She was sorry, too, but she'd come to accept it. "It was depressing to hear that news when the doctor told me, but I'm okay with it now. Dan and Eva's twins have adopted me as their auntie, so I'm glad to be a part of their lives."

The conversation was getting entirely too heavy and too sad to deal with after such an amazing bout of love-making. And while Ray might have said that he hadn't wanted to put a damper on things, he'd done just that.

She rolled slightly, moving away from him. Then she slipped out of his arms, climbed from bed and headed for the bathroom.

"Are you okay?" he asked.

She turned, glanced over her shoulder and offered him her brightest smile. "Of course."

But she *wasn't* okay. She was struggling with rejection, disappointment and the sudden reminder that she'd never have a baby of her own. Not that she'd expected to have one with Ray, but at least for a moment or two while making love, she'd entertained the brief fantasy of having it all someday: a husband and children, a home in the suburbs. Yet for some reason, and without any warning, that dream fell apart before it could even begin.

She had to find some solid ground on which to stand and some time to ponder what they'd just done, what she'd briefly imagined it to be and what she would do about it now.

When she'd kissed him, when she'd agreed to make love, she'd only thought of it as a sexual act. Yet thanks to the chemistry between them, it had been even better than she'd anticipated. Amazing, actually. And it had seemed to be a whole lot more than physical.

Surely, she'd only imagined the emotional side of it— at least, on her part. So until she could sort through it all and figure out a way out of it, she needed to be alone for a while.

If that darn pickup wasn't having engine trouble, she'd tell Ray that she was driving back to the ranch tonight. But as it was, she was stuck here until morning.

After their lovemaking last night, Catherine had stayed in the bathroom for what had seemed like hours, although it was probably only a matter of minutes. She hadn't seemed the least bit concerned about pregnancy, which should have made Ray feel better. But for some reason, it hadn't helped at all. He'd still been uneasy about the whole thing.

Not that he regretted making love with her. The time spent in her arms had been incredible, a real fantasy come true. But now that the new day had dawned, so had reality.

A relationship between the two of them, which had seemed so feasible in the heat of the moment, was no longer viable. The possibility had dissipated the moment Catherine had returned to the bedroom, only to curl up on her side of the mattress, rather than cuddle with him.

Now, as he lay stretched out on the bed, trying to set aside the uneasiness that had niggled at him all through the night, he tried to focus on the memory of their lovemaking. Of course, any sexual encounter would have been great after a two-year dry spell.

Or would it?

When he tried to imagine being in bed with another woman, each time he gazed into the fantasy woman's eyes, he saw Catherine smiling back at him, urging him on.

He told himself that was because the memory of their lovemaking was so fresh in his mind, so *real*. In that one, amazing moment, when the two of them had become one, climaxing at the same time, he'd wanted to hold on to her and never let her go. He'd also been tempted to spill his heart and soul to her—if he'd actually thought that what he'd been feeling for her had been real. But as his heart rate and his breathing slowed to a normal pace, he'd realized that he'd neglected to use a condom, that he hadn't even had the foresight to purchase any ahead of time. And the irresponsibility left him completely unbalanced.

He appreciated the fact that pregnancy wasn't an issue, but he had other concerns, too. Like becoming emotionally attached to a woman who wouldn't be in Brighton Valley forever.

Besides, just because sex between a couple was absolutely incredible, especially the very first time, didn't mean that they'd be compatible.

When the bathroom door clicked open, and Catherine walked out wearing the clothes she'd worn to the community barbecue last night, she cast a friendly smile his way. Yet they really weren't friends at this point. In fact, he wasn't sure what they were to each other. He supposed they were lovers, but would that be true if this was just a one-night thing?

He had no idea. Still, he sat up in bed, determined to face the uncertainty of the day.

"Would you like to eat breakfast here or at Caroline's Diner?" he asked.

"If you don't mind, I'd really like to get back to the ranch. I promised Eva I'd help her with the kids this morning."

He wished he could say he was relieved, yet for some reason, he hated to see her go, which made no sense.

Nevertheless, he threw off the covers and climbed out

of bed. "No problem. I'll take a quick shower, then I'll drive you back to the ranch."

"Thanks."

Again she smiled.

And again, he sensed there was something missing in her expression.

He'd never seen her like this—wrapped up in some kind of invisible armor, her thoughts a million miles away.

She'd withdrawn last night, right after their climax. Had she been truthful when she'd told him not to worry about pregnancy?

Or was she angry that he hadn't been more responsible?

No, she couldn't be mad about that. She should have thought about the consequences of unprotected sex, too.

Was she kicking herself for letting it happen? He supposed he wouldn't know unless he addressed the issue.

"Is everything okay?" he asked.

"Yes, it's fine." She crossed the room and placed a kiss on his cheek as if trying to convince him, yet failing miserably.

Something still wasn't right.

"Are you sorry about what we did last night?" he asked.

"No, not at all." She offered him another smile he couldn't trust. "How about you?"

"I'm not the least bit sorry." Okay, so that wasn't entirely true. He wasn't sorry about having sex—and he doubted that he ever would be. His only real regret stemmed from her mood change and the distance between them.

As Ray went into the bathroom and shut the door, he

tried to rehash everything that had gone on the night before so he could figure out what went wrong—and *when*.

The lovemaking itself seemed perfect.

When he'd rolled to the side and gazed at her, she'd been wearing a serene smile—a *real* one. And that proved that they'd shared the same pleasure.

It was only after she'd returned from the bathroom that things had grown a little…chilly.

Shouldn't he be happy that she wasn't putting any pressure on him, especially when she'd be moving back to New York soon?

Or had he begun to fall in love with an actress? A woman who pretended to be someone else?

By the time he got out of the shower, he wasn't any closer to having an answer than he'd been last night.

Even after he'd dried off and gotten dressed, he still wasn't sure what was going on between them—or how he ought to feel about it. But there was one thing he did know. He was in danger of falling in love with a woman who might not exist.

When he entered the living area, Catherine was seated on the sofa, waiting for him.

"You know," he said, as he grabbed his keys from the dinette table, "I was thinking. We've done a good job convincing everyone in town that I'm engaged. And after that announcement at the barbecue last night, people will know I'm off-limits. We probably don't need to be seen together constantly."

"You're probably right." She got to her feet. "Just give me a call at the ranch if you need me again."

For what? Another date to a community event he had to attend. Or for another night of lovemaking?

Damn. It almost sounded as if she was ending it all—

their employment, their friendship, their… What? Their star-crossed affair?

An ache burrowed deep in his chest, and he wished that he could roll back the clock twelve hours and start over. But it was too late to backpedal now.

"There's not much going on for another week," he said, "but I'm sure I'll need you again."

"No problem. Just let me know when."

He locked up his apartment, then followed her down the stairwell.

"How much longer do you plan to be in town?" he asked.

"I'm not entirely sure. But probably as long as you might need me."

For a moment, he was tempted to say that he'd like for her to extend her visit, that he had a feeling he would need her for a long, long time. But he couldn't say that. Instead, he thanked her for all she'd done to help him.

"And I'd also like to thank you for…last night. It was amazing. Maybe we can do it again sometime. But if not, that's okay, too."

"I feel the same way."

Did she?

He certainly hoped they weren't on the same page, because he hated not having a game plan. And he had no idea where to go from here.

Chapter 8

The drive back to the Walker ranch was fairly quiet, other than the sound of the music playing softly on the car radio.

Catherine hoped that she'd put Ray's worries to rest, although she wished she could say the same for herself. What had happened last night?

If she didn't know better, she'd think that she might actually fall for Ray—if she wasn't careful.

And if that was the case, then it really was for the best that they slow down their time spent together. Ray had made it more than clear that he didn't have any interest in striking up a romance—with *anyone*.

Besides, she had a life in New York. Getting involved with the Brighton Valley mayor wasn't a good idea. And if she let her feelings get in the way, their relationship— or whatever it was—could end in disappointment or heartbreak. And heaven knew she didn't need to risk having something like that happen.

When they arrived at the ranch, Ray kept the engine running.

"I have a meeting in Wexler with a couple of investors at noon," he said. "And while I'm in the area, I thought it would be a good idea if I talked to my foreman first. So, if you don't mind, I'm just going to drop you off. Can you tell Dan and Eva I said hello?"

"Of course."

His gaze zeroed in on hers, reaching out in a way that gripped her heart and nearly squeezed the beat right out of it.

"One more thing," he said.

She stiffened, and her breathing slowed to a near stop as she readied herself for whatever he had to say.

"Thanks again for last night. It was *amazing. You* were amazing. And it was both a gift and a memory I'll cherish."

Emotion balled up in her throat, making it difficult to speak. Yet, somehow, she found her voice and mustered a smile. "I thought it was special, too. And, for the record, I'm not sorry about it." At least, she didn't regret making love with him. It was the unexpected emotional fallout that had her scampering to make sense of it all.

"I'll give you a call in a day or two," he said.

"Sounds good." She lifted her hand in a wave, then watched him back up his SUV, as if he was backing out of her life forever.

She'd told him that she wasn't sorry, and in a sense, that was true. But now that she'd opened up to him, now that they'd shared a physical intimacy as well, she had to admit that she grieved for what might have developed between them. Because, if truth be told, she would have been tempted to remain in Brighton Valley indefinitely if he'd given her any reason to think that he'd wanted her to.

And how crazy was that? Her life and her career were in Manhattan. Giving up everything she'd ever wanted, everything she'd achieved, for a man was unthinkable. Yet the thought had crossed her mind just the same.

Catherine turned and headed for the ranch house. After climbing the steps and crossing the porch, she opened the front door and entered the living room, where Kaylee and a little red-haired girl sat beside a pink-and-chrome child's karaoke machine, five or six dolls surrounding them.

Upon seeing Catherine, Kaylee brightened. "You're home!"

She smiled, glad that she'd been missed. But at this point in time, she wasn't really sure where "home" was. Her apartment in Greenwich Village had been sublet for six more weeks, so she couldn't even fly back to New York if she wanted to. Still, she said to the child she thought of as a daughter, "Yes, sweetie. I'm home."

She watched the two girls set the dolls in a semicircle. "What are you doing, Kaylee-bug?"

"Me and my new friend, Shauna, are making a Broadway show for our dolls, just like you do. And after we practice, we're going to invite you and our moms to watch it. Well, not her mom. But her..." Kaylee turned to the red-haired girl. "Who is she again?"

"She's my foster mom, I guess." Shauna, a tall, gangly child who appeared to be a year or so older than Kaylee, gave a little shrug. "Her name is Jane Morrison. And she's a lot nicer than the last one I had before."

Catherine's heart went out to the girl, with big green eyes haunted by sadness.

In an effort to let Shauna know that her situation

wasn't all that unusual, Catherine said, "I'm kind of like Kaylee's foster mom, too."

"Yeah," Kaylee said. "When my mommy died, me and my brother lived with Catherine. Then we moved to the ranch with my Uncle Dan and Aunt Eva. But now that we're adopted, they're our dad and mom."

"Sometimes life gets complicated," Catherine said to the child, yet the reality of the words echoed in her mind, reminding her of Ray and of the awkward situation she'd created for herself.

"Shauna goes to my church," Kaylee added. "And on Monday, she gets to go to my school. I'm going to ask Mrs. Parker, the principal, to let her be in my class."

"It's nice to meet you," Catherine said. "And I'm glad you'll have at least one friend when Monday comes around."

"That's why Mrs. Morrison brought her to our house today," Kaylee said. "She's already gone to about a hundred different schools."

"Only four," Shauna corrected. "But that's okay. I'm used to being a new kid."

Catherine doubted anyone ever got used to being moved around that much or placed in new households, but she let the subject drop and asked, "Where's your mom, Kaylee?"

"She's in the kitchen."

Catherine set her purse on the bottom step of the stairway, planning to carry it up later. Then she made her way through the house, eager to find Eva and seek some advice—that is, if she had the courage to tell her what she'd done.

When she entered the kitchen, she spotted her friend standing at the sink, chopping vegetables to add to the Crock-Pot on the counter.

"Need any help?" Catherine asked.

Eva turned and smiled. "Thanks, but I've got it under control. How was the barbecue?"

"It was fun. The food was great, the music, too. And I really enjoyed the people I met."

"I'm sorry we missed it, but I couldn't take Kevin after he twisted his ankle."

"Where is he?"

"Dan took him to the Urgent Care in town to have an X-ray. We really don't think he fractured it, but it was still swollen and sore this morning. So we wanted to get a doctor's opinion—and to make sure he didn't have any serious tissue damage."

"I'm sorry I wasn't here earlier," Catherine said. "I could have watched the kids for you. Then you both could have taken him to the doctor."

"No, Dan can handle it. Besides, Kaylee has a friend over today, and it was important that I stayed home for that."

Catherine took a seat at the table. As she did so, she realized that the house was unusually quiet. "Where are the little ones?"

"Uncle Pete took them on a nature walk. Then he's going to put on a cartoon movie at his house and feed them lunch. I wanted Kaylee and Shauna to have some time alone so they could get to know each other better."

"Kaylee introduced me to her. She seems like a nice little girl, but I feel sorry for her."

"You don't know the half of it," Eva said, her voice lowered. "Her mother died when she was just a toddler. And somehow, she ended up with the stepfather. When he went to prison, she was placed in foster care. From what I understand, her maternal grandmother finally got custody, only to be diagnosed with terminal cancer a few months later. The poor kid has really been through a lot."

"I'm glad Kaylee is reaching out to her. How did you meet her?"

"Jane Morrison, one of the women in our church, is her new foster parent. And she asked if we could help with the transition." Eva turned back to her work long enough to put the veggies into the Crock-Pot, then she washed her hands at the sink. "How about a cup of herbal tea? I just put on a pot of water to heat."

"Sounds good."

Eva carried the sugar bowl, spoons and a variety of tea bags she kept in a small wicker basket to the table. Then she filled two cups with hot water, setting one in front of Catherine. She'd no sooner taken a seat when she asked, "What's the matter?"

"Nothing." Catherine opened a packet of Earl Grey, then dropped the tea bag into her cup of water. "Why?"

"I don't know. You look a little tired, I guess."

It was, Catherine decided, a perfect opening to tell Eva why she felt so uneasy, what she and Ray had done. But she wasn't sure if she was ready to admit to all of that— or if she'd ever be ready. So she said, "I guess I'm just a little tired. I didn't get much sleep last night."

"Sometimes that happens when you sleep in an unfamiliar bed."

"Yes, I'm sure that's it." Catherine glanced down at the steeping tea bag, wishing the leaves were loose instead of contained, wishing she could empty the cup and read her future.

"Uh-oh," Eva said.

Catherine glanced up at her friend, and as their gazes met, Eva cocked her head to the side as if she'd read Catherine's mind.

"I sense that something's either *very* right," Eva said, "or *very* wrong."

At first, Catherine assumed she was talking about the children, but when she caught the knowing look in Eva's eyes, she realized the conversation had taken a personal turn.

"What do you mean?" she asked.

"You and Ray might be faking an engagement, but you look good together. And you're both as nice as can be. If you lived in town, or had plans to stay, I'd probably encourage you to consider him as a romantic possibility."

"But I *don't* plan to stay in town," Catherine said, more determined to leave now than ever.

"I know." Eva took a sip of tea, and a smile tugged across her lips. "The two of you would make a great couple. And since you're both nursing broken hearts, it seems natural that one or the other or both of you would find the other attractive. And that in itself might be the cause for a restless night."

Yes, and so would the emotional aftereffects of great sex, especially when a romantic future didn't look the least bit promising.

Before Catherine was forced to either lie or to admit more than she was willing to share, Kaylee came bounding into the kitchen. "It's time for the show. Will you please come and watch us?"

"I wouldn't miss it for the world." Eva picked up her cup and looked at Catherine. "Do you mind bringing your tea into the living room? They've been practicing all morning."

"No, not at all." Catherine picked up her cup and saucer, then followed Eva and Kaylee back to the living room.

"There's going to be a talent show in our school cafeteria," Kaylee told Catherine. "And me and Shauna are going to be in it. We're going to sing and dance, just like you and my mommy."

Shauna kind of scrunched up her face. "It's Kaylee's idea. She wants me to be the singer, and she's going to dance."

"There's a talent show at the kids' school?" Catherine asked Eva. Could it be the same one she'd heard about while attending the hospital benefit with Ray? The one Dr. Ramirez had suggested she take part in?

"The Brighton Valley Junior Women's Club is sponsoring it," Eva explained. "There's been a lot of talk about building a center for the arts on the new side of town, and they'd wanted a fundraiser. They're even encouraging the school children who sing, dance or play an instrument to participate."

"That's really nice." Catherine would have loved getting involved in a community event like that when she'd been a girl.

"And Catherine," Kaylee said, "you can be in it, too. You could sing that song about the raindrops on roses, the one you used to sing to me and Kevin."

Catherine smiled, remembering the days when she lived with the twins. "You're talking about 'My Favorite Things' from *The Sound of Music.*"

"Yes, that's the one," Kaylee said. "Will you sing it at our school? And can you wear a beautiful costume like the ones you have in New York?"

Kaylee had been only five when her mother died, but she still remembered the times Jennifer and Catherine would take her backstage to see the costumes and props. One set in particular had been a pirate ship, and Kevin had loved the tour one of the stagehands had given him.

But Kaylee had especially enjoyed seeing some of the gowns up close.

"It would be really nice if you participated," Eva added, "especially since you're 'engaged' to the mayor. I'm sure he'd be pleased if you did."

Catherine wasn't sure what would please Ray these days, although she suspected he'd like the idea. And she missed performing for an audience—no matter what the size. But she didn't want to upstage any of the local talent—not when she was a professional.

"I don't mind getting involved with the talent show," Catherine said, "but I don't think it's a good idea if I compete with any of the local townspeople."

"I understand," Eva said. "It might not be fair to everyone involved. But maybe you could perform at the end of the evening. Or what if the grand prize was a voice or dance lesson from you?"

"It would have to be up to the committee heading up the event," Catherine said, "but I'm willing to do anything I can to help out."

"What about *us?*" Kaylee said. "You can give lessons to me and Shauna so we can be the winners."

"You'll always be a winner in my heart," Catherine said. "And I'd love to give you two a few pointers."

The girls clapped their hands with glee, then turned on the karaoke machine. Within minutes, they put on a darling show.

Shauna, who belted out a Hannah Montana/Miley Cyrus hit, had a natural talent that nearly knocked Catherine off her chair. On the other hand, Kaylee, bless her heart, hadn't inherited her mother's dancing ability.

Then again, maybe she just needed a few pointers. Either way, the kid had heart. And their performance brought maternal tears to Catherine's eyes.

When the "show" ended, the women broke into applause, praising both girls.

"I'll tell you what," Catherine said as she swiped at her watery eyes with her fingers. "I'd be happy to coach you girls for the community talent show."

Kaylee squealed in delight, while Shauna smiled.

"And I'll make the costumes," Eva added as she placed her hand on the red-haired girl's shoulder. "I'm also going to ask Shauna's foster mom to help me. This is going to be so much fun."

She was right. Catherine was going to enjoy helping the girls. She was also looking forward to having something to do over the next few weeks that would help to keep her mind not only off Ray, but off the mess she might have made out of their budding friendship.

After dropping Catherine off at the Walkers' place, Ray had driven twenty minutes to his own ranch to talk to Mark Halstead, his foreman. He could have used his cell phone rather than make the trip in person, but he'd needed to get some perspective, and there was no better way to do that than to step onto the old family homestead, to breathe in the country air, to see the cattle grazing in the pastures.

The bluebonnets his mother had loved dotted the hillsides these days, and while seeing them wasn't the same as entering her kitchen and finding her baking homemade cinnamon rolls as a treat, it was the best he could do.

He'd hoped that once Catherine had gotten out of his Escalade, he'd be able to sort through what had happened, and then decide what he wanted to do about it— if anything.

All morning long, he'd been beating himself up, although he wasn't sure why. He wasn't sorry they'd had sex, although it had definitely changed things between them. And he had no idea if that change had been good or not.

For one thing, he'd come pretty damn close to falling for Catherine Loza, another city girl who'd never want to be a rancher's wife. And to make matters worse, she would be leaving soon—and taking a part of his heart with him, if he was fool enough to offer it to her.

You'd think that after all the hell his ex-wife had put him through, he'd be fighting to remain single and unattached for the rest of his life. Not that he would ever broach the idea of a commitment with Catherine.

Besides, she'd said it herself. *It was just a physical act, something we both needed.*

And she'd certainly been right about that. He'd needed the release more than he'd realized. Maybe he'd needed the intimacy, too. He'd come from a very small but close family who'd been both loving and supportive. But as each family member had died, one after the other, he'd slowly lost parts of his connection to someone who'd loved him unconditionally.

He'd actually hoped that Heather would have stepped up to the plate in that respect, but whatever connection they'd had began to fray the day she'd moved in with him. And that was fine with him. He'd learned to get by without those family ties.

Besides, he had good friends who'd been supportive, like Dan Walker and Shane Hollister.

Yet in just a few days, he'd begun to feel that bond and the sense of kinship again—*with Catherine,* as strange as that might seem. Their whole relationship, whether they were friends or lovers, had been based upon a lie. So how could he place any value on whatever feelings he might be having for her, especially when he had no idea how much—if any—of the real Catherine she'd actually revealed to him. She could be putting on one hell of a show, and he wouldn't know the difference.

Still, he couldn't quite bring himself to let her go. It might be foolishness on his part—or a bad case of lust—but he didn't like the idea of ending her employment just yet. If he did, he'd have to explain their breakup to everyone in town.

Okay, so that's the excuse he was making to continue their charade—and he hadn't even reached the family homestead yet or breathed the country air that seemed to clear his mind.

As he neared the feed lot, which was only five miles from the long, graveled driveway that led to his ranch, he began to realize that he had another reason for maintaining the phony fiancée plan, and it wasn't nearly as practical.

Or maybe it was. He'd been yearning for something elusive, something he seemed to have temporarily found with Catherine.

Call him a fool, but after allowing them both some time to think, some time to put things into perspective, he was going to ask her to attend another function with him.

So what was next on his calendar?

The only thing he could think of was that birthday dinner at the American Legion Hall to honor Ernie Tucker.

Ernie, who'd been the first sheriff in Brighton Valley, was going to be one hundred years old on the fourteenth of the month. So the town had planned to have festivities all weekend long, beginning with the fancy dinner. There was going to be a parade down Main Street on Saturday, and finally, on Sunday morning, the Brighton Valley Community Church would have an ice-cream social in his honor.

If you asked Ray, it seemed a bit much. Poor old Ernie was going to be plumb worn out from celebrating come Monday. But not many folks could claim to reach a milestone birthday like that, especially when they were still spry and sharp as a tack.

So now he had a good reason to call Catherine and set up another date—so to speak.

Why was it that he couldn't wait to distance himself from her just moments ago, yet now he was thinking about seeing her again?

He wasn't going to ponder the answer to that, but attending a birthday celebration with her seemed safe enough.

When he spotted the three oak trees that grew near the county road, marking the property line at the southernmost part of his ranch, he imagined being with her on the night of Ernie's dinner party, walking down the quiet city street, feeling the heat of her touch as his hand reached for hers.

And as he let the fantasy take wing, he imagined taking her back to his apartment, this time with a game plan that included a night's supply of condoms, a room full of candles and anything else he could think of to create the perfect romantic setting.

It was a risky thing to do, he supposed, especially since any kind of a relationship between them would last as long as an icicle in hell.

But then, tell that to his libido.

Every day that following week, after Kaylee and Shauna got out of school, Catherine worked with them on their dance steps, as well as on the song they planned to perform for the talent show. Eva had insisted that the other children stay out of the way so the girls could practice without interruption. And while there were a few complaints from the younger twins, they forgot their disappointment as soon as Eva suggested a new outdoor activity to keep them occupied.

As a result, Kaylee and Shauna worked hard. It didn't take Catherine long to realize they stood a chance to win, especially if the competition was divided into age groups.

"Shauna," she said, "I think it's time you tried to sing without using the karaoke screen."

"I don't know about that." The shy, gangly girl bit down on her bottom lip. "I'm not sure I can do it without the words."

Catherine smiled. "Actually, you haven't been relying on the screen that much anyway. Why don't you give it a try and see how it goes?"

"O-kay."

Before Catherine could start the music, her cell phone rang. She would have ignored the call completely, but it might be Ray. And she...

Well, they hadn't seen each other since last Saturday, although things seemed to be okay both times they'd talked on the phone. So she was eager to...

What? Hear his voice?

She clicked her tongue as she glanced at the lighted display, and when she recognized his number, her heart stopped momentarily, then spun in a perfect pirouette.

You'd think she'd been waiting for days to hear from him. And, well...okay, she *had.*

"Excuse me, girls. I need to take this call." As she prepared to answer, she walked out of the living room and onto the porch, telling herself he probably had something work-related to say and nothing that would require her to seek privacy. But she still didn't want an audience, just in case.

Once she was out of earshot, she said, "Hello."

"Hey, it's me." They were just three little words—not even three that held any real importance, yet the deep timbre of his voice shot a thrill clean through her.

"Hey, yourself," she responded.

"Am I bothering you?"

"No, not at all."

"Good. I called to ask if you were available to attend a few functions with me next weekend."

Not until then? She shook off a tinge of disappointment. "Sure, what's up?"

"There's a birthday party at the American Legion Hall on Friday night for Ernie Tucker, one of Brighton Valley's oldest residents. There's also a parade in his honor on Saturday and an ice-cream social at the community church after services on Sunday. Can you attend all of them with me?"

She didn't see any reason why not.

"You're welcome to stay with me in town," he added, "if you'd like to."

Her heart thumped and bumped around in her chest like the worn-out rods and pistons in the ranch pickup she'd driven into town last week. The one that hadn't been safe for her to drive home.

You're welcome to stay with me in town...if you'd like to.

Oh, she'd like to all right. Her thoughts drifted to the night she and Ray had slept together, and she was sorely tempted to agree. At least her body was eager. But her heart and mind were telling her to slow down and give it some careful thought.

Was he actually suggesting that she spend three days and two nights with him in his apartment in town?

"We can always figure something else out," he added.

"I can take you home between the events—or you can drive yourself. It's really up to you."

"Let's take one day at a time."

At least that would give her time to think things through.

"By the way," she said, "what's the dress code on Friday night?"

"Whatever you're comfortable wearing. Some people will be casual, while others might get dressed up. I'll probably wear a sport jacket."

"And for the parade?" she asked.

"Slacks, I guess. Or maybe jeans, if you'd prefer. Nothing fancy."

"How about the ice-cream social?"

"Well, that's casual, too. But I suspect some people will have on their church clothes." He paused for a moment, as though wanting to say something else.

When it became apparent that he had nothing more to add, she said, "I'll be glad to go with you. Why don't I meet you in town on Friday evening?"

"You mean at my apartment, right?"

She wasn't sure what she meant. "Okay, I'll meet you there. We can talk about the sleeping arrangements later."

He paused a beat. "Fair enough."

There was so much left unsaid that the silence filled the line until it grew too heavy to ignore. But instead of mentioning the chasm their lovemaking had created between them, she told him goodbye and promised that they'd talk again—soon.

Yet thoughts about the future followed her back to the living room, where the girls had continued to practice without her.

She'd no more than taken a seat when her cell phone rang again. She glanced at the display, thinking Ray might have forgotten to tell her something, but she recognized Zoe Grimwood's number.

"I'm so sorry," she told the girls. "But I need to take this call, too."

As Catherine returned to the patio, eager to hear what was going on in Manhattan, she greeted her friend.

"Guess what?" Zoe said. "Word is out that Paul De Santos has managed to pull things together financially. And he's going to start casting parts for *Dancing the Night Away.*"

That was the show Erik had been producing when he'd left town, taking several large investments with him.

"I saw the script," Zoe added. "And the lead would be perfect for you."

Erik had said the same thing—before he'd talked Catherine into investing fifty thousand dollars of her own money into the project. The man she'd trusted had burned her in many ways when he'd left. The most difficult, of course, had been facing the irate investors and telling them she had no answers for any of their questions.

"I'm not sure how Paul would feel about me auditioning for any of the parts," Catherine said. "He probably blames me. Erik left him holding the bag. He had to deal with the investors who'd lost their money and try to make things right."

"Paul can't hold you responsible," Zoe said. "You invested in the project, too."

Still, Catherine had been dating Erik, so she should have been able to see through him. If Paul considered her guilty by association, she'd never land the part. So, no matter how badly she wanted it, why should she even audition?

"I'll have to think about it," she said.

"Why? That part was made for you. And Paul has to know it."

She was certainly tempted. If she went back to New York and landed a role in the very musical Erik had been trying to produce, it might vindicate her in the eyes of everyone she'd ever known or worked with on Broadway.

Catherine crossed the porch and peered through the window, into the living room, where the girls continued to practice their dance steps.

"I've got a commitment here for the next couple of weeks," Catherine said. "I can't come immediately."

She also had a commitment to Ray, the job he'd asked her to do. And then there was their budding romance or whatever they'd been tiptoeing around.

Tiptoeing around? That sounded as if they were both considering some kind of relationship, when she didn't know *what* either of them were actually thinking, let alone feeling.

She slowly shook her head. She'd better get the stars out of her eyes, or she could end up brokenhearted again. Ray had made it clear that he didn't want to date anyone. Otherwise, he wouldn't have hired her to keep the women at bay.

So what made her think he'd be interested in her—other than the fact that she was safe and would be leaving soon?

And worse, what if she was wrong? What if he actually considered striking up a romance with her? And what if she were foolish enough to go along with it?

She might end up married to the guy—and stuck in a small town forever.

"How's your knee?" Zoe asked.

When Catherine had been in New York, she'd been having a little trouble with it. She'd considered seeing a specialist, but the downtime had really helped. "It's a lot better than it was—in fact, I think it's completely healed, although it's still a little stiff."

And that reminded her. If she was going to return to Broadway, she'd have to start working out again. She'd also have to lose a couple of pounds.

"Okay," she told Zoe. "I'll do it. Once I have my flight scheduled, I'll give you a call."

At that moment, Kaylee ran out to the patio and tugged at Catherine's sleeve. Then she pointed toward the living room, where Shauna was belting out the song.

"She's not looking at the screen," Kaylee whispered, her eyes bright. "She's doing it, just like Hannah Montana!"

Catherine smiled at the child she thought of as a daughter and gave her a wink, then returned to her telephone conversation with Zoe. "I can return in a little over two weeks, but I won't have access to my apartment for another three. Will you let me stay with you for a while?"

"Absolutely."

"Okay, then. It's all set."

As she ended the call, she told herself it was time to go home. It was the right thing to do.

The *only* thing.

Chapter 9

On Friday night, twenty minutes before the birthday party was scheduled to start, Catherine arrived at Ray's apartment.

And he was ready for her.

He'd stocked a box of condoms in the drawer of his nightstand—just in case. He also had two selections of wine—a nice merlot lying on its side in the pantry, as well as a pinot grigio chilling in the fridge.

Not that he was going to try and seduce her. But this time, he was prepared for a romantic evening, especially since he hadn't been ready the last time.

As he swung open the door, he found her waiting for him, her striking blond hair glossy and curled at the shoulders. She'd chosen a festive red dress for the party, one that was both modest and heart-stopping at the same time.

What other woman could pull off something like that?

The moment their eyes met, all was lost—every thought, every plan, every dream he'd ever had.

What was it about Catherine that had him wishing things were real? That their feelings for each other were mutual? That their engagement wasn't just an act?

"I'm sorry I'm late," she said. "I'd meant to get here sooner."

"No problem." He slipped aside and let her in. "The American Legion Hall is just a short walk from here. We ought to arrive in plenty of time—that is, if you're ready to go."

In the soft living room light, he scanned the length of her one more time, deciding she was as dazzling as ever in that simple red dress and heels.

Yet when he spotted the little black clutch she carried and realized it was too small to hold much of anything, even a toothbrush, a pang of disappointment shot through him.

She'd said that they could talk about the sleeping arrangements later, although he suspected she'd already made up her mind. That is, unless she left an overnight bag in her car—just in case.

A guy could hope, he supposed.

"Do you want to come in for a drink or something?" he asked. "Or do you want to head for the party?"

"I'm ready whenever you are."

"All right, then." He lifted his arm in an after-you manner, then stepped out the door, locked up the apartment and followed her down the stairs.

She looked hot tonight—like a model striding down a runway, all legs and sway. And for the next couple of hours, she was all his.

Another pang of disappointment shot through him. What he wouldn't give to know that she was here because she wanted to be. Would she have come if he'd actually asked her to be his date?

He supposed he'd never know, because he sure wasn't going to ask her.

As they continued out onto the sidewalk and started down Main Street, she slowed in front of the florist shop, where a variety of potted orchids were displayed in the window.

"I love exotic flowers," she said.

He'd have to remember that.

When they reached the beauty shop, which had a Closed sign in the window, Ray came to a stop. "I'm sure you'd never consider getting your hair done in a small town like this, but you ought to check it out sometime. Darla Ortiz, the owner, used to be a Hollywood actress back in the sixties. And she's decorated the place with all kinds of memorabilia."

"No kidding?" Catherine stopped, too, then peered through the window and into the darkened shop that had closed an hour earlier.

Ray caught a whiff of Catherine's floral-scented body lotion, something exotic, something to be handled with care—or cherished from a distance like those orchids at the floral shop.

He did his best to shake it off, as he stood next to her and looked into the darkened hair salon.

"It's pretty cool inside," he said. "Darla has a wall full of framed headshots of various movie stars who were popular forty and fifty years ago. Some are even black-and-whites from the post–World War II era. And each one is autographed to her."

"I'll make a point of stopping by to see them," Catherine said.

Feeling a little too much like one of the older women in town who worked for the local welcoming committee or a fast-talking real estate agent bent on selling the community to a new buyer, Ray said, "Come on. We'd better get moving."

As they started down the street again, he couldn't help adding, "Brighton Valley is a small town with a big heart."

"I've sensed that."

He wanted to say that the same was true of most of the residents, including the mayor, but he decided he'd better reel in his wild and stray thoughts before he went and said something stupid. Something he might not be able to take back.

Instead, he decided to enjoy the evening with Catherine—whatever that might bring.

The Ernie Tucker birthday committee had gone all-out in decorating the American Legion Hall for the celebration, complete with red, white and blue balloons and matching crepe-paper streamers. Several picture collages on poster board had been placed at the entrance, as well as in various spots around the room.

Each board had a slew of photographs—old brown and whites, a few Polaroids and some in color. They each provided a view of Ernie's life from the time he was a baby until present day.

"There's a lot of history here," Ray said.

"I can see that."

One particular photograph caught Ray's eye. Ernie was a kid, standing barefoot next to the original Brighton Valley Community Church.

"For example," he said, pointing to the picture. "That

church burned down nearly sixty years ago. And the congregation rebuilt it in its present location on Third Street."

"How did it happen?"

Ray chuckled. "Fred Quade and Randall Boswell who, according to my grandmother, never did amount to much, snuck out of Sunday services one summer day. They hid out in the choir room, where they decided to drink a beer and light up a smoke. Before long, they were both sicker than dogs and ran outside, leaving two smoldering cigars next to the robes hanging in the closet. And before long, the church was on fire.

"It seems that old Reverend McCoy was giving one of those fire and brimstone sermons. My grandmother said there were a few people who thought that brimstone was raining down on Brighton Valley."

Catherine smiled, then pointed at a picture of Ernie receiving a Hero of the Year award from the city council back in the 70s. A young boy, Danny Marquez, stood next to him. "Is that Ernie and his son?"

"No, it's the kid whose life he saved. There'd been a car accident, and the vehicle slammed up against a brick building. When it caught fire, the boy was trapped inside. His mother was thrown from the car, but she was seriously injured and couldn't get to her son.

"Ernie came along and, using a tire iron, broke out the front window and pulled him to safety. Ernie suffered some burns in the process, but he became a local hero that night."

"The community must love him." Catherine scanned the crowded room. "Looks like quite of few of them have come out to celebrate his birthday."

"Yep. Ernie has always been one of the white hats, as far as people in Brighton Valley are concerned. Not only was he the town sheriff for nearly forty years, he was also a veteran of World War II and received a Bronze Star. There are a lot of people in town who will tell you that they don't make 'em like Ernie Tucker anymore."

Ray's granddad had been a local hero, too, and if he'd lived to be one hundred, the town would have also come out in droves. But Ray didn't see any need to comment. This was Ernie's big day—and one that was well deserved.

"Come on." Ray nudged Catherine's arm. "Let's go wish ol' Ernie a happy birthday."

They did just that, and for the next two hours, Ray and Catherine made the rounds at the party, talking to one person or another.

Finally, after cake and ice cream had been served, Ray and Catherine wished Ernie the best, then made their way to the door and out onto Main Street.

Just as they were leaving, Kitty Mahoney, one of the local matrons who'd been trying to set him up with her daughter, stopped them and congratulated them on their engagement.

"You're a lucky gal," Kitty told Catherine.

Ray wrapped an arm around Catherine's shoulder. "I'm the fortunate one. I thank my lucky stars every day that this lady agreed to be my wife."

For a moment, he actually believed it—that they truly were a couple, that they had a future together.

Kitty smiled, then went about her way.

Ray loosened his hold on Catherine, letting his hand trail down her back before releasing her altogether. They might have been more affectionate before—the hand-holding, the starry-eyed gazes. But it wasn't so easy pretending anymore, and he wasn't sure why.

He supposed it was because he was having a hard time deciding what was real and what wasn't.

Once they'd stepped outside, where a full moon lit their path, Ray said, "That was probably a boring evening for you, so thank you for being a good sport."

"It wasn't so bad. I've never had the chance to meet a man who was a hundred years old before. That's actually amazing, don't you think? And he seems so sharp."

"He sure is."

They continued their walk down Main Street, which was fairly quiet, now that the stores had all closed. Yet they weren't doing much talking, either.

Ray wondered if she was pondering the sleeping arrangements—or if she'd already made up her mind.

When their shoulders brushed against each other, he had the strongest urge to reach for her hand—and he might have done it, if she hadn't been holding her small handbag between them.

Was that on purpose? A way to keep her distance?

When they neared the drugstore and the entrance to his apartment, he slowed and nodded toward the front window. "Have you ever been inside?"

"Of the drugstore? No, why?"

"Uriah Ellsworth runs the place, and he just refurbished the old-style soda fountain in back. It's kind of a treat to go in, sit at one of the red-vinyl-covered stools and sip on a chocolate milkshake or a root beer float. I'll have to bring you here one day."

"That sounds like fun."

Did it? Was she enjoying herself in Brighton Valley? Did she have any longing whatsoever to stick around town?

And more important, did she suspect that Ray would like it if she did?

When they reached the stairwell that led to his apartment, Ray slowed to a stop. "Why don't you come up and have some coffee? Or maybe even a nightcap?"

"I'd really like to, but I need to get home. I promised to help Eva work on the girls' costumes for the talent show."

"What girls?"

"Kaylee and her friend Shauna. They created an act, which is pretty good. I choreographed the dance steps for them and have been coaching them."

"No kidding?"

Catherine cocked her head slightly. "What do you find hard to believe? That the girls are actually pretty good? Or that I'm helping them?"

"A little of both, I guess. But I mean that in a good way."

She smiled. And in the golden glow of the streetlight, he could see the pride shining in her eyes. Could he see something else in there, too?

Either way, it didn't seem like something he should put too much stock in. Her feelings—whatever they might be—would only complicate the issue. So he said, "I'm glad you're helping out. It's…a nice thing for the mayor's fiancée to be personally involved in one of the community events. So you can bet I'll be at the talent show, cheering them on."

"Thanks. The girls have really worked hard. I think you'll be pleasantly surprised."

"I already am." And not just about the girls.

He paused for a moment, giving her a chance to change her mind about coming upstairs with him. When she didn't, he said, "Come on, I'll walk you to the parking lot."

They continued to the intersection of Main and First,

then they turned left and headed for the alley where she'd left her car.

"You'll never guess what else I'm going to do," she said.

She was full of surprises this evening, it seemed.

"I have no idea," he said. "We haven't had a chance to talk much this past week."

Okay, so maybe that was partly his fault. He'd made a point of not calling her each time he'd thought of her, each time he remembered the night they'd made love.

Her steps slowed as she reached Eva's minivan, and she turned to face him with a bright-eyed smile. "I'm going to help out in the Fine Arts Department at Wexler High School starting next Monday."

She'd been right—he wouldn't have guessed that in a week of Mondays. Maybe he'd been wrong about her hightailing it back to New York and leaving him in the dust. Maybe she was finding her niche in Brighton Valley.

"How did that come about?" he asked, wondering if it meant she had plans to stay in town indefinitely.

"A couple of days ago, Jillian Hollister stopped by the Walker Ranch. I was in the living room, coaching Kaylee and Shauna on their routine. She watched for a while, and then she suddenly lit up and told me that the Wexler High dance teacher is out on maternity leave. Apparently, some of the kids in class had wanted to perform in the talent show, but the substitute teacher they'd brought in has no dancing experience—if you can imagine that."

Actually, he was still trying to wrap his mind around the idea of her taking on a job like that. "So you volunteered to help?" Ray asked.

"Well, when Jillian asked if I'd work with them, I told her I'd be happy to—at least until the night of the talent show."

That was great news. And promising. He liked thinking that she was getting more involved in the community. Maybe she wouldn't be so eager to leave town.

"Sounds like you're settling in," he said.

Settling in?

Oh, *no.* Catherine didn't want him to get *that* idea. Her life, her career, her very identity was in New York. And with *Dancing the Night Away* now a go, she had no reason to stay in Brighton Valley much longer.

Well, no reason other than Ray and the twins she'd come to love. And standing outside with him in the silver glow of a lover's moon, she was almost tempted to reconsider.

Almost.

As she struggled to shake off the sentiment that tempted her to change her course and ruin her chances to ever perform on the Broadway stage again, Ray placed his hand on her back, sending a spiral of heat to her core.

"Are you sure you don't want to spend the night with me?" he asked.

No, she wasn't sure. In fact, she wasn't sure about anything at all right now, especially with that blasted full moon shining overhead and the musky scent of Ray's cologne taunting her with the promise of another wonderful evening spent in his bed.

But if she weakened, then where would she be?

As if he might somehow hold the clue, she looked into his eyes, where the intensity of his gaze dared her to change her mind about staying with him, not only tonight, but in Brighton Valley indefinitely.

Yet how could she give it all up—the dream career, the bright lights, not to mention the culture-rich opportunities in a metropolis she'd grown to love?

As they continued to study each other in silence, his

hand remained on her back. He stroked his thumb in a gentle caress, setting her heart on end.

How could such a simple movement be so arousing, so alluring?

She pressed her lips together, forcing herself to remain strong. After a beat, she said, "Staying with you tonight isn't a good idea. My life is in Manhattan. And I'll be going back one day soon. When that happens, it'll be easier if we haven't grown too attached to each other."

His thumb stopped moving, then his hand slowly lowered until he pulled it away altogether. The loss of his touch stirred up a chill in the night air, leaving her to crave his warmth.

And to crave him.

"You're probably right," he said.

Under normal circumstances, she would have been happy to have him agree with her. Yet there was something bittersweet about being right, especially on a night like this.

As they faced each other in the moonlight, Ray reached out again, this time placing his hand along her jaw. His thumb brushed her cheek, warming her once again and deepening her craving for more of him.

"Would it also be a bad idea if I kissed you goodnight?" he asked.

She opened her mouth to tell him yes. But would it be so bad to end their evening together with a kiss?

Oh, for Pete's sake. Her better judgment, which had been battling desire as if her life depended upon it, lost the will to fight any longer and surrendered to temptation.

She slipped her arms around his neck, and with her lips parting, raised her mouth to his. The moment their tongues touched, the memory of their lovemaking came rushing back, making her relive each stroke, each caress, each ragged breath until she was lost in a swirl of heat.

This was *so* not a good-night kiss. Instead, it whispered, *Take me to bed and stay with me forever.*

When they finally came up for air, Catherine's head was spinning.

Really spinning.

She blinked, trying to right her world, yet a burst of vertigo slammed into her. As she grabbed on to Ray to steady herself, her fingers dug into his shoulder. Still, she swayed on her feet.

If he hadn't caught her, she might have collapsed on the ground.

What in the world was happening to her?

"Are you okay?" he asked, humor lacing his voice as if he thought the kiss had a bigger effect on her than it had.

Again, she blinked. Moments earlier, when she'd been kissing him, she'd been so overcome with passion and desire, that she might have described it as head-spinning and knee-buckling. But the buzz she was feeling right now was much more than that.

She was actually dizzy.

Was there any chance she might faint?

"Are you sure you're okay?" he asked again, this time taking her reaction a little more seriously.

As her head began to clear, she managed a smile and tried to downplay whatever had happened. "I guess I lost my head for a moment."

"Me, too. And you can't tell me that's a bad thing."

Sure it was. Losing her head might lead to losing her heart, and that would be a *very* bad thing.

But she wasn't sure where the dizziness had come from. It seemed to be easing now. But was it safe for her to drive home? The winding road that led to the ranch was pretty dark in spots.

"You know," she said, "I'm feeling a little lightheaded. I must have eaten something that didn't sit right with me. Maybe I should stay the night."

He brightened. "If that's the case, you shouldn't be driving."

"But I'll sleep on the sofa," she added.

He stiffened, as if her sudden change of course took him completely aback. But then, why wouldn't it? She'd been struggling with her feelings for him ever since the night they'd slept together. And she was still vacillating when it came to knowing what to do about it.

"No," he said, slowly shaking his head. "You take the bed. I'll sleep on the sofa."

"But I'm the one making unreasonable demands," she said.

He placed his hand on her back, disregarding her comment. "Come on. Let's go inside."

She didn't know what he would expect of her once they entered his apartment, but she'd meant what she'd said. She would stay the night, but they wouldn't be sleeping together.

Too bad her hormones were insisting otherwise.

Chapter 10

Once inside the apartment, Ray told Catherine to sit on the sofa. Then he went into the kitchen, filled a glass with water and took it to her.

He watched her take several sips, all the while checking out her coloring, which was a little pale.

"Are you feeling any better now?" he asked.

She nodded. "That dizzy spell seems to be over. If I wait a little while, I can probably drive home—"

"You're not going anywhere. There's no need to risk driving home in the dark when you can stay here."

She nodded, then glanced down at the glass of water she held. When she looked up, her gaze snagged his. "Thank you, Ray."

"For what?"

"I don't know. Understanding, I guess."

To be honest, he didn't understand any of it—her dizziness, of course. But her reluctance to make love again, when it had been so good between them, confused him. So did her change in attitude toward him, the distance between them, the stilted conversations that had once flowed so smoothly.

What had happened to the old Catherine, the woman he'd hired to be his fiancée, the one who'd at least pretended to hang on his every word and to gaze in his eyes with love?

He'd come to appreciate that woman. Not that he didn't appreciate the new Catherine. He just didn't understand her, that's all.

Was she playing some kind of game with him?

He hoped that wasn't the case.

"Listen," he said. "There's something we need to talk about."

His comment hung in the air for a couple of beats, then she slowly nodded. "You're probably right."

Then why was it so hard to broach the subject, to throw it out there? To encourage her to share her thoughts?

Finally, he said, "I miss the camaraderie we once had."

"So do I. But making love...changed things."

It certainly had. He supposed it always did—no matter who the couple was or what their stories.

"Why do you think that happened?" He had his own ideas, of course. But how did *she* feel about it?

"Because a relationship between us won't work. I mean, your life is clearly in Brighton Valley, and mine is in Manhattan. So even though the sex was incredible—and we seem to...care and respect each other—getting any further involved will only make it difficult for us when I leave."

She had a point, because he would damn sure miss her when she left town. And while it made sense that they protect themselves from getting in too deep, he couldn't help wishing that things could be different. That she would decide to make a life for herself in Texas.

But that was as unlikely as him selling his ranch and moving to New York City.

It would never happen.

"Are you sorry we made love?" he asked.

She smiled, her eyes filling with a sentiment he couldn't quite peg. "No, I don't regret that at all. But I do regret knowing nothing will ever become of it."

The truth in her words poked a tender spot inside him, just like a spur jabbing him in the flanks. And he had to concede that she was right.

"At this point," she added, "we can walk away with a nice memory. But if we get any more involved—or if that involvement is emotional—it might be tough to say goodbye."

It might be tough to do that anyway. But he shook off that thought as well as the implication that she could actually develop feelings for him.

"You've got a point," he admitted. "We don't live in the same worlds."

"If we did, things would be different."

Again the truth she spoke, the reality of the situation in which they'd found themselves, gave Ray another spurlike jab.

If he could come up with any kind of argument, he would have laid it on the table. But there wasn't one to be had.

"I'm glad we got that out of the way," he said. "Now all we have to do is decide on the sleeping arrangements. And like I told you before, I'm taking the sofa."

It had been an easy decision to make—the only one.

Yet three hours later, Ray lay stretched out on the sofa

in the living room, trying his best to sleep and not having any luck at all.

She'd told him that she didn't want to risk an emotional involvement with him. And he could see the wisdom in that.

But each time he closed his eyes and tried to drift off, he wondered if he'd already gotten in too deep.

If so, she'd been right.

It was going to hurt like hell when she left town.

Over the next two weeks, Catherine got so caught up at Wexler High School with the talent show rehearsals, as well as with Kaylee and Shauna, that she hadn't been able to spend much time with Ray or go to many of those social engagements he'd been paying her to attend.

Okay, so that was the excuse she'd been giving him.

He didn't seem to mind, though. And that made things easier. After the heart-to-heart chat they'd had the night of Ernie Tucker's birthday dinner, their conversations had been better, but they were still…a bit awkward.

They'd attended the parade in Ernie's honor the next morning, but that afternoon she'd felt a little nauseous and had decided to drive back to the Walker ranch instead of staying over to attend the ice-cream social on Sunday.

"I must have picked up a bug of some kind," she'd told Ray, as she got ready to leave the parade. "First the dizziness last night, and now an upset stomach."

"Take care of yourself," he'd said.

And she had. She'd gone straight home, slipped into her nightgown and taken a nap.

The dizziness and nausea had plagued her off and on for a while, although never enough to make her consider calling a doctor. And the busier she kept herself, the better she seemed to feel.

Still, if she didn't kick that bug soon, she'd have to make an appointment with a doctor, and she hated to see someone she didn't know in Brighton Valley. But she'd deal with that if and when the time came.

Now, as she prepared to walk up the stairwell to Ray's apartment, she reached into her purse for the key. She'd told him she'd meet him at his place so they could attend an auction tonight, and she was a little early. But she'd just finished working with the high school dance troupe and couldn't see any reason to drive all the way back to the ranch, then to town again.

She carried a garment bag that held a dress she'd borrowed from Eva, as well as a pair of heels. So she had to transfer everything to one hand so she could fit the key into the lock.

Once inside, she carried her change of clothes to the bathroom, where she would get dressed.

Thirty minutes later, she'd taken a shower and slipped into the light blue dress. Then she'd freshened up her makeup and swept her hair into an elegant twist. By the time Ray arrived, she was ready to go.

"I'm sorry I'm late," he said as he entered the apartment. When he spotted her in the kitchen, pouring herself a glass of club soda, he froze in his tracks. As his gaze swept over her, an appreciative smile stretched across his face. "Nice dress. Is it new?"

"Merely borrowed."

Something borrowed, something blue…

Shaking off the thoughts of the wedding day ditty, she asked, "Did you have a good day?"

"I sure did. And better yet, I heard that Jim Cornwall is doing much better and would like his job back in the not-so-distant future."

She took another sip of her drink, wishing it was ginger ale instead. Her stomach was feeling a little woozy again. "Have I met Jim?"

"No, not yet. He's the elected mayor, the one I've been filling in for."

Oh, that's right. He'd fallen off a ladder while trimming a tree in his yard and had been seriously injured—a skull fracture if she remembered correctly.

Catherine offered Ray a smile. "So that's good news, isn't it?"

"You bet it is. I had no idea how demanding the job would be, especially when it comes to all the social events I have to attend—like this one tonight." Ray nodded toward the bedroom. "Give me a minute, and I'll change clothes. Then we can go."

Catherine didn't have to wait long. True to his word, Ray returned within minutes, wearing a sport jacket and tie. And they were soon in his car and on the way to the Wexler Valley Country Club.

Tonight's event was a dinner and an auction, which would benefit a local Boys and Girls Club that serviced both Brighton Valley and Wexler, the neighboring town.

"You know," she said, as they turned into the country club, "you make a great mayor. And the townspeople really seem to like you."

"Thanks. It's been a good experience. But I'm eager to go back home and be a rancher again."

She could understand that.

Ray parked his SUV in the lower lot, and the two made the uphill walk to the main dining room, where the dinner and silent auction would take place. As he opened the door for Catherine, they were met by the sound of a harpist playing just beyond the entry.

"The music is a nice touch," Catherine said.

"Isn't it?" He smiled, then placed his hand on her back

as if nothing had changed between them. "That's got to be Margo Reinhold, the wife of one of our councilmen. She's the only one I know who plays the harp."

They'd no more than entered the main dining room, when Margo's husband approached Ray, taking time to greet Catherine first.

Ray turned to Catherine. "You remember Dale Reinhold, don't you, honey?"

"Yes, I do." She reached out a hand to greet him. "It's good to see you again."

After a little small talk, Dale said, "You heard the news about Jim Cornwall, didn't you?"

"I sure did." Ray lobbed him a bright-eyed grin. "And I'll be counting the days until he comes back."

"Maybe so. But you've been a darn good mayor. You really ought to think about running in the next election."

"Thanks. I'll have to give it some thought."

Catherine had expected Ray to bring up all the work he needed to do on his ranch, but he didn't. Was that because he'd actually enjoyed his stint as mayor?

Either way, she had to agree with Dale. Ray had been doing a great job as mayor. And he was clearly respected by everyone in the community.

As the men continued to talk, a waiter walked by with a tray of hors d'oeuvres—something deep fried and wrapped in bacon. The aroma snaked around Catherine, setting off a wave of nausea.

Oh, dear. Not again. And not here.

"Would you…" She cleared her throat, then issued an "Excuse me" before dashing off to find the ladies' restroom.

Thankfully, just putting some distance between her and the waiter's tray was enough to settle her stomach.

Good grief. What was that all about? Why hadn't she kicked that flu bug?

When she spotted a matronly woman wearing a tennis outfit, she asked where she could find the nearest restroom and was directed to her left.

Once inside, she found a sitting area and took a seat in an overstuffed chair. Her game plan had been to call a doctor once she got back to New York if she hadn't gotten any better. But maybe she ought to see someone while she was in Brighton Valley. What if the nausea and dizziness were symptoms of something other than a bug, something serious?

If she hadn't already been told that her chances of getting pregnant were slim, she might even wonder about that. But she'd learned a long time ago not to pin her hopes on having a child of her own.

Minutes later, the nausea passed. As she got to her feet, a silver-haired woman entered the room wearing a cream-colored dress and heels. Catherine had met her a time or two, but to be honest, she'd completely forgotten her name or her connection to Ray.

"Well, hello," the woman said. "What a lovely dress. That color really brings out the blue of your eyes."

"Thank you."

"I haven't seen you around lately," the woman added, offering a friendly smile. "It's good to see you and our mayor together."

"I've been busy," Catherine said.

"I heard that." The woman brightened. "You've been helping out with the high school dance group. That's a wonderful thing for you to do. But then again, you are the mayor's fiancée, so it makes sense that you'd jump right in and get involved in the community."

Catherine returned her smile, although she was still at

a complete loss when it came to remembering the woman's name. Was she the wife of one of the councilmen?

Maybe she was a councilwoman herself.

"Have you and Ray set a date for your wedding?" the woman asked.

"No, not yet."

"I couldn't wait to set a date when Roger and I became engaged."

Catherine wasn't sure what to say to that.

"June weddings are always nice," the woman added. "Roger and I figured that early summer would be a nice time to take a vacation, if we ever wanted to celebrate our anniversary out of town."

"Now there's a thought."

"Well, all I can say is that you're going to make a beautiful bride."

"Thank you." Catherine fought the urge to check her watch. Ray had to be wondering where she was.

"I hope you plan to have a big wedding."

"Why?" Catherine asked.

"Because everyone in this county loves Ray. And they're going to want to attend so they can wish the two of you their best."

"You're probably right." Catherine offered the woman her sweetest smile, then excused herself and left the bathroom.

She and Ray were going to have to talk about dates all right. Dates for their breakup.

And they'd also need to come up with a good reason for a perfect couple to split and go their own ways.

Catherine had been fairly quiet all evening, which really shouldn't surprise Ray. She'd been introspective ever since they'd made love. Even the heart-to-heart talk they'd had the other day hadn't made things any clearer.

She'd been right about not getting emotionally involved, but that didn't mean he was happy about the decision to take a step back—no matter what the future might bring.

Ray reached for his steak knife, cut into the filet mignon and took a bite. He'd eaten his share of fancy meals, but he had to admit the chef at the Wexler Valley Country Club had gone above and beyond tonight.

"Are you sure you don't want to have some of my steak?" he asked Catherine.

She'd passed on dinner, choosing only the salad with lemon instead of a dressing. She'd mentioned watching her weight, which he thought was silly. If ever a woman had a perfect shape, it was Catherine. But he decided it wasn't his place to tell her what to eat.

When the people at their table had finished their meals, the wait staff brought out cheesecake for dessert.

"Would you like a bite?" Ray asked Catherine.

"No, thank you."

She certainly had a lot of willpower. Heather, his ex, would have taken her spoon and at least had a taste.

After the waiter picked up the empty dessert plates, Ray placed his hand on Catherine's. "Are you ready to go, honey?"

"I am, if you are."

He nodded, then stood and pulled out her chair.

One nice thing about these public dinners was being able to pretend that everything was still good between them—even if there really wasn't a "them."

Still, he had to admit that it would have been nice if they really were a couple, if their fake relationship was real. There was something very appealing about being with Catherine, sharing an intimacy he'd never known with anyone else—even if it was all an act.

Would he ever share that kind of relationship with anyone? He hoped so.

Somewhere, deep inside, he was sorry that it might be with a woman he hadn't met, a woman who wasn't Catherine.

After saying their goodbyes to the others at their table, they made their way to the entrance.

"How much money do you think the auction brought in?" she asked.

"Quite a bit. Last year they made ten thousand dollars, and I suspect they did better this time. There had to be at least twenty more people. And they had a lot of nice donations for the silent auction." Ray opened the door, and when he asked Catherine to step outside, she swayed on her feet.

He reached out and grabbed her arm, steadying her. "Are you okay?"

His first thought was that she'd lost a heel or something.

"Yes," she said. "But can we stand here a minute?"

"Sure. Why?"

"I'm a little dizzy again."

His gut clenched. "*Again?* How often have you been having these spells?"

"A few times. Maybe three or four."

He'd been with her on two of those occasions—both of them in the evening. "Where were you when you had the other dizzy spells?"

"Once I was in the bathroom at the Walker ranch. And then it happened again when I was at the high school. But if I sit down for a while, it passes."

He hated the thought of her being sick. "That's a little worrisome, don't you think?"

"I suppose so. But in this case, I didn't eat much for dinner, so maybe that caused me to be a little lightheaded. I probably need to have some protein."

She might be right, but that didn't make him feel much better. What if there was something wrong? Something serious?

"I'll fix you a ham sandwich when we get back to my place," he said.

"That might be too heavy. If you have any cottage cheese, I might have a spoonful."

He never ate cottage cheese, let alone put it on his shopping list. And even if he did, he would insist that she eat more than that.

"I'll tell you what," he said. "Once I get you to the car, I'll go back inside and ask them to put one of those steak dinners in a take-home box."

"Please don't bother the chef with a request like that. I'll find something to eat when we get home."

Home. Just the sound of the word coming from Catherine's lips made Ray wonder what it would be like if the two of them actually lived together, but given their different ways of life, that would never happen.

"Do you think you can walk to the car now?" he asked.

She nodded. "Yes, let's go."

He slipped an arm around her—just in case she wasn't as steady on her feet as she implied she was—and walked her to the lower parking lot, where he'd left his SUV.

"You're staying with me tonight," he added.

She didn't object, which was good.

The next step was to insist that she make a doctor's appointment first thing Monday morning—whether she wanted to or not.

* * *

Once they'd gotten back to Ray's apartment, Catherine gave Eva a call and told her she'd bring the minivan back in the morning.

Ray had insisted that she make an appointment with one of the doctors at the Brighton Valley Medical Center on Monday morning, and she promised to do so—if she had another dizzy spell.

"I'm sure it's nothing to worry about," she added, although she wasn't entirely convinced of that. "I was probably just a little lightheaded from not eating much today."

"Then come into the kitchen with me," he said. "I'll fix you a sandwich."

"All right. But if you don't mind, I'd like you to leave it open-faced. No mayonnaise, please. And can I please see the nutrition label on that ham?"

He reached for her hand and gave it a warm, gentle squeeze that nearly stole her breath away.

"Okay," he said, letting go. "But you need to understand something. I'm worried about you skipping meals—or relying on rabbit food to keep you going. And while we're on the subject, I'm not sure why in the hell you think you have to diet. You look great."

"I… Well, thank you." She rubbed the hand he'd been holding just moments before. "But just so you know, I've put on ten pounds since arriving. And I don't want it to get out of hand."

She also needed to lose at least that much if she wanted to land the lead role in *Dancing the Night Away,* but she wasn't ready to tell him that.

"You can lose that extra weight without starving yourself." He nodded toward the open kitchen. "Come on. Let's get you some nourishment."

After pulling the ham from the fridge, he handed it

over to her to look at the packaging. Then he took a loaf of bread from the pantry.

Catherine read the nutrition label. The deli meat was a low-fat version, so she decided not to stress about it.

Within minutes, Ray had made the sandwich, just the way she'd asked—with one slice of bread and no mayo. He also added some lettuce and tomato, leaving them on the side. Then he carried her plate to the dining area.

"Thanks," she said, taking a seat at the table. "It actually looks pretty good."

"I'm glad." Ray removed his sport jacket, then he carried it into the bedroom, leaving her to eat.

When she'd popped the last bite of the sandwich into her mouth, she took the empty plate back to the kitchen and put it in the sink.

Ray, who'd come out of the bedroom, slipped up behind her. She'd heard him coming, then caught a whiff of his musky aftershave as he placed his hands on her shoulders and slowly turned her around.

"Now that you've eaten," he said, "I have another request."

"What's that?"

His gaze, as intense and arousing as she'd ever seen it, locked on to hers, causing her heart to rumble and her pulse to kick up a notch. But it was the husky tone of his voice and the suggestive words he uttered that nearly dropped her to her knees.

"I want to sleep with you tonight, Catherine."

If she were going to be honest—with him, as well as herself—she would admit that there wasn't anything she'd like better. But making love with him, as star-spinning and mind-boggling as it had been, had left them both on edge around each other. And if she weren't careful, she could ruin whatever friendship they had.

And Ray knew how she felt. He'd even agreed with her.

Of course, that didn't mean she wasn't sorely tempted to make love with him again. And obviously, he was dealing with the same temptation.

The hormones and pheromones that swarmed around them became so strong, so heady, that she could almost see them. But she forced herself to hold steady. "I told you that, under the circumstances, having a sexual relationship wasn't a good idea."

"I said *sleep*. Not make love."

She paused for a beat, thinking about it—and actually liking the idea.

"Even if we don't ever become lovers again," he added, "I'd like for us to be friends. I care about you, Catherine. And I want to share my bed with you."

She cared about him, too. Way more than she dared to admit—to him or to herself. But she would be leaving soon. She'd even purchased her flight back to JFK for the day after the talent show, although she hadn't told Ray yet.

And why hadn't she?

Maybe because she was afraid he had some warped idea that they might actually have a future together. That he'd ask her to stay in Brighton Valley, to be his real fiancée.

If he did, what would she say?

Could she give up her life and her dreams for a man? Maybe.

And maybe not.

Yet a better question might be: Could she give it all up for Ray? And if so, would she grow to resent him in the long run?

Her heart clamored in her chest, begging to get out

and to have a say about it, urging her to agree to more than just sleeping with him, to make love one more time.

And maybe even to cancel her flight back to New York.

But she had to go. And leaving Brighton Valley—leaving *Ray*—was going to be tough enough without running the risk of an emotional attachment, which she feared she already had.

Yet against her better judgment, she said, "Okay. I'll sleep with you."

She told herself she'd made that decision because she hated to have him sleep on the sofa, and she knew he'd insist that she take the bed.

But in truth?

If she was leaving on Sunday, she wanted to sleep next to him tonight.

And even more than that, she wanted to wake up wrapped in his arms.

Chapter 11

Ray woke the next morning with Catherine's back nestled against his chest, his arms wrapped around her.

He'd thought that once they'd drifted off to sleep last night, they'd end up on their own sides of the bed, but he'd been wrong. They'd cuddled together until dawn.

As Catherine began to stir, he took one last moment to breathe in the faint floral scent of her shampoo, to relish the feel of her breasts splayed against his forearm.

She turned, adjusting her body so that she faced him, and smiled. "Good morning."

He returned her smile. "'Morning."

"How'd you sleep?"

"Great." Much better than if he'd slept on the sofa, holding on to his pillow. "How 'bout you?"

"Not bad."

"Are you feeling any better?" he asked.

"Yes. I guess I just needed a bite to eat and a good night's sleep."

He hoped so. He'd been worried about her last night. "Do you want to use the shower first?" he asked.

"All right."

After she climbed from bed, he headed into the kitchen, where he brewed a fresh pot of coffee and searched the fridge for something to make for their breakfast.

He settled on bacon and eggs, although he figured it might be best to ask what she'd like to eat. Maybe she'd rather go to Caroline's Diner.

Minutes later, Catherine entered the kitchen, fresh from the shower.

"Coffee's ready," he said. "Would you like me to make some scrambled eggs? Or would you rather go down to Caroline's? She makes the best cinnamon rolls."

"I'll pass on a big breakfast," she said. "Coffee will be fine for now."

There she went with the dieting again. Hadn't she learned her lesson?

He crossed his arms and leaned his weight onto one leg. "Remember what happened last night? You need more than that to get by on. I don't want you getting dizzy again."

"Okay," she said. "I'll have an egg."

Just one? What was he going to do with her?

Love her came to mind. But he shook off that thought as quickly as it had popped up. All he needed to do was to fall for a woman who was supposed to be leaving town in the near future.

"There's something I need to tell you," she said, taking a seat at the dining room table.

"What's that?" He pulled two mugs from the kitchen cupboard, his back to her as he filled them with coffee.

"I've made plans to return to Manhattan."

His pulse, as well as his breathing, stopped for several beats, and when it started up again, he turned to face her. "When?"

"A week from next Sunday."

Eight short days from now.

"I hope that's okay with you," she added.

Wouldn't it have to be? He'd known it was coming, although it still took him by surprise and left him unbalanced.

"I know we had an agreement," she said, "but the length of it had been indefinite. And, well, I have an opportunity to audition for the lead in a musical, one I'd really like to have."

His heart sank to the pit of his stomach. Not only was she leaving Texas, but she was going back to the life she'd created for herself, the life she loved.

He couldn't fault her for it, but it still...well, it hurt to know she was leaving—and before he was ready to let her go.

Her news had jerked the rug right out from under his feet, toppling the phony world they'd created for themselves in Brighton Valley.

"We'll have to come up with a reason for our breakup," she added.

It would have to be a damn good one. Everyone in Brighton Valley seemed to like her—and to think of them as a couple. A perfect one at that.

The phony engagement may have worked like a charm, but now he would have to deal with the repercussions of ending it.

Too bad one of those repercussions had just hit him personally like a wild bronc coming out of the chute.

"Are you okay?" she asked.

Hell no. He wasn't okay. But he didn't want her to

know that. Or to think that her leaving was going to be any more than a little inconvenience to him. So he glanced at his bare feet, then back up to her face. "I'm sorry, Catherine. I didn't mean to ignore you. I had a couple of things scheduled for later in the month, and I was trying to figure out how I'd manage without you. But you're right. We'll have to concoct a story for everyone—something believable that won't make either one of us look like the bad guy. Can I have some time to think about it?"

"Of course. I'll try to come up with an excuse for our breakup, too."

He handed her a cup of coffee, then grabbed his and took a drink of the rich, morning brew. He hoped the familiar taste, as well as the caffeine, would right his world again.

Three sips later, it hadn't helped a bit.

He'd known this day would come. Why hadn't he planned for it? Why hadn't he realized they'd need an explanation?

Or *did* they?

Compelled to drag his feet, he asked, "Would it be so bad to let things ride a while?"

"What do you mean?"

"Well… Maybe we can tell people you had to go to take care of business in New York. We can let them think you'll be returning. That would keep the marriage-minded women in town at bay for a bit longer. And by then, maybe Jim will be back on the job as mayor, and I'll be at my ranch more often than not."

She seemed to chew on that for a moment, then began to nod. "That sounds like it might work."

It also bought him some valuable time. Time for Catherine to change her mind about leaving. Or, if she got to

Manhattan and missed the small-town life and wanted to return to Brighton Valley, it provided them with an opportunity to pick up right where they'd left off.

At least that's the excuse he seemed to be hanging on to.

What the hell was happening to him? Why the uneasiness about her plans to leave, especially when that had always been part of the plan?

Why was he missing the idea of having her around, when she'd never even hinted that she was looking for a husband or a home, let alone relocating to a town that must seem like Podunk, Texas, after living in a metropolis?

Damn. If he didn't know better, he'd think that he'd fallen in love with another woman who didn't share the same affection for him. And if anyone ought to know better than to imagine a woman having loving feelings where none existed, it was Ray. Heather hadn't placed any value on love, marriage or promises. And when she left the ranch, she'd never looked back.

Of course, Catherine wasn't at all like his ex-wife. She didn't have a selfish or greedy side. At least, not that he'd noticed.

Catherine lifted her cup and took a sip. Then she grimaced and set it down.

"What's the matter?"

"I don't know. It doesn't...taste very good."

"Really? Mine tastes fine." And just the way he liked it, just the way he made it every day.

"I guess it just isn't hitting the spot." She picked up the mug, carried it to the sink, then poured it out. "I'm sorry. I can't drink it."

"Would you rather have some orange juice?"

"I'm not sure. Maybe."

"It would be a lot more nutritious." He strode to the fridge and pulled out the container. "Wouldn't that be better?"

"I think so."

As he poured her a glass, he wondered if she was having any reservations about leaving. Maybe second thoughts, instead of the coffee, had left a bitter taste in her mouth.

Or maybe that was just wishful thinking on his part.

Either way, he was going to have to get used to the idea—no matter how much it weighed him down.

As he handed her the glass of OJ, he thought of something his grandma used to say: *You don't miss your water until the well runs dry.*

It hadn't been the case for him when Heather had moved out. By then, he'd actually been glad to see her go. But that certainly seemed to be the case now. He felt empty, just at the thought of Catherine going away.

"You know," she said, "if we put our heads together, I'm sure we can think of a good reason for us to break up."

He'd rather come up with a reason for her to *stay.* But she was right. They lived in two different worlds. Forcing her to clip her wings and remain on a ranch or in a small town like Brighton Valley would destroy a part of her—maybe even the part that appealed to him most.

But how was he going to get by without water, now that his well had gone dry?

The night of the talent show finally arrived, and no one was more excited than Catherine. Working with Kaylee and Shauna had been an amazing experience, and so had coaching the Wexler High School students.

Ray had been tied up at a meeting all afternoon, so he

told her he'd meet her there and asked her to save him a seat. He'd also mentioned that he had something to talk to her about and suggested she bring an overnight bag so she could stay in town with him.

If her flight had been another week out, she might have refused, fearing that her resolve to leave might weaken. As it was, she'd be flying out of Houston on Sunday afternoon—just a little under twenty-four hours from now.

In all honesty, she was going to miss Ray when she went to New York—more than she'd realized. And certainly more than he would ever know.

So what harm would there be in having one last evening together?

After dressing for the talent show and telling Kaylee she'd see her there, she borrowed one of the ranch pickups and drove to town. Instead of going straight to the theater, she first stopped at the florist shop on Main Street.

Three days ago, she'd ordered two bouquets of red roses to give to her favorite stars after tonight's performances. Wouldn't Shauna and Kaylee be surprised?

Next she drove to the Lone Star Theater, which had been built sixty years ago. When the owner died, his widow hadn't been able to find an investor or a buyer. Upon her death, she donated it to the city.

From what Catherine understood, it wasn't used very often. But it certainly made a perfect place for a talent show, with its old-fashioned curtain, stage and lighting.

Catherine sought a seat in the front section that was reserved for the families of those performing.

Eva and Jane, along with the parents of the younger contestants, had been allowed backstage to wait with the girls. That left Jerald Morrison, Dan and Hank Walker, as well as Kaylee's siblings to sit in the same row as Catherine.

Knowing she would need to get up and present the flowers to the girls, Catherine took an aisle seat, then placed her purse on the one next to it, saving it for Ray. Rather than hold the flowers and be unable to clap or to read the program, she slipped the bouquets under her chair, where they'd be safe.

Ray, who'd just arrived, greeted the others in the row before slipping into place, next to Catherine. Then he reached for her hand and gave it a squeeze. "Would it be appropriate for me to say 'Break a leg' to the dance coach?"

"Absolutely." She returned his smile.

Moments later, the show began, and Catherine sat back, waiting for the act she hoped would win in the ten-and-under division.

When the time came, and the girls finally stepped onto the stage, looking darling in the costumes Eva had made, Catherine sat upright and leaned forward. Her heart soared at the sight of them, at the smiles on their faces.

Eva and Jane had come around to the front part of the theater and knelt in the aisle, taking pictures. Somehow, even Jerald Morrison had managed to get out of his seat and film the girls using the video camera on his cell phone.

It was nice to see Shauna's new foster family being so supportive of her. The poor kid certainly deserved to finally have a stable, loving home. It was also high time someone recognized how sweet she was, how pretty and talented. And Catherine was thrilled to have the opportunity to encourage her.

As the girls performed on stage, it was clear to everyone that all their practice in the Walkers' living room had paid off. Shauna, who also had a solo part, brought down the house when she belted out the song's refrain.

And no one's heart swelled as much as Catherine's. In a way, she was paying it forward, encouraging young talent to reach their dreams.

When the song ended, Ray rose from his seat, clapping and cheering with all the rest. Yet when his eyes met hers, they seemed to tell her how very proud he was...of *her*.

In all her many performances, going back to those in the high school auditorium, on to college and even those on and off Broadway, no one had cheered like that for her. Sure, she'd been proud of her own success. And so had Jennifer Walker. But it wasn't quite the same as...

Shaking off the sentiment and the memories, Catherine reached for two of the small bouquets she'd set under her chair, but couldn't quite get a grip on them. So she stood and bent over to retrieve them.

The dizziness that had plagued her earlier in the week struck again as she stood upright. But she couldn't miss the chance to offer roses to Brighton Valley's newest and youngest stars. As she headed for the stage, she blinked her eyes, trying to clear her vision.

When she reached the bottom of the stage, she handed one bouquet to Kaylee and the next to Shauna.

"I'm so proud of you two," she said, realizing she would have given anything to have had someone say the same thing to her—and to truly mean it.

The lights up front glared, causing the dizziness to increase. Wanting to find an empty chair in which she could sit until her head cleared, she made her way to the far side of the stage.

In the meantime, Jane Morrison, who was standing in the wings, snapped a photo of the girls holding their roses. The camera's flash set the theater walls spinning.

Oh, God. No, Catherine thought as everything faded to black.

* * *

It had taken Ray a moment before he realized that Catherine had disappeared from his vision, and only half that time to see that she'd collapsed on the floor.

He rushed forward, nearly knocking over a couple of parents with cameras. He mumbled an apology, but all he could think of was getting to Catherine. The thought that she was hurt, that she was sick, nearly tore him apart.

When he reached her side, she was just starting to come to.

"What happened?" he asked, his gaze raking over her, trying to assure himself that she was okay.

"I…" She blinked. "When I…bent to pick up those roses…I got a little dizzy. I probably should have asked you to…pass them out for me. But I…wanted to be the one…"

Ray turned to a guy who'd been holding a cell phone, taking a video of the two girls on stage. "Hey, buddy. Will you call an ambulance?"

"Oh, Ray," Catherine said. "Please don't let anyone interrupt the show. If you want me to see a doctor, I will. Can't you take me?"

"Yes, of course." He scooped her into his arms, holding her close to his chest. The thought of losing her, of…

Hell, if she went back to New York, he was going to lose her anyway, and the truth nearly tore him apart. Because either way, he didn't want to let her go. He…

He loved her came to mind, but he couldn't even consider telling her, not when he knew she was leaving.

The man using his cell phone to film the girls, who Ray now realized was Jerald Morrison, said, "I've got my truck parked right outside the door, Mayor. I'll give you the keys, if you want to take it. I can ride home with my wife."

"Thanks." Ray knew his vehicle was several blocks away, thanks to his late arrival. And he was eager to get her to the E.R. as soon as he could.

"I don't think the girls saw anything," Catherine told Jerald. "But if they did, tell them that I'm fine."

"Don't you worry," he said. "I'll reassure them." Then he reached into his pocket and handed Ray a set of keys. "It's a black Dodge Ram."

Ten minutes later Ray had placed Catherine in the borrowed truck and driven her to the E.R. at the Brighton Valley Medical Center. He parked as close to the entrance as he could.

"I can walk, Ray. The night air has cleared my head. I'm not feeling dizzy anymore."

He agreed to let her give it a try, but he wrapped his arm around her for support and held her close.

Upon entering the two double doors, they headed for a triage area, where they spoke to a nurse. Catherine told her about the fainting spell, the dizziness and the occasional bouts of nausea.

After making note of it, the nurse sent Catherine to the registration desk. There she provided them with the pertinent information, as well as her insurance card.

Fortunately, the waiting room was fairly empty, which was unusual for a Saturday night. But that, Ray realized, could change in a heartbeat.

They chose seats near a television monitor that was set on the Discovery Channel. Catherine seemed to tune in to whatever show was on, but Ray couldn't help thinking about the various diagnoses that they might hear— things like brain tumors, aneurisms...

He supposed it could also be something less scary, like an inner-ear problem. He certainly hoped it was something that minor with an easy fix.

When his cell phone bleeped, indicating a text, Ray read the display and saw that the message was from Dan and read it.

How is Catherine? Dan asked.

So far, so good, Ray texted back. *Waiting to see the doctor.*

Let us know what he says.

Will do.

Kaylee and Shauna won the ten-and-under competition, Dan added. *Both families are thrilled. Please tell Catherine.*

After typing in *OK,* Ray turned to Catherine and gave her Dan's message.

"They won?" A broad smile stretched across her pretty face, lighting her eyes and making her look well and whole again. "I had a feeling they would. They worked so hard."

Ray reached out and caressed her leg. "They did a great job. You did wonders with them."

"Thanks, but it was my pleasure to help out. I really enjoyed watching Shauna come out of her shell. I'm so glad she found a loving home. Jane, her foster mom, has been *so* supportive. And did you see Jerald? He's taking an active paternal role, too. Hopefully, she can remain in the Morrisons' home until she's able to move out and live on her own."

"I hope so, too. The Morrisons raised three kids of their own. When the youngest went to college, they signed up to become foster parents."

While Ray was happy to know about Shauna's good fortune, he couldn't help worrying about Catherine. In fact, he'd been concerned about her ever since she'd had that first dizzy spell on Friday night. And while he hadn't seen her again until this evening, he'd called her every day to ask how she was feeling.

According to Catherine, she hadn't been dizzy since Ernie's birthday dinner. At least, that's what she'd told Ray. And he had no reason to doubt her. But then it had happened again.

Ray glanced at his wristwatch. What was taking so long? He really wanted Catherine to see a doctor.

Twenty minutes later, a tall red-haired nurse called Catherine's name, and Ray got right to his feet.

The nurse let them inside, then took them down one hall and then another. "Here we go," she said as she pulled back a screen and pointed out the hospital exam room assigned to Catherine. "Why don't you take a seat on the bed while I get your vitals."

After taking Catherine's temperature and blood pressure, the nurse checked her pulse, then made note of it on a temporary chart.

"The doctor will be here in a minute or two," she said, before whipping back the curtain and walking off.

That minute stretched out to ten or more. Finally, a lean young man wearing glasses and a lab coat pulled back the curtain and introduced himself as Dr. Mills. He talked to Catherine about her symptoms, then looked at the nurse's notes.

After listening to Catherine's heart and examining her ears, nose and throat, he took a step back. "Everything appears to be normal, but I'm going to ask a lab tech to come in and draw some blood. As soon as I get the results, I'll be back to talk to you."

"Thank you," Ray said.

When the doctor left and they were alone, Ray was

finally able to relax long enough to take a seat near Catherine's bed.

"I'm sure it's nothing to worry about," he said, although he wasn't nearly as confident as his words and his voice might imply.

He prayed silently, *God, please don't let it be anything serious.*

Moments later, a balding, middle-age man came in and drew Catherine's blood, then he took the vials to the lab.

To pass the time, Ray tried to make small talk, to keep both their minds off the possibility that there might actually be something seriously wrong.

Earlier today, when he'd told her to bring her overnight bag and stay with him after the talent show, he'd planned a romantic evening alone. He'd hoped to talk her into making love one more time before she left for New York.

Now, with her health in doubt, he wouldn't think of suggesting sex, which was out of the question. Instead, he'd be content to sleep with her and hold her all night long.

Damn. What was taking so long?

In what seemed like forever, but was less than an hour, the doctor returned.

Catherine, who was sitting on the bed fully dressed, her feet hanging over the edge, bit down on her bottom lip, preparing for whatever news he had to give her.

Ray got to his feet and made his way to her side, taking her by the hand.

"Well," Dr. Mills said, sitting in the swivel chair and wheeling a little closer to Catherine. "I think I have an answer for what's been causing the dizziness and the nausea."

Ray hoped for the best, but braced himself for the

worst. Yet nothing prepared him for what the doctor announced.

"You're pregnant."

Chapter 12

Pregnant?

Catherine wasn't sure she'd heard him correctly. There had to be some mistake. The other doctor, her gynecologist in New York, had said that it was unlikely she'd conceive, that...

"Are you sure about those results?" Catherine asked Dr. Mills.

"I'm afraid so. You're definitely pregnant, Ms. Loza. And that's probably what's causing you to feel dizzy and nauseous."

Yes, of course. That made sense. But still...

She was pregnant?

Her mind was awhirl. A *baby.* She would have a child of her own, a family...

But what about the upcoming audition? No way could she consider taking the role, even if they offered it to her.

So what would she do? How would she support herself in New York?

"She's been dieting," Ray told the doctor. "That can't be good for her."

Oh, goodness. *Ray.* Did he realize the baby was his? And if so, how had he taken the news?

She shot a glance his way, saw the seriousness of his expression. But then, why wouldn't he be uneasy? He'd been so stressed about the fact that they'd had unprotected sex, so worried about an unexpected pregnancy.

And now this…

On the bright side, he was still holding her hand. And he hadn't scrunched her fingers in a death grip.

"I don't think the dieting is a problem," Dr. Mills said. "At least, not as long as she starts eating nutritiously from now on. You can ask one of the resident obstetricians about that, but I suspect it's fairly early in the pregnancy. When was your last menstrual cycle?"

"I…" Catherine tried to think. "I guess it's been a while. I've been so busy that I haven't even thought about it."

"She's only about four weeks along," Ray said.

He was right, of course. Catherine, whose mind was still reeling in awe at the news—she was going to have a *baby?*—nodded her agreement. They both knew the exact night it had happened.

"We have several good obstetricians at the Brighton Valley Medical Center," Dr. Mills said. "So if you'd like me to refer you to someone, I can."

But Catherine wouldn't be staying in Brighton Valley.

Of course, if she couldn't dance or act on stage, she had no idea how she'd support herself and a child in New York. Things were horribly expensive there.

Jennifer Walker had faced the same dilemma when

she'd gotten pregnant with twins, but Catherine had stepped in to help her out.

When Catherine didn't answer the doctor right away, Ray said, "We'd like you to give us those names."

Surely Ray didn't expect her to stay in Brighton Valley, did he? Supporting herself and a baby here wouldn't be easy, either. What would she do?

Or was he still playing the role of her future husband—just in case word of this got out into the community in spite of all the privacy laws.

Uh-oh. Speaking of their role-playing, what were they going to tell everyone now? "Breaking up" was one thing. But when there was a baby involved? People might not be so understanding of those involved.

Boy, had things gotten complicated.

She and Ray certainly had a lot to talk about, a lot to decide. But he'd paid her to pretend to be his fiancée while she was still in town, so she'd continue to do that, at least until they came up with a breakup plan.

"We won't need those names," she told the doctor.

Ray stiffened, as if she'd somehow challenged him, threatened him. But she hadn't meant to.

"I already know which doctor I'd like to see," she explained. "It'll be Dr. Ramirez, Eva's obstetrician."

Ray relaxed his stance, as well as his grip.

Still, the enormity of the problem facing them was staggering.

"I have to admit," Catherine finally said, "this is quite a surprise for both of us. We're going to have a lot to talk about when we get home."

But where was home? New York? Brighton Valley? Someplace altogether different?

Life as she knew it was over. Maybe not in a bad way, since she was actually thrilled to learn about the baby. But she had no idea how the father-to-be felt about the news.

She shot a glance at Ray, the man who ought to have a say in all of this, the man who was probably going through his own emotional turmoil right now, but she didn't have a clue.

On the other hand, Ray was still trying to wrap his mind around the fact that Catherine was pregnant.

He supposed he'd better thank the good Lord that she was healthy and whole, since that had been his prayer earlier. But she was also expecting his baby.

His baby.

Talk about major dilemmas…

"I'm sure you're right," the doctor said, getting to his feet. "You do have a lot to talk about. I'll finish up the paperwork. Once you check out, you're free to leave."

"Thank you," Catherine said.

Neither of them spoke until after they'd left the hospital and climbed into his car.

"I'm sorry about this," she said.

About what? Getting pregnant?

"Do you plan to keep the baby?" he asked.

"Absolutely. I didn't think I would ever conceive, but that doesn't mean I didn't want a child—or a family."

That was good, wasn't it? He wouldn't have wanted her to consider adoption or anything else. Because even if he didn't have a wife or have any plans to get married again, that didn't mean he never wanted to have any kids.

So that was one hurdle solved.

"I'd like to be a part of the baby's life," he added.

"That might be a little difficult," she said.

Not if she stayed in Brighton Valley.

"Are you still going to leave tomorrow?" he asked.

"I don't know. I'd planned to audition for a part, but if I'm pregnant, there's no way I'll get it."

He wished he could apologize, but he wanted her to stay here. How the heck could he be a part of their child's life if he had to fly back and forth to New York every other month?

"There's a lot to think about," she added.

She had that right. He sucked in a breath, then blew it out again. "Here's something else you ought to consider."

"What's that?"

"We can always get married."

She turned to him, lips parted, as if the suggestion had taken her completely by surprise. Hell, by the look on her face, she'd either been swept off her feet or shocked by the preposterous notion.

But then again, he hadn't expected to propose to her this evening, either. Not when he feared the answer would be no.

"What's the matter?" he asked. "Was the idea too wild for you to even ponder?"

"No, it just took me aback, that's all."

Yeah, well he was a little off-kilter, too. But he didn't like the idea of losing her, especially when he'd be losing his child, too. How was he going to parent a kid who lived in New York?

"You're offering to marry me so the baby has your name?"

For starters, he supposed. He'd kind of like her to have his name, too.

"Marriages should be built on love," she said, "especially if they're meant to last."

"That's true." Sarcasm laced his tone as he thought about the woman who'd promised to love him until death, the woman who'd felt no such thing.

Trouble was, he knew darn well that Catherine wasn't anything like Heather. And he suspected that if she made a commitment to love someone, she would keep it.

But she hadn't said anything about love. And while he'd begun to realize that's what he was feeling for her, he didn't want to lay his heart on the line, then have her throw it right back at him.

Then again, he now had a son or daughter to consider. And he had a chance to have a family again.

"Marriage is still an option," he said. "I care for you. And I think you have feelings for me, too. To top that off, if we did get married, neither you nor the baby would lack anything. In fact, it might even solve some of our problems."

At least when it came to the phony engagement they'd created, it would help.

"You'd go so far as to marry me?" she asked, the sadness in her voice leaving him a bit unbalanced.

Did she think marrying him was a step down from what she deserved? Heather certainly had.

"Do you want to be a single mother?" he asked.

"At this point, I really don't mind. I'm actually glad to know that I was able to conceive. Being unwed and pregnant doesn't have the stigma it once did."

Maybe not. But what were all the townspeople going to think when they learned that Ray had fathered a baby and didn't marry the child's mother, especially when the woman was one who'd charmed her way into their hearts within a matter of weeks?

And it wasn't just the townspeople he worried about. His parents and grandparents would rise from their graves and haunt him like crazy if he didn't do the right thing by the woman he…*loved.* What was he going to do without her? Just thinking about losing her hurt like hell.

But what options did he have? He couldn't hire Catherine to be a *pretend* wife.

"It's really not a big deal," she added.

Oh, no? It seemed like a very big deal to him. After all, the woman he loved was taking his child and leaving him. And that hurt far more than anything Heather had ever said or done to him.

"I guess we can talk about it more when we get home," he said.

Silence stretched between them for a mile or two, and as he neared Main Street, she said, "You know what? I'm really exhausted. I'd like to go back to the ranch tonight. Would you mind dropping me off at the theater? I left Dan's truck there."

"I thought we had a lot to talk about."

"It might be better to sleep on it and talk tomorrow."

He glanced across the console at her, only to see her looking out the passenger window, her thoughts as far from him as the mountain in the distance.

What had happened? What was bothering her?

Ray was tempted to ask, but hell. He'd already had one city woman turn on him. What made him think Catherine wasn't doing the same damn thing?

He'd been down that painful road before. And he knew how badly things could end when two mismatched people said "I do."

But were they really mismatched and destined for heartbreak?

He wished he could say for sure. And while he was tempted to ask her to reconsider, he wouldn't.

The only thing worse than losing the love of his life would be chasing after her and begging her to stay when she was dead set on leaving.

So after dropping Catherine off at Dan and Eva's, he

walked her to the door. Instead of the goodbye kiss he'd been tempted to give her, if she'd seemed to be willing, he gave her something to think about instead.

"No matter what happens, I want you to know that I'm happy about the baby. The pregnancy might have blindsided me, but I'm getting used to the idea of being a father. And no matter what you decide, I want to be a part of the baby's life."

"That might not be easy."

"Yeah, well, sometimes the best things in life are worth fighting for."

She seemed to think about that for a moment, then said, "Thanks, Ray. That helps."

He hoped so, because it certainly hadn't seemed to help him.

"Good night," he said. "I'll talk to you in the morning."

Then he climbed into Jerald Morrison's truck, which he was going to have to return tomorrow, and drove back to his ranch.

Still, as he entered the empty, sprawling house, he was glad to be home, the memory-filled place where he'd grown up.

It was odd, he thought. When he and Heather had split, and she'd left him alone in this house, he hadn't been swamped in memories of childhood, of fishing with his grandpa or riding fence with his dad.

Instead he'd been angry and driven to shake every last thing that reminded him of her, every dream he'd ever had, every memory he'd ever cherished.

If it came right down to it, he might have run for city councilman as a way to get off the ranch, to shake the reminder of a marriage gone bad.

But Catherine had changed all that. And now, walking through the living room, where his mother used to sit with her knitting needles, crocheting baby blankets for the various expectant mothers she knew from church, Ray remembered it all.

And he missed it more than he'd ever thought possible.

Why was that?

What had Catherine done to him?

Somehow, in the midst of all the playacting, the pretending, he'd found the love of his life. Thanks to Catherine, he'd shaken all the anger, all the bad memories. And he was ready to reclaim all that had once been good and right.

As he climbed the stairs and headed for his bedroom, he wondered if he'd ever have a loving marriage with a woman who would stick by him through thick and thin.

As much as the dilemma perplexed him, he couldn't help wanting to make things right with Catherine—and by that, he meant making them real.

After Ray had dropped Catherine off at the ranch, Eva and Dan met her at the front door, worry sketched across their faces.

"Are you okay?" Eva asked. "What did the doctor have to say?"

Catherine might have kept the news to herself, but she'd been alone and on her own for so very long that she needed to confide in someone. And Dan and Eva were more like family to her than her many siblings.

"I'm not sure how Ray will feel about me telling you this," Catherine began, "especially so soon, but..." She took a deep, fortifying breath, then slowly blew it out. "I'm pregnant."

Dan blinked and cocked his head, as if he'd been as surprised by the news as she'd been.

But Eva, who'd known that Catherine hadn't expected to have a baby of her own, even though she'd secretly longed for one, wrapped her in a warm embrace. "I'm so happy for you."

"Thanks."

As Eva slowly lowered her arms, she gazed into Catherine's eyes. "You *are* happy about the baby, aren't you?"

"Yes, of course I am. But it certainly complicates things."

"Does it change your plans to leave?" Dan asked.

"It changes *everything*—and in ways I can't quite comprehend right now." Catherine blew out another heavy sigh.

"How does Ray feel about it?" Eva asked.

"He's taking it pretty well—at least for a man who went so far as to hire a fiancée so the single women in town would realize he wasn't interested in love or romance."

"Sounds like he wasn't too down on the *romance* part," Dan said with a grin.

Eva gave her husband a little elbow jab, as if his humor might not be appreciated. But it's not as though there'd been any seduction going on. They'd both been willing.

"It just...well, it just happened," Catherine said. "Neither of us planned on..."

What? Falling in love?

She certainly hadn't expected a feeling like that to develop. And what made it worse was that Ray had never given her reason to believe that he was feeling the same way about her.

Sure, he'd suggested marriage. But she'd be darned if she'd marry someone just because it was the honorable thing to do.

If he'd told her that he loved her, if he'd been sincere,

she might have considered accepting his proposal. But she couldn't get involved with another man who didn't love her. And she couldn't "pretend" that a wedding ring was the solution to their problem.

Speaking of rings, she glanced down at her left hand, at the heirloom Ray had loaned her to wear. She'd have to give it back to him before she left town. That is, if she left.

What was she going to do?

"Maybe I should put on a pot of chamomile tea," Eva said. "It sounds as if you might need it after all you've been through this evening."

As much as Catherine would like to have a confidant tonight, a woman who would understand why she couldn't accept Ray's proposal—if you could call it that since it had merely been a suggestion—she wanted to retreat to her bedroom, where she might be able to come up with a game plan she could live with.

"Thanks, Eva. But I'm really tired. It's been a taxing day and evening. And what I really need is a good night's sleep."

But even after Catherine had shed her clothes, put on a nightgown and climbed into bed, sleep had been a long time coming.

And morning arrived too soon.

Ray waited until nearly seven o'clock before driving to the Walkers' ranch. It was probably way too early for a Sunday morning visit, but he didn't want to wait much longer. Catherine was still holding a ticket for a flight leaving this afternoon, and he didn't want her to go before he had a chance to tell her what he had to say.

Last night, while he'd tossed and turned, thinking

about what all he stood to lose, he realized that he hadn't told Catherine how he'd come to feel about her. She might throw it right back at him, but it was a risk he had to take.

What if she left and he'd never told her how he felt? Would he regret it for the rest of his life? After all, what were the odds that he'd meet another woman who would touch his heart the way Catherine had?

Probably slim to none.

So he parked Jerald's pickup near the Walkers' barn, then made his way to the front door and knocked.

Kevin, who was still in his pajamas, answered. "My dad already went out to the barn. You can find him there."

Ray figured as much. Ranchers didn't lollygag over coffee, even on Sundays. "Actually, Kevin, I came to talk to Catherine. Is she here?"

"I think she's still asleep. Want me to wake her up?"

"Sure. Go ahead."

Ray took a seat on the sofa, but he didn't have to wait long. Catherine came into the living room just moments later, wearing a light blue robe over a white cotton gown. Her hair was tousled from sleep, and her feet were bare.

Ray stood, then nodded toward the door. "I need to talk to you. Do you mind going out on the porch with me?"

She fiddled with the lapel of her robe for a moment, then said, "All right."

As Catherine followed Ray outside, she couldn't imagine what he had to say. Would he bring up marriage again? Or maybe ask her to stay in town and give up her career?

She might have to do that anyway, although now, with a baby on the way, performing on Broadway had lost some of its appeal. Besides, she'd like to be near family when the baby came. And Dan and Eva, who'd become so much more than friends to her, held that place in her heart.

Maybe she could find her niche in a small town. She'd enjoyed working with the kids... And there was a theater that wasn't used nearly as much as it ought to be.

But that was wishful thinking. Ray didn't love her. And he didn't really want a wife. So how could she consider staying, especially when people learned she was carrying the mayor's illegitimate baby?

Once the door to the house was closed, and they were standing on the porch, Catherine asked, "What did you come to say?"

"Something I should have told you last night."

"What's that?"

He waited a beat, then said, "I may have hired you to be my fiancée, but along the way, I fell in love with you, Catherine. And I should have told you that when I suggested we get married. I liked the roles we played. And I'd want them to be real."

She liked being with Ray, too. And she'd even begun to like the woman she'd pretended to be, thinking that might be the person who lived deep within. But did she dare hope... Did she dare believe...

"You *love* me?" she asked, trying to wrap her heart and mind around his confession, needing to hear him say it again, wanting to believe him.

"Yes, I love you. And even if that doesn't make any difference to you, I wanted you to know."

"Why didn't you say anything last night?"

"Because I couldn't believe a woman like you would love a guy like me. And with you leaving..."

"You *love* me?" she repeated. That was even more amazing than finding out they were having a baby.

He smiled, and a glimmer lit his eyes. "I think I fell

for you the first day I saw you and spotted all those stickers on your face."

"You're kidding. I think that's when I started falling for you, too."

He cocked his head slightly, his smile fading into seriousness. "Are you saying that you feel the same way about me?"

"Yes, Ray. I love you, too."

He let out a whoop that might surprise any of his conservative constituents. "Then it looks like we've pretty much worked through all the complications that matter."

That was true. And she was beginning to believe that she could finally have it all—marriage to the man she loved, a wonderful father for her baby, the family she'd always wanted.

"So does that mean you'll marry me?" he asked.

"If you're asking me again, then I'm saying yes this time around. There's nothing more in the world I want than to be your real wife and the mother of our baby."

Then she wrapped her arms around him and kissed him with all the love in her heart.

The love they professed, the love they felt, was the real deal—and it promised to be the kind to last a lifetime.

* * * * *

Barbara White Daille lives with her husband in the wild Southwest, where they deal with lizards in the yard and scorpions in the bathroom. A writer since before she knew how to spell, Barbara loves creating home-and-family stories—with cowboys!—for Harlequin American Romance. When not writing, she can be found near books and chocolate. Please visit her at barbarawhitedaille.com.

Be sure to look for other books by Barbara White Daille in Harlequin American Romance—the ultimate destination for romance the all-American way! There are four new Harlequin American Romance titles available every month. Check one out today!

HONORABLE RANCHER
Barbara White Daille

In memory of F. D. White
an honorable man himself
and
as always, to Rich,
the best man for me

~~~~~~

I reckon there are many ways
to call a man a hero.

Chapter 1

Always a bridesmaid, never a bride.

Ben Sawyer had heard folks say that of some women. Not the one standing on the far side of the banquet hall from him, though. The one who'd done her best all day to avoid him.

Dana Wright had once worn a long white gown and walked down the aisle to meet her groom. *He* should know, as he'd stood up near the altar holding the ring his best friend would slip onto her finger.

Now, if the saying held true for the male side of a wedding party, he surely fit the bill.

Always a groomsman, never a groom.

Always losing out.

No sense worrying over it. He'd made his decisions a long time ago. Still, he had to fight to keep his eyes from tracking Dana's every move.

Twirling the stem of his champagne glass in his fin-

gers, he watched the couples two-stepping past him. After
plenty of turns on the dance floor himself this evening,
he'd decided to sit this one out. Every once in a while,
in a gap between the couples, he could see the opposite
side of the hall. Just then, he caught sight of Dana dis-
appearing through one of the glass doors to the terrace.

The newlyweds danced toward him.

"Having fun yet?" Tess asked.

"Absolutely," he confirmed. "Like everyone else."

Except Dana?

Tess's groom, Caleb, swept her away.

Ben set his glass on a nearby waiter's tray and began
circling the room. Every few feet, someone stopped him.
While he always enjoyed a good conversation, the inter-
ruptions came more often than he would've liked right
now.

Finally, he eased away from a small group and edged
over to the doorway Dana had exited through.

In the light from the carriage lamps outside, he saw
her standing alone near one of the stone fountains flank-
ing the club's entrance. He frowned and went through
the door, pulling it closed behind him without a sound.

Her back to the building, she stared down into the
water pooling in the base of the fountain. Lamplight and
moonlight combined to make the silver combs in her
blond hair sparkle. The combs held her hair up, exposing the smooth, pale skin of her neck. A row of buttons
that matched her long pink dress marched down to the
point where a bunch of lacy fabric covered the sweet
curves of her hips.

His mouth went dry. He'd have welcomed another
glass of champagne at the moment. Hell, he needed it
to wet his tight throat. To occupy his hands. His fingers
itched to touch those buttons now taunting him.

How had she managed to get into that dress all by herself? Would she need a hand getting out of it?

He shook his head at the stupidity—and the futility—of his questions. Of his dreams. Nine-year-old Lissa had probably buttoned her mother's dress and would unbutton it, too. In any case, Dana certainly wouldn't want his help. She didn't want his assistance with anything.

That gave him trouble, in view of the promise he'd made to his best friend. A promise he aimed to keep.

For a moment, he stood there considering his next move. Unusual for him. Folks teased that he'd talk to a tree if he couldn't find a person handy to listen to him. Yet, for the first time in his life, he didn't know what to say.

He took a deep breath and let it out again. Not wanting to startle her, he called her name in a low tone.

Without turning to look, she raised her chin a notch. She'd recognized his voice and gone into defensive mode. Hadn't he known she would? The sight should have made him turn around and leave. Instead, he smiled.

He never could pass up a challenge.

He ambled across the open space to stand by her side. Her head barely reached his shoulder. He caught the faint scent of a flowery perfume. When she neither lowered her chin nor looked at him, he gestured toward one of the small stone benches near the fountain. "How about you relax and we call a truce for tonight? After all, we're here to celebrate with Tess and Caleb."

She glanced from the bench to the country club as if assessing the lesser of two evils. "You're right, it's their night." With a small sigh, she took a seat.

The bench proved narrower than he'd expected and put him closer to her than he should've risked, truce or no truce. Their arms touched. Their elbows bumped. It

would have made sense for him to wrap his arm around
her shoulders. They were friends, weren't they? But once
he'd touched her, could he keep it at that?

Her expression softened. "Caleb went all out for Tess,
didn't he?"

"Renting the biggest hall within a hundred miles of
Flagman's Folly? I'll say. Good of him to invite all the
folks from town to the wedding, too."

"He seemed surprised that everyone accepted. But I
know they wanted to wish him and Tess well." She smiled
softly. "Tess makes a beautiful bride."

You did, too. Without missing a beat, he changed the
words that had come so quickly to him. "You're looking
good in that maid of honor dress yourself."

"Matron," she said. "Being a widow makes me a matron of honor."

*Which makes you a woman alone with three little kids.
So, why won't you accept my help?* He couldn't ask that
tonight. Not after he'd called for a ceasefire between
them. He probably wouldn't ask that ever, as nine times
out of ten, the shots came from Dana's side of their conversations. She'd never acted so defensively with him
before Paul died.

"What is it they're calling Nate again?" he asked. Nate
was the bride and groom's nine-year-old tomboy and the
best buddy of Dana's daughter Lissa. Like the girls, Tess
and Dana had been best friends all through school.

"A junior bridesmaid." She laughed. "Nate stopped
fighting over wearing a dress the minute Caleb said he'd
get her a pair of boots made to match his. She held her
ground about being a flower girl, though."

He chuckled. "That sounds like her. Well, Sam's little
girl had a good time dropping those petals in the church
aisle. I heard you made her dress. And yours. Nice."

Damn him for using the compliment, but it gave him a reason to touch her lacy pink sleeve.

She shied like a filly come eye to eye with a rattler.

He clasped his hands together and stared down at them.

When he looked at her profile again, he found her gazing into the distance, unblinking. The moonlight showed her lips pressed together in a straight line, the way he'd noted much too often lately. Her cheekbones had never looked sharp before now.

Nothing could make her less beautiful to him, but it shocked him to realize she had lost weight.

She'd driven herself after losing Paul. Trying to handle everything alone *had* to be too much for her. He needed to stop thinking about himself—about what he wanted and could never have—and figure out some way to be of help to her.

He'd already bought the building where she rented office space so he could give her a break on the rent. There had to be something else he could do.

Right now, he just needed to get her talking. He cleared his dry throat. "Caleb's fired up about his new property. I've got to hand it to you for that one. Nobody could've done a better job of selling that ranch, especially considering it's bigger than every spread around here."

She waved her hand as if to brush his words away. "That was Tess's effort, mostly. I just stepped in to handle the paperwork when we knew she'd become half owner. Besides, she had to focus on getting married."

"Whatever the reason, I know she was happy to have you help wrap everything up in time for the wedding."

He knew Dana accepted help in return from Tess, too, when she needed it. Why wouldn't she take it from him? They'd all been friends forever, through high school and beyond. Not Caleb, who at some point had fallen a year behind. But he and Tess and Dana. Sam Robertson. Paul Wright.

He thought of his best buddy often, recalling him as young and full of life. As part of almost every memory he'd forged since the day he started school. He tried not to think about Paul's death a year and a half ago. Impossible to avoid that thought at the moment, with the man's widow sitting on the cold stone bench beside him.

In all the years since grade school, nothing had ever come between Paul and Dana. He had always honored that. Now he had to make doubly sure not to cross the line. "Today has to be hard for you," he said, keeping his voice low.

"Seeing Tess and Caleb so happy? Why should that cause me any trouble? I'm glad they're finally together."

She meant it, he knew, though her words sounded as brittle as the chipped ice in the banquet hall's champagne buckets. In the moonlight, her eyes glittered. Had she tried for a lighter tone to fight back tears? Or to prove how comfortable she felt around him?

Why did she have to prove anything? Why the heck couldn't she enjoy his company, the way she always used to? If she'd just give him that, he'd feel satisfied.

Sure, he would.

She'd grown quiet again, and he gestured toward the fountain. "What brought you out here? Wanting to make a wish?"

She shook her head. "No. Those are for people who aren't willing to work hard to get what they want."

"I can't argue with you there." Still, he felt tempted to toss a coin into the water for a wish of his own—that for once, she'd let him make things easier for her. "But there's such a thing as working too hard, you know."

"Ben, please." She gathered up her dress and stood. "You called the truce yourself, remember? I know you only want to help. For Paul. And because we're *friends*." Her voice shook from her stress on the word. "We've had this conversation before. Now, once and for all, I'm doing fine." As if to prove her point, she smiled. "And I have to go inside. Tess will be tossing her bouquet soon. I wouldn't want to lose out on that."

A tear sparkled at the corner of her eye.

Missing the chance to catch a handful of flowers couldn't upset her that much. He knew what she really missed—having a husband by her side. Her husband.

His best friend.

But neither of them would have Paul back in their lives.

Before he could get to his feet, she left, running away like that princess in the fairy tale his niece asked him to read to her over and over again.

No, not a princess. The one who took off without her glass slipper—Cinderella.

Dana was no Cinderella. She hadn't left a shoe behind. Hadn't even dropped a button from that pink dress as something for him to remember her by. As if he could ever forget her.

She'd been the heroine of a story he'd once created long ago, a story he'd had to write in his head because he hadn't yet known how to spell all the words.

How did it go? Like in his niece's storybook…

Once upon a time, that was it.

Once upon a time, in the Land of Enchantment—otherwise known as the state of New Mexico—Benjamin Franklin Sawyer had high hopes and a huge crush on the girl who sat one desk over from him in their class-room every day.

No other girl in town, Ben felt sure, could beat Dana Smith, and most likely no other woman in the world could compare to her, either. In any case, without a doubt, she was the cutest of all his female friends in their kinder-garten classroom.

Unfortunately, when the teacher moved his best friend, Paul Wright, to the desk on the other side of Dana's, Ben saw his hopes dashed.

The crush, however, continued. For a good long while.

As for Benjamin Franklin Sawyer's hopes...

Well, not every story had a happy ending.

Not even Dana's.

Since Paul's death, they had seen less and less of each other. By her choice, not his.

She needed time, he had told himself. Needed space. So he'd waited. He'd talked himself down. He'd exercised every horse in his stable enough to cover every inch of the land he owned. When none of that worked, he'd bought the danged office building. And even that hadn't brought him peace.

Seeing her now had.

He never could stand to watch her cry, but tonight, he welcomed those tears in her eyes and the way she'd hurried away from him. *Doing fine,* she'd said. Like hell. Her actions revealed more than she would willingly tell him. More than she'd ever want him to know.

She needed his help, though she refused to accept it.

The help he had promised Paul he would give her.

No matter how firmly she dug her heels in and how often she turned him down, he was damned well going to keep that promise.

* * *

After one last breath of fresh air to calm herself, Dana slipped back into the banquet hall and sought safety at one of the tables.

"Hey, Dana, over here!"

Even above the music, she heard the familiar voice and fought to hide her cringe of dismay.

No safety for her tonight, anywhere.

Forcing a smile, she hurried toward the table halfway around the dance floor. Anything to keep from standing near the door. If Ben found her there, he would assume she had waited for him.

For the past year and more, she had done just the opposite—tried her best to keep out of his way. A ridiculous goal in a town the size of Flagman's Folly, where you couldn't step out your front door without meeting someone you knew.

Then he'd bought the building that housed her office, and she'd had to work twice as hard to avoid him. Ten times as hard to ignore her feelings. Because it wasn't only anger and irritation that made her insist she was fine. And that had sent her running from him now.

Reaching the table, she smiled down at Tess's aunt Ellamae. "Everything okay?" she asked. "Did you need something?"

"Everything's fine," the older woman said.

Fine. That word again. She resisted the urge to steal a backward glance at the French doors. To look for Ben.

They'd been friends forever, yet she couldn't risk being near him anymore. Talking with him meant she had to raise her guard. Trying to make him understand how she felt made her frustrated, in more ways than she wanted to think about. Every time they spoke to each other, she left more shaken than before.

Even tonight, when she fled outside for a few minutes alone, she'd found no escape from him. Worse, sitting beside him in the moonlight, she'd had trouble catching her breath. And that had nothing to do with the formfitting bodice of her gown.

"We were wondering what you'd gotten up to," Ellamae said.

She jumped. "Up to? Nothing. I'm the matron of honor, that's all. It's a busy job."

"Yeah. So, it's funny you found time to run off like that."

Ellamae's weatherworn face and gruff tone made most kids in town antsy around her. Her job as court clerk only increased their anxiety. But like a prickly pear cactus, her rough exterior covered the softness beneath.

Years of spending time around Tess's family had taught Dana that. She could handle Ellamae. "I just went out for a quick breath of fresh air."

"Not so quick, was it?"

She blinked. On the other hand, the woman's tendency to see all and want to know all made *her* a bit antsy, too.

Especially when she had so much to hide.

The man on Ellamae's other side broke in. "Glad you're back, anyhow," Judge Baylor said. "Wouldn't want to miss Tess throwing out her bouquet."

"Oh, I think I'll pass."

The judge's bright blue eyes met hers. "Well, now. Can't have you doing that, can we? It's tradition."

As Ellamae nodded vigorously, the bandleader made the announcement. At the tables around them, women jumped up from their seats.

Knowing enough not to protest, Dana swallowed a sigh. Everyone had respected her year and more of mourning, but with the folks of Flagman's Folly, tradition was practically the law. And between them, Ellamae and the judge *were* the law in town.

"Time you got back into the swing of things," Ellamae said.

Trust her to speak her mind. She now shooed Dana into the crowd with as much enthusiasm as little Becky Robertson shooed her chickens into their new coop.

Giving up, Dana joined the women surging toward the dance floor. Laughter broke out from behind her, and she looked back.

Ellamae stood waving a well-used baseball catcher's mitt. She hurried to Dana's side. "C'mon, girl, let's move it. I got done out of catching the bouquet at Sam Robertson's wedding, but I'm not missing a chance at this one."

Almost the same words Dana had used to escape from Ben. Time to make good on her excuse. Refusing to look for him, she took her spot with the women. From the middle of the crowd, Lissa and Nate turned, grinning, to wave at her. She waved back.

Ellamae nudged her, making elbow room.

Dana laughed and edged a few steps away. Though she stayed on the fringes, she held her hands up as everyone else did and matched their wide smiles.

The bride listened to her guests, all telling her how and when and where to toss her bouquet. Dana knew each woman in the group hoped to become the lucky winner—especially Ellamae, who stood waving her mitt-clad hand above her head.

Good luck to her. And to anyone else on that dance floor.

As long as she stayed behind all the other women, the bouquet shouldn't come anywhere near her. Just the idea that she might win the toss made her heart thud painfully.

Unable to stop herself, she glanced across the room.

Ben stood near the French doors, gazing at her, and she hurriedly turned away. Knowing he watched only made things worse.

The sigh she swallowed bordered on a sob. Of all the folks in town who worried her, good old Ben topped the list. Not only because he kept offering to help her.

But because he would be the person most hurt by the secrets she kept.

"Everybody set?" Tess called.

The crowd murmured in anticipation, and Dana forced herself to focus. If she didn't, it would be just her luck not to realize the bouquet had come right at her until too late—after her reflexes had kicked in and she had caught it.

Tess swung her arm as if winding up for a baseball pitch, then let the flower arrangement fly. It skimmed the fingertips of one woman after another, bouncing its way across the crowd.

To the amusement of everyone in the hall, Ellamae made a valiant effort to snag the bouquet in midair. The cumbersome baseball mitt let her down. The flowers slipped from her grasp, tumbled in Dana's direction, bounced off her shoulder, and landed in the arms of five-year-old Becky Robertson, who squealed. Jaw dropped and eyes wide, she looked up at Dana.

Sam's little girl was deaf. Glad his wife had taught folks some sign language, Dana fluttered her hands in the air, using the gesture for applause. Hearing Becky's high-pitched laugh made her smile. Dana held her right-hand palm turned inward a couple of inches from her own face. Tilting her hand, she pulled all her fingertips together. *"Pretty."*

Clutching the bouquet, Becky nodded energetically,

then ran toward her daddy, who waited at the edge of the dance floor.

"There goes one happy young'un," Ellamae said, shaking her head. "Well, after seeing that smile, guess I can't begrudge the girl. Better luck next time for the rest of us."

Not for me, Dana thought with relief as the other women drifted away and Ellamae stomped off in a pretend sulk. Her good fortune had come from *not* getting stuck with that bouquet.

Then she made the mistake of looking at Ben. No smiles there. No luck for her, either. He had started across the room toward her.

Chapter 2

Had Ben read her thoughts in her face from all the way across the room? Had everyone in the entire banquet hall noticed her relief at not catching the bouquet?

Casually, she hoped, Dana glanced away from Ben at the tables clustered around the dance floor. No one seemed to pay any special attention to her—except the bride, who marched up, shaking her head. "What in the world do you call that attempt? You didn't even try to catch it."

"I most certainly did. Ellamae made me nervous."

"Yeah, I'll bet." Tess frowned. "Are you having a good time?"

"Of course."

"I wonder. I wish we could have matched you up with a more eligible partner."

"Don't be silly. Sam and I are perfectly happy to act as a couple for the day."

Tess laughed. "You know, Caleb planned to ask him to stand up for him anyhow, but Sam beat him to it. He insisted Caleb choose him. Since he'd just gotten married, Sam claimed he would be the *best* best man Caleb could ever find."

No, he wouldn't. Dana had to bite her tongue to keep the words from spilling out. Of all the males in the room, Ben Sawyer would make the best man. He'd proven that ever since her own wedding. And in all the years before it.

He'd always been there for her, had always played such a big role in her life. Right now, though, she felt sure he planned to steal the show. Or at least, to make a scene. One she didn't want Tess to witness.

"Speaking of Caleb," she said quickly, "he's trying to get your attention." She gestured toward Tess's new husband, who had pulled a chair into the middle of the dance floor.

Tess gave an exaggerated groan. "Oh, no. It's garter time." She murmured, "Tradition is all well and good, but we have to draw the line somewhere. I've got the garter around my ankle." She grinned. "I hope he's not too disappointed."

Dana forced a laugh. "You have no worries there." The band played a few bouncy chords. Copying Ellamae, she made shooing motions toward Tess. "Go on. Everyone's waiting."

Single males, including Ben, flowed onto the dance floor. But as Tess returned to the front of the hall, he broke from the group and veered toward Dana.

"Did Tess tell you what she thought about your pathetic try at that bouquet?" he asked.

She exhaled in exasperation. They certainly had an audience now. She caught several people watching them, including Judge Baylor, who had taken pride of place in the center of the floor.

If she had to, she would smile until her cheeks hurt. But she wouldn't take a lecture from Ben. "Yes, Tess gave me her feedback. So I won't need any from you. Thanks, anyway."

"But I had my entire speech planned."

She laughed. "Save it for someone else. And for your information, as I told Tess, Ellamae made me back off."

His brows rose. "That's a switch." He smiled as if to soften his words. "I thought you could handle anyone who got in your way."

"Anyone but you, Ben," she muttered after he'd left to rejoin the other men.

At the front of the room, teasing his blushing bride, the groom tugged at the hem of her gown. As the other wedding guests cheered him on, Dana's mind wandered—directly to the dark-haired man whose shoulders strained the fabric of his well-cut tuxedo.

After Paul's death, Ben had offered to do anything he could to make things easier for her. His attention smothered her. His kindhearted attempts to help threatened to do even more. To make her needy and dependent and weak.

She couldn't let that happen. Not after all the years she'd heard those words from another man—the one she had mistakenly married. Paul had forced those words on her, had done his best to convince her they truly described her. She couldn't fall for that again, either.

And so, it had been easiest—best—to turn away from Ben. To *stay* away from him, when she wanted to do just the opposite. When everything in her longed for—

Laughter rippled around her. She sagged in relief, genuinely glad for the interruption that kept her from going down that mental road. She couldn't go anywhere with Ben. Shouldn't even think about him.

Outside, alone with him in the moonlight, sitting beside him on that bench, she'd wanted just to close her eyes and lean against him and see what would happen next. But she couldn't. Too many responsibilities and too many bad memories would keep her from ever relying on any man again.

Especially Ben.

As if she had called his name, he turned. Her breath caught. It wasn't until he approached her that she realized the garter toss had ended.

The music changed from the bouncy rhythm to a slower beat.

"May I have this dance?" he asked. He stood so tall, she had to look up to see his dark eyes staring down at her.

At the thought of stepping into his arms, her heart lurched. A dangerous road... A risky decision...

Somehow, she had escaped having to dance with him at Sam and Kayla's wedding the year before. She had managed to avoid that tonight, too. Until now. But they had an audience all around—all the folks from Flagman's Folly—scrutinizing their every move.

She blurted the only thing that came to mind. "Why not? We're friends, aren't we?"

His expression solemn, he nodded and held out his hand.

She couldn't have refused his invitation. Couldn't have turned him down. And he knew it. Of course, the matron of honor would dance with the ushers, too.

Why was she trying to kid herself? She wouldn't have turned Ben away at all.

But she should have.

He took her hand and settled his free arm around her waist, holding her in a light but steady embrace. As he led her expertly around the crowded floor, she tried desperately to focus on her movements. One trip over her own feet, and she'd make a fool of herself. One slip on this dance floor, and she'd wind up even closer to him than she stood now.

If that were possible.

She was nearly nestled against him. Her head swam, and she strained to keep her focus on the lapel of his dark tuxedo. She would not look up at him. She would not meet his eyes. She was too afraid of what he would read in hers.

There were other senses besides sight, though.

His warmth enveloped her, relaxing her even as it made her heart beat triple-time.

Loving the scent of his spicy aftershave, she inhaled deeply…and caught herself just as her eyelids began to close. Wouldn't that have made a pretty picture for all the wedding guests to see!

She shifted slightly in his arms. Her hand brushed the edge of his collar, her fingertip catching the faint sandpaper prickle of five-o'clock shadow on his neck. A shiver ran through her.

"You okay?" he murmured, tilting his head down.

"Fine," she whispered. So many uses for that one little word. So many lies.

He moved his arm from around her waist and rested his hand flat against her back. His thumb grazed the skin left exposed by her gown. For a moment, she felt sure he'd done it deliberately.

Silly wishful thinking. Yet she had to swallow hard against the small, strangled sound that had risen to the back of her throat. She *should* have turned him down.

No matter how much she longed for him to hold her.

The musicians brought the song to an end. With a sigh of relief, she dropped her arms and stepped back. Instantly, she missed his warmth.

"Thank you for the dance," he said.

Reluctantly she looked up, more unwilling than ever to meet his eyes. Instead, she focused on his mouth. On any other man she might have taken the curve of those lips as a complacent smile. Or even a self-satisfied smirk.

Not on Ben.

"Thank you, too," she murmured. She saw Tess approaching and turned to her.

"Dana, didn't you say P.J. and Stacey are staying with Anne all night?"

"Yes." The casual question helped clear her head. She had made special arrangements with her babysitter. "Anne's keeping them at her house, since I knew Lissa and I would get home so late."

"Good. But Lissa's now staying at the Whistlestop with Nate."

Dana frowned. Tess's mother had turned their family home into a bed-and-breakfast inn a couple of years earlier. Lissa spent the night at the Whistlestop Inn as often as Nate stayed at their house. But... "Roselynn doesn't need an extra—"

"No buts, please. I checked with Mom first." Tess leaned toward them and continued in a lower voice, "Nate's having a hard time adjusting to us going away. I invited Lissa."

"In that case, then, of course."

"Great." Tess turned to Ben. "We've had to do some rearranging and the limo's now overflowing. You won't mind taking Dana back to town, will you?"

"Of course not."

"But—" Dana started.

"Gotta run," Tess interrupted. Again. "Caleb's waiting." She turned away, her gown swirling behind her.

"I can find another ride—"

"No need," Ben said.

He closed his fingers around her elbow as if she planned to hurry after Tess. She did. "Duty calls," she said, tugging her arm free. "After all, I'm Tess's matron of honor tonight."

"No problem," he said easily. "I'll be waiting for you when it's time to go."

A few quick steps, and she'd left him behind. If only she could have left her own treacherous thoughts on the dance floor, too. On the long ride to Flagman's Folly in the quiet darkness of his truck, she'd better put those thoughts out of her mind. Or even safer, put herself to sleep. Then she wouldn't be tempted to think…to say… to do…anything she'd regret.

Silly to worry about that. What harm could come from a simple ride home with him?

Good old, dependable Ben. She could count on him to be there for her. To be her friend, always. To never do anything inappropriate.

It was enough to break her heart.

A red gleam from the road up ahead caught Ben's eye. The headlamps of his pickup truck reflected off the tail-lights of a vehicle pulled to one side of the road.

"Ben," Dana said, her voice tight with concern.

"Nothing to worry about." Even if he hadn't seen the car days ago, he'd have realized that. The coating of yellow dust from bumper to bumper and the dingy handkerchief hanging from the antenna told him it had sat there for a while. "I noticed it when I came this way last week."

No need to check for anyone stranded inside the vehicle. Still, habits died hard. He slowed for a look as he drove past. Around here, with towns few and far apart and where the sun parched everything it touched, folks kept an eye out for others.

Just as he watched over Dana.

"I'm surprised you didn't notice it before tonight," he added. "You're on the road often enough."

"Not lately." She sounded irritated.

"In fact, that could've easily been your van broken down back there. And what would you have done by yourself?"

"Called for a tow truck, of course. Besides, when I leave town, I'm usually not alone. I have clients with me."

She shifted in the passenger seat.

She hadn't said much so far on their way home. He'd even caught her with her eyes closed a few times. No surprise, considering the clock read ten past midnight.

Cinderella hadn't made it home on time.

Between her last-minute duties at the banquet hall and the long ride back to town, they'd only come to the outskirts of Flagman's Folly now.

"Sleep well?" he asked, smiling.

"Just resting my eyes."

In the dim light from the dashboard, he could see the line of her cheekbones. Again, he noted the weight she'd lost. Still, she looked beautiful. But tired. "With all the kids away, maybe you can get some extra rest in the morning."

"Not a chance. I'm picking up P.J. and Stacey at seven."

"So early?"

She laughed softly. "I wouldn't inflict P.J. on Anne and her mother any longer than that."

It had been a while since he'd seen the kids. Once, he'd had the run of Paul's house. He swallowed the bitter thought and kept his eyes on the road. "He's still a chatterbox, huh?"

"*Always been* a chatterbox," she corrected.

"He takes after his mama."

"He does not."

His laugh sounded much more loud than hers had. "Now, don't try pulling that one on me. I grew up with you, remember?"

"How could I forget?"

She didn't sound happy about it. "Was it that bad?"

"Don't be silly." She sighed. "I didn't mean that. I was just thinking in general about growing up here."

"The best place in the world," he said.

"Mmm."

"What? You don't agree?"

"Of course, I do. It's just…you know how people are here. *They* don't forget a thing, either."

"Works for me. It's nice to have folks around who know all about you." *Nice, except for their long list of expectations.* He stayed quiet for a while, listening to the tires whip the road. "Well," he said, finally, "I'd hate to live in a town where nobody knew his neighbor. Wouldn't you?"

She didn't answer. He smiled. She'd gone back to resting her eyes again. Her lashes left shadows on her cheeks. Her lips had softened. He wanted a taste. When he'd held her in his arms tonight, he'd had to fight like hell to keep from pulling her closer and kissing her.

Before they'd left the banquet hall, he'd thought about polishing off a whole bottle of champagne. He hadn't had but two glasses, hours before. Maybe some extra would have given him justification for what he wanted to do now. To step outside *everyone's* expectations. Especially hers.

He'd rejected the idea of more champagne, though. He'd never been much of a drinking man, and he wouldn't use liquor as an excuse for his behavior.

Besides, he didn't need alcohol to explain why he felt the way he did about Dana.

Glancing across the space between them again, he noted the way the pink lace of her dress lay across her shoulders. Then he forced his gaze to the road, where it belonged.

He had no right to look at her as she slept, unaware and vulnerable. No right to look at her at all. He was obligated to watch over her, to take care of her, as he'd promised his best friend he would do.

She'd made that damned hard for him.

He thought back to the day Paul had stopped by the ranch house on his last leave. The day Paul had asked him to watch over his family. Stunned by the request, Ben still had his wits about him enough to agree in an instant.

Paul and Dana and their kids were as close as family to him. He loved Lissa and P.J.—Paul Junior—as much as he loved his niece. He felt the same now about Stacey. Of course he would watch over them. All of them.

He had to keep that promise. Had to make sure he stayed close to Dana and the kids.

Staring at her with lust in his eyes probably wasn't the best way to get her to go along with that.

She woke up again just as they reached Signal Street, the town's main thoroughfare. He managed to smile at her briefly without making eye contact.

A few minutes later, after he'd turned onto her street and pulled into her driveway, he found himself grasping the steering wheel, as if his tight grip could rein him in, too. "Here we are," he said inanely, his voice croaking.

When he rounded the truck and opened the passenger door, she gathered her dress in both hands. Balanced on the edge of her seat, she hesitated.

The light from the streetlamp a few feet away turned her face pale as whipped cream and her hair buttery gold. Her eyes sparkled. He stood, one hand palm up, heart thumping out of rhythm, the way he'd waited after he had invited her to dance.

Finally, she reached out to him. Though he'd had the heater on low for the ride home, her fingers felt cool. Automatically, he sandwiched her hand between his. "You should have said something," he reproached her. "I'd have cranked up the heat."

"It's okay." She slipped free and walked toward the house.

For a long moment, he watched the pink-skirted sway of her hips. Then he came to his senses. As she unlocked the front door, he caught up to stand beside her.

"Coffee?" she murmured.

Not such a good idea. He forced a laugh. "You're not awake enough to make coffee."

"Of course I am," she shot back.

He'd said just the wrong thing. Or had he? Had his subconscious picked just the *right* words to guarantee she would argue the point?

She frowned and pushed the door open. "It will take more than the ride home to settle me down after all the excitement today. And it's the least I can offer to say thank you."

You could offer me something else.

Fingers now curled tight around a nonexistent steering wheel, he followed her into the house and the living room he'd once known so well.

"Have a seat," she said. "I'll be back soon."

Obediently, he dropped onto her couch and sat back as if he didn't have a care in the world.

Yeah. Sure. At least he'd gotten the obedient part right. No one in town would have cause to argue with him about that. Not even Dana.

He knew what folks thought of him—he'd lived with the knowledge his entire life. Good old Ben Sawyer. Well-behaved, safe, trustworthy Ben. Ben, the boy-next-door. All compliments, all good qualities to have.

The trouble was, not one of them appealed to him now.

The moment Dana went through the doorway into the kitchen, he sat up. He needed to pull himself together. To get control.

Not much chance of that, all things considered. Since grade school, he'd struggled to get a handle on the crush he had on her. Struggled—and failed. Years ago, that calf-love had turned into a powerful longing. And tonight, holding her in his arms had shot all his good intentions to pieces.

No matter how long or how hard he fought, he would never win.

Because no matter how wrong it made him, he wanted his best friend's wife.

Chapter 3

Leaving Ben as quickly as her pink high heels could carry her, Dana escaped to the kitchen, seeking safety in her favorite room in the house. But once there, she felt the walls closing in. As a tenant, she couldn't make permanent changes, but she'd decorated with blue-and-white towels and curtains to match her dishes. The normally soothing colors did nothing for her now.

Throughout the room, she'd hung so many houseplants Lissa often said they ate their meals in a garden. *A jungle,* five-year-old P.J. insisted every time.

An appropriate description at the moment, as she roamed the room like a tiger on the prowl, too tense to sit while the coffee brewed. Too aware of Ben just a few yards away.

After the dance, the ride home in the car and the sight of him sitting comfortably on her couch, nothing could calm her. And she had to go back into the living room and make polite conversation with him—at this hour! Why hadn't she said goodbye at the door instead of inviting him in?

Not wanting to admit the answer to that, she gathered mugs and napkins and turned the teakettle on.

Ben would only want coffee, though. She knew that about him and a lot more. His coffee preference: black, no sugar. His favorite food: tacos. Favorite cookie: chocolate chip. Favorite ice cream: butter pecan. What she *didn't* know about Ben Sawyer wouldn't fill the coffee mug she'd set on the counter.

What he didn't know about her...

She stared at the teakettle, which took its sweet time coming to a boil. Maybe better for her if it never did. Then she wouldn't have to go into the other room and face the danger of getting too close to him and the disappointment of knowing all the things she wished for could never come true.

This reprieve in the kitchen couldn't last much longer. Unfortunately. She had to stop obsessing about Ben.

She had to think of her kids. And her husband.

The reminder froze her in place.

Not all that long ago, her marriage had become about as solid as the steam building up in the teakettle. She and Paul had both known it, but before the issues between them could boil over, he announced he had enlisted. No warning. No compromise. No discussion. She'd barely had time to adjust to the news when he'd left for boot camp.

She had tried to see his decision as a positive change, a chance for him to come home a different man. For them to work things out. She owed her kids that. But the changes didn't happen for the better. His letters slowed to a trickle and then stopped arriving altogether.

When he came home on leave, the brief reunion was more uncomfortable than happy. Their final time together, she'd made one last attempt to save their relationship—an attempt that had failed. By the end of his leave, they'd agreed to a divorce. And to keep that between them until he returned after his discharge.

Only, he hadn't returned at all.

She'd been left with kids she loved more than life, a load of debt she might never crawl out from under, and renewed determination to hold on to the truth. A truth she had sworn no one—especially Ben Sawyer—would ever learn. A determination that Ben, so full of kindness and concern, undermined with almost his every breath.

Beside her, the teakettle screeched and spewed steam. *Like a dragon,* P.J. always said.

She looked at it and shook her head. Dragon or no, the kettle didn't scare her. Neither would Ben.

As long as she didn't get too close to either of them.

With an exasperated sigh, she moved across to the coffeemaker and poured a full, steaming mug. She was stalling, delaying the moment she'd have to face him again, whether he scared her or not. Quickly she poured her tea. Then she stiffened her spine and stalked toward the doorway to the living room. There, she faltered and stood looking into the room.

Tall and broad and long limbed, he seemed to take up much more than his share of the couch. He had left his jacket in the truck. While she had gone to the kitchen, he'd undone his tie and the top few buttons on his shirt. The sight of that bothered her somehow. Maybe because he hadn't hesitated to unwind, yet she remained strung tight.

He turned his head her way. His dark eyes shone in the lamplight. A smile suddenly curved his lips.

"I made myself comfortable," he said.

"So I see." Obviously he felt right at home, while she felt…things she definitely shouldn't allow herself to feel.

"You haven't changed much."

Startled, she stared at him. Then she saw he hadn't meant her at all. His gaze roamed the room, scrutinizing the well-worn plaid fabric on the couch and chairs, the long scratch on the coffee table where P.J. had ridden his first tricycle into it. Ben had been there that Christmas afternoon. He had bought that tricycle. Was he thinking about that now, too?

Nothing in the house had changed since he'd last visited. But she had. "No, not much different in here," she answered with care, as if he would pick up on the distinction.

With equal care, she handed him his coffee. For a moment his fingers covered hers. She nearly lost her grip. The hot, dark liquid sloshed dangerously close to the point of no return. When he took the mug, pulling his fingers away, she gave a sigh of relief mixed with regret.

Still, she hesitated.

She glanced across the room at her rocking chair, so nice and far from the couch. But with such sharp edges on the rockers, ready to pierce the lace of her dress. She'd lost even that small chance of escape.

One of P.J.'s dinosaurs sat wedged between the couch cushions. She plucked it free and dropped it on the coffee table. Then, cradling her tea mug, she took a seat.

"Your hands still need warming?" he asked.

Again she stared. If she said yes, would he take her hand between his again, the way he had when she'd climbed from his truck? Her palms tingled at the thought. But of course he hadn't meant that as an offer. How desperate must she be, wanting his attention so badly she

found it where none existed? At least, that kind of attention?

She shook her head to clear it as much as to answer
his question.

From under her lashes she watched him set the mug
down on his thigh, holding it in a secure grip, as if he
didn't want to risk spilling coffee on her old couch. Or
on his tuxedo pants.

He had large hands with long, strong fingers, firm to
the touch from all the hours—all the years—he'd spent
working with them. No town boy, Ben Sawyer. He'd always lived on his family's large ranch on the outskirts
of Flagman's Folly.

Working with real estate, she knew to the acre how
much land Ben Sawyer owned. Not as much as Caleb
Cantrell now did, but a good deal more than most of the
ranchers around here. She knew to the penny the worth
of Ben's land, too.

Not as much as his worth as a man. Or as a friend.

She took a sip of her tea, understanding she was stalling again. She could list Ben's good points forever, but
now she used them to keep her mind occupied so her
mouth couldn't get her into trouble.

"How's the ranch?" she asked finally. A safe subject.

"Still there, which says something in this economy.
You haven't come out since we raised the new barn."

So much for safe. "Work has kept me busy."

"I'm sure. Well, I'll need to have another potluck one
of these days, before the weather turns."

Again she wondered if his words held a hidden meaning. No. Not Ben. But she couldn't be quite as open with
him. Since Paul's death, she'd made it a point of visiting
Ben's ranch with the kids only when he had a potluck.

When there would be plenty of folks there. And even then she felt uneasy. Unable to trust her judgment around him.

Just as she felt now.

"We've got a couple of new ponies the right size for Lissa and P.J."

Her laugh sounded strangled. "Please don't tell them, or I'll never get Lissa to stay home and focus on her homework."

"Is she struggling with it?"

"Some. Mostly math. I try to help her, but a lot of it's over my head. It's gotten tougher since we were in school."

"A lot of things have." He sounded bitter. He smiled as if to offset the tone. "I can stop by and give her a hand."

Oh, no. She had to nip that bad idea before it could blossom into another problem. "Thanks, but she started going for tutoring. With Nate. I think they're catching on."

"Good." But he sounded disappointed.

Refusing to look at his face, she stared down at her tea. She couldn't risk having him come around here, getting close to the kids again. Sending her emotions into overdrive every time she saw him.

"Well." He gestured to the coffee mug. "What happened to my cookies?"

She looked up at him in stunned surprise. That was no casual question, was it? That was a direct quote of his own words, something he'd once said to her time and time again, beginning with the first week of her eighth-grade cooking class.

He sipped from the mug.

His averted gaze gave him away, proving he'd asked that last question deliberately. He'd meant to remind her.

Hadn't he?

Yet, truthfully, everything he said and did, everything he was, only made her recall their long history.

Everything she thought and felt only made things worse.

"Sorry," she said. "I'm all out of cookies."

"That's no way to say thanks for a ride home, is it?"

"If I'm remembering correctly—" she paused, cleared her throat "—I offered coffee, not dessert."

"A man can dream, can't he?" Now, over the rim of his mug, his eyes met hers.

Her heart skipped a beat. He couldn't be flirting with her. Not Ben. He couldn't want more.

Even though she did.

"Sure," she said finally. "Dream on." She looked down at her mug and blew lightly on the inch of lukewarm tea that remained, pretending to cool it. Needing to cool herself down. Needing to get him out of here—before she gave in to her own imaginings and made a fool of herself. Her cheeks burning, she added, "Speaking of dreams, I…I guess it's time for me to turn in. And for you to go. Before it gets too late."

"It already is."

She stared at him.

He shrugged. "It's nearly one o'clock, and I'm usually up by four. It doesn't seem worth it even to go to sleep, does it?"

"Not for you, maybe. But I intend to get a few hours in before I pick up the kids."

He nodded. "I'd better go, then."

Relief flowed through her. Two minutes more, and she'd be safe. She set her mug on the coffee table and rose from the couch. She had turned away, eager to lead him to the door, when he rested his hand on her arm. She froze.

"Before I go," he murmured, "you might need some help."

"I don't think so. I can manage a couple of mugs."

"That's not what I meant." He tapped her shoulder lightly. "Did you plan on sleeping in this dress?"

"No," she said, hating the fact that her voice sounded so breathless. That she *felt* so breathless. She must have imagined his fingertip just grazing her skin. "I thought Lissa would be here."

"She's not."

"I know."

She swallowed hard. Why had she ever wanted to make a dress she couldn't get out of herself? Why did she not regret the decision now? She could have saved herself some heartache.

She turned to him, and their eyes met. Unable to read his—unwilling to let him see what she knew he'd find in hers—she spun away again. "Well, you can unbutton the top two buttons. That ought to get me started."

Behind her, he laughed softly. He touched the low-cut edge of the back of her gown. Her breath caught. As he undid the top button, his knuckles brushed the newly exposed skin. She clutched her lace overskirt with both hands and hoped he had touched her deliberately.

He undid the second button, his fingers following the same path along her spine. Warmth prickled her skin.

When he reached for the next button and the next, she closed her eyes, wishing he'd meant to set off the heat building inside her.

After he'd undone the back of her gown, she turned, already planning the quick farewell that would send him on his way. With one look at him, her words disappeared before they reached her lips. Now she could read his eyes clearly. Could read naked longing in his face.

A longing she recognized too well.

In those endless months when she'd known in her heart her marriage to Paul was over, she had begun to yearn again for all the things she had always wanted in her life. All the things she had hoped Paul would be but never had been.

A solid, steady, dependable partner.

A husband she could truly love.

A daddy who would willingly raise her children.

A man...

A man just like Ben.

"Think I've gone far enough?" His voice rumbled through her. No sign of laughter now. His chest rose and fell with his deep breath. He looked into her eyes, then let his gaze drift down to her mouth.

She had spent the entire evening wanting him to kiss her—and she couldn't wait for him to kiss her now.

Slowly he reached up and rested his warm hand flat against the back of her neck. She tilted her chin up, let him cradle her head in his palm, allowed her eyelids to drift closed.

His breath fanned her cheek.

The brush of his lips against hers came with the lightest of pressure. Not tentative, but restrained, as if he touched her in awe and disbelief. That sense of reverence made her eyes sting. Made her heart swell.

He cupped her face, his fingers curving beneath her jaw, fingertips settling against her neck. He couldn't miss her rapid pulse.

His head close to hers, he murmured, "You know, I've had a crush on you since kindergarten."

"No."

"Yes. Although I admit," he added, his voice hoarse, "I didn't think about this until a few years later." He slid his hand from her neck and wrapped his arms around her, holding her close.

When she opened her eyes, she found his face mere inches away. "You're only looking for cookies," she teased.

"Oh, no. Not when I've just had something much better." His mouth met hers again. "You taste like wedding cake."

She smiled. "You taste like champagne."

"Only the best for you, darlin'. Always."

Always. The way he'd been there for her.

Yet through all the years she had known him, she'd never imagined they would ever kiss. During the recent months when she'd begun to dream about him, she'd never dared to let those dreams bring her this far.

She had to clear her throat before she could speak again. Still, her voice cracked. "Are you trying to sweet-talk me, cowboy?"

"*Sweet?* No, ma'am." He shook his head. "I'm thinking more like hot." He slid his hand into the unbuttoned back of her gown, pressing his fingers wide and firm against her. The soft material slipped from her shoulders.

Not breaking eye contact with her, he trailed both hands down her arms. Like the water bubbling in the country club's fountain, the gown fell in a froth of pink satin and lace.

When he took her hand and sank onto the couch, she went with him, wanting to get even closer, to brace herself against his solidness, to absorb his warmth. Wanting to hold on to a reality she wasn't yet sure she believed.

A few minutes later, though, she believed in him with all her heart. Despite his words, he was gentle and kind and sweet. And yes…later…he was hot, too.

He gave her everything she'd ever dreamed of. And more.

An even longer while later, she reached up to slide her hands behind his neck and link her fingers against him. As she held on, unmoving, he explored once again, running his hands down her sides, cupping her hips and holding her closer.

When she sucked in a deep breath, one side of his mouth curled in a smile. "This isn't what I expected when I drove you home tonight."

"That makes two of us." Like a schoolgirl, she struggled to hold back a giggle of pure joy at being two halves of a couple with him.

"And," he said, "this isn't what I expected when I promised to take care of you. But you don't hear me complaining."

Her throat tightened, and the giggle died. "No," she said, "I don't." Goose bumps rippled along her skin.

To accompany the chill running down her spine.

"In fact—"

"Wait," she interrupted, meeting his eyes. "You said 'take care'?"

He nodded. "Of you *and* the kids."

She tried to keep her tone even, her voice soft. "And you made that promise to…?"

He shifted, as if the question she'd left hanging caused him considerable discomfort. A small gap opened between them, and her body cooled.

"To Paul," he said.

"I see." She sat up, needing more distance between them. When he let her go, she grabbed her gown from the floor and slid into it, heedless now of the fine lace, of the delicate satin. "That's the reason behind everything?" she asked. "Because you made a promise to Paul?"

He leaned against the arm of the couch. "What 'everything'? You mean us, here?"

"We've never been 'us, here' before tonight." She wouldn't—couldn't—think about that now. It took twice as much effort to keep her voice level as it had to stifle that foolish giggle. "No, I mean everything you've done. Trying to help me. Stopping by my office unannounced. Buying the office building. All that—because of what you promised Paul?"

Frowning, he nodded. "Yeah. But I'd have done those things anyway. Why wouldn't I? I told you, you've been the girl for me since kindergarten."

"How long ago did you have to make that promise?"

"The day he shipped out at the end of his leave. But there was no 'have to' about it. I willingly gave him my word."

"I'm *not* willing to let you take care of me."

"It's too late for that."

She frowned. "Why?"

"I've watched over you for years. Ever since we were kids in school."

"Then it has to stop. We're not kids anymore. And as I've told you before, many times, I can take care of myself—and my children. I don't think you'll ever understand that." She tugged the bodice of her gown into place. "And I think it's time for you to go."

For a few long moments he didn't move. Then, slowly, he curled his fingers into fists and stared at her, his eyes narrowed.

She had no fear. This was Ben. He was good and kind and meant well. And because he was so good and kind, because he felt so determined to take care of her, she'd hurt him.

After he'd just made love to her as if—

She couldn't finish that thought. She couldn't sit here and watch him walk out.

Instead, she rose from the couch, then crossed the room. "Good night," she said over her shoulder. Her voice shook.

"Running away won't help anything," he said.

"I'm not running," she answered, climbing the stairs without looking back. Without stopping. "I'm just standing on my own."

On legs no steadier than her voice had been and that threatened to give way at any moment.

From the upstairs hallway she listened to his movements below.

When he left, she went down again to lock the door.

Then she sank onto the rocking chair. Her heart thudded painfully. She had wanted to stop him. Wanted to call him back. But she couldn't. She had to make him leave, had to force him to understand she didn't need him.

She had to force herself to accept a painful truth, too. For all this time, Ben had considered her his responsibility.

She couldn't allow that to continue.

No matter what she had heard for years from another man, no matter what that man had tried to make her believe, she wasn't anyone's burden. Never had been—and as long as she lived, never would be.

Especially not Ben's.

Chapter 4

Dana dropped Stacey off at the day-care center, then drove toward the elementary school. She needed the Monday-morning routine after spending most of Sunday agonizing over Ben. Again and again, she'd replayed what had happened between them.

Cheeks flaming, she glanced in the rearview mirror at Lissa and P.J. She needed to think about her children, not Ben.

Taking a deep breath, she looked at the kids again. Thought of her routine.

Of course, when she needed a distraction more than ever before, her office would be quieter than usual with Tess, her sole employee, away on her honeymoon. That meant she'd have plenty of time alone. Plenty of time to obsess over Saturday night—and then to forget it had happened.

But how could she ever forget anything about Ben

when everywhere she looked, she saw reminders of him? Even the squat, redbrick school building and the bus pulled over in the parking lot brought back memories.

Years ago, Ben and the younger kids from the outlying ranches only came into town when they rode the bus to school in the morning. As soon as the final bell rang, they immediately rode the bus home. With their parents busy working, the kids didn't get to hang out in Flagman's Folly until they could drive themselves back and forth.

Ranch families had the same problem today. She and Kayla Robertson already had a plan in the works, one Ben would eventually hear about thanks to his seat on the town council. She dreaded having to face him the night they would present their proposal.

"Mom, stop," Lissa shouted from the backseat. "There's Nate." In the rearview mirror, Dana saw her point off to one side of the schoolyard, where her best friend had just jumped down from Tess and Caleb's SUV.

Dana blinked in surprise at seeing Tess in the driver's seat. The newlyweds had spent a couple of days in Santa Fe but were scheduled to leave that afternoon for a cruise. She unbuckled her seat belt and climbed out of the van with the kids.

The two girls walked away, chattering and hiking their backpacks up on their shoulders. Carrying his lunch box and scuffling his feet, P.J. trailed behind them, unwilling as always to have anyone see him arrive with the girls.

Dana shook her head, then turned to Tess. "What are you doing here? Isn't your ship sailing?"

"Yes, but we have plenty of time before our flight for the coast. We decided to come back and surprise Nate and Mom at breakfast before Nate left for school."

Relieved, Dana nodded, unable to hold back a smile. "On Saturday, you said Nate was the one dealing with separation anxiety. But you're the one missing her already, aren't you?"

Tess shrugged. "It's silly, but you're right. I've never been away from her before."

"It's not a bit silly. I'd feel the same way." Happy to have something to keep her mind—and Tess's—off Ben, she said, "She'll be all right. Your mom and Ellamae will keep a close eye on her. She's got plenty to keep her busy. And Lissa can't stop talking about the sleepover in a couple of weeks."

"I know. Nate reminded me about it three times on the way over here this morning. Well, I'd better get going. I left Caleb back at the Whistlestop, making a few last business calls before we head out. Dana…"

At Tess's hesitant tone, she frowned. "What?"

"He's not happy leaving before the closing on the ranch."

Dana stiffened, sure she knew where Tess was going with the conversation. A former bull-riding champion turned ranch owner, Caleb Cantrell had invested his money wisely and had plenty to spare. He also now had a wife and daughter to spend it on.

Dana felt Tess's happiness as if it were her own.

Which meant she could also understand her friend's worry for her. She worried, too. For the sake of her children, she had to find a way to lighten her own load. A permanent solution. The commission from the sale to Caleb would definitely feed her hungry checkbook. But that money was just one more thing in her life…like love and marriage…that wouldn't last forever.

Hoping she sounded unconcerned, she laughed and shook her head. "You two need to stop worrying over everyone else and go enjoy your trip. Tell Caleb I'll survive till you get back."

"It wasn't only your survival he was thinking about. He's eager to get his hands on that ranch."

"He should be focused on getting his hands on his new wife."

Tess laughed. "We're taking care of that. Oh, before I forget, he wanted me to tell *you* something. A friend from his rodeo days is going to get in touch to look at property. His name's Jared Hall."

"Great."

Tess nodded. "But really, Dana, Caleb said he'd cut an advance check on the commission—"

"Enough. Quit trying to mother me." She smiled to soften the words. "I'm not Nate. But like her, I'll be all right until you're home again. Now, just stop. And," she said, faking a threatening tone, "if you *don't,* you're fired."

"Okay, okay. I definitely want my job. By the way, did you have a pleasant ride home with Ben the other night?"

She couldn't help flinching at the change of subject. Or more truthfully, at the mention of his name. She forced herself to meet Tess's eyes and raise her brows in mock-surprise. "'Pleasant'? You've never used that word in your life. Of course we had a 'pleasant' ride. What else would you expect?"

"Since you've asked…the two of you have seemed awfully uncomfortable with each other lately."

"We're fine."

"Maybe you are, at that," Tess said, her face suddenly as blank as P.J.'s when he was caught up to mischief. "I admit, you looked pretty relaxed in his arms on the dance floor the other night." As Dana opened her mouth, Tess raised her hands palms out and grinned. "I'm not asking anything about it. I'm just saying…whatever's going on with you two—"

"There is nothing going on. And I can handle our landlord. Very *pleasantly,* too."

Tess laughed and gave her a quick hug. They said their goodbyes, and Tess waved as she drove out of the parking lot.

Dana climbed into the van and slumped back against the driver's seat. No one else watched her. She was trying—and failing—to hide from herself.

How could she have lied like that, and to her own best friend? She *couldn't* handle their landlord. She couldn't deal with her emotions about him at all. Worse, she couldn't believe where those emotions had led her. And the risk they had caused her to take.

Everyone in town made it plain they would always consider her Paul's wife. They would always worship Paul. Only two days ago she had worried about their reaction to seeing her dance with Ben at the reception.

What would folks say now, if they knew the widow of their beloved army hero had slept with his best friend?

Ben looped Firebrand's reins around one of the posts of Sam Robertson's corral. The stallion's dark chestnut coat gleamed in the setting sun, giving credence to his name. Ben patted the horse's flank. As if in resignation, Firebrand snorted and nodded his head. Then he stood and stared over the corral rail.

Squinting against the sun, Ben waved to Becky, out near the barn with her puppy. Sam's little girl waved back. Pirate yipped a couple of times, then settled down at her feet again.

Seeing Becky and her dog led him to think of P.J.

That took his mind straight to P.J.'s mama. No surprise at the leap—or at what followed. Guilty thoughts flew in his brain like the flies buzzing around Firebrand's twitching tail.

Sam came out of the house carrying two long-necked bottles. "Here. Have a seat."

Ben nodded his thanks and took his time swallowing some of the ice-cold beer. It felt good going down.

It felt good to sit on the picnic bench in Sam's yard and watch the sun sink. He'd spent the past few days working hard, and he needed a break from the ranch. He needed a break from himself.

No matter how much he'd tried to keep busy with work, he couldn't stop himself from going over what had happened at Dana's house just a few days ago.

What the hell kind of friend would make a move on his best friend's wife?

"She's got a few new tricks, too," Sam said.

Ben started. "What?"

Sam chuckled. "Man, your mind must be a thousand miles away from here."

No, just taken a ride into town.

"I was telling you about Becky and Pirate," Sam said. "She's taught that pup some more tricks."

"Good." He nodded. "Good for kids to have a dog."

"Yeah. I just said that." Sam looked him in the eye. "Obvious enough you didn't catch a word of it. What's the trouble?"

He shrugged. "No trouble. I'm unwinding." He gestured to the catalog Sam had dropped onto the picnic table. "Is that the breeder's article you wanted to show me?"

Sam nodded, and the talk turned technical, lasting the length of their first beers and requiring a backup.

When Sam suggested a third, Ben shook his head.

"That's enough for me. I've got to get back to the house and check on that new mare."

"Have you talked to Dana this week?"

"No." He picked at the label on his beer bottle. "Was there a reason for me to?"

"No idea. Kayla mentioned you at suppertime. She's going into town to see Dana tomorrow, and I guess the office put the thought of you into her head. You don't need to do much there, though, do you? Besides collect the rent."

"There are things that need some attention. But all in all, it pretty much takes care of itself."

"Sounds like you made a good investment, then. I wish the ranches could run themselves, too."

"No, you don't. We've got to do something to earn a living."

They laughed at that, but later, as he headed homeward on Firebrand, he thought of the comment again. And of Dana and the tough time she was having.

There had to be something he could do to help her. Some way to keep in touch with her—without *touching* her. A way to take care of her without ticking her off.

If that could ever be possible again.

Through the years, guilt over his feelings for her had grown like the wild, choking kudzu that would take over his spread if he and his cowhands didn't keep a handle on it. The prettiest flowers you'd ever want to see, that kudzu. But deadly to the stock that grazed on his land.

And now with that load of guilt increased ten times over, it just might be the end of him, too.

Dammit, but he should have known better. Trying not to think of the other night, he took Firebrand into a gallop. His thoughts caught up with him anyway.

Dana had looked so beautiful in that pink dress.

And—for the first time in his life—he'd found her within his reach.

He couldn't keep from touching her, couldn't help but want to get her out of that gown and into his arms. Couldn't stop himself from making love with her.

For the only time in his life?

He leaned into Firebrand, urging him to fly as if a monster nipped at their heels.

Early Friday morning, Dana sat at her desk at Wright Place Realty. Outside the storefront window, Signal Street was bathed in September sunshine. Inside the office, she felt swathed in a sense of gloom heavy enough to cut with a knife. She missed having Tess around. She missed seeing Ben—though that was the last thing she should want.

Thank heaven, Kayla had shown up for their meeting, giving her a much-needed break from her wayward thoughts. She leaned back in her swivel chair and looked across the desk. "This idea's sounding better and better every time we discuss it."

Kayla smiled in satisfaction. "I know it is."

They wanted to convince the town council to build a playground for the children of Flagman's Folly, a place where kids of all ages could come together. At the moment, the town's limited options included the day-care center, with its small fenced-in area, and the sneaker-worn plot of grass running behind the elementary and high schools.

"We've got some time till the next council meeting," she told Kayla, "but we need to start looking for locations. First, though, we should check zoning ordinances."

"I can take care of that. You might have your hands full with Ben."

She stiffened. "Ben?"

"Yes. He told Sam last night he's thinking about doing some work in here."

She tried not to groan. When he had bought this building, he had promptly lowered her rental fees. If he planned to sink money into the property, would he feel the need to raise the rent again? Would he do that regardless, as a way to get back at her for what had happened between them?

No, not Ben.

Still, by the time the newlyweds returned, she could be in big trouble. Maybe she should have agreed to Caleb's offer of an advance. But accepting, after the way she'd denied needing it, was out of the question—even though Tess had probably seen right through her. After all, they had both been in the same precarious financial situation until just recently. Well, fingers crossed, Caleb's friend Jared would prove himself a real, live customer.

Avoiding Kayla's eyes, she straightened the paperwork on her desk. "I'm sure, sooner or later, I'll hear what he's got in mind."

"I'd go with sooner." Kayla sounded amused. "He's just about to walk in the door."

"What can I do for you today?" Dana asked.

Seeing her through the office window had cranked up the heat inside Ben. But now he winced as a chill settled over him. One that had nothing to do with the air that swept into the room as Kayla pulled the door closed on her way out.

Come to think of it, she'd left in a hurry. Maybe she hadn't much cared for the chill around there, either.

Behind her desk, Dana looked cool all over, too, from her blond hair to her blue blouse to the bare hands she had folded in front of her. A big difference from the way he'd seen her last, with her hair loose and her pink dress unbuttoned and her pale skin peeking through the back of the gown as she'd run up the stairs. She had just sent him on his way and, still, it had taken everything in him to keep from following her.

He tightened his grip on the clipboard in his hands and swallowed hard. *Steady, now. Just friends.*

Her icy question, one she would've aimed at anyone who walked through the door, said she might not even consider them that. "Uh. Listen, about the other night—"

She turned red to her hairline. "Please." She coughed and began again. "That's…something we shouldn't mention. Forget the other night. I have."

He nodded. She'd forced her tone to go along with the whole cool package, telling him she had no intention of making things easy between them. Well, he'd already taken on that job. To make things better. Not to argue with her but to help her.

Whether she wanted his help or not.

Of course, with the way she felt about that, he couldn't tell her outright. He raised his hand, waving with the clipboard he held. "I need to take a few measurements."

"What for?"

Her question took him aback—until he saw the small indentation between her brows. After all these years, he could read her every expression. The tiny frown meant something worried her. Keeping his tone level, he said, "I'm thinking about putting down new tile in here."

"There's nothing wrong with the floor."

"An upgrade might be nice, don't you think?"

She shrugged. "If you want the truth, I think it's fine the way it is."

Why had he bothered to ask? "Thanks for the input."

As nicely as he could, he added, "Think I'll go with the new tile. Might look good to your customers."

She sighed. "We don't have any clients, Ben."

He stilled. That sentence told him what had caused the worry line between her brows. Hearing it took the irritation right out of him. The sudden wry smile she sent his way made his pulse jump.

"You know, if Caleb hadn't bought that ranch," she added, "I'd be up Sidewinder Creek without a paddle."

"We've done that once before, haven't we?"

She laughed. "Yes, I guess we have."

Their eyes met. For a moment the shared memory from their grade-school days brought them close again.

"And," she continued, "you'd think I would learn from my mistakes."

She meant more than that day long ago. "Well," he said, unwilling to go where that would lead, "the thought of getting caught right now can't be so alarming, considering the creek's about a foot and a half deep from the drought."

"You know what I mean."

"Then all the more reason to try to lure customers for you."

She stared at him. The close moment ended as abruptly as if she had slammed the office door between them. "Thanks," she said finally. "But I can manage."

"How?" he asked, gripping the clipboard. "You're not expecting another Caleb Cantrell to just happen along, are you?"

"Maybe. A friend of his is flying in next week to look at property. But—"

"Yeah, Caleb mentioned that."

"—my business isn't your worry."

"Fair enough." No, it wasn't fair at all. Her words

stung, and he fought to shrug off his frustration. "This office *is* my concern, though. So is the entire building. And if I see improvements needing to be done, I'll make 'em."

"Fine. As long as you're aware I'm not obligated to pay you anything more than the rent we decided on. And that was no gentleman's agreement we made."

"Couldn't have been, since I'm no gentleman." He gave a rueful smile. "Neither were you, last time I looked."

No matter the chilly tone she'd forced earlier, no matter the blank expression on her face now, he could start a campfire with the tension sparking between them. He could start something more.

Give them time alone again—

"We have a lease," she said, her voice shaky. "Signed and sealed on the dotted line."

"I'm not arguing that."

"Good." She rose, marched across the office and flipped the hanging sign on the front door. From the outside, it would now display Closed.

She must have read his mind.

"Well, then," she said, "as there's nothing else to discuss, I'll leave you to get your measuring done."

Disappointment jolted him. "No need for you to go."

"Oh, but there is. I've got customers to lure in, and all that. Please lock up on your way out." Clearly all too eager to get away, she went through the door and closed it behind her even more quickly than Kayla had done.

He slapped the clipboard against his palm and shook his head. What the hell had he been thinking, wanting to get her alone? Hadn't that led to enough trouble?

So much for his plan of working around here—every time he would come in to do something, she'd just take off again. He couldn't ask her to stay at her desk, anyway, when her job required her to keep on the move. But he wasn't beaten yet.

She didn't know what a mistake she'd made by walking out on him. By forcing his hand. By making him twice as determined to find a way to make things easier for her.

He smiled, turning another idea over in his mind, one he liked much better than hoping to corner her in her office.

An idea he'd stake his ranch on she wouldn't like at all.

"I didn't do it, Mama!" P.J. called the minute she walked in the door late that afternoon.

Now what?

After Ben had invaded her office, seeming to take up all the oxygen in the room, she'd found it hard to breathe. Needing to go somewhere—*anywhere*—to escape, she'd spent a long morning researching at the local library. Then she'd spent an even longer afternoon back at her desk, searching for listings, hoping to find something to tempt Caleb's friend next week. Yet somehow, as she worked, she could still see Ben in the room.

Coming home to P.J.'s vehement denial gave her an instant diversion. Chances were, he *had* done whatever it was. She just hoped it wasn't something too serious.

"Didn't do what, P.J.?" she asked.

Instead of answering, he took her by the hand and led her to the downstairs bathroom.

Water trickled from beneath the vanity. Puddles saturated the tiles. The loose edges of a half-dozen vinyl squares had already started to curl. She groaned. "P.J., where's Anne?"

Dana couldn't ask for a better babysitter. She willingly picked up P.J. after kindergarten and nine-month-old Stacey from day care. And she was always available in the evening when Dana had to show properties to her clients.

When she had clients.

Best of all, Anne loved the kids. And that mattered most.

"She's in the backyard with Stacey," P.J. said.

Chances were almost guaranteed that Clarice, her elderly next-door neighbor, would have her eye on the yard, too. "You go out there with them, please, while Mama cleans up this mess."

After walking barefoot through the rising water on the bathroom floor, she tied a rag around the leaking pipe and put an empty bucket beneath the joint. Finished, she looked around and shook her head. *This* was the floor—and not to mention, now the pipe—that should be replaced, not the perfectly good tiles Ben wanted to change in the office.

The floor and the plumbing headed a long list of things that needed fixing around here. She couldn't afford the repairs. At this point, she couldn't afford to move anywhere else, either. In any case, she didn't own this house, only rented it.

In the kitchen, she grabbed the phone and punched her absentee landlord's number. Despite numerous reminders about repairs, she'd let George slide, knowing he had his own financial worries. She tried to ignore the issues, but her list had grown to a couple of pages, the minor fixes had given way to major problems, and this new situation threatened her family's safety.

She would never ignore that.

Frustrated at getting George's answering machine, as usual, she left a short but specific message. If she didn't hear from him by the end of the day, she would pack up and move out.

As if.

She'd just finished mopping up the last traces of water when the phone rang. *George, already?* Maybe miracles did happen.

And maybe, if she'd gotten tougher with him from the beginning, the miracles would have occurred sooner, and the minor fixes wouldn't have become major issues.

But it wasn't George returning her call.

Instead, she heard Kayla's voice. "Dana, my sister's flying in next Saturday. Sam and I want to surprise Becky. His mom has plans. Could we leave her with you until we get home?"

"Of course. Lissa has the girls here that weekend, and—"

The doorbell rang. *Another chance at a miracle?*

"This might be my landlord. I'll talk to you again, but definitely plan to bring Becky here that day."

She ended the call and hurried to the front of the house. But when she threw open the door, the man standing there was not George.

"Ben?" She couldn't stop the thrill that shot through her at seeing him on the doorstep. His gaze moved over her shoulder to the living room, where the couch sat just a few short yards away. Gripping the doorknob, she fought to keep herself and her tone steady. "What are you doing here?"

Like five-year-old P.J., he could be a man of few words when the situation warranted it. He simply held up a toolbox and a roll of duct tape. Then he moved past her and headed down the hall. She closed the door and followed slowly, feeling no less confused.

In the bathroom, he was on his knees in front of the sink, with his broad shoulders inside the vanity as he assessed the leak. *She* assessed the well-worn jeans pulling taut all over. After a good look, she croaked, "How did you know about the plumbing?"

"George called me." His voice sounded muffled.

Well, of course. The obvious answer, if only she'd paused to think. But somehow, thinking and analyzing and acting rationally had gone out the window lately. At least, every time she found herself in Ben's company. The formfitting jeans didn't help. Still, she could focus enough to know that something here didn't add up. "Why in the world would George call you?" she demanded. "Why didn't he come here himself?"

"He's out celebrating."

That response made no sense at all. "Celebrating what?" As if it mattered.

"Freedom from foreclosure." He'd deliberately deepened his voice, making the words ring hollowly in the enclosed space. He backed out from beneath the vanity, sat on his boot heels and looked at her. "I've taken a huge load off George's mind."

"How?" Unable to look at him, she moved her gaze to the sink. Turning on the faucet wouldn't be a good idea right now, but her throat desperately needed water.

"You're a real estate agent," he said. "Can't you figure it out?"

Of course she could. She already had. *Believing* the awful idea was something else. "You bought out George's loan?"

"I sure did." He grinned. "As of this morning, I'm the owner of this house."

Chapter 5

Dana parked her van in front of the house and waited while the girls in the backseat gathered their belongings.

"Don't forget your overnight bag," Lissa said to Nate.

Dana glanced toward the garage and Ben's dusty, dented ranch truck. Sighing, she shook her head. In the week since his shocking announcement, he'd nearly become a fixture in her home.

No, that word didn't fit. *Fixtures* stayed still and remained quiet and made life better for people, not worse. Nothing on that list of features came anywhere near to describing Ben's impact on her life. He'd done nothing but upset her routines, her thoughts, her balance.

In short, he'd upset *her*.

"Hey, I know that truck," Nate said. "Ben's here?"

"He's here *every* day," Lissa informed her in a tone Dana couldn't quite read.

"Cool."

Not so cool, in her opinion. Not when reality forced her to face the *true* reason for her upset.

Every afternoon she longed for a reprieve from dealing with Ben. And with every arrival home she caught herself in the lie. Because the sight of his truck outside the garage never failed to excite her.

Still, she stared at that dusty pickup truck in despair. What was wrong with her? She was a grown woman. A mother with small children. She had put behind her all the memories of…that incident with Ben.

Yet she showed every sign of a schoolgirl with her first crush. Relief. Elation. The heart-pounding attack of nerves that came with knowing she would soon see "him" again.

The girls tumbled out of the van, backpacks slung over their shoulders. Nate carried her overnight bag, too.

Anne came out of the house holding Stacey. From the open doorway, P.J. took one look at the girls running in his direction and went back inside. As Lissa and Nate raced into the house, Dana started more slowly up the path.

Anne met her halfway and handed Stacey to her. "All yours. I've got to get going."

After kissing the baby's fair hair, she looked at her sitter in surprise. "I usually have to pry you away from the kids to send you home. Everything all right?"

The teen's cheeks turned bright red. "Got a date," she mumbled. "With Billy. From Harley's."

Dana smiled in understanding. Billy was a tall, blond forward on the high school basketball team. From what she'd seen on her trips to Harley's General Store, where he worked after school, he was in demand. "Very nice, Anne. You'll have all the girls in Flagman's Folly envious tonight."

She giggled. "It's our first date," she confided. "We're going to the early show."

"Well, have fun. Be careful. And I'll see you on Monday."

"Okay." Anne chucked Stacey under her chubby chin, grabbed her bag from the porch step and took off down the sidewalk.

Watching her go, Dana cradled the baby against her and sighed. What she wouldn't give to be that young and innocent again. That hopeful.

Or would she?

She'd had her own man-in-demand, and look where it had gotten her. Her infatuation with Paul had disappeared a long time ago. Along with her love for him.

Stacey squirmed in her arms, and guilt flooded through her. Paul had given her three wonderful children. For that alone, she owed him more than she could ever have repaid.

"You planning on staying out here all night?"

She turned back to the house to find her new landlord standing in the doorway. He wore a pair of scuffed cowboy boots, threadbare jeans and…a smile.

This was good old Ben? It had to be, but she needed to look him over one more time, just to make sure. Her gaze got hung up somewhere between his belt buckle and his chin, lingering on his flat belly, taut chest and tight nipples. That night with him, she'd touched every bit of that goodness.

Her palms itched for the pleasure again.

She forced her gaze upward, reaching his mouth. His smile had disappeared. His eyes looked wary, yet they suddenly glittered. He was recalling that night, too.

She hadn't realized she'd held her breath until she exhaled in a rush. The blast ruffled Stacey's hair. Her daughter giggled. The sound broke whatever spell had transfixed Dana.

No matter what had happened between them such a short time ago, he was *still* good old Ben. For heaven's sake, she'd seen him in swim trunks every summer of her life. Well, at least until a few summers ago. He had seriously buffed up since then.

Or else her memory was going.

"Actually," she said, finally getting to his question, "I would like to go inside, if you don't mind."

"That can be arranged." Stepping back into the house, he held the door open for her and Stacey.

That was the trouble with Ben. He was always too willing to arrange anything he thought she wanted. Reluctantly, she climbed the steps and moved past him, trying not to inhale as the scent of his aftershave wafted toward her. Trying to ignore the sound of his footsteps as he followed her into the living room.

She set Stacey onto her blanket on the floor. The baby immediately grabbed her favorite teething ring.

"You're home late," Ben said.

She turned to him and felt relieved to note he had put on the blue T-shirt she'd seen hanging on the stairway banister. "Realtors work all kinds of hours," she told him. "I don't punch a time clock."

"Anne must have forgotten that." He dropped into her rocking chair. "I didn't think she'd make it till you got home. She was about to wear a trench into the front walkway, with all her pacing up and down."

She straightened one edge of the baby's blanket. "Anne was eager to go get ready for a date. I didn't know that or I'd have tried to get home sooner. We stopped to pick up a guest. As you've probably figured out."

"Nate?"

"Nate. She's staying with us for the weekend." She pushed the box of P.J.'s dinosaurs into the corner beside the couch. "They've got more friends coming later tonight and sleeping over till Sunday, too. Things will be hectic around here. Which reminds me…" She paused, trying to find the right words.

He raised one brow as if in question.

"I appreciate all you've done these past few days," she said finally. Truthfully. Every improvement to the house and yard only made things better and safer for her children. But she'd have to speak carefully now, so as not to give herself away. "I understand you want to fix up your property. But can't you do the repairs during the day, when I'm—" she grit her teeth and tried again "—when the kids aren't here underfoot?"

Now both brows shot up. "Not hardly. I've got a ranch to take care of, too."

It was that little word *too* that pushed her past the limit. "You *are* busy, aren't you? First a ranch, then an office building, and now this house and a family, as well."

"Family?" He looked puzzled. "You mean, your kids?"

"Yes, mine." She sank to the couch and pulled the afghan over her lap in a vain attempt to protect herself from her own emotion. "Ben, I know you have only our best interests at heart, and I know you want to help. To keep your promise." Her breath caught. She couldn't think about that. "But it's not necessary. Though I thank you for wanting to try," she added hastily, seeing the look on his face.

She didn't want to hurt him. She just wanted him to leave her alone to do what she had to do. As if she'd spoken the thought aloud, he rose from the rocking chair. She bit her tongue, not wanting to give him any reason to change his mind.

Finally, he nodded. "You're right."

She had braced for a farewell argument. His response made her sag against the couch in surprise. And relief. Thank goodness, at least she wouldn't have to worry about *him* underfoot this weekend. As it was, she would have enough to do trying to keep P.J. happy in a houseful of females.

"I *am* busy with the ranch," Ben admitted. "That takes priority."

"Absolutely," she agreed.

"But not tomorrow. I'll be back in the morning. Bright and early."

"Ben—"

"Look. This has nothing to do with helping you. Do you want to see my deed for this place? It's signed and sealed on the dotted line."

She winced, recognizing the words she'd said to him that afternoon in her office. The afternoon he'd bought her house. "All right." She gave in—since she didn't have a choice. "What time should I expect you?"

"We start at sunup out on the ranch."

She stared at him for a long moment, then got up to spread the afghan over the back of the couch. When she'd taken enough time to make it clear she didn't plan to respond to his ridiculous statement, he said goodbye and left.

She plopped back onto the couch and looked at Stacey.

Her daughter took the teething ring from her mouth and made a noise that sounded like "Pffftttth."

"My thoughts exactly, sweetie."

Resting her head back against the cushion, she closed her eyes and thought again of what she and Ben had done on this couch.

The memory alone left her breathless. But other

memories, much older and much sadder, made her chest tighten and her eyelids prickle with tears she refused to shed.

Long ago, she'd made the mistake of falling for the wrong man. One who had eventually taken her love for him and turned it to his advantage. Who had tricked her into believing she needed him and couldn't survive without him. He'd laid his trap and snared her. But she wouldn't ever let herself get caught again.

Not even by Ben Sawyer, a good man. The best man. A man who, in his own way, caused her more trouble and heartache than Paul had ever done.

Ben was laying a trap for her, too. One baited with kindness and concern, with kisses that made her heart melt, and caresses that made her pulse pound, and words she yearned to believe.

A trap more dangerous than the first one because she found it so tempting.

Ben had mentioned sunup only as a way of getting a rise out of Dana. When she didn't jump down his throat, he'd felt oddly disappointed. Somehow, having her snap at him seemed a whole lot better than that long, silent look she'd given him. A look that said she thought he was out of his mind.

While he didn't actually intend to show up at the crack of dawn, he found himself ready long before nine o'clock the next morning, with everything that needed doing already done. He didn't mind the work, because he loved this ranch. He enjoyed going through the routines his daddy and granddad had once taught him. Still, long years of practice meant he could finish up quickly.

Now he paced the floor in the ranch-house kitchen

much the way Dana's babysitter had paced in front of the house last night.

Considering Anne had expected Dana home by then, he'd grown concerned about her absence, too. That old van of hers had broken down more than once in the past year or so. And she was so independent, so sure she could handle everything on her own. He'd be damned if he'd let her get away with that.

He couldn't.

He couldn't stay away from her, either.

After grabbing his keys from the counter, he headed out to the hall. There, he paused only long enough to yank on his boots and pluck his Stetson from its hook on the coat stand.

Eager to get to town, he made the short trip in record time.

As he stood on Dana's front porch and rang the bell, a sense of discomfort washed over him. Not from tension. Not from guilt. From something he couldn't find a name for. Maybe he didn't want to identify it. He'd already felt too many things this week since buying Dana's rented house out from under her.

But, whatever else he didn't know, he felt certain of that decision.

The front door opened. Paul Wright, Jr., stood on the doorstep staring up at him. He'd known P.J. since birth. Yet as often as he'd played catch and checkers and cards with the boy, he'd never seen him just the way he was right now—looking the spitting image of the five-year-old friend Ben remembered.

The sight took him aback. The thought that came right on top of it took his concerns about his own actions away. How did Dana handle seeing her husband in P.J. every day?

The boy gave a huge yawn and rubbed his eyes with his fists. "I didn't sleep last night, Ben," he announced, walking away.

Ben shut the door behind them. "Why is that?" he asked, though he could have hazarded a fairly accurate guess.

"Girls."

P.J.'s opinion of the fairer sex matched the way Ben felt about cattle rustlers. "It must be tough on you, being the only man in the house."

"Yeah. Not like when my daddy was here. But he went to the army, and now he's not coming back anymore."

He sucked in a deep breath. He'd talked often enough with Dana's kids about their daddy, but never about his death.

He sure hadn't given much thought to Paul, either, when he'd held Dana in his arms the night of the wedding. Maybe that explained the discomfort he'd felt while standing on the doorstep.

"Yes, I know," he said finally. "Your daddy won't come back." But, lately, he'd felt as though Paul had never left.

P.J. climbed onto the couch, pushed aside a blanket covered with pictures of brightly colored dinosaurs and flopped back against a small mountain of pillows. Evidently, he had spent the night in the living room.

"And now," the boy said, yawning again and closing his eyes, "there are all these *girls* around here."

"Maybe they won't stay long."

P.J. opened one eye briefly. *"Ha.* They'll be here till *tomorrow."*

An awfully long time, from a little boy's perspective. Not that short in Ben's view, either. Last night, *tomorrow* had seemed very far away.

So had Dana and her kids.

He shook his head. He had to stop these kinds of thoughts. They'd bring him nothing but trouble. Maybe they already had.

P.J. lay with his mouth open, snoring gently. Smiling, Ben leaned down and settled the blanket over him. Finished, he turned toward the kitchen. And found Dana standing in the doorway, watching him.

He returned her scrutiny, taking in the pair of denim shorts that stopped way up on her long legs, her Flagman's Folly High School T-shirt, and the hair she'd pulled into a ponytail.

"While you're at it," she said, "don't forget to check out the dark circles under my eyes."

"What dark circles?"

"*Ha*—as P.J. would say." She turned back toward the kitchen.

He followed her through the room and out the door onto the back porch. "So you heard our conversation."

"Yes." She leaned over to pluck something out of a laundry basket, and those shorts rose even higher on her legs.

He felt like rubbing his eyes the way her son had. Glad for the reminder, he said, "What does P.J. know about Paul's death?"

"What you heard." She shook out a small towel and hung it on the clothesline strung from the porch rail. "It's enough for him now, at his age. I'm not sure he remembers a lot about his daddy. He wasn't even four yet the last time Paul was home."

"And Lissa?"

"Lissa knows more." She jabbed at the line with a clothespin. "She remembers a lot more, too."

"She misses him?"

"Of course she does."

The question seemed to surprise her. He'd bet the next one would leave her stunned. He asked it anyway. "What about you?"

She froze. The bedsheet she held up momentarily hid her face. Then she lowered the sheet and he saw her eyes again.

Dark circles or none, it didn't matter. She'd always had beautiful blue eyes.

"Ben, we've been friends all our lives," she said slowly. "But that's not a question you should be asking me."

"Why not? I'm trying to get a handle on your thoughts, since you're unwilling to come right out and tell me. You said it yourself, we're friends. What's wrong with acting like one?"

"That's just it," she burst out. "It seems like you're always acting with me. And then the night of the wedding, one minute we're friends, and the next we're—" She stopped short, her cheeks reddening. She clutched a damp towel against her. "Never mind. That night was just as much my fault as yours. But you—" Her voice broke. "I can't understand you anymore. I don't know what happened to the friend Paul and I grew up with."

He was the one left stunned now.

She shook out the towel. "Look, it's probably just me. It's been a long night, and I got even less sleep than P.J. did. Let's just forget what I said and agree to another truce, okay?" She gave him a crooked smile. "Don't you have some work to do around here? I know I do."

"Mama?"

At the unexpected voice, they both started. Lissa stood just inside the kitchen doorway. She wore pajamas and had her hair twisted into a handful of braids. Frowning, she looked from him to her mama.

"Stacey just woke up."

"Thanks, sweetie," Dana said. "I'll get her right now."

"Okay." Lissa stared at him for another moment, then left.

So did Dana.

Alone on the porch, he rested against the railing and looked out across her yard. She was right. He had been acting with her for a very long time. For the past year and more, as he tried to keep his promise to Paul. For nearly his whole life, while he hid his feelings for her. And now…

How could he blame her for not knowing what he was trying to do? He'd lost the answer to that himself when he'd gotten roped and tied by his own guilt.

Chapter 6

An hour later, when she heard Kayla greeting the girls in the backyard, Dana sighed in relief. "C'mon, sweetie." She gave Stacey a hug. "Let's go out to your swing."

Kayla stood in the yard, still talking with the girls. Becky had already joined them at the picnic table. Though the five-year-old was much younger, Lissa and the rest of the girls got along well with her. Surprisingly, P.J. did, too. He especially enjoyed her visits when she brought her lively little puppy along.

Today, she'd come without Pirate. Still, her arrival might help him settle down and accept that he needed to be nice to Lissa and the other girls.

She hoped Kayla's arrival might help *her* settle down, too.

After her uneasy conversation with Ben earlier, he had gone upstairs. As he worked in Lissa's bedroom, directly over the kitchen, every squeak of a floorboard made her hold her breath, waiting for his step on the stairs. Every pound of his hammer reassured her she didn't need to worry. For that moment.

On the shady back porch, she strapped the baby into the swing, wound the crank and gave the seat a gentle push. Stacey waved her arms and giggled.

P.J. sat on the top step. He gestured toward the potted plants and gardening tools that took up one end of the porch. "Mama," he said, "there's no place for my dinosaurs to walk."

"I know, sweetie," she said. Most of the plants should have been hung, but she hadn't found time to put up the hooks she'd bought. "I'll make space for them one day soon."

Earlier she had seen him keeping watch on Lissa and her friends, who had gathered at the picnic table. Now that Becky had arrived, he looked almost with longing at the group. "Why don't you go and sit with them? Becky will be happy to see you."

He shook his head. "Nah. I don't wanna play with girls."

"Oh." She smiled. Now wasn't the time to explain that Becky fell into that dreaded category. As she went down the steps, she ruffled his hair.

Kayla had crossed the yard to talk to Dana's next-door neighbor, Clarice, and Tess's aunt Ellamae.

Dana joined them. "Good morning, ladies."

"A loud morning, too," Clarice said.

Her tone surprised Dana. Clarice never minded the kids' play in the yard. And truthfully, the girls hadn't made much noise at all after coming outside this morning. Then her neighbor's gaze drifted to the second floor of Dana's house. The sound of hammering rang through the open bedroom window.

"Ben's here," Ellamae stated.

Dana nodded.

"He's been here quite often lately," Clarice said.

"Stands to reason, doesn't it, since he bought the house?" Ellamae asked. Not waiting for an answer, she sent Dana a sideways glance and added, "He'd help out whether he owned the place or not. In fact, I reckon he's volunteered a time or three before now. That's just his way."

At this obvious attempt to fish for information, Dana clamped her jaw tight. But for a second, doubt assailed her. Ellamae always knew everything. Maybe she was hinting at something. But she couldn't know what had happened here the other night.

There was no use arguing over the older woman's assumption about Ben. Her good opinion of him would never change. Besides, she only said what everyone else in town thought.

"Gotta hand it to him," Ellamae went on. "Ben Sawyer's always been such a good, steady boy. A good thing he bought the house, too. No offense, Dana, but I'll bet there's plenty needs fixing up. That lazy George would let the place fall to ruin. Of course Ben will take care of things over there."

Of course. That was the problem. No one in Flagman's Folly thought twice about Ben helping her. In fact, they expected it. She shivered, thinking of what they would all say if they ever suspected what had happened between the two of them.

"Ben is a *very good* friend to Dana," Clarice said. "He was like a brother to Paul. And you couldn't find a better man than Paul. My Vernon always said so. Rest both their souls..." A loud buzzer almost drowned out her hushed words. When the noise stopped, she said in a normal tone, "Well, that's the dryer." She hurried away.

"Before I forget," Ellamae said, "Roselynn wants y'all to come over tomorrow to welcome the newlyweds home. Two o'clock. Nothing fancy, just burgers. Kayla, you'll tell Sam?"

"Sure. Roselynn mentioned it the other day."

Ellamae turned to her. "You and the kids'll come?"

"Of course."

"Good. I'll leave it to you to extend the invitation to Ben—seeing as he's here more than he's home lately." Ellamae nodded and headed toward Clarice's back door.

Dana bit her tongue. She should have realized Ben would be included in the invitation. But she couldn't back out now.

She and Kayla walked over to stand near the porch. Overhead, Ben's hammering continued.

"Sounds to me like those ladies attempted to say something without coming right out with it." Kayla smiled. "And I can make a good guess what that was. I don't know about Clarice, but Ellamae, at least, wouldn't pass up a chance to do some matchmaking—as Sam and I have good reason to know."

They did. So did Tess and Caleb and a few dozen other couples Dana could name. But she shook her head. "Not this time. Matchmaking would be the last thing on their minds. That was their not-so-subtle reminder."

"Of what?"

"Of the fact Ben was my husband's best friend." As soon as the words left her mouth, she wished she could call them back. Kayla's puzzled expression only emphasized her need to watch what she said. She waved at Stacey, happy in her swing, then forced a laugh. "They just couldn't pass up an opportunity to sing Ben's praises. That's a tune I've heard all my life."

"Maybe he's worth singing over, if he puts all this effort into everything he does. Besides, you've been friends forever, too, haven't you?"

"That's exactly what those two want me to remember." The hammering ended abruptly, and her words sounded loud in the sudden quiet. She lowered her voice. "And it explains why they're so interested in what's going on over here. I'll guarantee they're peeking through Clarice's curtains right now."

Kayla glanced over at the house and smothered a laugh. "You're right."

"I knew it." She sighed. "Kayla, you don't know what you walked into, moving to Flagman's Folly from the big city."

"I'm not sure I'd agree with that. We had our...interested neighbors in Chicago, too."

"Busybodies, you mean. Not like this. It's one of the biggest drawbacks of a small town. Your life is not your own."

"Actually, I love that." To Dana's relief, Kayla held out the plastic file folder she'd been holding and changed the subject. "Here are the copies of the ordinances. I'll leave them with you. Thanks again for keeping Becky while we go to the airport."

"My pleasure. She'll be happy playing with the girls till you get back." She took the folder and tucked it under her arm. "I'll look at this during the week. By then, we should be down to just a final read-through on the proposal. No worries, though—the idea's so perfect, the council won't be able to turn it down. The members will all vote yes the minute they hear about it."

"Is that so?"

She and Kayla both jumped at the sound of the deep voice booming from over their heads. Ben stared down at them from the porch, his hands braced on the railing in front of him.

"What is it we're going to be so all-fired excited about?"

Dana froze. She needed to remember to watch what she said around him, too. Especially around him. Naturally, as chairman of the town council, he would take an interest in any new proposals. "We're not ready to discuss it yet."

"Why not, if you already know which way the vote will go?"

Smiling, Kayla moved a step away. "Gotta run. I'll leave you two to sort this out. Sam and I need to pick up Lianne." She crossed to the group at the picnic table. As she said goodbye to the girls, she signed her words to Becky.

The little girl answered, hands flying in the air.

Dana watched for a moment, smiling. Then, knowing she couldn't avoid Ben forever, she turned and trudged up the steps to the porch.

Arms crossed, he rested against the railing. He'd kept his T-shirt on—thank goodness!—but even through the fabric she could see the muscles of his chest and upper arms flex. *Good old Ben.* The reminder only made things worse. He didn't look a bit old—but he sure looked good.

She could look, couldn't she? Just as long as she didn't touch? As she waved goodbye to Kayla, her fingers trembled.

He glanced across the porch to where P.J. still sat on the top step playing with his toys. "Dinosaurs are fine," he said, his voice low enough that her son didn't hear. "But they're just toys. All kids ought to have a dog."

"Maybe." Shrugging, she glanced at P.J., too, then quickly away.

"Remember Buster Beagle?" Ben asked.

She had to laugh. "Of course. You know I *adored* him. I'd love to have another dog—someday. That just won't work for us right now. I wouldn't want the poor thing cooped up in the house when we're gone all day. And I can't see staking him to a tree in the yard, either." She frowned. "Besides, there are plenty of other things we need around here first."

Like school clothes. A washing machine to replace the one on its last legs. A nest egg to cover all the incidentals she and the kids needed. To pay off all the debts she owed.

Army survivor benefits only took her so far. And if not for Caleb's new ranch, the income from her real estate office wouldn't have taken her anywhere this year.

Ben looked out toward the picnic table. "With all the girls around here," he said, his voice still low, "he could at least use a few other boys around."

P.J. pushed the cardboard box he used as his dinosaur "cave" closer to their side of the porch steps. To get within hearing distance of their conversation, she was sure.

"There aren't any boys his age close by," she said. "And it's hard for parents to set up playdates, especially when they don't live in town. I don't have to convince *you* of that." Why she also didn't want to share her plans, she didn't know…

All right, she knew very well. Once he'd heard about the project, he'd make it one more thing he wanted to help her with.

"It's easier over the summer," she added, "when the kids have more free time. Right, P.J.?"

He nodded, confirming her thought about listening in.

"He went for art classes the past couple of years." She smiled. "That's where we first met Becky and Kayla."

"Yeah, I recall that. Speaking of Kayla, don't you two want to start collecting votes for that proposal you're working on?"

He must have taken fishing lessons from Ellamae. She forced a smile. "Since your eavesdropping told you I'm so sure about the proposal, you must know I'm not worried about votes." Not meeting his gaze, she lifted Stacey from the swing. "You'll just have to wait till the next Town Hall meeting."

"If that's the way you want it." He sounded irritated. "Then I've got a proposal of my own."

She stiffened, her arms unconsciously tightening around the baby, who squirmed. "What are you talking about?"

"I *propose* to take a ride over to the Double S and pick up some tacos to feed this gang lunch."

"Thanks, but I—"

P.J.'s hand on her arm cut her off. He hauled himself to his feet. "Can I go with you? I can help you carry the tacos."

"Sure," Ben said. "Pick up your dinosaurs first, though. You wouldn't want them getting trampled."

"Okay!"

To her surprise, P.J. immediately began scooping the dinosaurs into their cave. He'd reacted with more enthusiasm than he ever showed when she asked him to straighten up his toys. Maybe the lunch menu had given him the incentive. He loved Manny's tacos, but with her need to watch her pennies so closely, they hadn't eaten out in a while.

Over his head, she met Ben's gaze again. Trying to

ignore the sparkle in his dark eyes, she said, "I had lunch planned."

"Not enough for me, I'm sure."

None for you at all. But she couldn't say that with P.J. just inches away.

As it was, he looked up, his forehead wrinkled in concern. "We'll bring a taco home for Mama, too, right, Ben?"

"We sure will. *Two* for your mama," he promised. "After all," he continued, eyeing her as P.J. finished gathering his toys, "I'm working here through the afternoon. We might as well all eat together." He glanced down again. "C'mon, P.J., let's go see how many tacos the girls want."

"Okay." This time, her son took Ben's hand to haul himself to his feet. P.J. lowered his voice and confided, "I can count high. But don't tell the girls if I have to use my fingers."

"No problem, buddy," Ben said as they started across the sun-drenched yard. "Your secret's safe with me."

On the shadowed porch, Dana shivered. Ben's words rang in her head. She didn't want to think about secrets. At least, not her own. But his comment reminded her of the truth she'd kept from her family and friends all these years—the truth about her husband that no one, especially Ben, would ever accept. Because it wouldn't agree with their image of Paul.

Snuggling Stacey even closer, she breathed in the calming scents of baby powder, a laundered playsuit and just plain baby.

Over at the picnic table, Becky looked expectantly at Nate. The older girl raised her eyebrows and curved her hand into a claw, then ran her fingertips down her stomach. *"Hungry?"*

Becky bobbed her fist in the air emphatically. *"Yes!"*

Dana smiled. A shadow in Clarice's living room window caught her eye. The twitch of the curtain confirmed the two women still had her yard under surveillance.

Her smile slid away.

No matter what Kayla said, she couldn't really know what it felt like to live her entire life under a microscope. Dana did.

She loved her hometown and could never see herself leaving it. But even as a child, she'd realized there were things about growing up in Flagman's Folly she'd wished she'd had the power to change.

Such as knowing your past would always haunt you because no one would ever let you forget it.

"Dana went back inside with Stacey," Clarice reported, peering around the edge of the window curtain. "Ben's out in the yard with P.J. and the girls. That man is wonderful with those children. But I'll tell you, Ellamae, he's spending a good deal of time over there. What will people think?"

To tell the truth, Ellamae didn't much care about anyone's opinion but her own. "We covered that, didn't we? He owns the house now. You ought to be happy. Considering all the work he's putting in, he'll raise the property values of the entire neighborhood."

"You think so?"

"Who mails out the town tax statements?" she asked, not expecting an answer. They both knew very well that *she* did.

"Ben's taking off in the truck now," Clarice said. "But he's got P.J. with him, so they'll be back again." She let the curtain fall into place and went over to her recliner.

"I'd like to know what those girls are up to," Ella-mae said.

"Lissa and Nate?"

"No. Dana and Kayla. I heard Kayla came into Town Hall the other day to look up some zoning ordinances."

"What for?"

"I don't know." The admission bothered her. She liked keeping up with what went on in her town. "The judge and I were in court at the time, and nobody in the office asked her." That would never have happened if *she'd* been at the front desk that day.

And she would have asked Kayla outright when they'd all stood outside just a bit ago, if she hadn't been busy working on a more important plan. Or trying to, anyhow.

"I was talking with Kayla just before you pulled up," Clarice said. "She mentioned a proposal for the council."

Ellamae stared at her. "A proposal to do what?"

Clarice shrugged. "She didn't say."

Ellamae bit her tongue. The other woman did her best. Not like some folks who just didn't have a proper curiosity bone in their bodies at all.

As if she'd heard Ellamae's thoughts, Clarice said, "I'll see if I can find out from Dana."

"Good luck with that." Her own lack of progress still rankled. She cared for Dana almost as much as she did her own niece, Tess. One way or another, she'd find a way to get through to that girl. "When it comes to talking, she could give Ben competition. Except when there's something she doesn't want to discuss."

"She's got a hard life, raising those three children on her own. But she never says a word of complaint. Some people like to keep their troubles to themselves."

"Well, they shouldn't," Ellamae said flatly.

Clarice stared at her.

"I mean, they shouldn't be closemouthed with their friends." She ought to be more careful about what *she* said, though. Clarice didn't always understand what she was getting at. And worse, the other woman didn't always agree with her aims. "Talking over troubles is what friends are for."

"Maybe she's doing all her talking with Ben Sawyer now." Clarice shook her head. "I don't know. Maybe him stopping over there isn't so bad. They're friends, aren't they? They'll always have that connection, through Paul. And you know what my Vernon always said, rest his soul. You couldn't find a better man. And wasn't he right? Paul turned out to be a real hero."

"He did, didn't he?"

When Clarice picked up her knitting, Ellamae sat and brooded. Some of the woman's comments had caused her to reconsider her strategy.

"You know, Clarice," she said after a while, "I think on my way home later, I just might stop at Town Hall and look up a few ordinances myself."

"It's Saturday. Town Hall is closed."

Ellamae smiled. "Not to me it isn't."

Chapter 7

Ben loaded his tools into the back of the pickup. "Almost done," he said to P.J. His half-pint helper had trailed him around all afternoon. "I've got just a few more things in the house."

"Don't forget this." With obvious reluctance, P.J. held out the plastic container of washers Ben had given him to carry.

"Hmm." He pretended to deliberate, then said, "Why don't you hang on to it? We'll need it next time I come by."

P.J. grinned. "Okay. I'll go put this on my dresser right now." He rushed away, not even hesitating when he passed the girls still gathered around the picnic table.

Ben followed more slowly.

As he approached Lissa, she looked at him. "Are you staying for supper?" she asked.

Her expression didn't tell him whether she wanted a

yes or no. The thought made him realize that lately, for the first time, he'd had trouble reading Dana, too.

Before he could respond, Nate spoke up. "Of course not, Lissa. Ben's not here for the sleepover. Besides, he came to lunch. If he stays for supper, too, he'd just wear out his welcome. Right, Ben? That's what Aunt El always says."

He smiled. Funny how the two girls seemed to have exchanged their mamas' personalities. Always the outspoken one, Nate took more after Dana, who'd never lacked for something to say.

Except recently.

He nodded at Nate. "You're right. Don't think I'll try pressing my luck tonight."

Still, as he turned toward the house again, he wondered what would happen if he hung around until Dana called the kids in to supper. She couldn't ignore him if he stood right there in front of her. Or could she? He recalled how she'd sidestepped the proposal question.

Worse, out in the yard at lunchtime, he could see how uncomfortable she'd felt around him. A few times, the conversation—and his heart—had lightened after she'd met his eyes. But for the most part, she had kept her gaze averted and had made sure the handful of kids stayed between them.

He entered the house and checked the first-floor rooms. All empty. He made his way upstairs and picked up his tools from Lissa's bedroom. The sound of Dana's voice coming from her own room drew him forward, tugging him as surely as if she'd thrown a lasso to pull him toward her.

Damned wishful thinking.

"I think we'll go have a—"

When he stopped in the doorway, she broke off whatever she planned to say to Stacey, who looked up at her from her walker. Mouth shut tight, Dana eyed him almost warily and eased back a step, stopping short against the bed he'd helped set up years ago. The bed he'd like to help her into right now.

Again, he damned himself. He'd already risked too much with her downstairs on the couch. How could he think of taking her here in the bedroom she once shared with Paul?

The baby smacked the rim of her walker with a plastic rattle. He knelt to chuck her under the chin, and she giggled. "I finished fixing the shelves in Lissa's room," he said.

"Thanks." Her gaze focused on the dresser, the open closet, the light switch on the wall. On anything but him.

Had she read *his* thoughts in his face? Probably not, or she'd have left the room. And still, he wanted to tumble her down on that bed. Rising, he shoved his hands into his back pockets. "I saw Ellamae leaving Clarice's earlier. She said you had a message for me."

Watching the baby, she said, "Roselynn invited folks over for tomorrow. To welcome Tess and Caleb home. Two o'clock."

"Sounds good. Want me to pick you and the kids up on my way over there?"

"That won't be necessary." At last, she looked at him, her brow wrinkled. "Why didn't Ellamae just tell you herself?"

He shrugged. "Maybe she was in a hurry to get home. Does it matter?"

"I don't know. But have you ever known her *not* to have some motive for anything she does?"

Her question reminded him of her claim that he acted with her. He acted now, pretending this conversation could distract him from the thoughts going through his mind.

She picked up the baby. "I'm going to put Stacey in for a nap." She walked around him and out of the room, leaving him standing there staring at that big empty bed.

After a minute, he shook his head and turned to leave.

Lissa stood in the hallway, her frown a match to Dana's and suspicion written all over her face. "What are you doing?"

"Talking with your mama."

Her eyes widened. She leaned into the room to inspect it. "There's nobody in here."

"I know—"

"Lissa?" Dana called. "Are you looking for me?"

"Yes," she answered, but she still stared at him.

Dana appeared in the doorway. "Ben? I thought you'd left. I guess we'll see you tomorrow at the Whistlestop."

So much for an invitation to supper. "Yeah, you sure will."

She and Lissa stepped back from the doorway, and he took his leave. As he went down the hall, he could feel their gazes boring into his back.

Nate had hit it right. He'd outworn his welcome here.

Dana crossed to her dresser and began brushing her hair. Faintly, she heard the front door close downstairs.

"Ben's here a lot now, isn't he?" Lissa asked.

Dana turned. Lissa had always been her quiet child, so unlike P.J. She very seldom talked about anything that bothered her. Both the look on her face when she'd stood staring at Ben and her hesitant question now made Dana's stomach twist.

She couldn't let her feelings for Ben jeopardize her children's relationship with him.

"Why does he have to be here?" Lissa demanded suddenly.

Choosing her words with care, she replied, "Well...he bought this house, and he needs to make a lot of repairs."

"Why? George never fixed anything."

"He did, once in a while. But Ben is eager to get things done."

And that was another thing about Ben Sawyer. His take-charge attitude. A wonderful quality for a man to have—and Ellamae hadn't lied about George. He didn't have it. Neither had Paul. She just wished Ben didn't feel the need to take charge with her.

Lissa frowned. "Nothing ever went wrong in our house when Daddy was here."

"Sweetie, that's not true. Lots of things needed to be done around here, but your daddy didn't always have the...the time."

"Ben sure does."

She nodded. "Yes. He makes the time and goes out of his way to help other people."

"He always helped Daddy, too."

She gripped her brush more tightly. "That's right, he always did."

"But Daddy's gone and he's not coming back. Why does Ben still have to come here?"

She swallowed her surprised gasp. "I told you, he owns our house now. Besides, even though he has work to do here, he likes to have the chance to come and see you and P.J. and Stacey."

"I don't care. I don't want to see him."

How could she tell Lissa that she didn't want to see him, either? She couldn't. Instead, she said softly,

"I know it's hard for you to have Ben over when your daddy's not here anymore. But Ben would be very sad if he couldn't come and see you."

"Then how come he hasn't been here all along?"

"Because he lives on his ranch. You know that. We've visited there many times." But that wasn't what her daughter meant, and she knew it.

"He's not like Daddy," Lissa said. "He didn't go into the army. And he's not like Nate's daddy, either. Caleb was gone being a rodeo star. Ben didn't go anywhere."

"Of course not. He has to take care of his ranch." Although it didn't seem like that lately. She forced a smile. "That's enough talk for now. I think we'd better get downstairs to your guests, don't you?"

Lissa left the room.

She followed, one hand pressed to her stomach, as if that could ease the weight in the pit of it.

The talk with Lissa had only made her feel worse. Every response she gave her daughter reminded her of yet another of Ben's many good qualities.

And of something more.

Once, she had worried herself sick over how little Paul did with their children, how infrequently he even bothered to talk to them. Ben had treated the kids so much better—and had spent more time with them.

All these months she had avoided him, all the days she'd made excuses to prevent him from stopping by the house, she hadn't realized just how much his absence had affected her children. Until now.

P.J. had latched on to him as if afraid he would disappear from their lives again. Lissa had once trailed at Ben's heels, too. And now he'd become a stranger to her; she didn't want him around.

All because Dana had acted out of desperation, trying to save herself from heartache.

A heartache she hadn't managed to escape, after all.

Dana shifted on the picnic bench in the crowded back-yard of the Whistlestop Inn. Most of the townsfolk had showed up to celebrate the return of the happy newly-weds.

The party had started in midafternoon, and the sun now drifted toward the horizon like a worn-out birthday balloon. Still, everyone lingered. Most of the adults had gathered at one end of the yard, while the children played games at the other end. As usual, the women had settled at the picnic tables nearest to the house so they could keep an eye on replenishing food and drinks.

Almost against her will, Dana had found herself keep-ing an eye on Ben.

Now, even as she tried hard to focus on Tess's story about the honeymoon cruise, part of her attention wan-dered a few tables away to where Ben sat with Ellamae's boss, Judge Baylor.

The two men had settled in with a couple of mugs of lemonade and a bowl of chips. They seemed less inter-ested in the food, though, than in what they were dis-cussing. Their gazes occasionally shifted to the tables where the women sat.

More than once, Ben's eyes had met hers. Each time, she looked away hurriedly, yet she couldn't help won-dering what he was thinking. Couldn't help wishing she could turn into a fly and land on their table to listen to their conversation. Or maybe even better, manage to fly away from here altogether.

Too restless to sit still, she jumped up from the bench. "I'll go in and get some more lemonade." She hurried toward the house. Just as she finished refilling the pitcher, the kitchen door opened.

Tess slipped into the room. "Finally!" she exclaimed. "I've waited all day for a few minutes alone with you." She sank into a chair and grabbed a handful of paper napkins. "My excuse for coming inside. Sit a minute. Fill me in. What have I missed?"

Dana took a seat. "Not a lot. Though, thanks to Caleb, the best news is we've lined up a possible new client."

"Yes, he told me Jared's flying in Tuesday. He'll stay with us here. We've got plenty of vacant rooms, unfortunately. But at least that'll keep him handy." Tess laughed. "I can just imagine what Nate and Lissa will say once they hear we have another rodeo star living in Flagman's Folly."

"If we find something to suit him."

"We will. I'll be in early tomorrow to get started."

"You're *that* eager to leave your new husband?"

"Well…actually, he needs to go to Montana for a couple of days. Some trouble with his ranch foreman up there. Believe it or not, though, I *am* ready to get to work again. And it's so nice to be home."

"And to see everyone, I'm sure. Especially Nate."

"That, too. You were right—she survived fine without me. I hear she had a great time at your house with the girls." She raised her brows. "I also hear they weren't the *only* ones spending time with you."

Dana tried not to sigh. Of course Tess would have found out immediately. "I suppose you mean Ben buying the house."

"I do. What a surprise. Mom and Aunt El couldn't wait to *share the news.*"

Despite the situation with her new landlord, Dana responded with the second half of their inside joke. *"Of course not,"* she said, managing to keep a straight face until Tess rolled her eyes. Then they both burst into laughter.

"Anyhow," Tess continued, "I know George wasn't the greatest landlord, and he certainly didn't keep up with all the house repairs. You must be so glad to have Ben there."

Glad? If she only knew...

The kitchen door opened, and Ellamae peered from around the edge of it. "You girls planning to stay in here all afternoon? We've got thirsty people outside waiting for that lemonade."

"Coming right up," Dana said, grabbing the pitcher again. The interruption couldn't have come at a better time—because she couldn't have come up with a decent response to Tess's comment if they *had* sat at this table all afternoon.

Her best friend would never understand why she didn't want to have Ben around. No one would, unless she told the truth about Paul. And she couldn't do that.

Without a word, she followed Tess and Ellamae outside.

A couple of the men had joined the group of women at their picnic tables. Not Ben, though.

No matter how she tried to stop herself, she immediately found herself seeking him again.

Before she could glance away, he turned his head in her direction. For a long moment, she *couldn't* look away. Like a scene from a movie, everything around her—the conversation, the laughter, the movement—all seemed to stop. As if, for just that moment, only the two of them stood in the yard.

Which was ridiculous.

She forced herself to turn toward the nearest table. Hands shaking, she grabbed a paper cup and filled it with lemonade. As she sipped the drink, she glanced around her. No one seemed to have noticed anything. Yet again, she gave in to the urge to look in Ben's direction. He now sat leaning forward, listening to Judge Baylor.

Could she have imagined that frozen moment?

Fortunately, she didn't have time to think about it.

"Over here, Dana," Ellamae called. "Bring that pitcher."

Happy to oblige, she chose a seat across from Tess and Caleb, putting her back to Ben and the judge.

At the next table, Kayla sat with her sister, Lianne. With their long, honey-blond hair and blue eyes, they could have passed for twins. Like her little niece, Becky, Lianne was deaf. Unlike Becky, she used her voice and could read lips when people faced her directly as they spoke to her.

At the moment, Lianne was carrying on a conversation with Becky, Lissa and Nate, who had just slid onto the vacant bench at their table.

Caleb had draped his arm around Tess, and she leaned into him, her face the picture of contentment. Dana's heart swelled at the sight of her friend's happiness.

"So, Caleb," Ellamae said, "you decide yet what you're doing with that new property you're buying?"

"Running it as a working ranch, for one thing, raising cattle. Maybe some horses."

"Rodeo horses!" Lissa said eagerly, speaking like a true rodeo fan.

"And then we can come out and ride them!" Nate said. "Right, Becky?" She put her thumbs against her temples with the first two fingers of either hand extended. *"Horses!"*

Becky laughed and fluttered her upright hands in the air. *"Yay!"*

Tess laughed, too. "Gee, I wonder where this little once-upon-a-time city girl caught the horse bug?"

From hanging around with Nate, Lissa and the other girls, of course, who had all long ago been bitten by the rodeo bug.

"That's an idea," Caleb told the girls, smiling at them. "A ranch can always use more horses."

"How about a dude ranch?" Kayla asked. "You could bring in vacationers from the city, too."

Ellamae, Clarice and a few of the other older women told her what they thought of that—nothing at all.

"City folks who come to stay are one thing," Ellamae said. "Dudes are something else."

"I have an idea," Lianne said. "What about a kids' camp?"

Caleb's brows shot up. He turned so she could see his face. "Not a bad suggestion, Lianne."

Other folks at the table nodded agreement.

"That's not the only good idea around here this afternoon," Ellamae announced. "Dana, we've been talking about you. Or rather, reckon I should say we were talking about Paul."

Dana had just topped off a cup of lemonade for the woman next to her. For a moment, she froze with the pitcher in midair.

"Yes," said Clarice, "we think it's high time folks in town did something to honor him."

"Sounds good," Caleb said. "What do you have in mind?"

"Not sure yet," Ellamae said. "We've just started planning it. We're thinking of setting up a statue in his memory."

Dana wrapped her hands around her cup and stared down at the pulp swirling in the lemonade. Her insides felt as though they were swirling, too. She desperately needed a drink but didn't feel sure she could swallow.

"We'll need to get folks on board," Ellamae continued. "Talk up the idea, do some fundraising."

"Count me in."

Startled, she gripped her cup so tightly, it threatened to buckle. Ben had spoken from directly behind her. Having the women talk about her husband was bad enough. Having him add his two cents was almost more than she could bear.

"Isn't it, Dana?"

He had moved to stand at the end of the picnic table near her. She shifted on the bench, hoping to hide her reaction from everyone. "What?"

"I said the statue, or whatever the group decides on, is no more than Paul deserves."

"You're right there," said Ellamae, directing attention her way again.

As the conversation continued, Dana slowly let out the breath she'd been holding and gave silent thanks to the older woman for saving her from another awkward situation. From having to respond when she had no clue what to say.

She had no idea how to handle her reaction whenever Ben came near her, either. The past year and more had already strained her nerves. The past couple of weeks had stretched them almost to the point of snapping. Here at the Whistlestop, at her office, and, worst of all, now even in her home, her frequent contact with him only made it harder for her to forget.

To forget what they'd done that night after the wedding.

To forget Paul, the best friend Ben had lost, the boy and later the man everyone in Flagman's Folly had looked up to. Paul, the husband she had stopped loving long before he had died.

She lived with that knowledge daily. She didn't need any reminders. And she certainly didn't want a statue— a solid, unmovable, *permanent* reminder—of memories she longed to forget.

From the end of the table, Ben frowned and watched her.

With a shaking hand, she raised her cup to her lips and took a cautious sip. Though she managed to swallow, the lemonade didn't do a thing to steady her. It didn't help calm her racing thoughts at all. It didn't give her a single solution.

How could it, when she had no way out of her dilemma?

Sometimes, she dreamed about telling folks the truth. About what Paul was like. About how he had treated her. But for her children's sake, she couldn't. For Ben's sake, she wouldn't. She was well and truly trapped, stuck forever in a web of deceit.

A web she had spun herself.

Ben downed another mouthful of lemonade. The tart flavor on his tongue almost hid the bitter taste Dana's reaction had left in him a while earlier.

Almost.

Across the picnic bench from him, Caleb said, "The statue for Paul sounds like a great idea."

Ben agreed. Too bad Dana didn't see it that way. "He deserves all the accolades we can give him."

"You're right," Caleb said emphatically, looking shaken.

Ben well understood that. Though Caleb had grown up in Flagman's Folly, he hadn't been around when they'd learned of the tragedy of Paul's death. He'd only found out on his return to town.

Folks here still hadn't gotten over the shock. No wonder Caleb looked upset. "You knew about his decision to join up?" he asked now.

"Yeah, he told me ahead of time. That's a day I'll never forget."

Because the announcement had come as a complete surprise.

"You get to talk to him after he enlisted?"

"Yeah. A few times. He came home one last time, too. He'd seen a lot of action, things he didn't want to talk about. You know Paul, though. He took on the role of soldier the way he did everything else." With determination and the desire to excel and an almost uncanny belief that nothing would get in his way. To that point, nothing had. "You should've seen all his medals."

They'd met up several times in that brief trip Paul had made home, and Ben was pleased when Paul stopped by the ranch again on his way out of town. That visit added one more entry…one final entry…to his store of memories of his best friend.

He'd been different that last time, edgy, uptight and distracted. Eager to get back to action, or so Ben had figured. Impatient to return to his new life or not, something had riled him up that day. He couldn't have known he would never see Flagman's Folly again.

Or, maybe he'd had a premonition of some kind, telling him he would never return.

Whatever he'd had on his mind, Ben suspected it had triggered the recollections Paul shared that day. Had prodded him to remind Ben about their past, to reinforce their long friendship. To talk about the bond between them.

A soldier, Paul said, needed to be able to rely on his platoon, to trust the men who had his back.

The way he trusted Ben.

That's when he had asked Ben to watch over his family, speaking with an intensity that gave his request the weight of a solemn oath. With the same determination Paul had shown all through his life, Ben took that oath, knowing he would let nothing get in his way. He had never anticipated having to carry it out.

And then...

"Tess told me how it happened," Caleb said. "About the evacuation."

"Yeah. They got the women and kids out of the village, saved them all."

And then Paul's platoon was ambushed. In the chaos that followed, Paul dragged one of the downed soldiers to safety. Yet he hadn't been able to dodge a bullet himself.

In an instant, his best friend was gone.

"Paul died a hero," he said flatly.

And Ben had been left to fulfill his oath.

He could never break the promise he'd made. Never betray his best friend's trust. Yet, hadn't he done that, after all?

Hadn't making love with Dana been the ultimate betrayal?

If nothing else would force him to keep his hands off his best friend's widow, that would.

His best friend's widow...

Again, his stomach churned at the sourness of the lemonade he'd swallowed, mixed with the remembrance of Dana's reaction earlier. She didn't like the idea of a tribute to her husband. He couldn't understand it.

How could she *not* want to honor Paul?

Chapter 8

"I don't know, El," Roselynn said, frowning as she loaded glasses into the dishwasher. "You might be wrong this time."

Ellamae looked sharply at her sister. The last of the guests had just left the Whistlestop, and they were alone in the kitchen.

"Wrong about what?" Ellamae demanded.

"The statue for Paul."

She glared. "When we talked about it last night, you thought it was a fine idea."

"And I still do. It's a wonderful honor for him. But I'm not sure what we should do about Dana. The poor girl looked like she didn't know which way to turn when you brought it up this afternoon."

Tess walked into the room with a load of serving trays. "Almost done," she said.

She didn't always care for what her aunt and mama

got up to. Ellamae kept her mouth shut until she had left the room again. Then she said, "Dana will get used to the idea."

"But if she's still suffering so much…"

Roselynn always had been the pushover. "I wouldn't do anything to hurt Dana," Ellamae said gruffly.

"Of course I know that. But we don't really know how she feels. And Tess is as unsure about this as we are."

We? Normally, she would have snorted at that. *She* was never unsure about anything.

But for the moment, she needed to be careful about telling certain things to softy Rose. And to Tess. She also needed to uncover a few additional facts herself. That didn't present a problem. She could always work her way around an obstacle, once she set her mind to it.

For a good cause, of course.

Tess came into the kitchen carrying a couple of table-cloths. "I'll go throw these in the laundry, Mom."

"Hold on, Tess," Ellamae said. "Got a question for you. How'd you like to be on our committee for the memorial for Paul?"

"Oh. Well…" Tess's gaze swung to her mama and back to Ellamae again. For a moment, she looked the way Rose claimed Dana had—like she didn't know where to turn. But she nodded. "Sure, I'd love to."

"Good." Ellamae smiled.

Yeah, she could always work her way around anything.

At noon on Tuesday, Dana walked the short distance from Wright Place Realty to the Double S. Her brisk pace and the warm sunshine on her shoulders made some of her tension ease. Not having seen Ben for a couple of days might have had something to do with that, too. She and Tess had worked late last night, rounding up properties for their client to view. When she arrived home, Anne said her landlord had left.

Now she turned the corner onto Signal Street and came to an abrupt stop.

Ben stood in front of the Double S, leaning against his pickup truck. Try as she might, she couldn't keep her pulse from fluttering.

After a long, deep breath, she walked up to him. "What brings you to town in the middle of a workday?"

"A long list of overdue errands. Then I figured, as long as I was here, I'd stop for a cup of coffee."

Obviously, he wasn't having issues with his ranch foreman, as Caleb was. But her heart sank. "You're just going in?"

He shook his head. "Just coming out. I've got a few things to do before I head over to your house."

"Well, so long."

She turned away. He put his hand on her wrist. His touch warmed her more completely than the sun had done—and every muscle it had relaxed now tightened again. She slid her hand free.

"What's your hurry?" he asked.

"I'm early for a meeting here, and I want to get some paperwork done."

"For your proposal?"

She should've known better than to hope he'd forgotten. That was part of the trouble with Ben. He had one of the best—and longest—memories she'd ever known. "No. I told you. We're not quite done with that yet."

"Ellamae and her buddies will be busy drawing up a proposal of their own. For Paul," he added, as if she didn't know what he'd meant. "I have to say, you didn't appear to think much about their idea the other day."

"I didn't expect to have to think about it at all," she said. "They sprang it on me out of nowhere."

"That's not much of a…reason for not showing a little more enthusiasm."

She gripped the handle of her briefcase. *"Reason?"* she repeated. "Why do I need to give you a reason for my feelings?"

He shrugged. "Okay," he conceded. "Maybe you don't. But as you've mentioned it, how *do* you feel about it, anyhow?"

She exhaled in exasperation and stared at him. "And why do you think you have the right to ask that, either?" She shook her head. "Ben, what's gotten into you?"

"I could ask you the same question. Paul is a hero, dammit."

Yes, she wanted to shoot back at him. *A hero to you and all the folks in town.*

Once, long ago, Paul had been her hero, too.

For as long as she had known him, he could do no wrong in anyone's eyes, including her own, from his grade school days all the way up through senior high. And after his success on the football team, he'd guaranteed his place in the town's history as their golden boy. But gold tarnished. Fame didn't last forever. Neither had her relationship with Paul.

She couldn't say that to Ben, who now stood glaring at her. She couldn't say that to anyone.

"Folks want to do something to honor him," he said, "and you don't seem to want any part of it."

His voice had risen a notch, and she cringed. She didn't intend to talk about this with him. Not now. Not ever. And especially not right here.

Footsteps sounded on the sidewalk behind her. She

only hoped whoever approached hadn't heard Ben's words.

"Dana?"

The deep voice so close behind her made her jump. Turning, she looked up at the new client she had met just that morning.

A very good-looking man, Jared Hall stood a smidge taller than Ben. But he didn't have Ben's broad shoulders. He didn't have Ben's sparkling dark eyes. And, she discovered to her dismay, he didn't thrill her the way Ben did.

"Jared Hall." He held out his hand.

Quickly, she introduced the men, who stood eyeing each other. "Well," she blurted into the silence, "I guess Jared and I should get to work."

"Yeah," Ben said, putting his hand on her wrist again. "I'll see you later."

Casual words. Words anyone might say to a friend. But his lingering touch and intimate tone gave a completely different impression. Before she could ward it off, a shiver of excitement ran through her. Disgust at herself immediately followed. He'd done that deliberately, as if to prove something to her.

Or to Jared.

Unsteadily, she turned away.

As she and Jared walked toward the Double S, she heard no movement behind her, no sound of a pickup door opening. Ben still watched them.

When Jared held open the door of the café, she looked up at him and…deliberately…gave him a wide smile. But as they entered, she didn't dare look toward the street.

Inside the café, Dori and Manny greeted her with their usual beaming smiles.

"I heard you had my pastries on Saturday," Dori said. "You enjoyed them, yes?"

"Absolutely," Dana assured her.

"Along with my tacos," Manny said. He and Dori had a friendly rivalry about which of their specialties brought customers into the Double S.

"Yes, along with the tacos," Dana said, laughing. She introduced Jared, then led him to a corner booth.

Dori followed, carrying the tea and coffee they had ordered. "Also," she said, "I hear there is big excitement in town about your Paul."

Dana tightened her grip on the paper napkin she'd just spread across her lap. "That's right. Ellamae and some of the other folks are planning something."

"Yes, it was Ellamae who told me this morning. A very good thing. Everyone here says the same."

"Yes," she murmured.

When Dori walked away, Dana lifted her teacup and smiled across the booth at Jared, not seeing him. Her mind had gone far away in time but just a few blocks away in distance, back a year and more ago to the day she had learned of Paul's death.

The news had left her reeling. Not because of what he had meant to her but because he no longer meant anything to her at all.

Not for her sake but for their children's.

The daughter who idolized her daddy. The son who looked the image of him. And the baby she had just, days before, discovered she carried inside her.

Ben couldn't have realized what his pushing about her feelings had done to her.

Deep inside, she recognized that Paul had given his life bravely and that folks looked up to him for that sacrifice. Yet she couldn't get past her own knowledge of him.

Of the man he had never been.

Not a day passed without a bitter memory of how she'd felt about her marriage. About her husband. Still trying to deal with her disappointment in both, how could she face the idea of a statue in his honor?

Ben got through the rest of his errands, then headed to where he wanted to be. Dana's house.

No, *his* house. Dana's home.

The sitter had already picked up the kids. When he drove up and parked near the garage, he found them all on the front porch. He could see Dana's van coming down the street. Couldn't have timed his arrival any better.

As he got out of the truck, P.J. ran up. "Am I helping you today, Ben?" he asked.

"You sure are."

"Good."

A second after Dana parked beside the pickup truck, the passenger door opened and Lissa and Nate spilled from the van.

Ben looked at Nate in surprise. "What are you doing here? I thought for sure you'd go right home from school to spend some time with your mama and daddy, now they're back from their trip."

"They're not home."

As the two girls ran off, Dana said, "Tess took Caleb to the airport. He's going to Montana for a couple of days."

"Did you get things taken care of with your rodeo cowboy?"

"No. In fact, we're getting together again tonight."

"Tonight? You mean, you're dating him?"

She raised her eyebrows. Well, all right, maybe he'd been a bit too blunt. But seeing the man with her hadn't set right with him. Not at all. Thinking of her going out with him...

"No, not a date. We're meeting at the office to go over some listings."

She pulled a sack from Harley's out of the back of the van.

Seeing that she'd come from the market gave him other things to think about. It reinforced the thoughts he'd had about her lately, about how much responsibility she carried now that Paul was gone. The list of jobs he'd found needed doing around this house only added to his concerns.

Since Paul's death, Dana had become a single mom, sole breadwinner and the person who needed to take care of her family. And her home. And anything else that might arise, such as the proposal she was working on. The one she still wouldn't tell him about.

She reached into the van for another grocery sack and slammed the door.

"Can I carry those for you?"

She shook her head. "It's okay, I can handle them."

Without your help, her words implied. Surprise at her attitude no longer registered with him.

P.J. had waited quietly but now burst out, "Mama, I have to help Ben today!"

"Is that so?"

"Yep." He nodded. "We can hang up the flowers you have out on the porch."

"The flowers?" she asked.

"Please, Mama." He nearly bounced up and down in his eagerness. "Then I'll have more room for my dinosaurs."

For a moment she looked distressed, and then she smiled at him and nodded. "Sure, that would be great."

"Good. But you gotta come help, too. You gotta tell us where to put the flowers."

"I do?"

Her gaze moved to Ben, as if she suspected he had put her son up to the idea. Turning, she walked toward the house, P.J. beside her. "I'll need to take care of the groceries first."

Obviously, the thought of helping them didn't appeal to her. He wasn't sure he much cared for it, either. He didn't need the torture of working that close and not being able to touch her.

By rights, he probably should stay away altogether. Yet he looked for any excuse he could find to see her again.

He ground his teeth together. He'd been seeing her all his life. Why the hell would he need an excuse to do that now?

Another concern to add to the list of those that had plagued him lately. Concern about loyalty to the best friend who had trusted him to watch over his wife and children. Concern about the compassion he felt for this woman he'd known forever and was beginning to respect more each day—this woman who had so much on her plate.

This woman who still grieved for her husband.

Clamping his jaw shut against the words he wanted to say, he followed the two of them through the house and into the kitchen.

Abruptly, P.J. backed toward the door. "I forgot. I gotta get my tools." He turned and ran from the room.

Dana began unloading the sacks. "I know he's upset about not having room to play with his toys. I intended to get around to those plants very soon." Her voice shook with anger.

"I have no doubt about that. And for the record, I had

nothing to do with the idea. P.J. came up with it on his own."

She squared her shoulders and stared at him in disbelief.

That did it.

"Hold off on those groceries." In a half-dozen strides, he crossed the room. "We need to talk about what's going on here."

"As in...?"

"As in, what is it with you? First, for all these months, you refused to let me do anything for you—I had to buy an office building and now this damn house to manage to help you at all. And now, you don't believe me about P.J.?"

"I didn't say that."

Once again, her voice shook. He could see the tears in her eyes. Maybe she felt as frustrated as he did. But there was something else in her face, something he had trouble reading.

That had happened more and more often lately. It bothered the hell out of him.

But right now, he didn't need to read her expression.

He put both hands on her shoulders and turned her to face him squarely. "Dana, what you said with your words and what you're saying with your body language are two different things. Why are you making this situation so hard for us?"

"Because *I* should be the one to give P.J. the space to play with his toys."

Baffled, he shook his head. "What's the difference who hangs up those plants? Not everyone wants or has the skills to do handyman chores. Or sometimes they can't do them alone. Look how many times I came over to give Paul a hand. How is my helping him back then any different from my coming here to help you now?"

"I don't—"

Need your help.

He could hear the words. Before she could say them, he reached up to touch his fingertip above her upper lip. It silenced her immediately—a good thing, because as the warmth of her skin jolted through him, he had to pull his hand away.

Later, he'd worry about the reaction. Now he couldn't let it distract him. He let the safer feeling of irritation take over again.

He leaned forward, looking into her wide blue eyes. "You can't turn away from more than twenty years of friendship. Or at least, I can't. If you won't take help from me for yourself, at least accept it for your kids."

"I have been, haven't I?" As if she suddenly fought a smile, one corner of her mouth twitched. "Lord knows, Clarice and Ellamae think you've become a permanent boarder here."

P.J. ran into the kitchen. "Ready!" He shook the plastic canister Ben had given him, making the washers rattle. "C'mon, let's go." He grabbed Ben's hand and tugged. "C'mon, Mama."

"As soon as I finish unpacking the groceries," she told him. "You two go ahead."

"Okay."

P.J. pulled harder, and Ben let himself be towed through the kitchen and out the door. Once on the porch, the boy kept busy running back and forth to the picnic table, moving his dinosaurs out of harm's way.

Ben welcomed the breathing space, the chance to get his thoughts together. If he could.

Before, he'd had a long list of questions. Those, he'd

understood. What he couldn't deal with now was the thought that had raced through his mind when he'd touched Dana. And the added wagonload of guilt that had followed.

He didn't want to be her boy next door any longer. He wanted a chance with her—and he aimed to get it.

Chapter 9

Between the two of them, Dana and Tess had kept Jared on the run to various properties all around the state. On Friday, they met at the office to plan their weekend strategy.

"He's mine for the rest of the afternoon," Dana said. "The owner of that property outside Tucumcari called, and we're going down there to meet with him."

If not for being away from the kids, she wouldn't have minded the long ride. On the other hand, it gave her something she wanted. An excuse to stay busy. In these few days since she had helped Ben and P.J. with the flowers out on the porch, she'd needed something to occupy her mind. To keep her from dwelling on that afternoon. Ben's reminder of all the times he'd come by the house to help Paul had stirred up too many memories for her to think about.

His touch had stirred up too many emotions for her to handle.

"You're awfully preoccupied," Tess said.

She'd spoken in a teasing tone. Still, the words startled Dana. She hoped the reaction hadn't shown in her face. That wouldn't do. She needed to be very careful with Tess. With Ben. With everyone.

"You also seem awfully eager to escort Jared around in the afternoons." Tess smiled. "And I heard you went out with him last night. Are you sure you're not angling for more than dinner invitations with him? He's a good-looking man."

Dana forced a laugh. "The only thing I'm angling for is to give you and Caleb more newlywed time now that he's back from Montana. After all, you're still pretty much on your honeymoon, aren't you?"

Now, it was Tess's turn to laugh. "Yes, that's true. So I guess I'll head back home. You'll be picking Jared up at the Whistlestop?"

She nodded. "I'll be right behind you."

"Okay. But you know…" Tess's tone turned serious. "It's not a bad thing if you're interested in a man again."

"Tess, please don't."

"Okay, I won't. For now. Then, on another subject, do you and Kayla plan to present your proposal Monday night?"

"Yes."

"Good. I can't wait till you get it approved. I don't know why no one else ever thought of building a playground in town. But it's a great idea."

"We think so, too," she said, pouncing on the new topic. "I expect you and Caleb will be able to make use of it one of these days soon. And I don't mean for Nate, either."

Tess grinned. "I sure hope so. But it might be a little while before we need to think about that. Anyhow, I'm sure the council will go for the idea, hands down. Speaking of which…" she paused, then went on "…I'm on the committee for the other proposal. For the memorial in Paul's memory—"

Dana tried not to cringe.

"—and they asked me to find out if you'd like to join us."

"Oh." Avoiding her friend's eye, she reached for the pen she'd left lying on her desk. "Please," she began, "tell them I appreciate that they asked, but…but I think it would be best for the group to make their decisions without me. Besides, Kayla and I already have our proposal."

Tess nodded. "I thought you might turn us down," she said softly, "but folks wanted you to know they'd offered."

After Tess left the office, Dana slumped back in her chair and groaned.

What had she set herself up for? What kind of a tangled mess had she made with her web of deceit?

With all her efforts to hide the truth about Paul, she had never expected things to come to this. To the bizarre twist brought about by her misplaced pride. And by everyone's misperceptions of her marriage.

She didn't want to be held up as the iconic war widow. She didn't want any part of their tribute at all.

How could she have said any of that to Tess?

She couldn't, and there was no use even thinking about it.

She pushed herself upright and grabbed the phone on her desk. Then she punched the speed dial for her home number and sat biting her lip while the line engaged.

Ben had said he would be by around this time. He might already have arrived. Fortunately, she was going far away in another direction, and he'd be long gone by the time she got home.

The babysitter answered the phone on the second ring.

"Yep, everything is fine here," Anne said. "And since you're going to be a little late tonight, I've challenged P.J. to a checkers marathon. That'll keep him from bothering Lissa."

"That's great, Anne, thanks. I'll have my cell on if you need me." Dana hung up the office phone and pulled her handbag out from the bottom drawer of her desk.

Time to head over to the Whistlestop Inn to pick up the man who had so recently entered her life.

Time to stop thinking about the man who had always been part of it.

Long hours later, Dana dropped off their client at the Whistlestop.

"Thanks for everything, Jared."

Their trip out of town had taken much longer than she'd anticipated. He and the ranch owner had hit it off, and their meeting had led to an invitation for a late, lengthy supper.

On the return trip, still hours from Flagman's Folly, the battery of her van had died. In the harsh, dry heat of the Southwest, batteries didn't last that long to begin with. Neither did a few dozen other parts of a vehicle. The wear and tear of a job that took her all over the state only added to the chances of something going wrong.

"I'm glad you weren't alone," he said.

"Me, too. This could've happened at any time. I was lucky."

"We both were." He smiled at her. "I enjoyed the trip."

She smiled back and watched him go up the steps of the inn. When the door closed behind him, she turned the van in the direction of home. They had been lucky, also, to find a mechanic willing to come and tow the van back to his garage, where she bought the new battery.

Between all that and the long ride home, it was now well after 2 a.m. She wanted nothing more than to get back to the house, kiss her kids and crawl into bed.

Again, she felt guilty about being away from the kids for so long, although since Paul's death, they'd gotten used to being left with a sitter in the evenings once in a while. Anne had put them to bed on more than one occasion.

She'd called home several times to check in and was relieved to hear that everything had been going well.

But after all Anne's reassurances, she now felt surprised—and concerned—when she pulled up in front of the house and saw Ben's truck still beside the garage.

Leaving her van in the driveway, she hurried across the lawn. If not for the time, the sight of the truck wouldn't have alarmed her. Ben always wanted to wrap up a project the same day, if he could. But he'd never stayed this late before.

She nearly tripped going up the steps. It took her a couple of tries to fit her key into the lock. When she finally pushed the door open, the sight in the living room froze her in place.

Ben lay sprawled on the couch, watching television. Seeing him so relaxed lowered her anxiety immediately. But why hadn't he left? Frowning, she asked, "Are the kids okay?"

"Fine. All upstairs in their beds, asleep."

"Good. But where's Anne? And what are you doing here?"

"She didn't want to let you down, but when you called and said you'd be home so late, she finally told me she had a hot date waiting. I volunteered to stay." He yawned widely. "To answer your question, I'm the replacement babysitter."

She bit her lip. Much as she wished she hadn't come home to find him here, she couldn't argue about his stepping in this time. Though she trusted Anne, this late at night, she appreciated having a responsible adult in the house.

Adults couldn't come much more responsible than Ben.

And men couldn't come much sexier.

His hair tumbled on his forehead as if he'd run his fingers through it a dozen times. His eyes looked heavy-lidded from fighting off sleep.

Slowly, quietly, she closed the door behind her and advanced into the room. "Thank you," she said.

"You're welcome." After tossing the television remote onto the coffee table, he scrubbed his face with his hands. "The van held out all the way back here?"

"Yes, as I told Anne on the phone, it was just the battery."

"Guess I'd better head home," he said. He yawned again.

"You don't look like you're in any shape to drive."

"I'll be fine."

She glanced toward the stairway, took a deep breath and looked back at him again. "Why don't you stay the night," she suggested. "That is, for what's left of it."

He stared at her for a long moment, his eyes half-closed, an unreadable expression on his face. Or maybe it was just fatigue.

"I'll be fine," he said again.

"I'd rather not have you take the chance." A sudden case of nerves made her babble. "You look dead on your feet—or you would if you could stand up, and I'm not completely sure you can do that. There aren't any empty beds in the house, but you can spend the rest of the night here on the couch."

Her final word hung in the air. Neither of them needed the reminder. But that was over. Done with. It wouldn't happen again. She *would not* think about it.

And it was crazy to feel this anxious about inviting him to stay. Late as it was, she'd planned to insist that Anne sleep over until the morning, anyhow. Did it really matter that Paul's best friend and not her babysitter slept in her living room?

"Honestly, Ben. I appreciate your helping out tonight, and I wouldn't want to feel responsible for something happening to you on the way home just because you stuck around to watch over my kids. You can have the couch—it's no big deal. You've slept on it before." She took another breath, let it out and added, "After all, we're friends, aren't we?"

And after all, it wasn't as though she was propositioning him.

His sudden piercing look made her wonder if he'd thought exactly that.

She dropped her bag onto the nearest chair. "You're staying," she said firmly.

After yawning once more, he shrugged and reached for the hem of his T-shirt. In one swift movement he pulled the shirt over his head, exposing lots of lean, tanned skin.

She moved toward the stairs. "I'll just run up and get you some linens."

Run described her escape from the room perfectly.

Even while staring at Ben on that couch, she'd managed to keep all the memories of their night together out of her mind. But once he'd pulled off his T-shirt... Once she'd seen him half-naked in the dark intimacy of the living room lit only by the glow of a small lamp and the television screen... The sight had done something wild to her pulse. And the memories had flooded her mind.

It's only good old Ben, she told herself, hands shaking as she sorted through her linen closet. But the reminder didn't work this time.

To her dismay, she had a feeling it would never work again.

Alone in her bed a little while later, Dana struggled to calm her breathing. And her racing thoughts. Awareness of her unexpected guest downstairs troubled her. But she had to confess Ben's nearness excited her, too.

At long last, she fell into a restless, dream-filled sleep.

She was abruptly awakened from it, first by the sound of P.J.'s bedroom slippers slapping on the stairs and then by his exuberant greeting. He'd just discovered Ben in the living room.

If the brightness of her room didn't tell her she'd overslept, one look at her alarm clock did.

She exhaled in exasperation. Seven-thirty. But after all, it was Saturday. By rights, she couldn't actually resent that Ben had slept in, considering he'd been up so late only to help her out. On the other hand, he should have been long gone before any of the kids were up.

Especially Lissa. Since their talk, Dana had kept a close eye on her daughter, who still seemed irritated by having Ben around. Finding him there when she first woke up wouldn't improve her disposition any! With luck, Lissa would sleep in as usual on a Saturday, and Ben *would* be gone by the time she came downstairs.

She slid her arms into her robe and tied it tightly

around her. Quickly, she went to the head of the stairs and looked down into the living room.

She could just see Ben on the couch with the sheets rumpled around him, the pale yellow fabric highlighting his dark hair and tanned skin. His hair was even more tousled this morning, making him look younger and bringing back a flood of memories.

Ben with his hair dripping water onto his face the day at Sidewinder Creek when they'd all learned to swim.

With his clothes tousled after the entire seventh grade had camped out on his daddy's ranch.

With his eyes shining when he'd come to visit at the hospital the night Lissa was born.

Those and other memories—too many memories— she didn't want to think about.

Instead, she went down the stairs and focused on P.J., who sat leaning against the arm of the couch, his feet braced on Ben's thigh. He gestured with both hands and spoke at top speed. "And we were on this *huge* checkerboard, Ben! There were dinosaurs all over, too. They *flew* down the mountain—and then they landed. And they *smooshed* all the flowers flat like pancakes!"

"Really?" Ben asked. His lips tightened. She knew he was holding back a laugh. "That's one heck of a dream, buddy."

"Yep. It was fun." Spotting Dana, he grinned. "Mama, Ben played checkers with me all night."

"Not quite. Only till bedtime," Ben clarified, exchanging glances with her.

"I guess I owe you another thank-you."

"Why? It's not like it's the first time I've played games with the kids."

She stopped those memories before they could start.

"If you feel the need for more thanks," he continued, "I'll take them for dealing with Stacey's diaper last night."

When he grinned, she bit her lip to keep from smiling back.

P.J. squealed. "You changed Stacey's *dirty diaper?*"

Ben nodded. "Sure did. I changed yours once or twice when you were her age, too."

"Ew-w-w-w."

The doorbell rang. Undoubtedly happy for the distraction, P.J. slid from the edge of the couch and ran toward the entryway.

The sound of the bell had made Dana anything but happy. Who on earth would come calling at this hour?

Ben raised one eyebrow, probably thinking the same thing. He sat back and rested one bare arm along the back of the couch as if settling in for a nice, long conversation with whoever had rung the bell.

She swallowed a moan. He could—and did—talk to anyone, anytime. But obviously he hadn't thought twice about who might find him sitting on her living room couch. Could she somehow casually ask him to leave the room? Or at least to put his T-shirt back on?

And call attention to the fact that she'd noticed—and been bothered by—his half-nakedness?

No, she couldn't.

She tugged on her belt again. P.J. looked through the side window and then rushed to throw the door wide open. He knew better than to do that with a stranger, which meant the visitor had to be someone he knew.

Did that make this situation better or worse? It wouldn't matter either way, if she could just keep the person outside. She hurried to join P.J.

Her next-door neighbor stood on the doorstep. Dana's annoyance evaporated immediately. "Clarice, are you okay?"

"I was about to ask you the same question. Just thought I'd check…" She looked Dana over from head to toe. Then she peered around P.J. into the living room. *"Ben?"* She proceeded to look *him* over from head to…torso.

In spite of the situation, Dana found herself holding back a laugh. Clarice's inspection had definitely come to a halt at chest level. Eighty-five years old, and the woman obviously still recognized a good thing when she saw it.

P.J. lost interest and wandered toward the kitchen.

Clarice's gaze met hers again.

For a moment she held on to hope that only idle nosiness had brought the older woman here this morning. Hopes that Clarice's suddenly steely gaze squashed flat as P.J.'s floral pancake.

"My goodness. And in front of the *children?*"

She gasped. "It's not what you're thinking."

"No, it's what I'm seeing. Ben's truck in the driveway. *All* night."

"I had some car trouble yesterday. He stayed with the kids for me." Her heart sank. Within the hour, Ellamae would hear about her overnight visitor. Then the word would spread all over town.

"You want to be careful." Clarice sent a meaningful glance toward Ben. "Both of you."

"Dana's right, Clarice," he said easily. "The situation isn't what you're thinking. And it would be a real shame to have rumors start just because I gave Dana a helping hand out of pure friendship. Wouldn't it?"

"Friendship?" She looked him over again and shook her head. "I need to get back home."

As she stalked away, Dana closed the door gently,

knowing she hadn't heard the end of this. And she had only herself to blame for insisting that Ben stay.

P.J. trotted in from the kitchen. "C'mon, Ben. Mama will make breakfast soon."

"We'll be there in a minute, sweetie," she said. "Get the place mats on the table for me, please."

"Okay."

When he had left, she walked slowly into the living room, looked at Ben and raised her brows. "I've watched you talk a nervous mare across Sidewinder Creek in the middle of a gullywasher," she said, "but I think you've lost your touch."

He rose from the couch. Suddenly she felt the overwhelming urge to hurry into the kitchen with P.J. Somehow she managed to stand her ground.

"What makes you say that?"

She choked on a laugh. "Do you really think Clarice will keep quiet about finding you here this morning?"

He shrugged and spread his arms wide. His biceps bulged and his triceps did something equally devastating, and suddenly she lost all desire to laugh.

"C'mon, Dana. What do I look like? A fortune-teller?"

"No. Like a man who had better put his T-shirt back on if he plans to eat breakfast at *my* table."

There. She'd said it.

And now, though she didn't quite flee, she racewalked into the kitchen, mentally kicking herself the entire way. She hadn't planned to invite him to stay for breakfast, but the words had come out of her mouth faster than she could think.

His half-naked state had driven her to it.

Grabbing a jar of baby food from the refrigerator, she pressed it against her heat-flushed cheek. The chilled glass helped cool her down a bit. But nothing could stop the rush of guilt and shame that filled her.

She and Ben hadn't lied. The situation *wasn't* what Clarice had thought—at least, not this morning. Still, her neighbor's suspicions hit too close for comfort. For safety.

Whether or nor Clarice had proof of an indiscretion didn't matter. She would never keep gossip like this to herself.

"Are we working today, Ben?" P.J. asked halfway through breakfast.

"We sure are." He ate a mouthful of French toast and considered the situation he found himself in.

Last night, after Dana and the client were safely on their way back to Flagman's Folly, he'd given a big sigh of relief. And he'd felt inordinately pleased at how the rest of his evening turned out.

It hadn't taken much effort to convince her sitter he didn't mind her going. Truth be told, if she hadn't left, he'd have stayed anyway. He didn't care to leave a teenager alone at that hour with the kids.

On the other hand, when Dana had finally arrived, he'd found he didn't much like the idea of being alone with her, either. In her dark, quiet living room, he'd gotten to thinking—probably about the same things Clarice had thought. Even though he owned this house, Dana would have kicked him out of the place if he'd tried to put those thoughts into action.

Still, he'd been happy to bed down on the couch for the rest of the night. It fit right in with his plans for the weekend.

Besides, she made a great breakfast.

"Do you want more bacon?" P.J. asked, pushing the platter toward Ben's end of the kitchen table.

"Sure. Thanks, buddy." He took another couple of slices and passed the platter to Lissa, sitting opposite her brother.

When she'd first seen him in the kitchen, she'd acted a little standoffish but now seemed to have warmed up to him again.

Dana, on the other hand, had gotten colder. She'd taken a seat at the far end of the table, next to Stacey's high chair. She hadn't said much once they'd all come into the kitchen. Come to think of it, she hadn't even made eye contact with him since they'd sat down.

His feeling of pleasure gave way to guilt.

Leftover guilt from last night, at the way he'd played up his sleepiness. Sure, he'd had a long day and could easily have nodded out on the couch, but he wasn't as tired as he'd let on.

Then more guilt this morning, at lounging around instead of getting up and heading out the door. Leaving when he should have wouldn't have changed anything as far as Dana's next-door neighbor was concerned, but at least Clarice wouldn't have woken up to see his truck still in the driveway.

That was six of one, half a dozen of another, though. He would've gone home, showered and eaten breakfast in his own kitchen. But eventually, he'd have come back.

He still had errands to run and chores to do at the ranch this weekend, but he intended to spend what time he could right here. The more Dana saw of him, the more she'd get used to having him around. And the easier it would make it for him to get closer to her.

Already his plan had begun to work—she'd invited him to stay for breakfast, hadn't she?

P.J. held the nearly empty bottle of syrup out to him. "We need more, please."

He smiled. The kids didn't need time to get used to him.

"I'll take care of it," Dana said.

He had already risen. "No problem. I've got it."

"Ben knows where to find everything," Lissa said matter-of-factly.

"That's true." On his way over to the pantry closet, he thought about all the time he'd once spent in this house. Even in the few months just after Paul's death, he'd been a constant visitor...until Dana had started coming up with reasons to turn him away.

"Mama, you went out with Mr. Hall yesterday, didn't you?" she asked.

"Yes, I took him to look at property."

"Like you did with Caleb?"

"That's right."

"He's a rodeo star, too, just like Caleb."

"Yes, he is," her mama agreed.

Lissa's eyes shone with the same rodeo fever Nate and the rest of their friends had caught. Having Caleb Cantrell return to town was probably the most exciting thing they'd ever had happen in their young lives.

In her mind, a plain, everyday rancher just couldn't compare to the excitement of a real, live rodeo star.

She put her hands flat on the table and leaned toward her mama. "You really think Mr. Hall will buy a ranch here, just the way Caleb did?"

"I certainly hope so."

He frowned down at his plate. Now that Dana couldn't rightly keep him out of his own house, he suspected she'd begun to use her job as a way to avoid him when he came here to work in the evenings. But she'd just sounded as eager as Lissa had about the idea of a new star in town.

Her tone reminded him how much she could use another big sale.

Why the hell that meant she had to have supper with the man, he didn't know.

"Mama," P.J. said, "Ben looks sad. I think you better make him more French toast."

He looked up to find Dana staring at him. Quickly, he glanced toward her son. "I'm not sad at all, just thinking of how many chores I'm going to have to do today to work off this good breakfast."

He'd thought of a few other things, as well. And he didn't much like the direction his mind had headed.

Maybe Dana didn't worry about the size of her commission when she drove her new client all over the state. Maybe she hadn't minded getting stranded with the man last night, either. Maybe her interest in him was just what she'd said to Lissa: she hoped he would settle down in the area.

Trying not to frown again, he pushed his empty plate away from him.

For the first time, he wondered if Dana had a touch of rodeo fever, too.

Chapter 10

Dana stared through the kitchen window into the back-yard.

Right after breakfast, Ben had taken P.J. to the far end of the property, where he had begun breaking ground to lay in a row of fence posts. He'd settled P.J. off to one side of his work area with a small plastic bucket and shovel.

After a couple of quick peeks through the kitchen curtains, she began to feel as bad as Clarice and El-lamae with their spying. But that didn't stop her from looking....

P.J. ran back and forth, filling his bucket and then emptying it at the base of a small tree.

The digging was dirty work. Hot work, too, even though it was still early morning. As she peered through the window again, she saw Ben had stripped off his T-shirt and stood wiping his forehead with the back of his hand.

Her own hand stilled on the insulated cooler she had

just filled with lemonade. She bit her lip in indecision. Half of her knew she should bring the cold drink to him. The other half warned she'd best not go outside.

Ignoring the warning, she picked up the cooler and a couple of plastic mugs and crossed to the kitchen door.

When he saw her coming, he set his shovel aside.

"Looks like you've been working hard," she said. "You've made a lot of progress."

"Yeah. Slow progress, but I'm not taking any chances on doing anything I shouldn't."

Good advice. She'd do well to take it herself. The skin on her neck prickled, as if Clarice stared at her from next door. But what could she find wrong in Dana offering her landlord cold lemonade?

Ben gave her a half smile that left her insides shivering. That answered her question, all right.

He took the mug and tipped his head back to drink from it. She watched the muscles of his throat work as he polished off the contents in one long, uninterrupted swallow.

Almost unaware of doing it, she swallowed, too.

When he'd finished, he swept his tongue along the splash of lemonade left on his upper lip.

Her mouth suddenly felt as dry and cakey as the dirt around them. She swallowed again and wished she'd brought a mug outside for herself.

P.J. tugged on her arm. "What about me, Mama? I worked hard, too."

Face flushing, she turned to him. How could she have let herself get so distracted, she'd neglected her own child? "Right here," she said, handing him the smaller mug.

Then she refilled Ben's and again found herself frozen, watching as he took another drink.

She told herself to stop staring—and her self argued back. *Why should I stop? I'll make sure nothing ever happens between us again.* Still, the thoughts she kept having about Ben, the reactions she kept fighting were all perfectly natural, perfectly normal—even if she *could* think back almost far enough to recall them both in diapers.

But those days were long gone. Now, she was a full grown adult female.

And he was one hot-looking male.

She ran her tongue across her lips. A sponge-dry tongue that left her longing to take a swig directly from the insulated cooler.

She could just imagine the uproar she'd get from P.J., who had heard her lecture on that more than once.

Wasn't this just wonderful! Not only had Ben shaken her normal reserve, he had managed to undermine her parenting skills—without even knowing he was doing so.

"You okay?" he asked.

She started, realizing that he had noticed her staring at him. She said the first thing that came to her mind. "You've got dirt on your face."

Looking down, he clapped his free hand against his jeans, raising a cloud of dust, and laughed. "I can't see myself worrying about a smudge or two when I'm covered head to toe in the stuff."

"I suppose you're right."

"P.J. said I'll need to take a shower when I'm done. Didn't you, buddy?" He directed the question to her son but kept his gaze fixed on her.

She had a sudden vision of a steamy shower door and Ben's naked body half-visible through it.

"Yep," P.J. confirmed. "Mama says when we come in dirty, we should go right in and wash up."

Ben raised one eyebrow, as if challenging her to deny her son's words.

She bit her tongue. Again, somehow, he had turned her parenting skills to work in his favor. This time, she felt certain he knew exactly what he'd done.

"I've got a couple of things to take care of around noon," he told her. "I'll plan to stop and shower up before then. I've got a change of clothes out in the truck," he added. "You won't even have to provide a towel. I've got one of those, too."

The image *that* brought to mind was not something she wanted to think about then. "Don't be silly," she snapped. "I can certainly give you a towel."

He grinned.

Clamping her jaw tight, she glared at him. No doubt about his challenge now. Whether or not she'd planned to offer him the use of the shower no longer mattered. Because now she couldn't refuse. She'd gone right along with *his* plan, just as he had intended.

He reached for the T-shirt he had tossed onto a mound of dirt and used it to wipe the sweat from his face.

Immediately, P.J. grabbed the hem of his own shirt and scrubbed his chin with it.

She tightened her grip on the cooler. "All done with that?" she asked, gesturing toward Ben's mug. He nodded and handed it to her. "I guess I'll get back to the house."

"I guess I'll be getting back to work. At least, until it's time for that shower."

Gritting her teeth, she walked away.

Trust Ben to find something to tease her with and run with it. He'd been doing that since he was four years old. She should have been used to it by now. She shouldn't have reacted.

He couldn't have meant to add sexual undertones to

their perfectly innocent conversation. Not after their run-in with Clarice earlier!

His teasing aside, though, Ben was a good man. She couldn't deny that. Again, she saw her son copying Ben's move with the T-shirt. He made a good role model for any little boy, and especially one like P.J., who no longer had a daddy.

It was the other images of Ben imprinted on her brain that had left her shaken. His wide, easy grin. His dirt-smeared but handsome face. His sweaty, hard-muscled body.

The body that would soon stand naked in her downstairs shower.

A while later, Dana found herself pacing the kitchen floor. She desperately needed something to help burn up her nervous energy.

Like baking.

Yes. Measuring and mixing ingredients would distract her. Inhaling the sweet smells of sugar and vanilla would settle her nerves. Would keep her from dwelling on thoughts she didn't want to think about. From obsessing over emotions she didn't want to feel.

Quickly she washed her hands and assembled what she needed for the kids' most often requested cookie, a recipe she'd created herself. She'd always loved to bake, and it seemed as though she never had much time for it lately. Going through the familiar motions relaxed her.

Until she heard the footsteps on the back porch steps. Solid footsteps. Not P.J. in his sneakers, but the heavier tread of an adult. She fumbled the measuring cup in her fingers, spilling flour across the breakfast bar. So much for settling her nerves.

Bracing herself, she turned.

It wasn't Ben on the porch.

Her next-door neighbor peered through the screen door.

And a different kind of tension filled Dana.

"Come on in, Clarice," she called. Swiping at the counter with a damp cloth, she cleaned up the spilled flour.

The other woman took a seat at the breakfast bar and placed a large leather-covered folder in front of her. "I've brought something to show you." She sounded grim.

"Give me a minute." Dana washed her hands, then came to stand beside her.

The folder turned out to be a double photo frame holding two glossy, black-and-white photographs. The left-hand photo showed a solemn-faced man with close-cropped hair wearing an army dress uniform, the jacket decorated with rows of medals.

"My Vernon," Clarice said.

Dana smiled and nodded. "I know. He didn't change much over the years, did he? Except for letting his hair grow out."

"He never could stand having that military cut."

The second frame showed him with his arm around a younger, glowing Clarice. Instead of an elaborate white gown, she wore a simple light-colored suit with a small corsage.

"I've seen these on the table in your living room," Dana said. "That's the Vernon I knew. He always had a smile."

"Yes, he did. And we had a wonderful wedding, though no one had many reasons for smiling in those days."

Those days, Dana knew, meant during World War II.

"We didn't have time to plan a formal reception." Clarice shook her head. "We didn't even have a real honeymoon. Not then. Vernon headed off to war three days later."

Dana put her hand on Clarice's shoulder and gave a gentle, comforting squeeze.

"And you're right about seeing these pictures," the older woman said. "I keep them in my parlor to remind me of Vernon." She looked sideways and added, "I've noticed you don't have a single picture of Paul around the house."

At the accusation in her tone, Dana stiffened. As casually as she could, she rounded the breakfast bar and reached for her wooden spoon. "It's...still difficult for me to look at pictures of Paul." On the surface, every word held nothing but truth. It was only the real meaning behind her statement that filled her with guilt. "The kids have photos of him in their bedrooms."

"That's good to hear. You can't let them forget what a good man their daddy was. Such a brave soldier, and such a big hero."

Not in Dana's eyes. But how could she tell that to Clarice, whose own war hero lived up to that praise?

"I know how you feel, Dana—"

She couldn't know. Not, as P.J. would say, in a million-bazillion years.

"—but you should have his picture out where you can all see it, as a family." Clarice's expression matched her stern tone.

More footsteps sounded on the back steps, this time clearly the slap of her son's sneakers accompanied by the thump of Ben's workboots. Several thuds followed, two heavy, two lighter.

"It sounds like they're leaving their dirty shoes outside," Clarice said. "At least you've got them *both* trained right."

Dana gritted her teeth at this easy assumption that Ben spent enough time here to be trained along with her son.

The screen door burst open and P.J. slid across the floor in his stocking feet. "Look at me—I'm ice-skating!"

"So you are," Clarice said.

Ben came into the room carrying P.J.'s lemonade mug. He closed the door softly behind him. His hair lay in damp waves. His chest held a sheen of perspiration.

Dana forced her gaze away. Catching P.J.'s eye, she glanced meaningfully at his socks and tried for a light tone. "It's a good thing I just mopped the floor this morning, isn't it?"

"Uh-huh. Makes better ice." He climbed onto the stool beside Clarice's. "Yippee! Ben, Mama's making her bestest cookies."

Ben moved up to stand beside her. He smelled faintly of a mixture of earth and clean, male sweat. Gripping her spoon more tightly, she berated herself for the silly thought. Was there even such a thing as "male sweat," anyway?

"I like cookies," Ben said. "What kind are these?" he asked P.J.

"Spice cookies. You'll like 'em, Ben. *Hey.*" P.J. leaned against Clarice's arm to look at the photo frame she had set to one side of the counter. "Is that my daddy?"

"No," she said, "it's—"

"I can show you my daddy." He slid from his stool and rushed toward the door.

"No running in the house," Dana called after him.

"Yes, indeed," Clarice said. "One wrong slip, and who knows what would happen." She looked levelly from her to Ben and back.

"What's that?" he asked, pointing at the frame.

Dana stared down, mixing her cookie dough. Keeping her thoughts focused on her son.

She didn't worry about P.J. carrying the photo from upstairs. He would bring the small, unframed picture he kept on the nightstand near his bed. The larger glass-and-wood-framed photo hung on the wall well out of his reach, and he knew better than to try to get to that.

Still, she didn't want him to carry down even that small photo of Paul. She didn't want Clarice to go on listing Paul's virtues. And she especially didn't want his best friend hovering near her elbow.

Just thinking of all she couldn't control made her hands shake. Trying to hide the fact, she worked doggedly with her dough, shaping the mounds into logs.

P.J. came back into the room. Lissa followed close behind.

"Here's my daddy!" He thrust the photo at Clarice.

As she took it from him, her eyes softened. Dana didn't need to guess why. The photo of Paul was almost a duplicate of the one taken of Clarice's husband, the standard, shoulders-squared pose of a soldier in full dress uniform. Like Vernon, Paul wore a row of medals on his jacket.

No matter what else he hadn't done, no matter that he'd never been the daddy her kids deserved, he'd left her children something they could view with pride.

"He's my daddy, too," Lissa said, her eyes shining. "And he's a hero. Isn't he, Mama?"

Startled, Dana mangled the log of cookie dough in her fingers. Again Ben stood watching her. This time he didn't turn away. He was waiting for her to answer. Wanting to know what she would say. She took a deep breath, hoping—praying—to come up with something that would satisfy him.

Before she could think of anything, Clarice wrapped an arm around Lissa and said, "Of course he's a hero, sweetheart. Just like my Vernon. Your daddy's someone you can be proud of. Someone we *all* need to respect."

Lissa nodded. "Just like Caleb. And Mr. Hall," she said. "They're rodeo heroes, aren't they, Mama?"

"Yes," she said, relieved to find something she could agree with. Happy to have had someone step in once again and help her by responding when she had no clue what to say. "Yes," she repeated. "They definitely are heroes."

And she definitely couldn't keep relying on other people to save her. She needed to stand up for herself. Besides, one of these days, her luck would run out—if it hadn't already.

Ben continued to stand and watch her as though he could read every thought that raced through her mind.

Tearing her gaze away, she went to the refrigerator. Once the dough had chilled, she would slice it into nice, even rounds. If only her life could turn out as perfectly. But hadn't she made sure it wouldn't? In fact, hadn't she gone out of her way to guarantee just the opposite would happen?

Her neighbor's certainty of Paul's virtues was no one's fault but her own. She ought to feel glad about it. After all, it proved that she had successfully done what she'd attempted to do—uphold the story of her ideal marriage.

A story based more on fiction than on fact.

"I need to run out to my truck," Ben said. "P.J., you'd best go and wash up."

The kids disappeared in one direction and he went off in the other. The screen door slapped closed behind him, leaving Dana with Stacey and Clarice.

The older woman didn't waste any time. "Dana," she

snapped, "how can you compare a cowboy who rides bulls for a living to a man who has given service to his country the way my Vernon did? And to a man who has given his life, as Paul has?"

"I didn't mean—"

"I just hope the town council sees fit to approve our memorial." She shook her head. "Your children need something to help them remember their daddy. They won't find it here."

"Clarice!" She tried to soften her tone. "I know you have their best interests at heart. So do I, and—"

"*Really?* I can't imagine how what *I* saw this morning proves you care for your children." Her eyes glittering, she snatched up the photo frame. "You should be ashamed. Their daddy's a hero and a veteran. And though he's barely settled in his grave, you're throwing yourself at his best friend."

Clarice stormed out the back door.

Struggling to catch her breath, Dana took Stacey from the high chair and hurried from the kitchen. She couldn't stay there and face Ben when he came back inside. She couldn't stay there when the older woman's words still echoed in the room.

Beneath all the fury, Dana had heard the frustration. She'd seen the gleam of tears. Clarice *did* have her family's best interests at heart.

Knowing that, how could she just ignore what her neighbor had said? She couldn't.

Not when all the folks in town believed it, too.

Not when she was guilty of each and every accusation.

Finished tucking in his T-shirt, Ben caught sight of himself in the mirror and nearly winced. Before his shower, he'd gone out to his truck for his duffel bag.

Clarice had cornered him there, her expression looking about as grim as his reflection did now.

When she'd arrived at Dana's doorstep that morning, he hadn't known whether to laugh or groan. He should've realized she'd see the truck outside. To tell the truth, maybe he'd wanted her to notice it. Like Dana, folks needed to get used to seeing him around here.

He hadn't anticipated the older woman's reaction then. And he hadn't been ready for her anger when she'd caught him outside. She'd torn a strip off his hide over finding him on Dana's couch. Over what all the folks in town would think about "Ben Sawyer cavorting with his best friend's wife."

He'd managed to calm her down again. He thought.

If only he could settle down himself. Could shake off the guilt that stuck to him like the damp hair clinging to his forehead.

As he finished loading up his duffel bag, P.J. came to the bathroom door, providing a much-needed distraction.

"Cookies are almost ready," he said.

"Sounds good." He straightened the bath towel on the rack and grabbed the bag. "Do you think I'll be able to eat more than you will?" he asked as they walked down the hall.

"No way! I can eat a million-bazillion."

The doorbell rang, and P.J. changed direction.

He and Lissa ran in a dead heat to the front door. Squabbling over who would get to open it, they both grabbed hold of the handle and yanked. Tess stood on the doorstep with Nate.

P.J. rolled his eyes and headed toward the kitchen.

The two girls plopped down on the couch. Dana had long ago taken away the sheets Ben had left in a pile at one end.

She had just come into the room. As P.J. passed her, she smiled and ruffled his hair, then looked at Tess. "Good morning. What are you two doing here?"

"My new husband hijacked our client for the day. Nate and I are on our way to the Double S for lunch."

P.J. stopped in his tracks. "Yay! Can we go, too?"

"P.J.!" Dana said in dismay. "Wait until you're invited."

Tess laughed. "That's exactly why we stopped here. You're all invited. Our treat. P.J., how did you know?"

"I'm a good guesser." He plopped into the rocking chair.

Ben turned to Tess. "I hear you're on the proposal committee for Paul's memorial." From the corner of his eye, he saw Dana stiffen. She refused to open up about her own proposal. The fact still rankled. That was only half of it, though.

After the discussion at the Whistlestop, he'd decided to let her think over the suggestion Ellamae had made. Almost a full week ago, and it seemed she hadn't gotten comfortable with the idea yet. How the hell much time did she need to accept something she should have approved in a heartbeat?

"Where did you hear the news?" Tess asked.

"From Clarice." He shot Dana another look. Her frozen expression said the woman had cornered her alone, too. "She was visiting here and mentioned it."

Tess nodded. "Instead of a statue, we're now thinking of a monument of some kind. Whatever we decide," she said, smiling, "Caleb said he would provide the funds for it."

"Hey," he protested, "I'm willing to foot the bill."

"Oh, I knew you would be. But Caleb volunteered.

He wants to repay folks for their kindness since he's come home."

Abruptly Dana turned and went toward the kitchen.

Startled, he stared after her. For the first time, his conviction wavered. Maybe he'd misjudged her lack of enthusiasm over the memorial. Maybe she'd had the same thoughts that had just slammed into his mind at Tess's words.

Caleb had returned to town.

But Paul would never come home again.

Dana reappeared carrying Stacey. "I've got the first batch of cookies done. I left you a plateful of cookies," she told him, not meeting his eyes. "Ready if you are, Tess."

"See you later," he said. He'd be back after he got his chores done.

In a whirlwind of movement and chatter, the kids went out the door. The women followed.

He stood rooted, feeling no inclination to get to work. Running his fingers through his still-damp hair, he stared across the room and through the long window beside the door. He caught sight of Dana as she walked past it. They had only a pane of glass between them, but so much more to keep them apart.

Clarice sure as hell had made certain to remind him of that.

Chapter 11

After lunch, Dana told Tess she'd buy ice cream for everyone. She was relieved when her offer was accepted. Her budget could stretch that far, at least.

Besides, she knew P.J. would savor his vanilla scoop in tiny little spoonfuls, as always, which meant she could delay going back to the house. Back to facing Ben and her memories of the conversation with Clarice.

Afterward, still not ready to go home, she suggested to Tess that they take a stroll along Signal Street.

Ahead of them, Lissa and Nate led the procession, with P.J. tagging behind, trying to listen in on their conversation.

"It will be nice when the playground's ready for the kids," Tess said.

"Hmm..."

"Dana, is everything all right?"

Surprised, she glanced sideways. "Yes, fine."

Tess's eyes narrowed. "Now, why do I doubt that?"

"Because you're imagining things?"

"I don't think so. You didn't even hear what I just said. And you didn't say a word when I was talking to Ben earlier. Are you upset that Caleb offered to pay for the monument?"

"No, of course not. Why would that upset me?"

"I don't know. Flagman's Folly has never done anything like this before, and everyone's so excited about the memorial." She paused, then said softly, "They're all so proud of how you're handling things on your own, too."

Dana stopped to watch P.J. run up the steps of Town Hall.

"Listen," Tess said, "it's just the two of us here now. I know there's something bothering you. You were fine yesterday, and only one thing has changed since then." She took a deep breath and let it out slowly. "If it's not Caleb, then are you upset because I'm on the monument committee?"

"Now you're being ridiculous."

At Tess's expression of relief, she tried not to cringe. She had meant what she said—of anyone in town, she'd have chosen her best friend to work on any project concerning her own family.

Except *this* project.

It wasn't Tess's participation on the committee that bothered her, but the fact that the committee existed at all.

"Talk to me, girl," Tess persisted.

Dana adjusted the light blanket over Stacey's legs. A useless delaying action because no one was going to come along to save her. And right now, she wanted that—no matter how many times she'd insisted to Ben that she could handle things herself.

She pushed the stroller forward again and sighed. The

kids had taken off again. She couldn't use them for a distraction.

Her luck had finally run out.

Then she met Tess's stare and recognized the uncertainty in her best friend's face. For that reason alone, she had to talk. Not about Paul. She couldn't, especially after what had happened with Clarice. But she needed to ease Tess's worry—and badly needed to confide in her about Ben.

She and Tess and Ben and Paul had all grown up together. Had known each other forever. If anyone could help her with this situation, Tess could.

"I wasn't very open with you when Caleb came back to town—" Tess began.

She shook her head. "That's not it at all, believe me."

"All right, then what *is* it?"

After a long, deep breath, she muttered, "It's Ben."

Tess gasped. "He's objecting to the monument?"

"No, it's nothing to do with that. It's… He's taken over my life." She tried to smile. "Or at least, it feels that way. It was bad enough when he just owned the office building. Now that he's bought the house, too, he shows up almost every day. Every time I turn around, he's there."

"He's being helpful. That's just Ben."

She could have screamed. How could she expect Ellamae and Clarice to back off, when her best friend felt the way they did? "I *know* that's just Ben. And he's very helpful. But he wants to do things for me—things I can do for myself—and it's getting on my nerves."

"It's that bad?"

"It's worse."

They walked for a few yards, then Tess said softly, "You know, I would feel lost if something ever happened to you."

Dana stared in surprise. "Same here. You know that."

"Well, then. Ben and Paul got to be best buddies back in kindergarten, just as you and I did. He probably feels lost now. Maybe he's trying to stay close to Paul through you and the kids."

She gripped the stroller. "I never thought of that."

"And you know how most guys are when it comes to talking."

"Not Ben. He's never had a problem with talking about anything."

"Except his feelings." Tess's voice rose. "I'm sure that's it. He's been quiet—different—for months now. I think you need to talk to him."

She clutched the handle with such force, her knuckles turned white. "Talk to him?" That's just what she wanted to avoid.

"Yes. Get him to tell you what's on his mind. That way, he'll start opening up."

"You could be right—" she began. *But I'll never know.*

Tess nodded emphatically. "I'm sure I am." She sighed in obvious relief at having come up with an idea that would help.

Dana tried not to cry in frustration. She should never have said anything, never have gotten Tess involved at all. Her suggestion *didn't* help. It only made things worse.

She had no intention of talking about Paul. And no desire for any heart-to-heart conversations with Ben.

But now that she had gotten Tess involved, now that Tess believed her suggestion had been accepted, she would want to know how things were going. She would expect to hear progress reports. She would be eager to learn what Dana had done to help their good old friend Ben.

* * *

All too soon, P.J. finished his ice cream and Tess drove them home.

As P.J. and Lissa climbed out of the backseat, Dana cradled Stacey in one arm. She handed Lissa the baby's car seat. "I'll see you in the office on Monday," she said to Tess. "Good luck with Jared tomorrow."

"Okay. And good luck with...you-know-who." Tess smiled.

"Thanks." Dana closed the passenger door and waved goodbye.

"Ben's truck is here again," Lissa pointed out.

She'd already noticed that. "Yes, I see it."

At that moment, the front door opened. Ben stepped out onto the porch as if he'd been lying in wait. Desire ran through her, followed by a breath-stealing surge of awareness. No getting away from it. Good old Ben was a good-looking guy.

After working in the yard that morning, he'd changed into a snug, soft green T-shirt that accentuated his muscles and played up his dark hair and eyes. Before lunch, she had walked into the living room and seen him standing there with the moisture from his shower—that shower she'd fantasized over—still dampening his hair. Her reaction to the sight had made her ten times more eager to accept Tess's invitation.

But now she was home, and there he stood again, looking as good as any hero from the romance novels she read. And leaning against the porch railing as if he owned the place. Now, annoyance mixed with desire until she reminded herself he *did* own this property and there wasn't much she could do about it.

"Did you have a good lunch?" he asked.

"We sure did," P.J. said. "And we went for ice cream."

"Yeah? Where's mine?"

"We didn't bring you any." Lissa's glance flew to Dana and then away.

Was she upset about finding Ben here again? Or that they'd left him out of their plans?

Dana still wasn't sure what impact his absence had had on her children. Or whether it had been wise for her to let him back into their lives. As *she* couldn't decide, it was no wonder if Lissa felt confused, too.

He shrugged. "Well, then, I guess it's only fair I ate up all the spice cookies."

"You *did*?" P.J. gasped, and raced past him into the house.

Lissa stared at Ben. "You didn't really, did you?"

"No, not really."

Dana followed her into the living room. "Lissa, you *do* know Ben was just teasing. He wouldn't do something like that."

She shrugged. "But...but *P.J.* didn't know that."

"That's true." And worse, she probably shouldn't have jumped to Ben's defense. Too late, she bit her tongue, thinking of the irony. Like Tess, she had fallen back on the old standard phrase, on the townsfolk's common cry: that's just Ben.

"Daddy wouldn't tease me or P.J. about the cookies." Frowning, she went up the stairs.

Resting her chin on the baby's head, Dana watched her go.

Ben stepped into the house and closed the screen door. She couldn't tell by his expression if he had heard Lissa's comment.

P.J. ran toward them from the kitchen. "You did *not* eat all the cookies!" he exclaimed. "Mama, can I have some?"

"Oh, I don't think so, young man. You just had a taco, tortilla chips and a dish of ice cream. That's enough for now."

He frowned but nodded. "Can we have some after supper, though?"

She tried to hold the kids to one sweet a day. But rules were meant to be broken—once in a while. "Yes, that will work."

"You gotta wait till after supper," he told Ben.

"No problem. I can do that."

She turned and stared at him. "I'm sorry, but...weren't you planning to go home before then?"

He rubbed the back of his head. "Well, to tell you the truth, I had every intention of it. But I heard how your washer sounded this morning, so I came back here and tore it to pieces."

"You didn't."

"I sure did."

She fought back a groan. The evenings she'd spent away from home this week, trying to avoid him, had forced her to do something she would never usually do. Let the laundry pile up.

Mentally, she began running through a list of all the wash she needed to get done, including the outfit she'd dug from the depths of her closet to wear to the meeting on Monday night. She needed her washing machine—in one piece.

"Good thing I took it apart, too," he said. "Left any longer, you might've needed a whole new tub. I'll have to go pick up a few parts. Judging by the pile of baskets next to the washer, I reckon you'll want it together again by tomorrow. Otherwise, it'll have to wait until Tuesday."

"Tuesday!"

He nodded. "Town council meeting on Monday. So I thought I'd keep working on it tonight."

"Good idea," she said faintly.

"That's what I thought." He turned to P.J. "Hey, buddy, how about we take a ride to the hardware store later, and then pick up a pizza for supper?"

"Yeah!" P.J. yelled.

"There's no need for that," she said. "I've got home-made soup thawing in the refrigerator. Unless you've already eaten it all?" The words, spoken half-jokingly, made her stop and think.

He laughed. "No, I didn't touch anything in the re-frigerator."

"What *did* you have for lunch, anyway?"

"Not a thing. Not even that plateful of cookies you left me. I came right back and got busy wrestling with the washing machine so I could find out what it needed."

Nothing like piling on the guilt. But she couldn't complain. A serviceman would cost a small fortune. At least Ben had offered to make the repairs. She would pay for the parts.

"I'll pick up the pizza," he insisted. "It's the least I can do. After all, you fed me breakfast this morning. Be-sides—" he grinned "—I'm already invited for dessert."

After supper, Ben took P.J. up on his request to read him a bedtime story while Dana put Stacey to bed and Lissa closeted herself in her bedroom.

Earlier that evening, Dana had made a big green salad and set out all kinds of vegetables to go along with their pizza. Seeing the food on the table had almost made him feel guilty for deliberately tearing her washer apart.

Almost. After all, the machine *had* made an awful

racket the last time he'd heard her using it. And he hadn't been kidding about the condition of the tub.

But most of all, fool that he was, he hadn't been able to pass up the excuse to hang around tonight.

Now, while he tinkered in the utility room, she worked not five feet away from him, washing dishes.

"P.J. sure called it right about those cookies," he said. "They were great. Better than any store-bought ones. Maybe you ought to go into business." Eyeing her over the washer, he saw a small smile touch her lips.

"Thanks, but I have a career. I'll keep the cookies for my kids. I don't bake for them often enough as it is."

Because she had that career. Because she didn't have a husband and had to take care of everything herself.

"Maybe that's not so bad," she continued. "You know what they say about too much of a good thing. And I could say the same about take-out food. We don't do that very often, either."

Because she was a good mama who wanted to make home-cooked meals for her family. And because she didn't have the money.

"The tacos last week. The pizza tonight." She looked over at him. "Those were real treats for them. Thank you."

At the sight of her smile—now wide and full and directed right at him—he nearly lost his grip on the wrench in his hand. He hadn't bought that food to earn her thanks. Or even to impress her. But if it would get him a reaction like that again, he'd clean out Harley's General Store to fill her kitchen cabinets.

Knowing he had to watch his own response to keep from scaring her away, he simply shrugged. "My pleasure. Nice for me, too, to have supper with you all now that my parents have gone."

"You must miss them." She stared down into the dish-water.

Damn. What a stupid thing he'd said. His parents had "gone" when they'd retired to Florida. A big difference from Dana, whose husband had died.

Again he wondered if he'd misjudged her over the memorial for Paul. Over the feelings she tried bravely not to let show.

He bore down so hard, the wrench slipped and flew from his hand. It went clattering into the space between the washer and the wall.

"Dang."

"Can you reach it?"

"I'm checking." He leaned over the machine and thrust his arm as far down as he could behind it. "I'll never get it without moving the washer. And I just leveled it off again."

"Maybe I can try?"

She came to his side and wiped her hands on a dish towel. Dropping the cloth on top of the dryer, she put her hands flat on the washer as if planning to boost herself up.

"You won't be able to get to it, either," he said.

"Is that so? Isn't that what you told me when your favorite marble rolled behind the bookcase in the school library?"

"Well…maybe." He grinned.

"Maybe nothing, mister." She laughed. "I saved your butt that day and you know it. Mrs. Freylin would've had a fit if she'd seen you trying to tip those shelves."

"Okay, okay. I admit, you saved me. But that was a long time ago. Your arms were thinner then."

"And they're still not as big as yours. I can probably—" She stopped.

He had reached out to keep her from climbing onto the washer. His fingers easily encircled her wrist. Her skin was firm yet soft, warm to his touch and still damp from the dishwater. Slowly he ran his thumb over the inside of her wrist, brushing away the moisture.

Her arm trembled against his fingers. Or maybe the tremor had gone through him.

No laughter. No smiles.

She looked away and took a breath so deep, her chest rose beneath her sleeveless blouse. She'd left the top two buttons undone, and in the shadows beneath the fabric he could see more soft, pale skin.

For sure now, his hands shook as he fought the urge to reach up and run his fingertip down into that deep V. But, damn—he wanted more than that. Not just the chance to touch her there. Not just her body, either.

He wanted *her*. He always had.

He reached up. Tilted his head down. And froze at the sight of her expression.

A split-second later he dropped his hand. "Dana, I—"

"No. Don't say it. Don't even think it. I'm sorry." She rushed from the utility room and through the kitchen.

He stood there, unable to believe what he had come so close to doing. Unwilling to admit the risk he wanted to take.

And damned unhappy to realize he'd caused that stunned look on her face.

Chapter 12

Dana held back a sigh of exasperation and despair. How could things keep going from bad to worse?

Last night Ben had tracked her down in the living room to let her know he needed another part for the washer. He had told her he would be back before noon today. And he'd assured her—more emphatically than she wanted to recall—that what had happened wouldn't get in the way of their friendship.

Then he had left. In a hurry.

How could she blame him, after that moment in the utility room when he'd caught her staring at him? Ogling him the way Lissa and her friends ogled Jared Hall—and Caleb, before he'd become simply Nate's daddy. And then, just as Ben had started to kiss her, she had run away.

With the mixed messages she kept sending, it almost wouldn't have surprised her if he hadn't come back today.

Almost, because of course, he would. He was Ben.

He would never back down after he'd given someone his word.

She needed to prep meals for the week but couldn't bear the thought of working alone with him in the utility room, just a few feet away. So she'd tempted the kids into the kitchen with more cookies.

Nothing had gone right this morning. Nothing had gone right in her life for a while. Her children didn't provide the distraction she'd hoped for. Her next-door neighbor had the best intentions, Dana knew that, and the truth in those accusations had crushed her. And Ben— good old Ben—still tempted her…with something even sweeter than cookies.

He came into the kitchen now as if her thoughts had brought him to her. As she pulled the first trays out of the oven, he moved to her side. "Smells good."

"Yes. How's the washer coming along?" she asked pointedly.

"Nothing to worry about. Got that all under control." He gestured toward the trays. "You planning any extras for me?"

"Ben," she said under her breath, "you're as bad as P.J. was when Tess invited us for lunch yesterday. You know you're supposed to wait until you're asked."

"Huh. If that's the case, I could be waiting an awfully long time."

She looked up, but he had walked over to P.J. and Lissa. Biting her lip, she turned back to the trays. It had been a long time since she had invited him into their home for any reason. And to tell the truth, if he hadn't bought the house, he wouldn't be here now.

Had Tess been right? Had he waited all this time—all the months since Paul's death—for an invitation that had never come? Had he bought the house as a last resort, only so he could see more of his best friend's children?

She swallowed hard past the lump in her throat.

He and the kids sat at the table, drinking milk and eating cookies still warm from the oven. Lissa hung around watching as P.J. and Ben played a marathon card game that appeared as though it would last until noon.

Not a problem for Ben, since P.J. had already made it clear he expected him to stay for their midday Sunday dinner.

Like the roast and vegetables cooking in the pot on the back burner, mixed emotions simmered inside Dana.

P.J. had become a different little boy in these past couple of weeks, more outgoing, more easygoing, more tolerant of Lissa and her friends. She couldn't deny she owed all that to Ben.

Between that and everything else he had done around the house, she couldn't begrudge him another meal. Could she?

Those simmering emotions threatened to boil over.

At the breakfast bar, she transferred cookies from the cooling racks to her largest cookie jar. He rose from the table and came toward her.

Tensing, she tightened her hold on the spatula. She wasn't going to take the chance of having another tool slip into an inconvenient spot, the way his wrench had fallen behind the washer last night. She wasn't going to risk allowing her true feelings to show again, either.

He reached around her, attempting to grab a cookie.

Pretending playfulness she didn't feel, she pushed his arm away. "Don't you think you've had enough?"

"Well, you know how it is. You get one taste and you just want more. Besides, it's not like I get to have your homemade cookies all the time. The kids'll tell you that—right, kids?"

"Right!" Lissa and P.J. exclaimed.

She forced a laugh. "And they'll tell you just what I tell them. No more, or you'll ruin your dinner."

"That's right, too," P.J. said, not sounding nearly as enthusiastic this time.

"You see?" She shifted just as Ben reached around her again. His outstretched hand skimmed her breast.

His dark eyes held her gaze for several heartbeats.

He recovered first, dropping his hand to the counter beside her and stepping back.

Quickly, she glanced over at the kitchen table. P.J. knelt on his chair, scooping up the scattered cards, not glancing their way. Lissa sat watching them, but as her chair was on the far side of the room, she couldn't have noticed. Not that the innocent collision had meant anything, anyway.

It was just another taunting reminder of something she couldn't have.

"'Scuse me," Ben mumbled, his breath tickling her ear. As he walked toward the table, he continued in a normal tone, "Since the cookie break is over, maybe I'd best get back to work."

"You can't," P.J. said matter-of-factly. "We didn't eat supper yet. And we have to finish our game."

"Well," he said, drawing the word out, "you're right there, P.J." He dropped into his seat again. "Always a good thing to finish what you start."

Dana stared at him. Though he sat looking at P.J., had he directed his comment to her? Was he really talking about last night, telling her he wanted to be more than just friends, no matter what he had said?

But friendship was all she could give him. No matter how much she longed for more, too.

"'Finish what you start'?" she repeated brightly. "As in, finish fixing the washing machine?"

"Oh, I got that done already." He grinned.

Well, of course he had. Why tell her about it? After all, if she'd known earlier that he'd finished his job, she might have found a way to get him out of her hair—*before* P.J. had invited him to eat with them.

This time, one look told her she'd figured out exactly what he was thinking.

She covered the cookie jar and dropped the spatula into the sink. "Oh, well, thank you so much. I guess now I can go and start a load of laundry."

"You sure can," he said, taking the cards P.J. held out.

She tried not to run from the kitchen.

In the utility room a few minutes later, she braced her hands on the edge of the dryer and took a deep breath. She felt as agitated as the load of clothes she had just tossed into the washer.

Ben made her think things she shouldn't. Made her wish for things she could never have. Made her weak when she needed to be strong, for so many reasons.

And just like the clothes in the washer, her guilt and need and obligations tumbled around and around inside her.

After their Sunday dinner, the card game started up again in the living room. Dana cleared off the kitchen table but kept her ears half tuned to the conversation.

"Can we play all day?" P.J. asked Ben.

"I doubt that. We've still got work to do outside."

"Daddy played cards with me *all* the time," Lissa said with more than a trace of smugness.

Sensing trouble, Dana edged toward the doorway.

"My daddy played cards with me, too," P.J. said.

"He did not."

"Yes, he did."

Over their heads, Ben's gaze met Dana's.

"No, he didn't," Lissa insisted. "And besides, you were too little when he was here."

"I was not—"

"You don't even remember him."

"Yes, I do." As if to prove his point, P.J. reached into his shorts pocket and held up the small photograph of Paul that he kept by his bedside. He slapped the photo on the coffee table. It was crumpled around the edges, as if he'd carried it since he'd brought it down to the kitchen yesterday. "*That's* my daddy. He's a hero."

"*You* only know that because I told you!"

"Lissa!" Dana said. "P.J. Both of you, stop."

"But P.J. doesn't know—"

"Lots of people know your daddy's a hero." Ben's voice cut across her words quietly but with such emphasis Lissa and P.J. snapped their mouths shut. "P.J. could have heard it from them. And he definitely heard it from me. Your daddy's a hero. That's why he's wearing those medals in that picture. He's an army hero."

"I know that," Lissa said.

He smiled. "There's something I'll bet you don't know. He was a hero in Flagman's Folly, too."

"He was?"

"Yep. The greatest hero the high school football team ever had. He led them to three state championships in a row. Nobody had ever done that before, and they've never done it since."

"*Wow.* Mama never told us *that*."

Ben nodded, in agreement with her or confirmation of his own statement, Dana didn't know.

Like a dark cloud, silence hung over the room. Or over her.

"Your daddy and I were friends for a long, long time," Ben said. "Your daddy and mama and I have all been friends since we were in kindergarten."

"Like me?"

Dana didn't have to look to know her son's eyes had widened in astonishment. She wished she didn't have to listen to Ben's response. Yet she couldn't force herself to step away.

"Yes, like you. Your daddy and I were best buddies ever since then. And nothing will ever change that."

Buddies. *Friends.*

Just as they were.

"Best friends do everything together," Lissa said, "like me and Nate."

"Yep," he agreed, "just like the two of you. In fact, your daddy and I used to have sleepovers, too. Until the time we let my garter snakes loose in the house."

"In the *house?*" Lissa screeched.

Again, Dana didn't have to look to know P.J. would have just the opposite reaction. "You had *snakes!*"

"Well, I sure didn't have them for very long after that. My mama feels the way your mama does. She doesn't like 'em a bit."

"Ben," Dana said warningly, "don't give him any ideas."

He laughed. "I'm not."

Turning away, she went to Stacey and lifted her from the high chair. She wrapped her arms around the baby and rested her cheek against her hair.

Maybe she *had* been wrong about having Ben spend

so much time with Lissa and P.J. The expression on her older daughter's face said she still wasn't sure how she felt about Ben. P.J.'s feelings, on the other hand, had been evident in the way he looked up adoringly at the man.

Life had gotten so complicated in the past few weeks.

No. Life had become complicated long before Paul had died. When she'd started weaving that web of deceit.

Dana tightened her hold on Stacey and the little girl squirmed. She rocked her gently and looked down at the baby she loved, the baby she had conceived in a mistaken effort to save her marriage.

She would never regret having Stacey. Still, she knew what her last-born child represented to the townsfolk of Flagman's Folly—and to Ben Sawyer. Her baby gave them additional proof of Dana's perfect marriage.

And gave her yet one more secret to hang on to.

With every story he told about Paul, Ben felt worse than ever. How could he have thought about trying to get anywhere with his best friend's wife?

Clarice had blasted him with her opinion about that.

Dana herself had told him to back off the night of the wedding. And she hadn't changed her mind. He'd seen that in her face just before she'd run from the utility room. The sight had stayed with him all night, and he hadn't shaken it yet.

But he'd had years to learn how to cover his feelings.

"Hey, buddy," he said easily to P.J., "we've got a job to do. How about you run upstairs and get into some work clothes."

"Okay." The boy took off.

Lissa hadn't said much while he was telling his stories, but she didn't seem to want to miss one of them. She sat now on the edge of an ottoman and rubbed at the carpet with the toe of her shoe. He waited, thinking again of how little she resembled her mama as far as jumping into a conversation. But she'd speak up when she got good and ready.

He looked toward the kitchen. Again, Dana stood in the doorway, this time holding Stacey. In an instant, his jaw tightened.

If her reaction last night hadn't told him all he needed to know about ever having a relationship with her, seeing her hugging the baby sure as heck did. Like P.J. keeping track of tacos on his fingers, he could count back the months. He wouldn't have to go very far to know Paul and Dana had conceived that baby when Paul had come home for his last leave.

"Ben?"

He tore his gaze away and looked at Lissa. "Yeah?"

She stared back. "You were *always* best friends with Daddy?"

He nodded. "In grade school and junior high, and all through high school, too. And I was best man at his wedding."

"What's a best man?"

"When a man gets married, he's called the groom—"

"I know that. Like Caleb. And Tess was the bride."

"Exactly. The groom's best friend is called the best man, and he gets to help the groom."

"You mean, like Becky's daddy did?"

"Yes. The best man stands by the groom in church and holds the wedding ring until the groom puts it on the bride's finger."

"Oh." She sounded relieved. "Then, the best man doesn't get married."

"Well…no. Not when he's helping the groom."

"That's good." She dragged her toe across the carpet

again. "Mama says you come here all the time again now because you bought this house and you need to fix it up."

The abrupt change in subject made him want to shake his head in confusion. But he didn't. Obviously, she had something in *her* head and knew where she was going with it. "Yeah, there's a lot that needs to be done around here."

She nodded. "I know. And now Daddy's gone, you're helping Mama. Like a best man, right?"

"That's right. I want to help all of you."

"Good. But you won't have to go to church to help Mama. Because she won't get married again."

He swallowed hard and told himself not to look over toward the kitchen. "She won't?"

"No."

He couldn't stop himself. When his gaze shot to the doorway, he knew Dana hadn't missed a word. She stood frozen, almost the way she had last night.

Before she had run from him.

He forced himself to focus again on Lissa, who sat shaking her head.

"Miss Clarice says *she* can't get married again, because Mr. Vernon was a hero. And she says nobody can take Daddy's place because he's a hero, too."

"She's right. He sure is." He hesitated, then said, "Is that what's got you all quiet with me lately? You're thinking I'm trying to replace your daddy?"

She shrugged and nodded. "Yeah."

"Well, don't worry about that at all. I told you, I was his best friend. And I'm here to help out."

She nodded. "Now you told me. Because you're Mama's best man." She looked over toward the kitchen. "Right, Mama?"

Ben looked that way again, too.

"Right," Dana said.

Smiling now, Lissa went upstairs.

Dana had disappeared from the doorway.

He sat there for a moment or two, but when it became clear she didn't intend to return, he got up and ambled into the kitchen. She stood leaning against the breakfast bar, her arms still wrapped around Stacey. When she saw him, she seemed to stiffen, but he didn't let it deter him. He headed directly across the room and came to a stop just in front of her.

"Is that what you're worried about, too?" he asked. "That I'm here trying to take over? Trying to replace Paul?"

She shook her head.

"Well, just in case, you heard what I said to Lissa. I'm here to help you and the kids."

"Yes, I know. You've said that all along."

"And you've never been happy about it. I can't say I understand that." He took a long, calming breath and reached up to stroke Stacey's hair lightly with one finger. Trying to keep his voice just as gentle, he said, "You know, these are Paul's kids, too. No matter how you and I feel about everything, maybe we ought to consider what he would have wanted."

Dana rested her chin in her hands and stared down at the tabletop without seeing it. A while ago, Ben and P.J. had left the house to go out into the yard to work. Lissa had gone onto the back porch with a book.

When Ben had started telling his stories, she had wanted to sink into a puddle and melt into the floor. Like the Wicked Witch of the West in the kids' favorite movie.

Oh—and wasn't that an appropriate comparison! Because she felt wicked. She felt awful. She felt racked with guilt and more. Clarice had seen right through her.

Wanting her husband's best friend made her ashamed.

Ben was so wrong about expecting her to take Paul's thoughts into consideration, though she could never tell him that.

Yet he was so right about everything else.

If she ever again lost herself in daydreams, no doubt he would be the first to remind her they could never come true.

And everyone in Flagman's Folly would back him up.

"Mama!" Lissa yelled from the porch. "P.J.'s hurt!"

Dana jumped to her feet. After a quick glance at Stacey, safely strapped into her high chair, she rushed across the room.

Outside, Lissa stood pointing to the opposite end of the yard. "He fell into the hole where Ben was digging, but Ben already saved him."

Even from this distance, she could see Ben kneeling beside her son, who stood chattering away.

"It doesn't seem like he's hurt. I'll take a look, though. Please go keep an eye on Stacey."

The screen door slapped shut behind Lissa as Dana went down the back steps. She watched Ben check out P.J.'s arms and legs under the guise of brushing loose dirt from his clothing.

"Everything all right?" Clarice had come outside, too, and rushed in their direction. "My goodness. I was looking out the window and when I saw him fall, I just—"

"Nothing to worry about," Ben interrupted. "He's fine."

He clapped his hands on P.J.'s pants legs. A dust cloud rose, sending her son into giggles.

Clarice took his hand. "Well, he may be fine, but he's

filthy. He can come along with me, and I'll clean him up a bit. And then maybe he'll help me make a dent in a gallon of ice cream taking up space in my freezer. How about that, P.J.?"

"Sure, Miss Clarice. I can do that."

Now he could think only of his treat. But without that, and given time to stop and dwell on what had happened, it wouldn't have taken much to send him into tears. And he did seem fine. Grateful for her neighbor's quick thinking, Dana mouthed a "thank you" to Clarice.

The older woman nodded stiffly. She hadn't forgotten their conversation. Or forgiven. But at least she wasn't taking her feelings out on the kids.

As she led P.J. away, he grinned and gave Dana a big wave. She waved back. Then, forcing a smile, she turned to Ben, who looked more upset than P.J. had right after his fall. "None the worse for wear."

He finished dusting himself off and shook his head. "I'm glad for that. Scared the hell out of me when I saw him slip. He was too far away for me to catch him."

"He's quick. And with all the time he's spent with you lately, I'm just amazed you haven't seen him take a spill before now."

"You sound like you expected it."

"It's more like I'm used to it. You remember, he had those stitches from falling off the coffee table when he was three."

"Yeah, I do remember. I guess he's a typical boy, huh?"

She laughed. "Nothing's typical when it comes to kids. Girls get into just as many scrapes. Lissa has had her share of bumps and bruises. And at the rate she's going, I'm sure Stacey will, too."

"It's a lot to deal with, isn't it? A big responsibility, watching over kids."

"So, you've noticed." She'd said the words with a hint of irony, but the fact that he *had* noticed pleased her. Maybe now he would give her some credit. Would accept the fact that she could take care of her kids.

"I never realized it involved so much worry," he said. "And so much work. Especially with three of them."

"It can be challenging. They're a handful at times."

"I see that." He shook his head. "And here you've been dealing with this on your own. I told you I'm here to help. You can depend on that, doubled. Or maybe I should say tripled. I'll make it a point to stop in as much as I can."

Here we go again. It was all she could do not to snap at him. "Ben, I appreciate that, thank you. But—"

"No thanks necessary," he interrupted. "Maybe you have managed all right alone. Now you don't have to." He stared her down. "At least, not around *this* house."

Obviously, he'd set his mind on that. And now he'd set his jaw, too. Eyes glittering, he stood taller and looked even more determined.

And very, very sexy.

She backed up a step, shaking her head, whether in response to her thoughts or his words, she couldn't tell.

"I'm going to pack it in for the day," he said. "I'll be seeing you tomorrow—"

"I don't think so—"

"—at the town council meeting," he finished without missing a beat.

"Oh, right." How could she have forgotten?

She couldn't think around him. And obviously couldn't convince him of anything.

She'd better have her head on straight tomorrow night. She and Kayla had so many dreams for the kids of Flagman's Folly wrapped up in the proposal they planned to present.

She could only hope that, unlike Ben, the rest of the council would listen to reason.

Chapter 13

"We believe Flagman's Folly should provide a common area for children to play in, such as the one we propose."

Dana stood at the small podium reserved for anyone who wanted speak at a town council meeting. She tried to put her conviction into her words as she addressed the men and women seated at the long conference table at the front of the room. Behind them loomed Judge Baylor's massive wooden bench, the focal point of the courtroom adding solemnity to the occasion.

She swallowed hard and continued, "We also believe the children would benefit greatly from this playground. In addition—"

At the sight of several heads nodding even before she had finished her speech, she shot a triumphant glance in Kayla's direction—and promptly came to a halt when she saw the look on her friend's face. Something was wrong.

They had arrived late to the meeting. At the first

break, she and Kayla had squeezed into the only seats left available, on the end of the front row beside Tess and Caleb Cantrell.

Kayla and Tess both sat staring at her in dismay. From the row behind them, Ellamae whispered into their ears.

"Dana?" Ben asked. "Are you with us?"

Quickly she turned her attention back to the council. Ben was the chairman, but so far she had managed to meet everyone's gaze but his. "Yes," she replied, still not looking at him. "As I started to say, in addition, based on the facts we've outlined, we propose the council allocate the lot northwest of the elementary school for the playground."

Now the whispers came from all around the courtroom.

Now a few of the council members looked dismayed, too. Not one of them would look her way—except Ben. She refused to meet his gaze.

"Excuse me." Ellamae rose from her seat and hurried to stand beside Dana at the podium. "Since Dana and Kayla missed the earlier proceedings tonight—"

"They had car trouble, Ellamae. They explained that." Council member Joe Harley, also owner of the general store on Signal Street, smiled at Dana.

She winced. The new battery had done its job, but something else inside her van had quit on their way to Town Hall. They'd had to push the van to the curb with some help from a couple of teenagers and then hurry on foot the rest of the way.

"I know the details," Ellamae said with exaggerated patience. "I was here helping to present the *other* proposal on tonight's agenda. Remember?"

As the town clerk, Ellamae felt as comfortable speaking her mind in this courtroom as she did anywhere else in town. It didn't help that she'd known Dana and Joe since they were born.

She turned to Dana. "Tess doesn't want to break this news to you, and you couldn't have been aware of it, of course, seeing as you weren't here—" she glanced at Joe "—due to your aforementioned trouble with your vehicle. But we already presented our proposal for the memorial for Paul."

Dana nodded stiffly. "I assumed that's what you meant."

"And the monument's going on that very plot of land near the school."

Dana's heart sank. She turned to the front of the room. "But that location's the only property available that—"

Ben held up his hand, cutting her off, and now she had no choice but to meet his eyes. He looked as determined as he had the day before. And yes, just as sexy.

He also looked annoyed.

"Hold on a minute," he said. But his annoyance didn't seem to be directed toward her. He had turned his attention to Ellamae. "Your proposal—your very *worthwhile* proposal—was presented. But the council hasn't voted on it yet."

"What does that matter? Ben Sawyer, you know darn well it *will* be approved."

"Not tonight, it won't. We'll table discussion on both proposals until the next meeting."

"Thinks he's the judge here," she muttered, low enough that only Dana overheard.

"Excuse me?" Ben said.

She grinned. "You're in charge here."

"Right. Then, as we've come to the last item on our agenda, I'll call this meeting adjourned."

His eyes narrowed, and the look of intense irritation

on his face made Dana's pulse skip a beat. This time it wasn't directed at Ellamae, but at her.

She hurried to follow the folks streaming through the double doors. Outside, Caleb moved ahead through the crowd, but Kayla and Tess stopped off to one side of the doorway to wait for her.

As soon as she reached them, Tess said, "If I'd had any idea we had chosen the same site for both proposals, I would have tried to suggest some other location to our committee."

"It's just an unlucky coincidence," Kayla said.

But the site is perfect for the playground. Dana couldn't say that. Obviously, Tess felt terrible. "You would have had a hard time trying to sway Ellamae if she had her heart set on it, anyhow."

"She did," Tess said.

One of the people exiting the hall came to a stop by Dana's side. The scent of spice told her who it was.

"Hey, folks," Ben said. "Dana, got a minute?"

She eased a step away. "No, actually. I can't stop to chat. I promised Anne I'd come right home after the meeting."

"Then I'll give you a ride," he said, "seeing as you don't have a vehicle. No argument." He smiled. "It's on my way."

"Great," Tess said. "We're taking Kayla home—and we've got to run before we hit a traffic jam. I'll see you at the office in the morning, Dana. Night, Ben."

The two women hurried off.

She sighed. "Thanks for the offer, but it's only a couple of blocks. And please don't say anything about walking alone at night. Flagman's Folly is the safest place in the state." She watched Tess and Kayla cross the street and added under her breath, "We don't have traffic jams here, either."

"With only one traffic light on Signal Street, how could we? But that reminds me. What about your van?"

"I'll call the garage when I get home."

"Then the sooner you get there the better, before Ron closes up shop for the night."

"Not necessarily," she said sweetly. "You know everyone in town has his home phone number."

Ellamae and Roselynn emerged from the building.

"Dana!" Tess's mother exclaimed. "You're still here? Why, I wonder how come Tess and Caleb didn't take you home. Ellamae's got her car. Can we give you a lift?"

"All taken care of, ladies," Ben said. "Thanks, anyway."

"That's our Ben," Ellamae said, nodding.

Before Dana could say anything, both women beamed at him, then moved down the steps. As soon as they had gone out of earshot, she hissed, "I could have accepted and saved you the trouble."

"No trouble. I've got to pick up some tools I left at your place, anyway."

She exhaled heavily. "Ben Sawyer, remind me. Did you ever in your life lose an argument?"

He laughed. "No. And I don't aim to start."

A noisy group spilled out onto the porch, jostling her. She and Ben stepped aside.

Now that he wasn't glaring at her with irritation, as he had inside the courtroom, she noticed how the streetlamp picked up the warm tone of his brown eyes. How it highlighted the darkness and fullness of his dark lashes. Women would pay a fortune for mascara that could give them lashes like that.

In the lower lighting, his face seemed different, too.

Harder. More rugged. Even more interesting with the play of shadows carving his cheeks.

She wanted to touch him. Again. Just a gentle graze of his jaw, the way his hand had accidentally brushed her breast. At those thoughts, at that memory, at the sudden darkening of his eyes, as if he might be recalling that moment, too, she started to shake inside.

"Come on," he said, his voice rough, "let's get you home."

Ben made the short, almost-silent trip back to Dana's house in record time. If she hadn't had to get home to tuck the kids in and call Ron at the garage, he might've pulled over to talk. As it was, he bit his tongue and focused on the road. He'd get his turn. He'd make sure of that. He wasn't going home until he'd found out the truth about that look he'd seen in her eyes just a short while ago.

A look that had finally given him hope.

When she opened the front door and went upstairs, he waited a second, then moseyed over to take a seat on the couch. Better just to wait until her sitter left. Then they wouldn't have anything or anyone to distract them.

As she and Anne came down the stairs, she took one look at him and narrowed her eyes. She'd probably expected him to leave after he'd gotten his tools...the ones he hadn't actually left behind.

Anne said good-night, and the two of them went outside.

When Dana finally came back in and closed the door, he sat waiting. Instead of crossing to the living room, she moved to peer through the long window beside the front door.

"Something interesting out there?" he asked.

"I'm just seeing that Anne and Billy get to his car."

"Why? Not twenty minutes ago, you told me this is the safest town in the state."

"I'd just like to keep an eye on them," she said without turning. "They *are* still only kids."

He walked over to her. "Is that why? Or are you putting off talking to me, the way you did in the truck on the way home?"

"That's ridiculous."

Gently he took her by the arm and turned her to face him. "Is it? Or are you afraid?"

"Afraid? Of you?"

He might've taken offense at her scathing tone, except her laugh sounded forced. She didn't plan to make this easy for him. Maybe it wasn't easy on her, either. But he had to know if he'd really understood what he'd seen in her eyes.

"Now," he said softly, "who's talking trash? You'll never have anything to fear from me, and we both know that. You're afraid of what you were thinking outside Town Hall."

She shook her head. "Ben, I hate to tell you this. You can't read minds."

"I can read eyes, though. And faces. Especially yours, since I've known you so long. Take right now. I'm reading annoyance, clear as anything."

She groaned. "Okay, I'll grant you that. At the moment, anyone in the world could see it." She sighed heavily. "You know, we seem to do this all the time. We're as bad as Lissa and P.J., bickering like a couple of kids."

"That's just what I'm getting at. We're adults, not kids." He slid his hand from her arm to her shoulder. "We can stop bickering all on our own."

She shook her head again, as if in pity. But beneath his palm, she trembled. "Somehow I doubt that."

"You know better. And you've known me just as long as I've known you." He held his breath, contemplating what he would do next. The action could ruin that friendship forever. But no matter what she said, no matter the look on her face the other night when they'd stood this close, he knew what he'd seen in her eyes just a while ago. He reached up and touched her cheek. "I'll bet my ranch you can read me right now, too."

"The question is," she said, her voice shaking, "why would I want to?"

He laughed softly. "I can think of a few reasons." He bent his head and touched her mouth briefly with his. So briefly that if he'd closed his eyes first, he might have missed it.

Her eyes went wild, like those of a colt he was trying to break, and again, like a colt, she reared. Her back hit the door behind her with a thud.

"No," she said, crossing her arms. "We can't do this. Didn't those run-ins with Clarice tell you that?" She sighed. "I'm sorry. There have been a lot of mixed messages and crossed signals being sent around here lately. But that won't happen again. I promise you."

Those last words chilled him as effectively as a plunge into Sidewinder Creek in midwinter. Made him see sense just as effectively. He took a step back and nodded. "Yeah, you're right. It won't happen again."

"We *are* friends. But that's all. Right?"

He heard the desperation in her voice, as if nothing in the world meant more to her than having him agree.

He could almost see them again at their kindergarten desks. Him. Dana. And Paul.

"Right." He took a long, deep breath and let it out. "I'm your friend. And honorary uncle to your kids. Then, of course, there's our business relationship. I own the house. You pay the rent. And we can't forget our other relationship."

She hesitated. "What other relationship?"

"I'm on the council, and I hold the deciding vote. You presented a proposal. Right?" he pressed, just as she had done a moment ago.

"Right." She shook her head ruefully. "That was a real coincidence, two proposals involving the same property. But the site's perfect for—"

He held up his hand, just as he had in the courtroom. "You had plenty of chances to talk to me before tonight. You didn't want my help. No sense trying to convince me now." He couldn't keep the bitterness from his tone. No matter how much his feelings for her tied his thoughts up in knots, his mind stayed clear on one thing.

She refused to honor Paul.

"You could be right about the site for the playground. But why isn't it an equally good place for the tribute to your husband?" He'd kept his voice low, yet she flinched as if he'd shouted the question at her. "And why is it, all along, you haven't supported the idea of that memorial?"

"That's *my* business." Her eyes flashed. "And it's got nothing to do with any of *our* relationships." She stepped aside. "Excuse me. I have to call about my van. You shouldn't have any trouble finding your way out, since you're a foot away from the door."

She moved past him and hurried to the stairs, leaving him standing there looking after her. Leaving him angry. Sick. And disgusted with himself.

The way he had felt for days now.

He didn't understand why she wouldn't accept the idea of the monument. Why she still refused to honor Paul. But hadn't he done the same—no, hadn't he done much worse—by lusting after his best friend's widow?

No matter how much he wanted Dana, even with the ghost of his best friend standing between them, he couldn't disrespect her by going against her wishes. Not even for the pleasure of a one-night stand.

Not that she'd give him that now.

And if she ever did, he'd have his one night in paradise, that's all. Because the next morning, she'd regret it, and that would be the end. Of everything.

She'd never take him on as a long-term lover. She might reject him even as a friend. He couldn't run that risk.

He needed her.

Chapter 14

Ben fiddled with the handle of his coffee mug, debating whether he should ask Dori for another fill-up.

Monday night, after the town council meeting and their talk at her house, he'd let Dana kick him out. He'd gone slinking off like a mutt with its tail between its legs—because he hadn't known what to say. A hell of a thing to admit, for a man who almost always had the last word.

He'd stayed away from her place yesterday. Tough to do, since he missed seeing the kids. But he fought against stopping by. He didn't want to run into her. Yet.

In the long run, the distance had done him good because he'd had time to figure things out. In all these months since Paul had died, he'd done his best to get close to her, trying to help her. Trying to make her his.

And in these few short days, he'd discovered he'd done every damn-fool thing possible.

"Coffee, Ben?"

He looked up at Dori and nodded. "Last one. Then I'll be getting out of your way."

"What is that, 'get out of my way'? You are always welcome at the Double S." She smiled as she topped up his mug. "It's good to have you visit us for supper again."

He'd come in with a couple of his ranch hands, who had left afterward to go have a few beers. Now he'd hung around so long, he'd outstayed all the other diners. But he hadn't worn out his welcome here, the way he had with Dana.

As if she'd read his thoughts, Dori said, "Tess and Dana came in this afternoon with their new client. That big rodeo man, what's his name?"

No use pretending he didn't know. He'd heard it often enough around Dana's house. "Jared Hall."

"Yes. They hope they will make a sale to him." She went back to the kitchen, leaving him with his coffee.

Yeah, as if he didn't have enough to think about, there was Jared Hall. Like Caleb Cantrell, another big rodeo star. Unlike Caleb, a man who'd caught Dana's eye. And maybe not just for the commission.

He scowled down at his coffee mug. Then he shook his head, knowing he was avoiding the man he needed to think about.

Paul.

He pushed his mug aside and dropped some bills on the table. They'd settled his check earlier so Dori could close up the cash register.

After a quick good-night, he went out to his truck and decided to swing past Dana's before heading to the ranch. As he'd told her the other night, it was on his way home.

After ten o'clock now, and the shops had long ago rolled up their sidewalks. The temperature had dropped below average for the month, and most folks had their doors and windows closed, too. But at Dana's, the front door stood open. A rectangle of light fell across the porch and down the steps to the sidewalk.

He frowned. As he pulled to a stop in front of the house, a figure moved in the shadows of the porch. Anne, the sitter.

She walked out to the curb. "Hi," she said. "Dana's not home yet."

"No problem. Just passing through. I saw the door open and wondered about it. Something up?"

She shook her head. "No. Dana said Billy could come by for a while because she's out so late with Mr. Hall."

Would he never get away from that name? Would Dana ever get away from the man?

"They're out on a date." She giggled. "Billy and I weren't, really, since we were just hanging out, y'know?"

Yeah, he knew. He had gone on his fair share of those kinds of dates, too. When he'd gone out with the whole gang. And sometimes, when he'd only tagged along with Paul and Dana.

"He just went around the corner. You must have passed him. I left the door open—" she jerked her thumb over her shoulder, indicating the house "—in case the baby cried. But the kids are all asleep, and Dana ought to be home soon."

"From her date," he said in a level tone.

She nodded.

In spite of his...irritation, he felt better knowing she wasn't off somewhere alone in a van that might break down.

They said good-night, and he drove on. He could've kicked himself now for driving by. He didn't need to hear the news.

Dana and Jared Hall, out on a date. Together.

The coffee he'd downed burned in his gut. But it told him what he'd been trying to ignore. Irritation, hell— he wanted to kick the man's ass for even daring to look at his girl.

And *that* told him the real reason for his bad attitude.

No matter what he'd said to himself the past few days, no matter what he tried to force himself to believe about staying friends with Dana, he couldn't do it.

That would never be enough.

Way back in kindergarten, he'd never had the nerve to challenge his best friend for her attention. Now he no longer had to hold himself up against a man who was gone.

Now all he had to contend with was a real, live rodeo star.

He turned onto Signal Street, empty of traffic, and coasted along. He didn't plan to go by the office. They were probably out of town, anyway.

But down the block, once again, he saw lights shining across a sidewalk. Lights from the real estate office. The office in the building he owned. He kept coasting along. He ought to make sure that no one had broken into the place—even though Dana seemed to find Flagman's Folly the safest darned town in New Mexico.

He pulled to the curb and looked through the storefront window. Inside the office, she sat at her desk. Alone.

Judging by the paperwork spread out in front of her and the tape trailing from her calculator down to the floor, she'd sat there for some time.

Whatever she needed to figure, he'd give her something else to add to her calculations. He'd always been there for her, and he wasn't going anywhere now. He wasn't walking away. He wasn't losing out again. Because he was as good a man as anyone—including her rodeo star.

She'd need some time to think that over before she could accept it. He'd give her that time, no matter how long she took.

What did a few more years matter, when he'd already waited since kindergarten?

Dana scribbled another number on her notepad and made a face at it. The total hadn't changed since the previous week. And Jared still hadn't made up his mind.

Sighing, she put down her pencil. He was an intelligent man, good at conversation, and with a face any woman would love seeing across the table at a cozy little Italian restaurant. She had loved it tonight, too, no denying that. But that's as cozy as she would get. He just wasn't the man for her.

When he'd asked for another date, she had turned him down gently, hoping it wouldn't affect his decision about buying property. Either way, she couldn't pin all her expectations on a sale to him.

After dropping him off at the Whistlestop, she should have gone home. On her quick detour to the office, the new stack of bills in the mail Tess had left on the desk distracted her.

But now, nothing could distract her from her new worries.

When she had arrived home from work yesterday, Anne never mentioned a word about Ben. Finally, she'd broken down and asked. Anne said he hadn't come by the house at all.

Frowning, she pushed the stack of papers away from her.

She ought to be grateful that he'd paid attention, for

once, and had stayed away. Landlord or not, he wouldn't show up on the doorstep as often anymore. Not after Monday night. She and the kids would do better not having him around.

The sound of a tap on the office door startled her. She looked up.

Despite everything she had just told herself, when she saw who stood outside, she couldn't stop her immediate rush of pleasure. But, instantly, another instinctive response took its place.

Self-preservation.

Oh, please, not now.

Her thought didn't make Ben leave. And *she* couldn't make him leave, since he'd pulled his own key out of his pocket and unlocked the door.

As if he planned to stay a while, he took a seat next to her desk.

"Don't get comfortable on my account," she warned. "I'm about ready to pack it in."

"Yeah, I can understand that, after another late night with your client."

She opened her mouth to answer, then abruptly changed what she'd planned to say. "What makes you think I was with Jared?"

"Anne said—"

"You asked Anne?"

"Well…" He shrugged. "Yeah."

"Ben Sawyer, I thought we had this settled. You don't need to check up on me. I'm fine. The van is fine. Ron said it was only a loose connection."

His eyes widened, as if in surprise. "Is that what you think I'm here for tonight? To check up? Nope. That's got nothing to do with why I'm sitting in this chair."

"Then what is it? What are you doing here?"

"Do you really want to know?"

She sighed. "Probably not, but I'm asking."

"Jealous," he said flatly.

"What?"

"That's what I'm doing here." He slapped his palm on the desktop. "You were out and it was late and I was driven here by worry mixed with plain, damn jealousy."

She shook her head in the hope of making sense of his words. That didn't work. "Jealous of what?"

"Not what. Who. That rodeo cowboy. Now that we've got that *settled*," he emphasized, throwing her own word back at her, "need any help with that?" He gestured toward her paperwork.

This wasn't the Ben she knew. He was different tonight. But she wasn't. From now on, she couldn't allow herself to be anything but a woman protecting her secrets. Taking a deep breath, she folded her hands on the desk in front of her. "Ben."

He sat back in the chair, stretched his legs full-length and crossed them at the ankles. Staring down at his boots, he said, "You remember kindergarten?"

She blinked. He definitely was not himself, and he was mixing her up. But she wouldn't let him see that. "Yes."

"You remember how, when the timer rang, that meant we had to clean up the classroom?"

"Yes." If this was a game of Twenty Questions, she didn't plan to lose.

"Who always goofed around and made everybody laugh, but never picked up anything?"

"Paul."

"And who carried those little plastic bins around while you put the scissors and the glue sticks and the crayons into them?"

"You."

"Well, there you go." He kept his gaze focused on his boots. His dark lashes hid his eyes.

Just as well he wasn't watching her, because her eyes had begun to water. She did remember those days. And so many that came after them. Swallowing hard, she clamped her hands together.

"Telling me not to help you," he said, "is like telling Firebrand not to run. Or Becky's pup, Pirate, not to bark. Or Sidewinder Creek not to flow. Nature has to take its course. And so do I."

"Ben!" He made her crazy. But she couldn't hold back a laugh.

He grinned, still looking at his boots. "Well, it's true."

"Okay, I give in. And I'll admit it. You did help me. You helped everyone."

"That's true, too." At last, he raised his eyes to look at her, and she felt no desire to laugh. "Folks help other folks they care about, Dana." He leaned forward. "And remember, I always helped you the most." Lightly, he drew his finger across the back of her wrist.

She caught her breath, recalling the night they'd stood in her utility room and he'd held her wrist in his fingers. The night they'd kissed on the couch and he'd held her in his arms.

He stroked her hand, his finger tingling her sensitized skin. She had to fight not to lean toward him.

Just as she lost the struggle and moved forward, he sat back in his chair.

She took a deep, shaky breath, needing desperately to clear her mind. It didn't work. She had to get away from him. If he wouldn't leave, she would. Hands trembling, she shuffled her paperwork together and stowed it in her desk drawer. "Time to call it a night."

"I'll trail you home."

She looked at him.

"I'm leaving town, and it's on my way."

She hesitated, then nodded.

He followed her the few blocks to the house, where she parked the van. With the engine still running, she clung to the key ring in the ignition. He'd want to come inside with her. And she knew what he'd want next. The way he'd touched her just minutes ago told her that. Heaven help her, she wanted it, too.

Would she be able to resist?

When she walked across the yard, he stayed in his truck at the curb. Still expecting him to join her, she opened the front door. He flashed his lights and waved in farewell. Her heart gave a funny little flip, whether out of disappointment or relief, she didn't know.

She waved back, feeling cool and collected on the outside, hot and needy on the inside, and all mixed up whichever way she examined herself.

For a long time, she stood watching him drive away.

Then she closed the door and turned around and discovered Anne standing in the living room with her arms crossed.

"Where have you been all this time, young lady?" the teen asked, attempting to frown. "And who was that young man who just drove you home?"

Dana forced a laugh. "We had separate vehicles."

"A likely story." Anne's wide grin put dimples in both her cheeks. "He tracked you down, huh? I knew he would."

"He just happened to drive past the office while I was still there."

"Like I just happened to need something from Harley's every day Billy had to work?"

"No, this is different. Ben and I are just friends."

"Yeah." Anne nodded. "That's what Billy thought about us."

Dana smiled. But after Anne had gone home with her father and Dana made her way upstairs, the sitter's words came back to her, and she shook her head. Unlike Anne and Billy, she and Ben *were* just friends.

She frowned. He hadn't acted like himself at all. But no matter what crazy notion he'd gotten into his head tonight, he'd soon regret the idea.

Yet another reason for her to feel guilty for the mixed signals she kept sending.

After she'd gotten ready for bed, she made one last trip to the kids' rooms. As she tucked the dinosaur quilt around P.J., he stirred and opened his eyes.

"Mama," he whispered. "Hey, Mama...Ben didn't come for two whole days. You think he's coming tomorrow?"

She clutched the edge of the quilt. "I don't know," she said honestly.

"Maybe he will. I like Ben, Mama. I want a daddy like Ben."

He closed his eyes again and rolled over while she stood there frozen, trying to figure out what she could have said that wouldn't have broken his heart.

Or hers.

The next evening, with the dishwasher running and the counters cleaned, Dana felt at loose ends. Lissa sat at the kitchen table doing her homework, and P.J. had gone upstairs with his dinosaurs.

Neither of them had talked much at supper.

No one had said a word about Ben.

After helping Lissa with a couple of her English sentences, she went out to straighten the living room. A few minutes later, the doorbell rang. She stilled with her hands on the afghan she'd been folding.

Somehow, she knew she would find Ben on the door-step.

Crossing from the living room to the entryway, she managed to take one normal breath. When she opened the door and saw what he held cradled in his arms, the small, polite smile she'd forced onto her lips slid away. "What is *that?*"

"A present."

She could hear P.J. running down the hallway up-stairs. He'd be disappointed to find she'd beaten him to the door. Especially when he saw Ben there. *And* when he saw what Ben stood holding.

"Go away," she said through gritted teeth. "You can't bring that in here."

P.J.'s sneakers hit the stairs. "Who's there, Mama?"

"Come on, Dana, it's for the kids."

She shook her head and closed her eyes. Maybe she could make *everything* go away.

"Hey."

She jumped, and her eyes flew open. Ben had whis-pered the word against her ear. From inches away, she met his gaze. The corners of his eyes crinkled when he smiled. "It'll be okay. I promise."

No, it wouldn't. It was just another promise she couldn't let him keep.

P.J. ran up behind her. "A puppy!" he shrieked.

Ben slipped past her into the house. She closed the door and rested her head against it. Behind her, the babble rose. The high-pitched yap of the dog. Excited questions from P.J. Squawks of astonishment from Lissa, who had come running in from the kitchen.

And above it all, a deep laugh of happiness mixed with satisfaction. Ben's.

Ben couldn't have come up with a more devious plan than trying to get to her by getting *himself* in good with her kids. Somehow, she would have to harden her heart against his scheme. And pray she'd have more success with that than she'd had in trying not to obsess over him.

She turned.

Lissa and P.J. sat on the edge of the couch. Ben knelt beside the coffee table with the whimpering dog in his hands.

"It's like Christmas." Lissa sounded entranced.

Ben handed the dog to P.J., who held the wriggling bundle carefully in both arms.

Lissa leaned over to pet one of the dog's floppy ears. Big, sad brown eyes stared up at her. "What is he?" she asked.

"It's a she," Ben said. "She's just a plain old hound dog."

"We have to name her."

"Duke." P.J.'s tone said he would accept no argument.

"You can't give a girl a boy's name," Lissa argued.

"Why not? Nate's a girl, isn't she? *She's* got a boy's name. I like Duke." The dog looked at him and yipped again. P.J. nodded emphatically. "See, she likes it, too. It's a good dog's name. *Duke.*"

"No—"

"How about Duchess?" Ben asked quickly.

P.J. frowned. "What's that?"

"It's a girl duke." He turned to Lissa. "You know, like prince and princess. Duke and duchess."

"*Oh-h-h.* Yeah. I like that. Okay, P.J.?"

"Okay." He grinned. "Thanks, Ben. Thanks a lot! I always wanted a puppy." His eyes shone.

So did the dog's.

And, when Ben looked at her, so did his.

But when he started across the room toward her, she blinked back the tears that threatened and braced herself, literally, against the door.

She had to get him to take back that dog.

The minute he reached her, she spoke, her voice low so the kids wouldn't hear. But she'd bet he would have no trouble reading the anger in her eyes.

"Ben, what do you think you're doing?"

"You said you'd like to have a dog."

"Yes, I did. But I said *someday.* I can't—" She choked on the word and had to start again. "I told you, we can't have a dog. I work all day."

"Clarice said she'll keep an eye on her for you."

Wonderful. The whole town would know what he'd done. "You told Clarice about the dog?"

"Clarice and Ellamae told me. When I said I wanted a puppy for the kids, they came along to help me pick her out at the pound."

Even better. Now all of Flagman's Folly would know *she'd* turned away a poor homeless puppy. A puppy who now yelped in the background. A puppy who had just made P.J. and Lissa laugh.

How would she manage to explain this to the kids?

"I don't want a dog cooped up in the house," she said.

"Let her out in the yard."

"It's too hot in the summertime. And there's no shade."

"So I'll build a doghouse and plant a tree."

She groaned. Would he never give up? "I don't like the idea of staking a—"

He raised his brows.

She snapped her mouth shut in instant understanding. "The fence," she hissed when she could speak again. "*That's* why you put up the fence, isn't it?"

He smiled.

He means well. He always does. Take a deep breath before you blast him.

Instead, she sighed. Blasting wouldn't work. She needed to be truthful and explain her most important reason for digging in her heels. She kept her voice low but made her tone uncompromising. "We can't keep the dog." Quickly, she put her fingers to his lips to prevent him from responding. The warmth of his skin almost made her forget what she'd planned to tell him. "I can't—" Her voice broke.

He smiled again, his mouth tickling her fingertips.

She snatched her hand away. Her cheeks burned, partly from allowing him to see her reaction and the rest from knowing what she had to admit. "I can't afford to feed him," she muttered.

"Her." He kept his voice low, too. "And she comes with a lifetime supply of dog food and unlimited veterinary care."

"I can't accept that."

"Why not? We're still friends, aren't we? Just like you said the other night?"

She swallowed a sigh of both relief and disappointment. So, they were back to that again. How quickly he'd managed to come to his senses.

With anyone else but Ben, she would have thought he'd repeated her words to hurt her. But, no, he meant them. Chances were, if she let him, he'd pay for her grocery and doctor bills, too. He only wanted to help.

She needed to remember that the next time her expression threatened to give her secrets away.

He moved closer. She could feel the heat radiating

from him. Had to look up to see his eyes. Had to curl her fingers to keep them by her sides.

"Dana." His voice rumbled her name. She would swear she'd felt it vibrate through her. "Let me do this. For them. Because, like it or not, I will be here for you and your kids for the rest of my life."

Chapter 15

"Have you had your talk with Ben yet?" Tess asked as they crossed the Double S parking lot.

Always busy on a Friday night, the café already had customers seated outside. Tiny lights strung around the patio twinkled like fireflies in the twilight.

Dana tried not to groan at her friend's question. She'd had plenty of talks with Ben. Too many talks. But none she could share with Tess. "No. Not yet. Jared has kept me busy."

"Well, now he's left town, he can't stop you from having your chat."

"No." She wished she could argue that point.

And when she followed Tess through the front door of the restaurant, she immediately wished she could turn around and leave. Even as the thought struck, Caleb waved at them from a booth on the opposite side of the café. Across from him, Ben turned to look and smiled.

They had held the closing for Caleb's new ranch earlier in the week, and he'd wanted to celebrate at the Double S. She hadn't realized he'd planned a party for four.

When she had walked over to the Whistlestop to drop the kids off just now and caught a ride here with Tess, her best friend hadn't said a word about Ben joining them for supper. Well, she'd give Tess the benefit of the doubt. Maybe he and Caleb had just run into each other.

Gripping her handbag with suddenly damp fingers, she took the seat beside Ben.

Caleb wrapped his arm around Tess. "Hey, Dana," he said. "You get Jared up to Santa Fe all right yesterday?"

"Yes, in plenty of time to catch his flight." In her effort to avoid Ben, she had volunteered to drive their newest client to the airport. "He hadn't made any decision before he left, though."

And Tess still hadn't let up with her teasing. "I'm surprised he left at all," she said now. "But he told Caleb he'll be back soon. He seemed to like your personal attention."

Beside her, Ben shifted, giving her more room. She dropped her bag on the seat between them. Refusing to look his way, she said lightly, "Well, you know what we tell all our clients. 'You've come to the Wright Place.'"

Caleb chuckled. "Yeah, I heard that not too long ago."

"And it turned out to be true, didn't it?" Tess asked.

"Yep. That's why we're here celebrating tonight."

She elbowed him. "I'm not talking about the ranch."

He dropped a kiss on her temple.

Ben turned to Dana. "Kids home with Anne?"

His voice sounded stiff to her ears, but the other two didn't seem to notice. "No. She has a date tonight."

"With her high school hero," Tess said.

Dana grabbed a taco chip from the bowl on the table and nearly buried it in the salsa.

"The kids are at the Whistlestop with Nate," Tess went on. "She had a fit when she heard supper was adults-only."

We're adults, Ben had said the night Dana had almost let him kiss her. Again. *We can stop bickering all on our own.*

But they couldn't.

"Mom promised her a barbecue," Tess continued, "so naturally, she wanted Lissa to come and stay the night. Mom and Aunt El are thrilled to have all the kids sleeping over, too. They were just complaining the other day about not sitting for them in so long."

Just as Ben had complained about not getting to see enough of the kids.

When Dori came to the booth, Dana ordered the first thing that came into her head. Tacos. A bad choice, reminding her of the day Ben had bought lunch for her family and Lissa's friends. Reminding her of all the days he'd spent at the house lately.

And bringing her thoughts to Monday night after the meeting. He'd gone from amorous to arrogant, in the space of a few heartbeats. All for the best, of course. His response had only made her more determined to keep her distance, before they did anything *else* they would both regret.

He seemed to remember the wisdom of that, too. When he'd dropped by the office the day before, he'd kept his visit all business and brief. Too brief for her liking.

Now, nothing seemed to satisfy her about their relationship. Maybe because the only thing she wanted was a *close* relationship. One everyone could know about. And she couldn't have that.

Sitting beside him, listening to his voice, hearing his

laugh… Every minute felt like a punishment for a longing she had no way to control.

During supper, she struggled to keep her mind on the conversation. At the same time, she counted the minutes until they would finish eating and she could go home.

Late in the evening, she caught Tess eyeing her, making her sit up and—belatedly—pay attention. What had she missed? And why did Tess look so uncomfortable?

"Aunt El's spent a lot of time pounding the pavement this week," Tess said. "To prove there's support for the monument, she's getting names on a petition and plans to bring it to the next council meeting."

"Has she?" Ben asked. "Going to be an interesting night."

"Kayla and I aren't worried." Dana spoke with an assurance she didn't feel. The council members would vote for the playground. They had to.

If she needed to depend on Ben and his deciding vote, she might as well put their proposal through the office shredder. He would never support her, even if she tried to win him over to her opinion. Besides, how could she get close enough to talk to him at all, when he claimed he could read her so well?

If he could truly see into her heart, what he found would drive him away from her. Would push him toward voting against her.

What did it matter? They could never come to an agreement.

He wanted to honor his best friend. And she wanted no part of the memorial.

Supper finished, the four of them strolled outside to the patio. Dana half listened as Ben told Tess and Caleb about a new mare he'd bought for the ranch. While they talked, she looked beyond the patio to a sky studded with stars.

A beautiful night, a night for lovers.

As if Caleb had heard Dana's thought, he pulled Tess close and said, "Since Nate's spoken for this evening, the two of us are going off for some alone time."

In the light of the tin lanterns on the patio tables, Tess blushed and looked at Dana, who swallowed her smile.

Caleb turned to Ben. "You don't mind taking Dana home?"

She caught her breath. Her earlier suspicions returned, and she shot another look at Tess. Did the color in her face really come from a blush, or had her cheeks flushed in guilty embarrassment? Had Tess known what Caleb was going to ask Ben? Had she put him up to it to begin with? Dana tried to push away the thought that Ben's invitation to supper had all been part of a plan. *Not Tess.*

Besides, as Dana had told Kayla, even Ellamae and Roselynn wouldn't have dreamed of matching her up with Ben.

"No problem," he said now. "I can drop Dana at the house."

And what could she say in return? She couldn't insist that the newlyweds drive her home. Feeling guilty for harboring even a fleeting suspicion of her own best friend, she simply nodded.

They walked out to the front of the café, where Tess had left their SUV and where Dana now noted Ben's truck parked up near the corner.

She wrapped her hands around her arms, chilled not from the October air but from the knowledge that she'd have to accept the ride home with Ben. After all the objections he had raised the night of the council meeting, she would never convince him to let her walk home alone.

Not at this hour.

Not even in the safest town in the state.

They said their farewells and walked away. Dana held her head high and kept her eyes focused on his truck. He claimed to be able to read her face. To see her feelings in her eyes. Though she wouldn't admit it then, even to herself, she acknowledged now that she knew exactly what he'd seen in her eyes on Monday night outside Town Hall.

The same thing he'd seen the night they'd stood so close together in her utility room.

Well, he wouldn't see it tonight. Not if she could help it. She continued to keep her eyes focused and her face forward and her tone light as they chatted all the way home.

All the way to the house Ben owned.

"Thanks for the ride," she said, her hand on the passenger-door handle.

"I'll walk you in."

That's not necessary had been her battle cry for weeks now, and where had it gotten her? Nowhere with Ben. He never listened to anything.

Other than that, she had to admit, he excelled at everything, whether it involved ranching or handyman chores or caring for her kids. And as a perfect gentleman, since he'd driven her home—not just followed her—of course he would insist upon seeing her to the door.

To her surprise, as they went up the front path, he said, "Since we didn't stay for one of Dori's desserts, I thought you might pour me a cup of coffee." From inside the house, the dog yipped. "I haven't seen Duchess in a couple of days. And," he added, "I'd like to talk for a bit."

"Talk?"

"Yeah, talk. You know, conversation. Words back and forth. You and me."

More than likely, he wanted to discuss something to do with the house or the office. "I don't know. The last time we tried that, things didn't work out very well." She held back a sigh of exasperation at herself. Did they really need the reminder?

"If you keep the cookies coming, we ought to be fine."

Shaking her head, she said, "You're as bad as the kids." But Duchess had begun barking in earnest now. Dana led him inside.

While he greeted the dog, she went to the kitchen to fill the coffeemaker and the teakettle. Duchess padded into the room and bounded into her bed in the corner.

"The cookie jar's in the utility room," she told Ben. "Second shelf on the left. Beside the box of cereal."

To quote him, those directions "ought to be fine," too. They would have to, because she wasn't venturing anywhere near that room with him again. Her face warmed, reminding her of Tess's flush earlier. Now she couldn't tell if her own warmth came from a blush or guilty embarrassment. But she knew the trigger came from her memory of what had happened in that utility room a few short days ago.

Crossed signals.

She'd attempted to make that plain to him, too. She'd tried to explain about the mixed messages between them, though she knew in her heart she was to blame for most of them—bickering with him one moment and staring at him like a starstruck schoolgirl the next. Staring openly enough to give him the idea she'd wanted him to kiss her. Again.

Yet, that night in the utility room, all he had done was touch her wrist, and she had melted against him.

Well…all right, she hadn't quite let herself go to that extent.

But she'd wanted to.

For sure, she had trembled. For certain, he had felt it. No denying that. She could tell by the way he'd looked her up and down and then stared, his expression frozen.

She'd wanted him the night of Tess's wedding, too.

She would want him forever....

"You okay?"

Startled, she placed a couple of dessert plates on the table with a clatter. "Yes."

"You look out of it. Maybe you need a good night's sleep."

"Maybe."

"Lucky for you, all the kids went to stay at the Whistlestop again." He lifted the lid of the cookie jar. "Chocolate chip, huh?"

She nodded, on the verge of nervous laughter. Obviously good old Ben didn't feel *he'd* gotten lucky. Or maybe he felt he had—with the cookies. She ought to be glad to have such an...honorable friend. She ought to be doubly glad he hadn't mentioned that other night when quiet surrounded the two of them and no children slept upstairs.

"You wanted to talk?" she prompted, pouring her tea and his coffee.

"Yeah."

He took a cookie from the jar. "Chocolate chip are my favorite. Remember when you used to make them for me in your cooking class in eighth grade?"

She remembered. She'd thought of it the night of the wedding, too, when he'd asked her about "his" cookies. Was that why she'd baked these yesterday before taking Jared to the airport?

"Not just for you," she said. "Tess and I gave the burned cookies to all the guys."

He laughed.

Turning from the counter with their mugs, she saw he had taken P.J.'s place at the table, which put him closer to her than usual. But if she walked all the way around to Lissa's side to get some distance from him, they would sit facing one another.

She took her regular seat next to the baby's high chair. "I'm sure you didn't come in to discuss the cookie of the week, even if they are your favorite. What do we need to talk about, the house or the office?"

"The memorial."

She had lifted her brimming mug almost to her lips. Her hand jerked. Boiling water sloshed onto her fingers. She nearly dropped the mug onto the table, then grabbed her napkin and dabbed at her hand.

"Did you get burned?"

He reached for her, but she jerked her hand away, deliberately this time. "Don't worry about it. I told you, how I feel about the monument is my business."

"I heard that. I can see it. Tonight at supper, Caleb and Tess could, too. Didn't you notice how they reacted? Do you want everyone else seeing it, too?" His voice rose.

Duchess yelped. He waited until she had settled down again before continuing in a lower voice, "I have to tell you, folks are damned excited about that memorial, and even more excited about the fact they're dedicating it to a man they admire. How are they going to feel, every time they make mention of it, when that man's own wife looks like she can't stand to think about it?"

"I don't look—"

"You sure as hell do. And is that what you want them to see? Is that what you want your kids to notice every time their daddy's name is mentioned?" He stood abruptly, the chair legs screeching on the kitchen floor. "Come with me."

"What?"

But he had left the room.

Angry now, she followed through the doorway. He was already headed toward the stairs. "Where are you going?"

"I want to show you something in P.J.'s room."

"What does he have to do with this?" she asked.

But he didn't answer.

Upstairs, he went into her son's room.

Following close on his heels, she came to a halt just inside the doorway.

Everything looked the same as usual, from the dinosaur-patterned quilt she had made for P.J.'s bed, to the row of baseball caps hanging from pegs on the closet door, to the plastic jar on one end of his dresser. The jar of washers he'd carried with him almost everywhere since Ben had given it to him.

Ben had replaced the overhead light fixture a couple of weeks ago, but other than that, she could find nothing different. "What is it I'm supposed to see?"

"This." He reached up between the dresser and the doorway and tapped a picture frame hanging on the wall.

Paul's photograph.

She took a half step backward, but he caught her hand and drew her into the room. Then he took her by the shoulders and turned her to face the photo, the original of the small picture P.J. had left on the coffee table downstairs.

"And this." He tapped the row of medals on the uniform. "Paul earned every one of these for skill and bravery and honor. For fighting to help people who couldn't help themselves. For saving lives. And if that's not enough for you, just think about what else he did. He gave *his* life for his country."

She heard him inhale and exhale slowly. Felt his breath ruffle her hair and his hands lift from her shoulders.

"That makes him a hero," he said, his voice hard now. "A hero in anyone's eyes—but yours."

His boot heels struck the wooden floor when he backed away from her, as if he couldn't stand to be near her. In the dresser mirror, she saw his reflection. His face looked pinched, his eyes sad. "You married that man and had children with him, but even for their sake, you can't honor him the way he deserves. You loved him, but—"

"I *didn't* love him."

"What?"

She looked at his reflection again and wanted to cry at the look on his face. At the truth of how she felt about him. At the memory of his reaction when he'd realized her feelings. And most of all, at the lies he and everyone else in her life believed about Paul.

The lies she had fed them.

She turned to face him. "I didn't love him," she said. "I did when I married him, but not...at the end."

He shook his head as if stunned. "He loved you."

"No, he didn't. Paul loved—" she flung her arm out and pointed at the photograph on the wall "—*that*. Being a hero. Being a football star. Being looked up to and admired and—and *honored*. Paul loved the image of Paul."

"You're wrong. He was my best friend, and I knew him as well as anyone could. Better than you did, obviously."

"You didn't know him at all." The words had tumbled out before she could stop them. He looked as if she'd slapped him. "He liked you, yes. But for the most part, he liked what you could do for him."

"No—"

"Yes. Think back. Who drilled history and geography into him when he didn't study for exams in grade school? Who covered for him with the principal when he got in trouble in junior high? Who always picked up the checks when we went to the Double S after the high school football games?" Her voice cracked, and she swallowed hard. "Who drove me home from parties when he couldn't stand to leave the crowd?"

"He was my friend. I didn't mind doing any of those things for him."

"You didn't have a choice. He may never have fumbled a ball in his life, but he'd have dropped you in a minute if you'd stopped providing what he wanted. I'm sorry, Ben, but he used you. The way he used me and anyone else he could."

"I don't buy a word of that. And how can you say those things about him? He was a damned good husband—"

"He wasn't."

That stopped him, but not for long. "All right, maybe not in your eyes. But he was a good provider and a good daddy—"

"He wasn't either of those."

"Oh, come on." He grimaced and shook his head. "Next thing, you'll be telling me he never existed."

"He existed, all right," she said. "He just hid the real Paul behind the image he let everyone see."

"Dammit, I don't believe this." He brushed past her. "And I'm not staying around to listen to it."

His boots thudded against the stairs.

She curled her fingers into fists, then winced as the skin pulled taut on her scalded hand. Her eyes blurred with tears. Not from the pain of her blistered fingers but from the irony of their heated words. She'd done such a good job of lying, Ben couldn't believe her when she told the truth.

Downstairs, the front door slammed.

The sound of it echoed through the quiet house, reminding her she would be alone all night.

Except for the dog.

Chapter 16

Halfway home again, Ben made a last-minute decision at a crossroads, swinging the truck onto a side road that would take him even farther out of town. His thoughts had swung twice as fast—several times over—since he'd barreled out of Dana's house.

Instead of leaving her at the door, as he probably should have, he'd gone inside. He'd wanted answers to all the things troubling him. Instead, he'd left there a hell of a lot more troubled, with way too many questions— old and new—in his mind.

Questions he had no plans to share with anyone.

This time on a Friday evening, he'd have found no one at the ranch to listen to him anyway. His foreman and all his ranch hands would have gone their own ways, maybe into town for the high school varsity game or out on the back highway to one of the bars for a brew. Neither of those choices attracted him tonight. He didn't want to be on his own—didn't want to give all those questions in his head free rein. Still, he disliked the idea of facing a crowd. Strange, since he usually liked being out with folks.

He and Paul both had.

A few miles later, he pulled up to a ranch house much like his own, knowing he'd have a good chance of finding a family man like Sam Robertson at home. Sure enough, Sam answered the door with his five-year-old peeking out from behind him.

"Hey, Ben, have a seat. Be right back. Becky and I were just going into the kitchen to see her mama." He turned to his daughter and signed the words as he said aloud, "Ready for your bedtime snack?"

Looking at Ben, she grinned and tapped the fingertips of one hand against her other palm.

"I know that one," he said, copying her motion. "Cookies, right?" He tried not to think about…the chocolate chips he'd just left behind.

Sam nodded. "Yep. Want a beer? Coffee? Sweet tea?"

"Tea sounds good." He didn't want to think about the coffee he'd missed out on, either. He took a seat on one of the living room couches and looked at the chime clock on the mantel. Earlier than he'd figured. The conversation he'd planned to have with Dana hadn't gone nearly as long as he'd expected.

Sam came back into the room carrying two tall glasses.

Ben took a swig and looked at Sam, who had settled back on the other couch. The two of them had been friends for a long time—as long as he'd known Paul. If anyone could swap memories with him, Sam could. If anyone would tell him the truth, Sam would.

And he wanted some truths.

Not about Dana. Those, he'd have to hear from her own lips, if she'd ever share them.

He swallowed another mouthful of tea. "I left the post digger out by the barn."

"Good timing. Caleb wants it for next week."

The two of them talked for a while, and eventually, as Ben had known it would, the conversation came around to Paul.

"Kayla told me about the monument," Sam said. "A good idea."

"Yeah." Too bad everyone didn't think so. He frowned, recalling what Dana had said about her life with Paul. What he had no intention of believing. "I'm glad folks came up with the proposal and followed through on presenting it to the council."

"Paul would have been, too."

"You mean that folks want to honor him?"

"And to look up to him like we always did."

The statement came too close to Dana's accusations for comfort. "We can't blame him for that."

"Of course not. He was used to having us all hanging around the biggest fish we'd ever had in our little pond. You'd know that more than the rest of us."

"Yeah." Just what did he know? Nothing, according to Dana. "Did you ever think he took all that attention for granted?" That was as close as he would go to asking a question he didn't really need an answer to. It was crazy for him to wonder about it. To let Dana's distorted thoughts affect his own.

But Sam laughed. "Ben, I think he took everything he could get and wanted more. And I'll tell you another thing. When they set up that monument, they'd better make sure it's something fancy, something big and hard to miss—just like him. That's what he'd have wanted, too."

Ben's memories rang true. He had to respect them.

Much as he hated to admit it, he had to allow Dana the right to her feelings, too.

But he had memories and feelings of his own, and they were all tied up with what that monument meant to him.

A physical representation of the honor Paul deserved. An honor he—as Paul's closest friend—would make every effort to uphold.

A permanent reminder that he had to do his best for Dana and her young family, though she fought him every step of the way.

A mocking remembrance that he'd waited too long to tell her the truth about his promise.

And a deathblow to any chance he might have with her.

Dana padded barefoot into the bathroom. Her feet stung from the cold tiles. Her eyes stung, too. As she switched on the light and opened the medicine chest, she avoided looking at her reflection. She'd already caught sight of her face in her bedroom mirror, and it wasn't pretty. Not surprising, after the night she'd put herself through.

Or half a night. When she'd rolled out of bed just now, her alarm clock had read 3:37 a.m.

Her face looked puffy. Her hair sprouted in different directions. Her blistered hand throbbed.

And she'd left the ointment in the living room.

Groaning, she went down the hall, headed toward the stairs. Halfway along, she stopped. After a long battle with herself, she went into P.J.'s room and turned on the lamp on his nightstand. Then she sat on the edge of his bed, took a deep breath and brushed her hand across a dinosaur on his quilt.

She didn't want to look at the other side of the room.

In any other photo she'd ever seen of Paul, he'd had his mouth curved in a confident grin and his chin held high, tilting his head into his favorite look-at-me-and-love-me angle.

And she had loved him. All through school, he was the boy of her dreams, and after graduation she had married him. Yet, a few years later she'd felt only relief when they'd agreed that their marriage was over.

When it came to being a husband and father, he'd left a lot to be desired. Then he had gone overseas with his platoon, where he'd earned all those medals he wore.

In everyone's eyes but hers, he'd gone from strength to strength, from golden boy to brave soldier to war hero. In the meantime, she'd kept up appearances, and when he came home on leave, she'd made that one last-ditch effort to save their marriage. Only days later, he was killed.

For the folks in Flagman's Folly, and especially for her children's sake, she could never do anything to destroy Paul's image.

Not when she'd spent so many years helping to preserve it.

She couldn't risk getting close to Ben, no matter how much she wanted to. As it was, she'd told him too much tonight.

At last she looked across the room at the photograph on the wall. Paul stared back at her with the most serious expression she'd ever seen on him in a photo. Or, come to think of it, in real life.

Sighing, she rose from the bed.

The doorbell rang. She gasped, then hurried to the stairs, her thoughts flying to her children. To the fear any mother would have when a bell pealed in the middle of the night and her child wasn't home.

To the sight of Tess standing on the front porch, waiting to tell her—

She flung the door wide.

Not Tess.

Ben.

"I thought—" she blurted. "The kids?"

"No," he said quickly. "No, nothing about the kids."

Exhaling in relief, she sagged against the door.

Duchess had run into the room and wove in and out between them. Only half aware of doing so, Dana stooped to pat the puppy. Duchess wriggled in excitement, accepted a head-scratching from Ben and then padded back to the kitchen.

Dana stood and looked at Ben, her eyebrows raised.

"I…saw your light on," he said.

"Oh." She blinked. "And you thought you'd…drop in."

"Well, I never did get my coffee."

She stared at him in disbelief. He wanted more than coffee. He wanted to pick up their conversation again. At this hour.

That was Ben, though. She knew him well.

He'd never give up on anything. Never break a promise. Never leave a friend hanging. Never want to let the sun go down—or in this case, come up—on an argument. It had both surprised and startled her when he'd slammed out of there last night.

Now they might as well get this over with.

Once and for all.

She stepped back. When he moved past her, she closed the door. "Have you been sitting outside the house all night?"

"No. I headed home and then…drove around for a while."

"Have a seat. I'll bring the coffee out here. Give me a few minutes."

Or a few hours.

At one point in her presentation, she stopped, realizing she was going through the same motions she had on the night they'd made love. Now, she shivered. Not in excitement or anticipation but in fear. Because she wanted Ben's arms around her again. *No matter what.*

Then she thought of her kids. Of Clarice and the rest of the townsfolk. Of seeing how only a portion of the truth had hurt Ben.

Compared to all that, what she wanted couldn't even make the list.

It wasn't until she brewed the coffee and returned to the living room and saw the way he looked at her that she realized she'd run downstairs in her sleepwear.

Oh, well. Serve him right for all the times he'd walked around here shirtless.

Too bad he'd get less of a thrill than she ever had eyeing him. Lissa had passed the nightshirt on to her, labeling it "babyish." It covered more of her than the gown she had worn for Tess's wedding…the gown Ben had unbuttoned later that night.

In any case, the picture of the smiling teapot on the nightshirt went perfectly with the plate she carried.

"Here," she said, holding it out to him. "You never got your chocolate chip cookies, either."

Dana had said she didn't want any of the cookies, so he polished them off. Once in a while, he sipped from his mug. She had taken a seat on the other end of the couch, and they sat there in silence. After all, he told her he'd come for the coffee. Why would she sit there and chat?

Why would he start a conversation?

Because he *had* to. Just as he'd had to come here again.

After talking to Sam, after spending hours driving the back roads in his pickup truck, he'd finally admitted he couldn't stay away. He had to know everything Dana had kept from him.

From the corner of his eye he took in her bare calf, the curve of her knee and the swell of her breasts beneath the soft nightgown.

Leaning forward, he set his empty plate onto the table. At the sight of the scrunched-up tube of ointment, he frowned, remembering. She had burned her hand in the kitchen earlier.

Looking over at the plate, she said, "I assume you want to talk again."

He waited until she turned his way. "That, too. But I also want to listen." Her eyes widened, revealing how much his words had surprised her. He waited, giving her time to get her expression under control again. Then he said, "Tell me about Paul."

"What do you want to know?"

Her shoulders went back, and he knew he'd better take it slowly. Better start with details less upsetting to her. He settled against the couch and rested his coffee mug on his thigh. "Tell me about the scholarship."

She frowned. "He didn't get one."

"That's what I meant."

She shifted, putting more space between them. Deliberately or not, he didn't know.

"He'd pinned his hopes on winning a scholarship somewhere. When he got passed over in the draft by his first choice and then his second choice and finally all his other choices, he decided to go to State." She looked down at her hands in her lap. "Even there, when he made the team, he couldn't get his star quarterback status again."

She'd lowered her voice, as if trying to soften her words. To ease his disappointment. To help him deal with the truth.

"Because he *wasn't* a star," she continued. "Here in Flagman's Folly, yes, where everyone had his back and made him look good. But not at State. There, he wasn't even a team player. They'd cut him before the third game."

He tightened his fingers around the coffee mug. "That's when he came home?"

"Yes."

"You said…" *He wasn't a good husband.*

Hell, he couldn't ask her about that, though he wanted to know. What happened between husband and wife had to stay there. But she'd told him something else, too. "You said he wasn't a good provider."

"No." She smoothed the afghan resting on the arm of the couch. "You know after he came back, he took the job at the dealership. Mostly because he liked the idea of being the superstar car salesman. And he did make some sales over the years. But with the economy so bad, he didn't make many."

He clenched his free hand into a fist. "Geez, Dana. He could've borrowed from me—"

"No, he couldn't. Because then people would know. They'd see the real Paul behind the image."

"I wouldn't have told anyone."

"No, you wouldn't." She sounded sad. "You'd have covered for him. The way you always did. And he knew that."

"Then why didn't he come to me?"

"Because I told him if he asked you for money, I would spread the news to everyone in Flagman's Folly."

"You—" He choked on the word. *"Why?"*

"Because he would have been using you, the way he'd always done. And I couldn't stand to see it happen again." Her fingers dug into the afghan. "Ben, he gambled away the commissions he made from the dealership."

He shook his head. "I would've known—"

"No, you couldn't have. He didn't do it here, just for that reason. *Folks would know.* He lost most of it in out-of-town casinos, and the rest he spent buying things on-line. Status symbols, to show off his wealth—what little he had left."

The longer she talked the faster the words came. He didn't want to hear any more. But he had to listen.

"When that ran out, he turned to me. The economy hadn't done much for real estate, either. Still, he took every penny he could get—every penny I could squeeze from my business without going under." She exhaled a shaky breath and met his eyes. Hers were filled with a pain he had no trouble reading. "He took food from the kids' mouths. But he didn't care, because no one would know."

"Damn," he muttered. *"I* didn't know. I—"

"Don't," she said. "It's the image he wanted you to see. We all have those. Just as we have things we want to hide."

Her words cut him with their toneless accusation, a reminder of the secret he'd kept from her. Of the promise he'd made.

He set his mug on the coffee table and rose from the couch. He had come back here again looking for answers. But he'd never expected to hear all this.

It mocked everything he had known about Paul. Everything he'd done for him.

Everything he hadn't done for himself.

All this time, he had stayed away from Dana, believing he couldn't touch her. Believing he owed Paul that loyalty.

Now, getting hit with all this…

He shook his head. "I can't believe it. The man died a hero, Dana."

Eyes gleaming, she looked away.

Chapter 17

Dana spent the weekend with the kids...and without Ben. Fortunately they had the puppy to keep them all occupied. Yet even Duchess couldn't hold P.J.'s attention full-time.

On Sunday afternoon, as she sat on the couch folding clothes, he'd climbed up to sit beside her.

"Where's Ben, Mama?" he asked. "He doesn't like us anymore?"

She'd expected something like that. Hadn't she known having Ben around the house so often wasn't the best thing for the kids? She had to swallow hard before she could respond. "I'm sure he's busy working on his ranch today."

"I miss him."

"I know you do," she'd said. *So do I.*

On Monday, with things so quiet, she suggested Tess take the day off for more honeymoon time, to run errands, for whatever she liked. And when Tess took her up on the offer, she sagged in guilty relief.

She welcomed the chance to spend the time alone in the office. But by late afternoon, the quiet had gotten to her. The walls had begun to close in. She'd had too much time to think.

She left work early for a quick trip to Harley's on her way home. And even there, standing at the head of the pet-products aisle, she found her thoughts straying to Ben.

He'd looked shell-shocked by everything she had said. It destroyed her to know how much she'd hurt him. But she couldn't keep the truth hidden any longer. Not from him.

That second time, he had left the house quietly. No slamming the door behind him. No puppy bounding in from the kitchen to investigate. That time, she had felt so much worse. Because his careful closing of the door made his departure final.

Yet it also made it more like Ben. That was his way. Not to make waves, not to cause trouble, just to be there, steady, reliable, safe. Always.

Though not for her, from now on.

"Excuse me," an unmistakable—and unmistakably teasing—voice said from behind her. Tess pushed her cart beside Dana's. Eyebrows raised, she pointed toward the aisle. "Don't you need to go down there?"

Tess's question didn't surprise her. "I hate to tell you this," Dana said, "but your expression of wide-eyed innocence stopped working in the third grade. And no, I don't need dog food. The puppy came with a good supply. As you probably knew before I did."

"Okay, I confess. You never mentioned her at the Double S the other night, but Mom and Aunt El did happen to *share the news.*"

"Of course." Dana forced herself to laugh along with Tess.

"That's just like Ben."

She winced. "Mmm-hmm." Hoping Tess hadn't seen her reaction or the sudden moisture in her eyes, she hurried to push her cart toward the checkout counter. "Hi, Billy."

The clerk looked from her to Tess and back again. "What are you doing here? I saw Anne on her way to pick up P.J. and Stacey. She said you had the council meeting today."

"Later tonight," she said. After she'd paid for her groceries, she stepped aside to wait for Tess.

She wanted to run out of the store immediately. To pass on attending the meeting altogether. To avoid seeing Ben. But of course she couldn't let Kayla down. Besides, where would she go? Everyone in Flagman's Folly knew she should be at Town Hall tonight. And unless she invented an excuse, she couldn't even hide out at home. She'd arranged for Anne to stay with the kids.

"Ready?" Tess asked her.

"Ready as I'll ever be," she said grimly.

Tess frowned, and Dana pushed her cart through the automatic doors. In the parking lot, they stopped behind Tess's SUV.

"Anyway," Tess said as she unloaded her groceries from the cart, "back to what I was saying inside. That was nice of Ben to take care of the dog food. *And* to get the puppy for the kids."

"Yes. He's a good friend."

"Is he? A *friend,* I mean?"

"Of course," she snapped. "We might have different

opinions over things, but that doesn't mean we can't be friends."

"Hey, girl."

Dana blushed. "Sorry. I was thinking about something else."

"I have a feeling it's all related." Tess leaned back against the SUV. "I won't give you the wide-eyed innocent look again. But around the time that stopped working for you, I think we discovered boys. Dana," she added softly, "you know what I meant by the emphasis on that word just now. It's obvious Ben wants to be more than a friend."

"He can't be."

"Why not?"

She looked around the lot, empty of other shoppers at that moment. Empty of a possible distraction. Trapped, she looked back at Tess again. "You know why. And he's only being nice because of Paul."

Tess shook her head. "Oh, no, he's not."

"We're just friends," Dana insisted. "Besides, if I… If we…" She gripped the handle of the shopping cart. "I could never live it down."

"Live what down?"

She groaned. "You're going to make me say it, aren't you? All right, then. Folks would never forgive Paul's wife and Paul's best friend for crossing that line."

"That's not true."

"Yes, it is." She sighed. "You should hear Clarice rant about it. She's appalled that Ben is at the house so often— and there's not even anything going on between us."

Not anymore.

"Clarice is a wonderful woman," Tess said, "but she's never gotten over losing Vernon. She's let his death affect too many things in her life. Don't let her get to you, Dana. Clarice is *not* the voice of Flagman's Folly."

Dana's guilt eased just the smallest bit. "All right, maybe not, but Ellamae is."

Tess laughed, and despite her mixed emotions—or maybe because of them—Dana couldn't keep from smiling, too.

"You're right," Tess said. "Or at least, Aunt El thinks she is. But she doesn't feel the way Clarice does. She and Mom think you and Ben make a perfect couple."

That statement made her reel. "No—"

"*Yes.* You know I wouldn't lie to you. Everyone in town thinks that."

"I don't believe it," she blurted, then shivered at her accidental echo of Ben's words. "No one has ever said anything like this to me before. Why not? And why are you saying it now?"

"Because they were giving you time. Letting you grieve. But I'm *your* best friend, and I'm saying it now because it *is* time."

"You mean, you think that, too?"

Tess nodded. "I'll confess, I have for years. I don't want to hurt you," she added, her voice soft again, "but I saw how things were with you and Paul. You've been ready for a while. You need to move on. You *and* Ben."

Dana stared across the empty parking lot. Everything Tess had said stunned her. Her final admission took her breath away.

She had a confession of her own to tell, but she couldn't share it with Tess now. She couldn't admit Ben had already moved on.

And the quiet closing of the door behind him said he wouldn't be back again.

* * *

Dana sat in the front row of spectators' seats in the courtroom and braced herself as Ben announced the next items on the agenda. The proposals.

Whispers broke out all around her, then quieted, until she heard nothing in the room but the blades of the overhead fan. Obviously the time had come to address the topic of most interest to folks this evening.

Which proposal had received Ben's all-important vote? Had he supported the playground? Or had he voted the way he had planned all along—to choose the memorial and stay loyal to his best friend?

No sense worrying about it, when she already knew what decision he had made.

She should have known from the beginning, from the night of Tess's wedding, when he'd told her about the promise he'd made. Now, weeks later, that news still made her breath catch. No matter what he claimed about being friends, for all these months since Paul's death, he'd thought of her as less than that. He'd considered her his *responsibility*. That knowledge hurt more than she could ever have imagined.

Just as she had hurt him with the truth about Paul.

They couldn't be…close. She'd made sure they couldn't be friends. And now he had decided against her proposal.

How could she expect anything else?

Still, holding on to hope, she had tried to talk to him since her arrival tonight. But like the previous meeting when she had refused to make eye contact, he now avoided her.

At the front table, he cleared his throat and moved his water glass aside. Nervous gestures that astounded her. In all the years she had known him, Ben Sawyer had never once felt nervous about speaking in public.

He couldn't face her because he'd decided against her proposal.

And she was going to live for the rest of her life with a permanent, public reminder of all the mistakes she had made.

"Folks," he began, "as you know, the council was recently presented with two proposals, both involving property adjacent to the elementary school." Reading from the paper in front of him, he said, "The first proposal recommends that a memorial be erected on that site to honor Paul Wright, one of our own local heroes. A man who gave his life for his country."

No one made a sound. Dana locked her fingers in her lap.

"The second proposal," he continued, "recommends the building of a playground on that same site, to provide a common area for the children of Flagman's Folly." He set the papers aside and looked up at his audience. "The council considered both proposals very carefully and came to—" he paused "—an impasse."

The whispers broke out again. He waited until they had trailed away. "As a result," he said slowly, "the council has an alternative suggestion to present to both committees."

She exchanged a glance with Kayla.

Then she looked across the aisle at Tess, who gave a tiny shrug. Beside her, Ellamae wore a disgruntled expression. Obviously neither her gossip-gathering skill nor the power of Judge Baylor had helped her this time.

Dana faced forward again. Ben sat looking directly at her. She jumped. Hoping he hadn't noticed, she pressed her fingers more tightly together.

He had always claimed he could read her face. She wished she could read his. But she couldn't—because there was nothing to see. No expression. No emotion. No feelings for her at all.

He looked away.

"The council," he continued, "recommends the committees meet on a middle ground. We would like to support the intent to honor Paul Wright with a memorial—" his gaze met Dana's again briefly, then moved out to survey the room "—by suggesting the two committees merge, name the playground after the Wright family, and dedicate it to Paul and Dana's children and all the children of Flagman's Folly."

A hush fell over the courtroom, as if everyone in it had taken a deep breath.

A similar quiet had filled the cemetery the day they'd laid Paul to rest. Dana did now what she couldn't do then.

Fight back tears.

After sending Anne home with Billy, Dana went to kiss all three of her sleeping kids. She patted Duchess, curled up in the bed that had somehow made its way upstairs to the floor in P.J.'s room. One corner of the dinosaur quilt trailed down beside the puppy, as if P.J. had tried to tuck her in for the night.

Downstairs in the living room again, she curled up on the couch, tucking herself in with the afghan. She tried not to think about the last time she had sat there with Ben.

The reaction to his announcement in the courtroom tonight left no doubt about how everyone in the room felt. After a quick conference with both committees, Ellamae immediately presented a revised proposal, which the council had unanimously passed.

Dana had left Town Hall as soon as she could.

She and Ben hadn't spoken a word to each other.

She pulled the afghan more closely around her. Through the long window beside the front door, she saw a truck glide past the house. The streetlamp gave off enough light to tell her the truck was Ben's.

Of course. He was on his way home.

Headlights flashed in the east window. He had turned into her driveway. She exhaled in a rush. Before he reached the steps, she had moved to the entryway and opened the door.

The cold night air made her shiver. Made her voice shake when she said, "I didn't want the bell to wake the kids."

Ben entered and closed the door firmly behind him.

When he said nothing, she asked, "You're just here to listen again?"

"At first, anyhow."

She nodded and led him into the living room.

He took a seat beside her on the couch.

She hadn't planned what she would tell him, if she ever got the chance to talk to him again. After tonight's meeting, she hadn't really expected to have the opportunity at all. But now that he had arrived, she felt no qualms.

This was Ben.

She took a deep breath. "I'll start. But first, there's something I need to know. You told me you had the deciding vote on the council."

He nodded.

"But there was a stalemate. That means you *didn't* vote."

"That's right."

"The committee's recommendation tonight—the compromise—that was your idea, wasn't it?"

"Yes. I knew how you felt about the memorial, but not

why. Not in the beginning." He shook his head. "If I had, I might not have pushed as hard as I did for you to tell me your reasons. But even once I knew, when it came down to it, I still wanted to see Paul honored. Now he is, and his name will live on the way it should. Through his family."

She nodded. That was Ben, too. Of course, he would stand up for what he believed in. Would stay loyal and true.

"You're right," she said softly. "He was your best friend, in the only way he knew how to be. You need to honor that."

"You're okay with it?"

"I'm okay with it." She had managed to hold back earlier, but now she couldn't stop a tear from running down her cheek. She wiped it away. "After I left Town Hall, I stopped by the cemetery to make my peace with Paul. Thanks to you."

"Me?"

She nodded. "At the end of his life, he was a hero. You were right about that, too, all along. And it's what I want the kids to remember about him."

"The good parts." He smiled sadly. "The rest of what you told me, they don't need to know. No one does."

"No. But I want you to know *all* the parts."

"There's more?"

"There's more." Not that long ago she wouldn't have been able to share this with anyone. "You know how upset I get at the thought of you wanting to take care of me."

"That would be an understatement."

"Paul…" She hesitated. Maybe she still had more qualms than she'd thought. Not about trusting Ben, but about having to show him how naive she'd been. "I told you he used me, too. He built his ego by tearing mine down. He started early, long before high school, and never let up. It was so subtle back then, I didn't realize it."

Ben's eyes glimmered.

She swallowed hard. "When he came back from State, he wasn't subtle anymore, just told me outright I needed him and would never get anywhere without him. And I...I bought into it." Her laugh sounded bitter. "I was that dumb. But I'd never been with anyone else, and we'd been together since grade school. When he came home on leave that last time, I thought maybe things had changed for the better. He seemed different, as though he cared."

"He *was* different," Ben said in a low voice. "He did care. I told you, that's when he asked me to watch over you and the kids."

She nodded. "I believe now he meant well. But what he wanted for me isn't what I want." She spoke as quietly as he had. "I want to be a good mother to my kids. I don't ever want to be weak and needy—the way Paul claimed I was."

"*Dana.* You've been running a business and raising three children on your own for years. There's nothing weak about you. You're the strongest woman I know."

Her heart soared. She'd been so wrong, for so long, about so many things. But not this. Of course, Ben was nothing like Paul. Of course Ben believed in her.

"After he left again," she said, "I finally came to my senses. I realized that, no matter what he said, I'd never been the kind of woman he claimed I was. And he'd long ago stopped being the man I'd once cared about. The man whose image I'd always tried so hard to protect." She took a deep breath and released it. "When he died, I felt I had to keep up that image. For the folks in town. For the kids. And especially for you. Because you were his best friend. And because...I love you."

Her voice broke, but she rushed on. "I know I shouldn't tell you, because we're just friends. But I can't help thinking that if I had said it months ago, we could have had a chance together. I could have had what I'd always wanted. A good daddy for my kids. A strong marriage. An equal partner."

"That's what I wanted," he said.

Wanted, not *want.*

Now her heart broke, too. She looked away.

"Dana." He took her hand. "A long time ago I made a big mistake by stepping back from what I wanted. Instead, I did what I could—for you and Paul—knowing you deserved the better man. Only now I know I'm the *best* man for you."

Slowly she turned to look at him.

He twined their fingers together. "Everything I stepped back from is what you've always wanted, too. The kids. The marriage. The equal partner. I wouldn't settle for anything less." Smiling, he added, "Since kindergarten, I wouldn't settle for anyone but you. I never changed my mind about that, and I never will."

He reached up with his free hand to brush away the tear running down her cheek. "I won't change my thoughts about taking care of you, either. I want us to take care of each other. Not because we're weak, but because that's what makes a marriage strong. That's what makes us equal partners. Can you see that?"

Not trusting herself to speak, she simply nodded.

"And I came up with that suggestion for the committees because I wanted you to understand a compromise would work. That you and I could reach our own middle ground." He tightened his fingers around hers and raised their joined hands. "We made it."

She laughed shakily. "Are you expecting me to argue with that?"

He shook his head. "No, just to love me. The way I've always loved you."

He wrapped his free arm around her and touched his lips to hers. His kiss was hot enough to satisfy the desire she'd fought for so long. Sweet enough to tell her he would *always* be the best man for her.

And filled with the kind of promise she'd want to hold him to forever.

Epilogue

One month later

On a cool, crisp Saturday morning, a week after their wedding, Ben stood on the playground holding Dana's hand. It was a nice day for the dedication.

Across from them, on a bench near the basketball court, Lissa sat watching them. When she caught him looking at her, she grinned and waved. Smiling, he waved back.

P.J. had joined a group of boys his own age playing kickball in the schoolyard.

Ben gently pushed the baby swing. Stacey gurgled, and he laughed.

"She's happy the committee let her christen the swingset," Dana said.

"Looks like it," he agreed. He caught his new wife's gaze. Just a short while ago, Ellamae had asked her to cut the ribbon for the dedication ceremony. "You're okay with your new job?"

"I'm glad for it," she said. "It will let me cut the ties to the past. The bad ties. And," she added in a softer tone, "it's a way for me to honor Paul."

His throat suddenly tight, he nodded.

Ellamae hurried up to them again. "Now, Dana, I hope you don't mind that Kayla's giving the dedication."

"Not at all. She did so much to make sure everything was ready for today, especially with all the additions."

He and Caleb and Sam had taken the initial proposal beyond just the play area for the kids. They would soon break ground for the new Flagman's Folly Community Center, too.

"I think Kayla deserves the pleasure," Dana added.

Ellamae looked at them both thoughtfully, then said, "They asked me to speak, but I recommended her." She laughed. "Between Becky and the new baby on the way, she'll have more to do with this playground than I will. Besides, I've taken care of enough around here already."

"You mean by joining the monument committee?" Dana asked.

"No. I mean, by *creating* the monument committee." She shook her head. "If I hadn't helped you two work through all those problems Paul caused between you, you never would've made a couple."

Dana's eyes widened in astonishment. "You knew about Paul?"

She nodded. "The way the Wrights spoiled their only son, there was no surprise he turned out the way he did," she said gruffly. "Besides, we'd had more than a few creditors calling Judge Baylor." She shrugged. "But all that's between us and the judge. And Stacey." She smiled at the baby.

Ben squeezed Dana's hand. "The important thing is," he said, "folks have always thought Dana and I should be together."

"Well, of course they have. Except Clarice. But don't worry, I'm working on her, and she's coming along." She gave an exaggerated sigh. "As usual, I'm the only one willing to do anything around here." She winked at them, then sauntered away.

He and Dana exchanged a glance.

He shook his head. "Think of all the time we wasted, and for nothing," he said.

"Think of all the time you waited," she countered, "and never stopped being my friend. Ben, there are so many things that haven't lasted for me. You will."

"Yep. Like nature taking its course." When she laughed, he wrapped his arms around her.

He'd never felt more content.

Just like the storybooks…

They would live happily ever after in the Land of Enchantment—otherwise known as the state of New Mexico.

Because Benjamin Franklin Sawyer had finally gotten his girl.

* * * * *

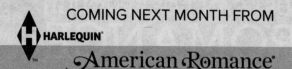

Ryder stood at the pasture fence, his leather dress shoes sinking into the soft dirt. He'd have a chore cleaning them later. At the moment, he didn't care.

When, he absently wondered, was the last time he'd worn a pair of boots? Or ridden a horse, for that matter? The answer came quickly. Five years ago. He'd sworn then and there he'd never set sight on Reckless again.

Recent events had altered the circumstance of his enduring disagreement with his family. Liberty, the one most hurt by their mother's lies, had managed to make peace with both their parents. Not so Ryder. His anger had not dimmed one bit.

Was coming home a mistake? Only time would tell. In any case, he wasn't staying long.

In the pasture, a woman haltered a large black pony and led it slowly toward the gate. Ryder leaned his forearms on the top fence railing. Even at this distance, he could tell two things: the pony was severely lame, and the woman was spectacularly attractive.

The pair was a study in contrast. While the pony hobbled painfully, favoring its front left foot, the woman moved with elegance and grace, her long black hair misbehaving in the mild breeze. She stopped frequently to check on the pony, and when she did, rested her hand affectionately on its sleek neck.

Something about her struck a familiar, but elusive, chord with him. A memory teased at the fringes of his mind, just out of reach.

As he watched, the knots of tension residing in his shoulders relaxed. That was, until she changed direction and headed toward him. Then he immediately perked up, and his senses went on high alert.

"Hi," she said as she approached. "Can I help you?"

She was even prettier up close. Large, dark eyes analyzed him with unapologetic interest from a model-perfect oval face. Her full mouth stretched into a warm smile impossible not to return. The red T-shirt tucked into a pair of well-worn jeans emphasized her long legs and slim waist.

"I'm meeting someone." He didn't add that he was now ten minutes late or that the someone was, in fact, his father.

"Can I show you the way?"

"Thanks. I already know it."

"You've been here before?"

"You…could say that. But it's been a while."

Look for HER RODEO MAN by New York Times bestselling author Cathy McDavid, available March 2015 wherever Harlequin American Romance books and ebooks are sold!

www.Harlequin.com

COMING NEXT MONTH FROM

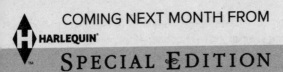

HARLEQUIN®

SPECIAL EDITION

Available February 17, 2015

#2389 MENDOZA'S SECRET FORTUNE
The Fortunes of Texas: Cowboy Country • by Marie Ferrarella
Rachel Robinson never counted herself among the beauties of Horseback Hollow, Texas...until handsome brothers Matteo and Cisco Mendoza began competing for her attention! But it's Matteo who catches her eye and proves to be the most ardent suitor. He might just convince Rachel to leave her past behind her and start life anew—with him!

#2390 A CONARD COUNTY BABY
Conard County: The Next Generation • by Rachel Lee
Pregnant Hope Conroy is fleeing a dark past when she lands in Conard County, Wyoming, where Jim "Cash" Cashford, a single dad with a feisty teenager on his hands, resides. When Cash stumbles across Hope, he's desperate for help, so he hires the Texan beauty to help rein in his daughter. As the bond between Cash and Hope flourishes, there might just be another Conard County family in the making...

#2391 A SECOND CHANCE AT CRIMSON RANCH • by Michelle Major
Olivia Wilder isn't eager for love after her husband ran off with his secretary, leaving her lost and lonely. So when she scores a dance with handsome Logan Travers at his brother's wedding, her thoughts aren't on romance or falling for the rancher. A former Colorado wild boy, Logan is drawn to Olivia, but fears he's not good enough for her. Can two individuals who have been burned by love in the past find their own happily-ever-after on the range?

#2392 THE BACHELOR'S BABY DILEMMA
Family Renewal • by Sheri WhiteFeather
The last thing Tanner Quinn wants is a baby. Ever since his infant sister died, the handsome horseman has avoided little ones like the plague—but now he's the guardian of his newborn niece! What's a man to do? Tanner calls in his ex-girlfriend Candy McCall to help. The nurturing nanny is wonderful with the baby—and with Tanner, too. Although this avowed bachelor has sworn off marriage, Candy might just be sweet enough to convince him otherwise.

#2393 FROM CITY GIRL TO RANCHER'S WIFE • by Ami Weaver
When chef Josie Callahan loses everything to her devious ex-fiancé, she leaves town, hightailing it to Montana. There, Josie takes refuge in a temporary job...on the ranch of a sexy former country star. Luke Ryder doesn't need a beautiful woman tantalizing him—especially one who won't last a New York minute on a ranch. He's also a private man who doesn't want a stranger poking around...even if she gets him to open his heart to love!

#2394 HER PERFECT PROPOSAL • by Lynne Marshall
Journalist Lilly Matsuda is eager to get her hands dirty as a reporter in Heartlandia, Oregon. The locals aren't crazy about her, though—Lilly even gets pulled over by hunky cop Gunnar Norling! But the two bond. As Gunnar quickly becomes more than just a source to Lilly, conflicts of interest soon arise. Can the policeman and his lady love find their own happy ending in Heartlandia?

YOU CAN FIND MORE INFORMATION ON UPCOMING HARLEQUIN® TITLES, FREE EXCERPTS AND MORE AT WWW.HARLEQUIN.COM.

HSECNM0215

SPECIAL EXCERPT FROM

H HARLEQUIN®

SPECIAL EDITION

*Matteo Mendoza is used to playing second fiddle
to his brother Cisco…but not this time. Beautiful
Rachel Robinson intrigues both siblings, but Matteo
is determined to win her heart. Rachel can't resist the
handsome pilot, but she's afraid her family secrets might
haunt her chances at love. Can this Texan twosome find
their very own happily-ever-after on the range?*

*Read on for a sneak preview of
MENDOZA'S SECRET FORTUNE by USA TODAY
bestselling author Marie Ferrarella, the third book in
THE FORTUNES OF TEXAS: COWBOY COUNTRY
continuity!*

***

Matteo knew he should be leaving—and had most likely already overstayed—but he found himself wanting to linger just a few more seconds in her company.

"I just wanted to tell you one more time that I had a very nice time tonight," he told Rachel.

She surprised him—and herself when she came right down to it—by saying, "Show me."

Matteo looked at her, confusion in his eyes. Had he heard wrong? And what did she mean by that, anyway?

"What?"

"Show me," Rachel repeated.

"How?" he asked, not exactly sure he understood what she was getting at.

Her mouth curved, underscoring the amusement that was already evident in her eyes.

"Oh, I think you can figure it out, Mendoza," she told him. Then, since he appeared somewhat hesitant to put an actual meaning to her words, she sighed loudly, took hold of his button-down shirt and abruptly pulled him to her.

Matteo looked more than a little surprised at this display of proactive behavior on her part. She really was a firecracker, he thought.

The next moment, there was no room for looks of surprise or any other kind of expressions for that matter. It was hard to make out a person's features if their face was flush against another's, the way Rachel's was against his.

If the first kiss between them during the picnic was sweet, this kiss was nothing if not flaming hot. So much so that Matteo was almost certain that he was going to go up in smoke any second now.

The thing of it was he didn't care. As long as it happened while he was kissing Rachel, nothing else mattered.

***

Don't miss MENDOZA'S SECRET FORTUNE
by USA TODAY bestselling
author Marie Ferrarella,
the third book in
THE FORTUNES OF TEXAS: COWBOY COUNTRY
continuity!

Available March 2015, wherever
Harlequin® Special Edition books and ebooks are sold.

HARLEQUIN®

A *Romance* FOR EVERY MOOD™

JUST CAN'T GET ENOUGH?

Join our social communities
and talk to us online.

You will have access to the latest
news on upcoming titles and special
promotions, but most importantly,
you can talk to other fans about your
favorite Harlequin reads.

Harlequin.com/Community

 Facebook.com/HarlequinBooks

 Twitter.com/HarlequinBooks

 Pinterest.com/HarlequinBooks